D1194432

SIN
WITH
ME

**Also by J.T. Geissinger**

Bad Habit Series

*Sweet as Sin*

*Make Me Sin*

The Night Prowler Series

*Shadow's Edge*

*Edge of Oblivion*

*Rapture's Edge*

*Edge of Darkness*

*Darkness Bound*

*Into Darkness*

Novella

*The Last Vampire*

J. T. GEISSINGER

Published by Montlake Romance, Seattle

www.apub.com



ISBN-13: 9781477824047
ISBN-10: 1477824049

Cover design by Eileen Carey

Printed in the United States of America

*To Jay. Who knew?*

*"The hottest love has the coldest end."*

*~ Socrates*

# Prologue

"Bless me, Father, for I have sinned. It's been thirteen years since my last confession."

I don't have to count the time. I remember exactly how long it's been since I've knelt in a small, stuffy confessional booth and stared through a tightly woven wooden lattice at a shadowed figure beyond.

I remember because it's the last time I trusted God.

The priest seated behind the screen murmurs, "The Lord be in your heart and upon your lips that you may truly and humbly confess your sins. In the Name of the Father, and of the Son, and of the Holy Spirit. Amen."

I make the sign of the cross over my chest, fold my sweaty hands together, and rest my elbows on the narrow ledge jutting from beneath the lattice. My heart pounds like I've been running a race.

But it's not a race that makes the blood roar through my veins. It's that old familiar demon I've spent half a lifetime with. The one that's carved its name deep into my heart.

Shame.

After a long, silent moment, the priest gently prompts, "Tell me your sins, my son."

"I . . ."

My throat closes. I swallow, fighting the claustrophobia that always follows me into small spaces. I envy everyone who's never felt this clawing, animal panic, this nauseating sense that all the walls are closing in. I feel trapped. Sick. On the verge of screaming.

Through sheer force of will, I manage not to leap to my feet and bolt. I clear my throat and start again. "I'm guilty of everything. I don't know where to start. Just . . . assume the worst."

The priest answers gently, "Try to think of one specific thing. Start with whatever is most bothering you today."

My grim laugh makes the priest tilt his head. I see him only in profile, the shadowed figure of a gray-haired man wearing black vestments. His posture indicates he's listening. He's interested. I wonder if he really thinks he can offer me absolution.

I wonder what he'd say if I told him he can't.

"A sin I committed long ago still eats at me, Father. And today . . . something happened today that reminded me of it all over again."

"Have you confessed this sin to God?"

"Yes."

His answer is swift. "If God forgives you, son, you must also forgive yourself. The sacrament of reconciliation washes us clean and renews us in Christ."

*Washes us clean? Bullshit. If I were clean I wouldn't be on my knees whispering my secrets to a stranger.*

I grit my teeth, draw a slow breath through my nose, and fight to keep my voice steady. "I don't believe that."

I'm startled to hear the priest chuckle. "Then why are you here?"

Uncomfortable, sweating, fending off a sudden sharp dizziness that makes the room tilt, I retort, "Old habits die hard."

The priest sagely nods. Though I can't make out his features or expression, I get the sense that he approves of my honesty.

I don't need his approval. I need an unbiased ear who's legally and morally obligated to keep his mouth shut. I need a guilt dumpster.

And if a Catholic priest isn't the perfect person for that, I don't know who would be.

"What is this sin you can't forget?"

When I remain silent, wrestling with the horror of saying the words out loud, the priest adds, "Some sins against other people can't be undone, but instead of hating ourselves, we can view it as a learning experience and an incentive to do good in the future instead of evil."

*An incentive to do good.*

My breathing hitches. I shift my weight, relieving the dull ache that's begun to settle into my left knee. "So doing good can help . . ."

"It can help you forgive yourself, even though God has already done so."

My ears buzz with a high-pitched sound, like a nest of wasps is hovering around my head. Forgiving myself isn't something I'm capable of. There's a reason shame and guilt exist. That reason is punishment.

Sinners *deserve* punishment. It's the one thing the Catholic Church and I wholeheartedly agree on. But his words have caught fire in my mind.

*Maybe the answer I'm seeking has nothing to do with me. Maybe it has to do with . . .*

*Restitution.*

Hope rises inside my chest like a cresting wave. "Do I tell this person what I've done?" I blurt.

Beyond the lattice, there's a weighted pause. "Only if it would be good for him or her. Would your admission benefit them in any real, concrete way? Because if disclosure would cause more pain than good, you should bear the weight of your transgression alone. A confession to another person motivated solely by a selfish desire to make one*self* feel better is, in itself, a sin."

My heart pounds. My hands shake. Water pools in my eyes, making my vision swim. I say hoarsely, "I don't know. I don't know."

The priest says, "Well, my son, until you know, hold your tongue and trust in God."

I can't trust in God. He abandoned me years ago. But I *can* hold my tongue. I've been doing that since the last time I confessed.

And until I find out if disclosure is the right way to go, I can do good.

I whisper the Act of Contrition. The priest recites words of absolution. I rise unsteadily, open the door of the confessional booth, and walk slowly past the empty pews, my heart thumping hard under my breastbone.

When my cell rings, I fish it from my pocket and answer it without even looking to see who it is. "Yeah?"

"Brody! Where the fuck are you, brother? We're all at the hospital. We thought you were following right behind us!"

I push through the heavy carved wooden doors at the front of the church and step out into a warm, brilliant Los Angeles afternoon. Even in February, it's a perfect seventy-two degrees. I close my eyes and lift my face to the sun. "I'm on my way, Nico. Just had to make a quick stop."

"Well, hurry the fuck up! Chloe's about to fuckin' pop! You gotta be here when the baby's born!"

"I'll be there in ten minutes. And Nico?"

"What?"

I open my eyes and look directly into the sun, letting it blind me. "Tell Grace . . ."

*Would your admission benefit her in any real, concrete way?*

"Tell Grace what, brother?" Nico says with a knowing chuckle. "That you like the way her brains fill out her sweater?"

"Just tell her I'm coming," I reply softly. "And that . . . she should call me if there's anything she needs me to pick up on the way."

I disconnect the call before Nico's stunned silence can turn into questions. Then I jog over to my car, parked in the church lot in the shade of an early-flowering magnolia tree. I feel the cold, familiar presence of my demon as he jogs along unseen behind me.

*Do good. Do good. Do good. God help me to do good.*

The demon's growling laugh follows as I tear out of the parking lot, tires squealing.

*God isn't listening, Brody-boy. But you already knew that.*

I press my foot hard against the gas pedal, on my way to seek the redemption that's eluded me all these years.

# Chapter 1

## Grace

"Grace, if you don't wipe that look off your face I'll slap it off," mutters Kat, standing next to me inside the luxurious private maternity suite that A.J. booked for Chloe's labor. The suite has three rooms, two bathrooms, freshly cut orchids stuffed into vases all over the place, and a flat-screen TV almost as large as the one in my living room.

Like everything else A.J. does for Chloe, it's completely over the top.

It melts my heart how that giant, surly caveman is such a teddy bear when it comes to his woman. They say music can tame a savage beast, but I have solid evidence that love is really the magic potion at work. Love can turn even the most terrifying beastie into a purring ball of fluff.

"What look?" I turn to my best friend with my brows arched.

She hisses under her breath. "The look like you're trying to hold in a monster fart during church! I know you're not big on babies, but this is Chloe's special day!"

"Oh stop, Dramarama." I wave a hand dismissively in her face. "For one thing, I wouldn't set foot in a church if God Himself descended from the heavens on a golden chariot and ordered me to. Churches give me the creeps. All that hypocrisy, guilt, and repressed sexuality—ugh. And for another thing, even if I *do* hate everyone else's spawn, I'm going to love Chloe and A.J.'s as if I produced it from my own vagina."

"Then what's with your *face*?" she presses. "Do you need to use the toilet?"

Instead of admitting I'm teary-eyed and emotional that this day has finally come and my normal resting bitch face is having problems maintaining its status quo, I say breezily, "I just can't stand the smell of hospitals."

That isn't a lie. Hospitals have a distinct smell—antiseptic with undertones of agony and dead things—that's burned into my memory.

In fact, it's one of the very first memories I have.

I dig a bottle of Clive Christian perfume out of my handbag and spritz it into the air. "And this place could really use more flattering lighting. No one wants to push a new human through her cooch under the harsh glare of fluorescents. It's uncivilized. I'll get some candles from the gift shop downstairs."

Kat snorts. "Oh dear lord. Please don't tell me you're gonna check the thread count on the bedsheets next."

I narrow my eyes at the hospital bed near the window. "Now that you mention it—"

"Here we are, ladies! All checked in! The nurse is bringing Chloe up in a moment!"

Grinning like mad, Chloe's father, Thomas, bustles past us into the room. As usual, he's impeccably dressed in a bespoke Brioni suit—this one a gorgeous navy blue—a crisp white dress shirt, and black Ferragamo loafers. He's also wearing a tie, a silk pocket square, and a watch worth north of one hundred thousand dollars. He's the only man I know who'd come to his first grandchild's birth dressed like he's having lunch in Cannes with the president of the European Union.

I expect it of Chloe's mother, Elizabeth, however. She's the daughter of a British countess and would literally rather die than be caught *en déshabillé*. She follows Thomas into the room, sailing by in pink Chanel, a cloud of Shalimar, and gleaming ropes of pearls.

"Grace." She takes my hands and kisses me on both cheeks. "You look *divine*, as always." Eyeing my necklace, she asks, "Is that the new Divas' Dream collection from Bulgari?"

The woman can spot anything expensive or couture from a thousand paces. It's no wonder we get along so well.

I nod, smiling. "It is. I bought Kat and Chloe one, too. Matching push presents for all of us."

Elizabeth pats my hand, clucking like a mother hen. "Such a good friend. Hello, Katherine." She turns to Kat and presents her cheek for a kiss. Kat obliges, and then Elizabeth hands Kat her purse as if she's the coat-check girl in a restaurant. As Elizabeth minces away and disappears into the bathroom, Kat looks at me and rolls her eyes.

I try not to laugh. Adopting Elizabeth's genteel accent, I say, "Dear, my shoes could use polishing when you have a moment—"

Kat elbows me in my ribs. "Shut up. And why are *you* the favorite? I've known Chloe's parents longer!"

I sweep my hair over my shoulder. "It's impossible to compete with perfection, darling."

Kat makes a retching noise and tosses Elizabeth's handbag onto a nearby chair.

Emerging from the adjacent sitting room he's just inspected, Thomas enthusiastically claps his hands. "So! What are we drinking? Scotch? Vodka? A little gin and tonic to get the party started? We've got a fully stocked minibar here, ladies. It would be a sin to let it go to waste!"

Knowing Chloe's father as well as we do, neither one of us finds it odd that his first order of business is distributing cocktails. He's an interesting mash-up of James Bond and Al Capone—always perfectly dressed and smooth as silk, with a martini in one hand while the other fondles a loaded gun stashed in his pocket.

He might be a wealthy and well-respected attorney, but I know a carefully crafted mask when I see one.

After all, I've got one, too.

Kat says, "I'm good, thanks." She glances at the small suitcase near her feet. "I want to get Chloe's stuff ready before she gets here." She makes her way to the bed, flops the suitcase on top of it, and then proceeds to unpack the few items of clothing inside.

Thomas looks disappointed, but shrugs. "Grace? What can I get you?"

I drop my handbag on the chair next to Elizabeth's. I'm not sure my nerves will make it through the next few hours without fortification, so I say gratefully, "I'd love a vodka rocks. Easy on the rocks."

He beams. "Coming up!"

As he disappears into the adjacent room, a nurse pushes Chloe through the doorway in a wheelchair. She's wearing a blue cotton hospital gown and a pair of white ankle socks. She's also pale, sweaty, and clutching her huge belly with one hand.

Holding her other hand, the enormous blond bulk of her fiancé, A.J., follows right alongside. Despite not being able to see even a foot in front of him because of the brain surgery he underwent last year that left him blind, there's a distinct swagger in his walk. His grin stretches from ear to ear. His chest is puffed out like he's about to pound on it with his fists and let rip a deafening Tarzan yell.

*Look at him. He's a proud papa already and the baby isn't even out yet. That man is going to be an incredible father.*

I quickly swipe at my eyes before anyone notices the water pooling in them.

The nurse, a curvy thirtyish brunette with alarmingly tall hair-sprayed bangs and penciled-on eyebrows, says soothingly, "Okay, Chloe, this is your maternity suite. You'll be here for a while longer until we're ready to go into the delivery room. Your doula will be here any moment to start timing your contractions—"

*"Fuuuck!"* Chloe doubles over in the wheelchair. Her face is contorted with pain.

Kat and I gasp. A.J. cries, "Angel!" and drops to his knees beside her. The nurse, who has obviously seen this all a million times before, says cheerfully, "Whoops, there's another one!"

While Chloe groans, Kat and I rush over to her, squawking and flapping our hands like a pair of hysterical pigeons.

"Honey, what can I do for you—"

"Deep breaths, Chloe, remember your training—"

"Do you need water—"

"Did you get your epidural—"

"Should we move you to the bed—"

"I started unpacking your clothes—"

"What can we do to make you comfortable—"

"Your father's making drinks—"

"Girls!" thunders A.J.

Kat and I instantly shut up.

More softly, he says, "Thank you." His unfocused gaze turns to Chloe. He rests his big paw on her shoulder and gently squeezes. "Chloe, sweetheart—are you okay?"

Panting, she says between gritted teeth, "There's a person the size of a watermelon trying to escape from my uterus. *No*, I'm not okay."

Above her, the nurse shakes her head and mouths at us, *She's fine.*

"Darling! Goodness!" Chloe's mother stands outside the open bathroom door, clutching her pearls.

A.J. says, "She just had a really strong contraction, Mom."

Another thing that melts my heart is how A.J. calls his future mother-in-law "Mom." The man has so many layers of sweet under that scary tattooed exterior, it really gives me hope for the rest of humanity.

"I was referring to the cursing!" says Elizabeth, dismayed.

Chloe growls, "I'm in *labor*, Mother."

Elizabeth sniffs. "There's no excuse for vulgarity, dear. I was in labor for a combined total of forty-six hours with you and your brother and I never once resorted to swearing. It's unseemly."

The way Chloe is looking at her mother makes me think something *very* unseemly is about to come out of her mouth, so to keep the peace I interject.

"A.J., why don't we move her to the bed? I think she'll be most comfortable there."

He's on his feet so fast he might as well have springs in his legs. "Arms around my shoulders, baby," he murmurs to Chloe as he lifts her. When she's securely in his arms, he says, "Lead the way, Grace."

While Kat scrambles to get the suitcase off the bed, I put my hand on his arm and guide him over to it. "Right here. Feel it?"

When his knee bumps the edge of the mattress, he leans down, gently sets Chloe on the bed, finds her face with his hands, and then gives her a soft kiss. "Tell me what you need."

"Just that," she sighs, settling back into the pillows.

"There's my girl!" crows Thomas, coming over with a drink in each hand. Beaming at Chloe, he gives me my vodka rocks. I proceed to drink half of it in one gulp.

This child birthing business is stressful.

A woman with long, flowy blonde hair and a gentle smile appears in the doorway. She gives the back of the door a hesitant knock. "Hello. My name is Nadine. I'm the doula?"

She says it as if she's not entirely sure it's true. Elizabeth looks her up and down, frowning at her Birkenstocks and untamed hair.

A.J. says, "Yes! Welcome! Come in!"

Thomas asks, "Would you like a drink, Nadine?"

Elizabeth says flatly, "Thomas."

Chloe groans. "Oh shit sticks! Here comes another one!"

Elizabeth exclaims, "Chloe Anne Carmichael!"

The doula moves to the end of the bed. "Let's take a look and see how dilated we are, shall we?"

I say, "Okay, kids, I think it's time for us to leave you to it! We'll be in the waiting room with the rest of the gang." I lean over and kiss Chloe's forehead.

She grunts. "What, you don't want to check out the gaping maw of my cervix?"

"Thank you for that disturbing visual." I grimace and take another swig of my drink.

Kat comes over, bumps me out of the way with her hip, and kisses Chloe's cheek. Very softly, she says, "You're gonna do great. Everything's gonna be perfect. Try not to stress out, just breathe. Okay?"

Chloe nods, and then her face puckers. She gasps. "A.J.!"

Kat and I leap out of the way before he flattens us.

"I'm here, angel. I'm right here."

When he starts to murmur something else into her ear, I turn away, smiling. Kat links her arm through mine. We say good-bye to Chloe's parents, gather our handbags, and quietly leave the room.

After we've closed the door behind us and are standing in the empty hallway, Kat heaves out a shaky breath.

"You doing okay?"

She swallows hard, closes her eyes for a moment, and then nods. "Yeah. It's just . . . fucking hospitals."

I know this must be taking an emotional toll on her. When Kat was a teenager, she got pregnant. She decided to go through with the pregnancy, arranged for the baby to be adopted, and even became friends with the couple who was going to be the adoptive parents.

Then life decided Kat hadn't already been fucked over enough by her father abandoning her on her eighth birthday, the baby's biological father abandoning her when he discovered she was pregnant, and her mother dying on the same day Kat went into labor, because her baby girl died three days after she was born.

"Fucking hospitals," I agree, meeting her eyes.

She stares at me a moment. "Are *you* okay?" she whispers, squeezing my arm.

Usually it's an incredible gift having a friend who knows me so well, but every once in a while it's a royal pain in the ass. I hate people guessing I might be made of anything but titanium.

I smile brightly. "Of course."

Her left brow climbs. Kat has mastered the art of the eyebrow arch. It always surprises me how a two-inch section of facial hair can so perfectly telegraph emotions ranging from curiosity to disbelief to withering disdain. Right now it's calling bullshit on me.

I insist, "I'm bulletproof, Kat. You know that."

"Sure thing, Pinocchio. But your nose is growing." She looks pointedly at the glass of vodka in my hand.

*Eagle-eyed witch.*

"Hey, don't blame me, I was just being polite. Thomas hates to drink alone."

"Thomas?" Kat mimics.

"Yes, Thomas. That's his name."

"That's funny, because I always call him Mr. Carmichael. You know, out of respect?"

I grin at her and again adopt Chloe's mother's voice. "Yes, dear, the help should always be respectful of their betters."

She barks out a laugh and shakes her head. "Screw you, Grandma."

"A delightful invitation, but I'm currently screwing a gorgeous and extremely well-endowed talent agent from CAA."

"No!" Kat exclaims. "Who is he? Why haven't you told us anything about him? Spill, spill!"

She's excited—and more importantly distracted from any more questions about my emotional state.

Exactly as I'd hoped.

I tell her about my latest conquest as I lead her down the hallway toward the waiting room, where the rest of our crew awaits.

With the exception of one Brody Scott, lead guitarist for Bad Habit, whose hauntingly intense green eyes I haven't been able to get out of my head in the year and a half since we first met.

Which is exactly why I won't go anywhere near him. An attraction that powerful is too dangerous for someone with no past or future, and who has a black hole in her chest where a living, beating heart used to be.

The moment Kat and I enter the waiting room, Kenji leaps to his feet with an ear-splitting shriek and collapses on us as if he's the one in labor and not Chloe.

"OmigodtellmewhatshappeningisshehavingthebabyrightNOW?"

It comes out in an almost unintelligible, breathless burst. Wearing a vintage red velvet smoking jacket over white leather pants paired with hot-pink combat boots, his nails painted as red as his lips—it's Valentine's Day after all—he hangs on to us, clutching our arms, swooning and fluttering his false eyelashes.

Being careful not to smudge his perfectly applied foundation, Kat plants a kiss on his smooth cheek. "It takes a little longer than that, honey."

He turns his big brown eyes to her. "How *much* longer?"

She lifts a shoulder. "Could be a few hours, could be a day."

His gasp alone is so dramatic he could win an Oscar for Best Performance. Combined with his look of utter horror and the way he recoils with his hands on either side of his face, it sets Kat and me off into gales of laughter.

"A *day*!" he squeaks, outraged. "That's *barbaric*! That's *inhumane*! That's cruel and unusual punishment just for riding the baloney pony! Oh!" He flops back into the chair he was sitting in when we entered and lifts a shaky hand to his forehead. "I'm so *glad* I don't have a vagina!"

Standing next to Kenji's chair with his hands on his hips and a grin on his face, Nico drawls, "Well, that's one mystery solved."

Kenji goes from fainting ingenue to smoldering seductress in one second flat. He crosses his legs, bats his lashes at Nico, and purrs up at him. "Would you like proof, you sexy thang?"

Amused, Kat crosses to Nico and wraps her arms around his waist. "Stop hitting on my husband, Scarlett O'Hara. This bad boy is *mine*."

Nico, spectacular in tight jeans and a black T-shirt that looks painted onto his muscular chest, takes Kat's face in his hands and kisses her. As usual, it's embarrassingly passionate. Those two take public displays of affection to a whole other level. Don't get me wrong, I'm all for sex in public places. But kissing? Snuggling? Lovey-dovey-ing?

Barf.

Kenji purses his lips and mutters, "He was mine first, bitch."

I hand Kenji the rest of my vodka. "Here. You need this more than I do."

He accepts it gratefully, sighing. "Oh, lovey, you're the only one of this rotten crew who understands me." He downs the drink in one gulp and then looks around hopefully. "Where's the bar in this joint?"

"Hospitals don't have bars in them, Einstein."

Kenji gazes up at me in consternation. "Then how did you get this?" He rattles the ice cubes in the empty glass in his hand.

"There's a minibar in Chloe's maternity suite, courtesy of her father."

He looks thoughtful. "Do you think they'll mind if I just pop in for a little refill? If I'm going to have to sit in this hideous mauve waiting room with Dolly Parton playing on the speakers for a *day*, I'm going to need booze or I'll go absolutely mad."

I chuckle. "Actually, I think Chloe's dad would be thrilled if you went up and asked for a drink."

Kenji pops to his feet and beams. "I knew I liked that man!" He lowers his voice to a whisper. "Even if he is a Republican."

He says the word "Republican" as if it's "murderer." I say wryly, "Sweetheart, I think you're the last person in the world who should be judgmental."

He tsks, waving me off as ridiculous. "Oh, honey, it's wrong to judge someone on something they're born with, like their race or sexual orientation. But if you *choose* to be an idiot, that's a different story."

"Right. Because no Democrat in history was ever an idiot."

He stares at me for a beat, and then says icily, "For the sake of our friendship, I'll pretend I didn't hear that." With a flourish, he turns and sashays away.

Looking around the empty waiting room, I ask Nico, "What happened to the guys?"

Barney, Nico's bodyguard and driver, and Ethan and Chris, the keyboardist and bassist for Bad Habit, are nowhere to be seen. We'd been having a barbeque at Nico and Kat's house when Chloe went into labor. We all drove to the hospital together, but somehow managed to leave Brody behind at the house.

Nico says, "In search of food."

"More food? I think Barney had about two dozen of those ribs you made."

His arm still around Kat, who's attached to his side like a barnacle, he laughs. "Yeah, that boy's got a big appetite. You should see him put away my hush puppies. I have to make an extra batch just for him."

Because life is entirely unfair, not only is Nico Nyx gorgeous, talented, loyal, and sexy, he can also *cook*. Kat had to step up her exercise routine from three to five days a week just to keep her weight the same after she moved in with him.

Suspiciously casually, Nico adds, "And I just got off the phone with Brody."

*Act natural. Act disinterested. Don't look at Kat.*

Busying myself with sitting in a chair, slipping off my heels, and digging through my handbag as if I'm in search of something important, I say, "Oh?"

"Mm-hmm. He's comin' now." Pause. "He said to tell you to call him if you need him to pick up anything on the way."

Startled, I abandon my fake rummaging. "What?"

Nico has these ridiculously disarming dimples that flash in his cheeks whenever he smiles, or is trying *not* to smile, as he's doing now. "You heard me."

Kat sends me her thousand-yard-expert-sniper stare. I know I'm in for some serious interrogating the minute we're alone together. To mitigate the damage, I laugh.

I aim for carefree, but unfortunately it comes out sounding a little panicked. "Oh, he's just playing with you. I don't even have his phone number."

Like the statement about hating the smell of hospitals, this is another suspicion-deflecting gem that also happens to be true. I don't have Brody's phone number.

Forget about the fact that he's tried to give it to me several times, I don't have it because I've refused.

"Are you seriously trying to pretend there's nothing going on between the two of you?" Kat straightens her spine and glares daggers at me. "I *saw* you at the house, Grace."

When I blink innocently, she rolls her eyes.

"After you said you were going to the bathroom and Brody followed you and then you both disappeared for like fifteen minutes and then you came back all red-faced and flustered and Brody came back looking like the cat that ate the canary?"

Nico whistles. "Ooo, she went there!"

"Yes, I did! And I will *not* have you keeping secrets from me!"

Kat stamps her foot. On anyone else that would look ridiculous, but somehow she pulls it off. Probably on account of her being exotically beautiful, which imbues most of the ridiculous things she does with effortless chic.

I say to Nico, "Is it me, or is she unusually bossy today?"

In his slow, Southern drawl, Nico deadpans, "Darlin', if you think I'm goin' anywhere near an answer to that question, you're crazy."

Fortunately the gods of distraction are on my side, because at that moment the guys stroll back into the waiting room. Chris and Ethan—dressed like twins in alligator cowboy boots, ripped jeans, and white T-shirts, their arms covered in tattoos—sprawl into a pair of chintz chairs opposite me and start chomping on cafeteria hamburgers while Barney, holding a sub sandwich in one hand and a Coke in the other, directs a question to Kat.

"Everything good?"

Kat nods. "She's all checked in. They're in the maternity suite now. Her contractions are already coming pretty close together, so we should get an update soon about how long they think it will be before the baby comes."

Barney looks satisfied. He takes a huge bite of the sub. He's wearing his standard-issue black Armani suit and white dress shirt open at the collar—the only outfit I've ever seen him in—and the gold Rolex that was a birthday present from Nico. He's got a perfectly groomed goatee and a full head of dark hair cropped short with military precision. Combined with his linebacker shoulders and piercing dark eyes, he's always struck me as what a proper mafia hitman would look like: dangerous.

He's also dangerously hot, if you like guys who wear guns under their suits and are named after purple dinosaurs.

Then Nico turns his head and breaks into a grin. He says to someone out of my line of sight, "Glad you could make it, slowpoke."

It's interesting the way my pulse spikes when I realize he must be speaking to Brody. Interesting and annoying, because I'm not the kind of woman whose pulse is easily spiked. I was once robbed at gunpoint by a crackhead and my reaction was to look at him and calmly say, "I'm happy to give you money for drugs, but what you really need is a hot meal, a hot bath, and a hug."

He took the money.

"You guys ran out so fast you left tire marks on the driveway." Brody rounds the row of chairs I'm sitting in, trades a back-slapping hug with Nico and a nod to the other guys, and then asks Kat, "How's Chloe?"

I'm too busy staring at him to hear the answer.

There's just something about him that's so . . . cool. I don't know how else to describe it. He's very good-looking, but in an approachable, boy-next-door sort of way. Unlike Nico, whose body looks carved by Michelangelo from a perfect piece of granite, or A.J., who's the size of The Hulk, Brody is slim and graceful like a runway model. His shoulders are lightly framed in muscle, his waist is narrow, his legs are long and lean. He has a lope like a wolf's, a Cheshire Cat grin, and a husky laugh that puts you in mind of the bedroom. The man is just plain *sexy.*

He also dresses like a Johnny Depp *GQ* ad, which sets my lady parts aquiver. A well-dressed man simply slays me.

Today he's wearing black Doc Martens and black designer jeans paired with a pale gray dress shirt—cuffs rolled up his strong forearms—topped with a fitted black silk vest. A leather cuff adorns one wrist. Around his neck on a leather cord is a small silver medallion. He's got a silver ring on his right thumb, a silver stud in his left ear, and a wicked gleam in his dark green eyes—

*Busted.*

I break eye contact with him and pretend to inspect the hideous still life of flowers on the opposite wall.

In a low voice, Brody says, "Grace."

That's it, just my name, but hell if it doesn't raise all the little hairs on the back of my neck and make my nipples hard.

Goddamn it.

"Hello." I continue to stare at the painting. Across from me, Chris and Ethan smirk around mouthfuls of burger and share a glance.

Apparently I didn't sound quite as disinterested as I was aiming for.

Nico clears his throat and tries to make some casual conversation to relieve the sudden odd tension. "So you said you had to make a stop on the way."

"I, uh, yeah. I did."

There's the strangest tone in Brody's voice, almost as if he's embarrassed. I glance at him and find him looking at the floor, squeezing the back of his neck with one hand. His face is turning red.

In my practice as a marriage and family therapist, I've seen a thousand men tell a thousand lies. I've become something of an expert at detecting them. Unlike sociopaths who can lie without batting an eyelash, a generally honest man with something to hide becomes very uncomfortable when questioned. He shows his discomfort in concrete, physical ways that he isn't aware of. A hard swallow. A shifting gaze. A nervous laugh. The list goes on, but one thing these tells all have in common is that they're unconscious, and uncontrollable.

And obvious as hell.

I don't think Brody's admission that he made a stop is a lie, but whatever the stop was is something he definitely doesn't want to talk about.

Well, good. One more reason to stay away from him. My two best friends got involved with men who had *massive* secrets, and I want nothing to do with that kind of drama. Some straightforward shagging followed by a quick exit is much more my speed.

Speaking of which . . .

I dig my cell phone from my handbag. As Nico smoothly turns the conversation to another topic, I send a text to my dick du jour, Marcus.

*My friend went into labor today. I'm at the hospital. Have to cancel dinner tonight.*

Because he's a talent agent to some big movie industry names and has to be available 24-7, his phone is always attached to his hip. So even though it's Sunday, it's no surprise when I immediately see three little dots appear on the screen, indicating he's composing his answer.

*I've never had sex in a hospital . . . ?*

There are some women who'd be insulted by that response, especially since today is Valentine's Day and it's supposed to be all about the hearts and flowers, yada, yada, yada, but his interest in casual sex as opposed to committed relationships is one of the top two things I most enjoy about Marcus.

I'll give you a hint what number one is. It has four letters, starts with C and ends with K, and is longer than eight inches.

I type: *I have. It's not as exciting as you might think.*

Unlike the man himself, his answer comes fast. *Quickie in the parking lot?*

I consider it, but decide to pass. I suppose I can forgo cock for a few hours for my best friend. This time.

*Can't. I'll catch up with you later. Send me a dick pic to tide me over.*

I have to wait a little longer for his answer, but my patience is rewarded by a gorgeous, close-up shot of Marcus's erection, jutting proudly from his unzipped trousers. I'm sure he's sitting behind the desk in his home office at this exact moment, reviewing some boring contract, but getting a boner is like his superpower. The slightest sexual innuendo will make the man's dick jump to life as if it's spring-loaded.

My thumbs fly over the keyboard of my iPhone. *Stroke it. I want video.*

The conversation continues around me but now I'm completely focused on the cell in my hand. I swear these things are mankind's greatest invention.

After about thirty seconds a video loads, opens, and starts to play.

Loudly.

As he strokes himself, Marcus's deep baritone blares from the phone. "You want my hard cock, baby, you got it—"

I yelp and try to get the video to stop. In my fumbling rush I hit the lock button instead. The screen goes dark, but Marcus's voice plays on.

"—right fucking here for you any time you want it—"

Kenji, whose timing is always impeccable, returns with his drink in hand just in time to hear Marcus say, "—you bad sexy girl, you make me so fucking hard, I want your sweet wet pussy on my face—"

"Jesus Christ!" I shout at the phone, frantically hitting the volume button on the side. I finally get it silenced, and blow out a relieved breath.

When I look up, everyone is staring at me.

Ethan, Chris, and Barney all have mouthfuls of food but have stopped chewing.

Kat's eyes are wide and unblinking.

Nico looks as if he might burst into laughter.

Kenji has a hand to his throat and has gone pale.

Brody's dark brows are lifted high on his forehead, but it's not from shock. It's from amusement, evidenced by the way his voice shakes with repressed laughter when he says, "I have so many questions."

My composure regained, I simply smile at them all and wave a hand as if I'm passing by in a royal carriage procession. "Oh, that's just a work thing. Research."

I stuff the phone back into my handbag and keep my serene smile on my face, even when Barney says in a husky tone, "If that's from your work, I need to change jobs."

I meet his penetrating gaze and wink. "I can always use another hand around the office."

Kat snorts. "'Use' being the operative word."

"My God, lovey," says Kenji, fluttering his lashes. "Who was *that*? And can I get an introduction?"

I press my lips together to keep from laughing. Marcus—all six foot four, two hundred thirty pounds of him—would break Kenji in half.

The appearance of Thomas interrupts any further questioning. He bursts into the room shouting, "Chloe's dilated to seven centimeters!"

With her brows pulled together, Kat exclaims, "Already? That's so fast!"

Concerned by the look on Kat's face, I ask, "Is that bad? What does it mean?"

Thomas chuckles. "It means she's swearing like a sailor and giving her mother fits."

Kat flashes me a look but doesn't say anything else. My concern deepens.

Thomas adds, "They took her into the delivery room with her mother and A.J. The doctor seems to think it won't be more than an hour or so before the baby's out."

"An *hour*," Kat repeats slowly.

While all the guys murmur their approval at how efficient Chloe seems to be at hatching new members of the human race, I watch Kat. She's gone pale and has started chewing on her lower lip, sure signs of distress.

I pity Nico. I know his wife's mama bear instinct is going to make her freak out with worry until she can see for herself that Chloe and the baby are both fine.

I slip my feet back into my heels and am about to go over and comfort her, but Brody beats me to it. He moves closer to Kat, bends his head down near hers, and says softly, "My sister's first kid came really fast, too. It's not that unusual."

Kat looks up at him. Her big, almond-shaped eyes fill with hope. "Really?"

Brody nods, smiling down at her reassuringly. "Chloe's gonna do great. She's strong and healthy. Everything's gonna be fine. I promise."

He sounds so confident that Kat actually lets out a relieved breath. "Thanks, Brody."

He nods, shares a smile with Nico, and then, whistling, casually strolls away toward a vending machine on the other side of the room, as if he didn't just prevent a nuclear meltdown.

As the rest of the group chats with Thomas, I follow Brody over to the vending machine. He's staring at the collection of candy and chips behind the glass like it's a maddening puzzle.

When I walk up beside him, he asks, "Salty or sweet?"

Without hesitation I pronounce, "Salty."

He grins, nods in satisfaction as if I've passed a test, inserts a bill into the machine, and presses a key for his selection. A bag of salt-and-vinegar potato chips falls from its shelf. Brody retrieves it from the tray and turns to look at me, his cocky grin still firmly in place.

I say, "Thank you."

He knows exactly what I mean. His shrug is dismissive. He tears open the package of chips, pops one into his mouth, and starts to munch.

I briefly admire the sun-kissed glow on his cheekbones, the copper and gold highlights in his finger-combed brown hair, and the way the muscles in his square jaw flex with every chew, before mentally slapping myself and getting back to what I was saying.

"No, really. *Thank you.* If Nico or I tried to reassure her it probably would've made her worry even more."

Brody swallows. He licks a fine dusting of salt off his lips. His full, sculpted lips, which now glisten with moisture, might as well be calling out "*Kiiisss meee*" in a sultry voice.

Stupid lips.

Looking straight into my eyes, Brody says in that low, sexy voice of his, "I didn't do it for her."

I think, *Holy sparkling unicorns. The way my hoo-ha is tingling, I might as well be watching Ryan Gosling prance naked through a Tiffany store in Paris. I need to never, ever speak to this man again.*

Then the clinically trained part of my brain muses, *Could this be what it feels like to lose your mind?*

My pulse accelerates, my palms start to sweat, and my stomach flutters like a flag in a stiff breeze, but I keep my expression neutral.

I'm excellent at that kind of thing, having practiced it every time I've been near him in the past eighteen months.

"Oh. Well, either way. It was a nice thing to do."

"Nice like when I kissed you in the bathroom at Nico's?"

My pulse zooms into Formula One racing mode. Naked Ryan Gosling dives into a pile of emeralds and rubies and comes up spouting gold coins.

*Steady, Grace. STEADY.*

"When you *tried* to kiss me," I correct.

Brody's gaze drops to my mouth. "I don't know, when two people's lips meet, I think that's technically a kiss." When he looks back up into my eyes, his own are burning.

This is how it's been since the first time our eyes met. That click, like something snapping into place, the aha! when you remember something you'd forgotten. Kat took Chloe and me to see Bad Habit play a gig at the House of Blues and there he was, up on stage, slinging his guitar around his hips like he was fucking it. He looked over at me standing in the shadows offstage and grinned at me, and I just about had a heart attack.

He was the sexiest man I'd ever seen. Every cell in my body screamed "*I want!*"

I've been avoiding him like the plague ever since.

"It's not a kiss if there's no tongue. Besides, you wouldn't know what to do with me." I was going for playful but there's a distinct edge to my voice, almost like a challenge.

*Wonderful. Even my voice has a lady boner for this guy.*

Brody moves closer so I can smell the soap he uses, the wind-clean fragrance of his skin. He leans in and whispers into my ear, "I know exactly what to do with you, Grace. And you know I do. So when you're done with your latest disposable boy toy and find the guts to give me a chance, you know where to find me."

Then he turns and walks away, leaving me flushed and flustered, heart racing, hands trembling, full of exquisite longing for something I know I can never have.

Fate doesn't play favorites with girls like me.

Exactly one hour later, just as Thomas is about to try to get an update on Chloe's progress, A.J. and Chloe's mother appear around the corner of the waiting room wall. She has her arm linked through his and is carefully leading him, murmuring directions in a low, somber voice.

A.J.'s cheeks are wet with tears.

My stomach drops. Everyone falls silent. Sitting next to me, Kenji grips my arm with a little gasp of horror. From one breath to the next, the mood in the room goes from happy to terrified.

If A.J. Edwards—biggest, baddest badass of them all—is crying, it can only mean one thing.

Disaster.

From the chair on my other side, Kat leaps to her feet. She cries, "A.J.?"

He exhales a long, shuddering breath. His mouth works, but no sound comes out.

Elizabeth pats his hand. She says quietly, "It's all right, dear. Tell them."

Everyone stands. No one makes a sound except for Thomas, who jerks forward a few feet and sputters, "What is it? What's happened?"

A.J. makes an awful choking noise. He drags the back of one hand across his eyes. Then he sucks in a deep breath and shouts at the top of his lungs, "IT'S A GIRL!"

A beat of silence.

Then we all start screaming and rush him, everyone talking at once.

I throw my arms around the huge bulk of A.J.'s shoulders. I hear the guys' gruff congratulations, Kat's happy wail, Thomas's curses of relief. Kenji's scream sounds like an air raid siren. We're a big ball of laughter and tears, arms entangled around one another, hugging, euphoric, jumping and jostling, making a scene, but not one of us cares.

Chloe and A.J. have a little girl.

For the first time I can ever remember, I start to cry.

"Congratulations, big guy," I whisper, my wet face resting against A.J.'s shoulder. "You're a daddy."

Blubbering like a baby, A.J. drops his forehead to mine. He's crying so hard his whole body shakes. "I'm a d-daddy," he repeats hoarsely, and then bursts into another round of sobbing.

I start to laugh through my tears. Happiness expands inside my chest, so hot and big it feels as if it might break me wide open.

Elizabeth says, "I hope we didn't scare you too much! A.J. wanted to be the one to tell you all, so I had to give him a moment to compose himself." She beams up at him, her eyes shining with pride. "He was a rock for Chloe in the delivery room, but as soon as the doctor put the baby into his arms . . . well. You can see."

A.J. sobs again.

I've never seen anything more adorable.

"How's Chloe?" I ask.

"Perfect," answers Elizabeth. "Her doctor said he's never seen such a fast, easy first delivery. She only pushed for seventeen minutes! And Abigail's already nursing. Things couldn't have gone better."

Gulping and hiccupping, A.J. nods emphatically.

"Abigail Aleksandra Elizabeth Edwards," whispers Kat, her voice shaky.

It's the name Chloe and A.J. had picked out if they had a girl, honoring their mothers with the two middle names. I meet Kat's watering eyes, and reach out for her. We clasp hands and squeeze hard, smiling at each other.

"When can we see the little muggle?" sniffles Kenji.

His face is blotchy. His cheeks are streaked with mascara. One of his false eyelashes is hanging askew. If he had any idea what he looked like, he'd faint.

"Chloe can have visitors as soon as she's ready. She's going back to the maternity suite in a few minutes. I know she wants to see you all right away." Elizabeth turns her gaze to me. "She really wishes you girls were with her during the delivery, but the hospital policy is two people maximum in the delivery room."

"We know." I swipe beneath my eyes with my fingers. Then from over my shoulder, a tissue appears.

I turn. Brody winks at me and wordlessly waves the tissue.

"Thanks." I take it, wipe my face, try not to like him even more for being so sweet and thoughtful, fail utterly, and then decide I need another drink because this day is far too emotional for me to handle sober.

"Thomas," I say, turning to him. "Do you have any champagne in that minibar?"

"Do I have any champagne?" he scoffs, squaring his shoulders and jutting out his chin. "You might as well ask if the pope has any funny hats!" He raises his arm in the air like a general giving marching orders to his troops. "To the maternity suite!" he cries.

"To the maternity suite!" everyone shouts back in unison.

Like a crazed horde of barbarians, we throng down the hospital hallway, hooting and hollering, scaring the shit out of several unsuspecting nurses and doctors on the way.

Blinking up at me in hazy, slack-mouthed confusion like someone awakening after a long night of hard drinking, the creature snuggled in a pink blankie in my arms is so astonishingly beautiful I can only stare at it in silent awe.

*Her*, I correct myself. I stare at her, little Abigail, feeling as if everything I thought I knew about life is complete and total bullshit.

Today is a day of two huge firsts for me: I cried, and I fell in love.

With a *baby*, of all things.

Next thing you know I'll be wearing sweatpants in public and taking in stray cats.

"She's so perfect," I whisper, marveling at the teeny fingers gripped around my thumb. She has her father's startling eyes—clear golden amber, the color of fine whiskey—but everything else about her is pure Chloe, from her rosebud lips to her long, elegant limbs, to the wispy blonde curls on the top of her head, fine as chick fluff.

Well, she did get one other thing from her father.

She's huge.

"This kid's gonna be an athlete," muses Barney, looking at Abby over my shoulder. "Swimmer, maybe. Or volleyball player."

"Or basketball star," pipes in Nico. "How long did you say she was?"

He looks at Chloe. She's propped up on a pile of pillows in the hospital bed, smiling dreamily, glowing and gorgeous like no person who's just shoved nine pounds and five ounces of infant through her birth canal has any right to be.

She says, "Like half a mile, I think."

A.J., sitting in the chair next to Chloe's bed and finally composed, chuckles. "Sixty-one centimeters."

Nico does the math faster than the rest of us. "Jesus. That's *two feet* of baby, brother!"

Equal parts horrified and impressed, we all stare at Chloe.

She says, "You're gonna feel even worse for me when I tell you that I was too dilated to get an epidural. I had her with no drugs."

Fanning himself and softly moaning, Kenji sinks into a chair on the opposite side of the room.

Kat glares at A.J. He can't see it, but it doesn't stop her. She barks, "I have one word for you Mr. Edwards! Diamonds!"

Smiling, A.J. lifts Chloe's hand to his lips and gently kisses it. "Already on it, Auntie Kat."

Hearing him say the words "Auntie Kat" makes her lower lip quiver. Mollified, she says, "All right, then." Her voice breaks over the last word.

Grinning, Nico pulls her into his arms and murmurs something into her ear that sounds like "big softie."

"Can I hold her?"

We've all taken turns holding the baby except Brody, who now stands in front of me with his arms out, wiggling his fingers in a "gimme" gesture. I carefully place Abby into his arms, and then step back and watch him as he starts to coo down at her, rocking her gently and making funny faces.

He appears to be very comfortable holding a baby. I wonder how close he is with his sister and her kids.

Then I wonder what the hell is happening in my uterus, because I could swear that watching him cuddle that child just made my ovaries twinge.

I abruptly turn away. "Thomas—more champagne, please!"

"Coming up!"

When he hands me a full glass of bubbly, I ignore the way Kat is looking sideways at me with narrowed eyes.

*That woman should be spying for the CIA!*

"Welp, I think we'll get going and let you get some rest," says Chris, speaking for himself and Ethan, who seem to operate as one unit, always arriving and departing together. They approach Chloe's bed and say their good-byes—each of them bending to give her a kiss on the cheek, then bumping fists with A.J.—and then trade hugs with Nico, Kat, and Barney. They then shake hands with Thomas and Elizabeth, who are both high as kites with pride and look as if they might go out dancing after this.

From his chair, Kenji lifts his bejeweled left hand in Chris and Ethan's general direction. Instead of the kiss it appears Kenji is expecting, Chris shakes his pinky finger. Grinning, Ethan does the same.

Kenji heaves a sigh and waves them off like a pair of misbehaving children.

Brody asks them, "See you at the housewarming next Saturday?"

Chris nods with so much enthusiasm I worry his neck might snap. "Dude, can't wait to see the new pad! We'll totally be there."

"What can we bring," chimes in Ethan, "besides hookers?"

At the same time, Kat and Chloe shout, "NO HOOKERS!" startling Elizabeth so much she jumps, sloshing champagne down the front of her Chanel jacket.

"Only kidding, dudes!" says Ethan, laughing. "Chill."

"I'll give you *chill*," growls Chloe.

A.J. puts his face into his hands and tries unsuccessfully to smother his laughter.

"You don't have to bring anything," says Brody, grinning. "I'm all set." He walks to Chloe and carefully places Abby in her arms, then turns back to the guys. "Four o'clock, okay?"

Ethan and Chris agree, trade fist bumps with Brody and hugs with me, and take their leave.

Which is when Brody turns to me and pins me in his stare. "You're coming, right?"

*Is it me, or was that a double entendre? And why am I hoping it was? God, I need to get away from this person as soon as possible.*

I finish my glass of champagne in one swallow. "I didn't realize I was invited."

"Of course you're invited," he says, as if I'm an idiot. "You're core."

"Core?"

He nods, making me admire the way his hair falls over the collar of his shirt. It's really quite pretty hair, glossy and thick, very soft-looking, meant to be touched—

*Oh for fuck's sake. I should just jump out the window and put myself out of my misery.*

I shoot a desperate glance at Thomas to see if he'll read my mind and offer a refill on my champagne, but he's too distracted with his new granddaughter at the moment, so I'm on my own with my raging hormones.

Brody says, "Yeah. Core. You know," he makes a lazy circle in the air with his forefinger. "Part of the inner circle."

And now, for the coup d'état, my vagina decides it would very much like to get acquainted with Brody's finger, because hearing him say "core" and "inner circle" in conjunction with that clockwise motion of his tapered finger sends a bolt of pure lust through me, making my pussy actually *throb*.

Finally my brain has had enough of this nonsense. It shouts at me in no uncertain terms, *STOP*.

Attraction is one thing. I understand attraction. It's simple, it's straightforward, everyone knows what to expect: bada bing, bada boom, now get your ass outta my bedroom. What I feel for Brody goes so far beyond attraction it's not even in the same universe.

Which is exactly why it's so dangerous.

And why I need to stop this madness before it has a chance to get worse.

My smile is pinched. Avoiding his searching gaze, I say coolly, "Thank you for the invitation, but I'm busy next Saturday."

I turn stiffly away from him, set my empty champagne glass on a nearby console, go over to Chloe, and kiss her on the forehead. "I'm leaving, too, but I'll be back tomorrow, okay?"

Chloe nods. "I'm not sure how long we'll be in here, so give me a call first. They might let me go home later tonight."

I'm aghast. "Already?"

She chuckles. "It's not a hotel, Grace. Plus I'm anxious to get into my own bed."

"Oh no!" I cry, remembering something.

Chloe looks startled. "What's wrong?"

"I never checked the thread count on the sheets or bought you candles from the gift store!"

Chloe shakes her head and laughs. "The things you worry about."

"I want you to be comfortable!"

Blue eyes shining, she gazes up at me. Her smile is the definition of angelic. She says softly, "Oh, Gracie, I'm more comfortable than I've ever been in my entire life."

I know she's not talking about the bed.

I stare at them for a moment—my beautiful friend and her perfect baby, the man who literally took a bullet for them seated by their side—and realize with a pang in my chest that today's firsts are still coming.

Because I'm experiencing another emotion I've never felt before. It's ugly, cold, and dangerous, like a snake unfurling inside my belly. I recoil from it exactly as I would if it were a hissing snake about to lash out and sink its fangs into my leg.

It's longing so sharp I can taste it, wanting so deep I feel it in my bones.

It's jealousy.

I'm flooded with shame and confusion. This isn't me, this person. This person who sheds tears and feels envy and can't manage to control her hormones around an attractive man.

I don't like this person. Whoever she is, I have to lock her in a box and throw away the key because she's far too volatile to be trusted.

I force a smile. "Love you, honey."

Chloe smiles back. "Love you, too."

I round the bed and give A.J. a hug. "You did so good," I whisper into his ear.

His expression is calm, proud, and extremely satisfied. He squeezes the arm I've got around his shoulders. "I didn't do anything. I'm just the luckiest motherfucker on the planet."

From behind us, Elizabeth scolds, "*Language*, dear!"

I go over to her and Thomas, give them both hugs, and say my good-byes. I do the same with Nico and Kat, who is watching me a little too closely for comfort, so I escape with a breezy smile as fast as I can.

And then I say good-bye to Kenji.

"Aunt Kenji," I pronounce, looking down at him in his chair, "you were fantastic today. I'm very proud of you."

"You are?" he replies, preening.

"Yes. You didn't make it all about you, you didn't complain . . . much, and you didn't faint once."

His eyes grow misty. He starts blinking rapidly as if he's got a speck of dust lodged under a lid. "Oh, lovey, that's so sweet of you. I don't care what anyone says, you *aren't* a man-eating ballbuster with a shard of ice in her chest where her heart is supposed to be."

And that, folks, is Kenji's version of a sincere compliment.

"Thank you. Considering the source, that means a lot." I lean down and kiss the cheek he offers.

When I turn for the door, I come face-to-face with Barney and Brody. They stand blocking the doorway, looking at me eagerly like they're in line to have a book autographed by their favorite erotica author.

I say cautiously, "Guys. Nice seeing you."

Brody says, "You, too, Grace. It's always great to see you."

He puts emphasis on the word "see." Combined with the twinkle in his eye and the way one corner of his mouth tugs up, I know he's referring to our brief interlude in Nico's bathroom, where he backed me up against the counter and tried to kiss me. I told him to get lost and gave him a laundry list of reasons why I wasn't interested, but not before spending a decent amount of time leering at the bulge in his jeans.

I mean, I might be cold but I'm not dead.

Barney says, "Yep. And, uh . . . I wasn't kidding before. If you ever need a hand around the office . . ."

He shrugs his broad shoulders, leaving the rest of his sentence dangling there between us like a dare.

Brody's expression sours. He shoots a sharp glance at Barney, and then focuses back on me. "If your plans change on Saturday, I'd love to have you."

An explicit picture of Brody "having" me pops into my head, complete with an audio soundtrack of our pleasured groans and the sound of a headboard slamming against a wall as Brody fucks me from behind while I'm on my knees in bed, my face buried in a pillow.

*Great goddess of peckermelons, get me out of this room NOW.*

I say primly, "Sorry. I have a date."

The smile on Barney's face is a little too smug. It irks me. Just because I'm shooting Brody down doesn't mean I want anyone else to be happy about it.

I turn to Barney. "And I *was* kidding before. I always work alone. Thanks for the offer, though." I shoulder past them both, retrieve my handbag from the little table just inside the entrance, and then leave without so much as a backward glance. I walk away briskly, my heels clicking against the linoleum floor.

Just before I'm out of earshot, I hear Barney chuckle. "Is she always that hard to read?"

Brody sighs. "Man, you have no fucking idea."

I walk a little faster before the wistful tone in his voice makes me turn around and run back in.

A few hours later I'm flat on my back in Marcus's bed, stuffed to the gills with his thick cock, taking it like a champ while he bangs the living daylights out of me, when he suddenly stops thrusting and sighs.

"What's wrong?" I ask, perplexed. "Why are you stopping?"

"Because if I wanted to have sex alone, Grace, I'd just jerk myself off."

He stares down at me with his brows lifted, daring me to contradict him.

I don't bother with a denial. I'm many things, but a woman who fakes an interest in sex isn't one of them. "You're right. I'm sorry. My head is just somewhere else."

It wasn't when I got here half an hour ago, but as soon as Marcus slid inside me, it was as if I mentally went offline. I've never composed a to-do list in my head during sex before, but here we are.

God, that's depressing. I'm filled with sudden empathy for one of my patients, who shared with me that she dislikes sex so much she recites Edgar Allen Poe's narrative poem "The Raven" while her husband is fucking her just to keep her mind off how disgusting she finds him.

Marcus offers, "You want me to go down on you?"

"You already did that."

"So you want me to go down on you again?"

I unhook my ankles from around his back, give him a friendly pat on his muscular shoulder, and shake my head. "I don't think it will help. I can tell I'm not going to get there, no matter what we try. It's not you."

He chuckles. "I know. But thanks for the vote of confidence."

He withdraws from my body, rolls to his side, then sits up on the edge of the mattress. With a practiced hand, he removes the condom from his erection and tosses it into the trash can next to the bed. Then he slowly runs a hand over his smoothly shaved head.

He was an athlete in college—running back for USC's football team—and over the past decade has kept his athlete's physique. I admire the way the muscles ripple in his back with the movement of his arm. I admire how beautiful his skin is, shining a deep, burnished brown in the low light, like polished wood. I admire the pure masculine physicality of him, his broad hands and strong thighs and thick neck . . .

And I admit to myself that while Marcus is in every way a perfect specimen of male beauty, at the moment I feel about as much enthusiasm for him as I'd feel if my doctor called to schedule me for a colonoscopy.

This is *not* good. If my libido deserts me I'll have to find something else to occupy all my free time.

And fuck if I'm about to take up knitting.

Marcus rises from the bed and lumbers into the bathroom. Without turning on the light, he runs the faucet and splashes water on his face. He leans over the counter for a moment, his hands braced against the marble. "You want to go get something to eat?"

I sit up, find my dress and underwear scattered on the floor, and step into my panties.

"No, thanks. I think I'll just hit it. I've got an early meeting tomorrow."

I put on my bra, zip up my dress, step into my heels, and comb my fingers through my hair. When I'm finished, I turn to find Marcus leaning against the doorjamb with his arms folded across his chest, watching me.

He says softly, "You don't always have to do that, you know."

"Do what?"

"Run away."

When I don't respond, he pushes off the door and comes to stand in front of me. He pulls me against his chest and winds his strong arms around me. "You could stay the night for once. It wouldn't kill you."

It probably would, but I decline to share that opinion with him.

"You know I don't do sleepovers, Marcus."

"I know. And you don't talk about your past and you don't date anyone longer than a month."

His tone isn't accusing, only factual, but I find myself feeling defensive anyway. I say into his chest, "I thought we were on the same page about all that."

"We were." He pulls away and looks at me. "Until I realized our one-month stand is almost up."

I frown, trying to remember when we met. "Is it? Honestly I haven't been keeping track."

Marcus brushes my hair off my face. "Yeah? That sounds like a good thing. I must be keeping you too preoccupied to watch the calendar." His smile comes on slow and sultry.

It was the first thing I noticed about him when we met, apart from his sheer size. He's got a killer smile, totally confident, totally sexy, totally effective on its intended target. I'm always amused when we're out somewhere together at how easily he can make a woman swoon with nothing but a well-timed flash of that rakish grin.

Absentmindedly, I reach down and fondle his cock. It's still stiff. "How many days do we have left?"

"Six."

His voice is thick. I know he loves it when I've got my hands on him. He loves to watch me jerk him off, loves the contrast in the colors of our skin, my paleness against his darkness, my small, soft palms gripping his big, hard dick.

I sigh. He really is a good one. Too bad our time is almost up.

Suddenly he takes my head in his hands and kisses me, hard. When he breaks away, he says, "Let's renegotiate our deal. Tack on a few extra days, see how it goes. What do you say?"

Cue the sound of screeching brakes.

"Marcus. Please tell me you're not catching feelings for me."

He blinks, the picture of innocence. "Feelings? What're those?"

When I narrow my eyes, he sighs. "I like you, yes. I'll admit that. We're very similar people. We're both focused on our careers, we both love sex, neither one of us wants a relationship. And to be totally honest, I haven't found that particular combo before. So I'm reluctant to give it up. That's it."

He pauses. His eyes search my face. "It's your turn to talk now."

"I'm trying to decide if you're telling the truth or just telling me what you think I want to hear."

His voice comes husky. "You've still got my cock in your hands, Grace. Do you have any idea how hard it would be to come up with a convincing lie right now?"

I tip my head back, look at him from beneath my lashes, and lightly squeeze his erection. "As hard as this?"

He smiles. "Maybe not *that* hard."

"I should take care of this before I leave," I say, squeezing him again.

His voice is unsteady when he asks, "Are you trying to distract me so you don't have to answer my question?"

I don't bother with an answer. I simply sink to my knees, apply my mouth, and get on with the distraction that never fails to bring inconvenient conversations with men to an abrupt end.

The night is crystal clear and cold. I drive with the windows of my Lexus down, letting the icy wind sting my cheeks and whip my hair, sweep the cobwebs from my head. I take the long way home, avoiding the I-405 that's always bumper-to-bumper, even at this late hour on a Sunday evening, and take the winding two-lane canyon road instead. It snakes through the Santa Monica Mountains, linking the inland valleys to the beach communities of Malibu and Pacific Palisades. It's the longer route, even with the freeway traffic, but I need to be alone with my thoughts.

And, truth be told, I dread going to sleep.

The nightmares never really went away, but they're much more frequent this time of year. In the weeks leading up to St. Patrick's Day, they appear almost every night with relentless ferocity, violent ordeals of screams and carnage that leave me shaking and sweating when I bolt upright in bed, staring wildly into the dark with my heart like a jackhammer inside my chest.

Nothing has cured them, not therapy or medication or time.

Everyone has their demons. Mine come out to play at night.

In the first months after the accident, the nightmares paralyzed me. It was like reliving the worst moment of your life over and over again, in surround sound and Technicolor. I slowly learned to accept them the way you accept that you have cancer. There was a lot of anger and denial at first, a lot of fear and bargaining, a desperate search for cures and answers that eventually yielded nothing but exhaustion and ultimately the realization that I was no longer in control.

Sleep was no longer my friend.

My own mind was a traitor to me.

Summer and fall are better. Quieter. The demons rest. But for me, the waning days of winter and the early days of spring are a living hell.

Pacific Coast Highway is gorgeous in the moonlight. The ocean is as black as ink, as restless as I feel. The traffic is light so I fly up the coast, listening to Nina Simone sing the blues in her raspy contralto.

By the time I get to my building in Century City, it's nearly midnight. I slow as I approach the high metal entry gate, and wave to the guard in the security booth.

"Evenin', Miss Stanton," he says, tipping his hat.

"Hi, Roy. How are you?"

He nods, smiling. "Better than I deserve. Have a good one, ma'am." He waves me through.

In the portico, the valet takes my car. Inside the elegant lobby of glistening glass and marble, the night concierge murmurs hello. Avoiding my reflection in the mirrors that line the walls, I take the private elevator to my floor. The doors open to reveal my darkened condo and a spectacular view of the Los Angeles night skyline through the living room windows beyond.

I set my handbag on the console by the door and step out of my heels. I don't turn on the lights. I stand there for a moment in the dark, watching the night sky, all the lights that sparkle like faraway diamonds.

I think of all the joy at the hospital today. All the love and warmth and happy tears.

Inside my living room, it's as cold and silent as a tomb.

At times like this, my loneliness is so raw, so sharp and burning, I have to fight to breathe.

This is one of the reasons I chose the career I have. I couldn't help myself. There was no cure for what ailed me, so I wanted to help others who might be going through something similar. I understand what drives people to stay in relationships long after the love is gone. I know why they accept less than they deserve, and put up with too much shit, and suffer for years rather than get out.

Because loneliness can kill you.

And even if it doesn't kill you physically—which it certainly can, disease of the psyche often leads to disease of the flesh—it can kill your soul.

Which, in all the ways that count, is actually worse.

Just ask me.

I pad in my bare feet into the kitchen, flip on the overhead light, pull a frozen dinner from the freezer, heat it up in the microwave, and eat it right out of the plastic tray, standing over the sink. Then I go to my bedroom. I wash my face, brush my teeth, get undressed, and get into bed. I watch television for as long as I can keep my eyes open, switching between late-night talk shows and old movies. Finally at 3:00 a.m. when I can no longer fight sleep, I turn off the TV.

Then, staring up at the ceiling with my hands clenched to fists at my sides, I wait for the darkness to take me.

At one o'clock the next afternoon, I'm eating a salad at my desk in my office when the phone rings. I pick it up, say, "Grace Stanton speaking," and laugh when the response comes, sharp as a tack.

"*The* Grace Stanton, marriage therapist to the stars, ultimate commitment-phobe and dedicated dickaholic?"

"Dickaholic?" I repeat, grinning. "That's a new one, Kat. Bonus points for creativity."

"It was either that or 'cock-gobbling meretrix.'"

"Meretrix? Have you been reading the dictionary again?"

"Aha!" she crows, pleased. "You don't know what the word means, do you, Ms. PhD from Stanford University?"

I look at the ceiling and sigh. "A meretrix was a registered prostitute in ancient Rome."

In my mind I see her on the other end of the line, sticking out her tongue and flipping me the bird. "I'm gonna get you one of these times."

"In your dreams, princess. And thanks for the compliment, by the way. It's so wonderful to have friends who ring you at work just to call you a whore."

"You're not a whore," comes the immediate response. "You just like dick more than any person I've ever met."

I smile. "So technically I'm a slut."

She protests, "If you were a man we wouldn't even be having this conversation!"

"Hey, you started it."

"That's not why I'm calling anyway," she says, changing the subject. "I just wanted to let you know that Chloe was released from the hospital late last night."

I stuff a bite of salad into my mouth and say between chews, "I know. I called this morning and they said she'd checked out."

"So d'you want to go visit her after work tonight?"

"Tonight? You don't think we should give her a few days to settle in, spend time alone with A.J. and the baby?"

Kat snorts. "Whose idea do you think it was that we come over? A.J. has already texted me like ten times trying to find out how soon we can be there. He's dying to show that baby off to whoever he can. I think he's dragging people in off the street!"

"I didn't get any texts from him," I say, surprised.

There's a short pause. Then Kat says, "You might be the only person on earth he's afraid of."

"Oh please! That man isn't afraid of anything!"

Kat's response is wry. "I hate to break it to you, Ice Queen, but you have no idea how intimidating you can be. I know a few mobsters who'd shit their pants if they had to go up against you."

Ice Queen? I'm not sure whether to be insulted or pleased, so I settle on neutral. Even if it does sting a little. "Well, good. It's better to be feared than loved."

This time the pause is longer. Softly, Kat asks, "Is it?"

*Oh shiznits. Here comes the lecture.*

"I can't tonight anyway. I've got plans with Marcus. How about tomorrow?"

"You have plans with Marcus? That's like twice this week, right? And you said you had another date with him this coming Saturday?"

I hear the hope in her voice, close my eyes, and pinch the bridge of my nose. It's hard having two best friends who so completely, utterly, and unreservedly believe in true love.

Not everyone gets the happily-ever-after.

"Kat. Please don't do that."

"Do what?" she asks, sounding hurt.

"You know what."

"Wanting you to be happy? Why is that so bad?"

"I *am* happy. We don't all need the white picket fence!"

It comes out harsher than I expected. I hear it in the silence that follows, in her offended little huff, so I backtrack. "I'm not saying there's anything wrong with the white picket fence. It's just not for me, that's all. You know that. It's how I'm built."

"It's how you *choose* to be built," she shoots back.

"I'm not fighting with you about this," I say firmly. "And I'm not defending my personal choices about my love life, either. Do you want to go together to Chloe's tomorrow night or not?"

After a tense pause in which I count every tick of the clock on the wall, Kat sighs. "You drive me to drink, girlfriend."

"Don't blame your chronic alcohol problem on me, dear."

"Gah. You're such a bitch."

She says it with love, though, so I know I'm forgiven. "Do you want me to drive? I can pick you up around six?"

"Fine. See you at six."

We say good-bye and hang up, but I have a bad feeling this conversation isn't over.

The next night promptly at 6:00 p.m., I push the button on the call box at the bottom of the long, gated drive that leads to Nico and Kat's place in the Hollywood Hills. When the buzzer sounds, I pull through the gate. When I get to the top of the drive I start to laugh, as I always do when I see their house.

"The Shack," they jokingly call it. It's an enormous compound of glass and stone, perched on the side of the hill with a spectacular view of the entire Los Angeles basin, from downtown to the sparkling Pacific to Malibu, far north. It's about as shack-like as the Taj Mahal.

I park next to the fountain in the middle of the circular driveway and head to the front door, a massive slab of redwood twice as tall as I am. It opens before I'm even halfway across the cobblestone drive.

Barney stands there waiting. He's looking at me over the rims of a pair of mirrored sunglasses, with his brows lifted and an expression like he hasn't eaten in weeks.

"Hey there, big boy," I say playfully when I reach the front step. "How's it hangin'?"

He smiles, exposing a set of gleaming white teeth. "To my knees, Angelface."

"Oh my. And I thought that was just a big gun in your pocket."

"Oh, it *is* big. And fully loaded."

We grin at each other.

"Your girlfriend's in the kitchen."

"Thanks." Then, just to see if he'll play, I add, "I'd ask you why you're wearing sunglasses indoors but then you'd probably tell me something dumb like your future is so bright you have to wear shades and I'd lose all respect for you."

His smile is blinding. He slides his sunglasses farther down his nose, looks me up and down, and drawls, "I know that's a line from a song. And honestly, sweetheart, it's not your respect I'm interested in."

"No?" I blink coyly, thoroughly enjoying myself. There's nothing like a little harmless flirting with someone who can give as good as he gets. "Then what are you interested in?"

I half expect him to say something creepy, but he surprises me when he deadpans, "I just want to say one word to you. Just one word. Are you listening?"

"I'm listening."

"Plastics."

It's a famous line from a movie. He's testing me to see if I'll get it. Which, because I'm a huge film buff, I do.

"Exactly how do you mean, Mr. McGuire?" I answer, playing the part of Dustin Hoffman's character, Benjamin.

Barney's face lights up. "You know *The Graduate*?"

"What, you thought I was just another pretty face?"

"I thought you were a pretty everything," he answers instantly. "But getting my stupid movie references makes me think you might actually have a brain, too."

I pretend to be insulted. "I'm a licensed therapist, Barney. I'll have you know I have an advanced degree!"

He's clearly not impressed. "Some of the stupidest people I've met have advanced degrees. Also, therapists are generally as much of a whack job as their patients are."

"Usually more," I agree, taking no offense because he's right.

"I'm glad we had this conversation," he says with a straight face, nodding. "Now I can masturbate to the thought of your enormous brain and not just your beautiful body. I'll feel much better about myself afterward. You know, women's rights and whatnot. I know you ladies like to be taken seriously."

"You're fun," I declare, charmed by this Armani-wearing, smart-mouthed thug. "Why didn't I know this about you?"

"Probably on account of the huge cloud of testosterone that surrounds me. Makes it hard to see me through all this"—he swivels his hips and waggles his eyebrows up and down—"machismo."

I throw back my head and laugh. "Yes. That's definitely it. Now let me in before I throw myself at you and ruin a beautiful friendship."

"Goddamn. Don't tease me like that, woman," he says, his voice gravelly and his dark eyes alight.

"You can take it."

I place my hand on his broad chest and gently shove. He steps back, grinning, his gaze raking over me, and lets me inside. As I walk by him, I say over my shoulder, "I know you're staring at my ass, Mr. Machismo, because I can feel it burning."

His husky laugh follows me all the way into the kitchen.

I find Kat perched on a stool at the huge marble island in the middle of the gourmet kitchen, staring at an open cookbook on the counter as if it just arrived from outer space.

I say, "Hey."

Without looking up she asks, "Lobsters can feel pain, right?"

"I don't know. I've never asked one."

She glances up at me, distress in her eyes. "Seriously. This recipe"—she points at the book—"calls for a *live* lobster to be thrown into boiling water. That's, like, torture!"

"Your warped sense of morality is torture. Where do you think those juicy steaks you like so much come from? *Murdered cows.*"

Kat puts her hands over her ears. "Stop it. I'll have nightmares."

I fake a dying cow staggering around the kitchen. *"Moooooo!"* I moan loudly.

"Cut it out!"

I stop when I realize she's freaking out. I cross to where she's sitting and give her a hug. "Oh, honey," I say, patting her silky dark hair. "It must be tough going through life with half a brain and a too-big heart."

"I don't even know why we're friends." She sighs, pushing me away.

I gently smooth her hair off her forehead. "Because Chloe only blows rainbows and sunshine up your ass and you need someone to bring you back down to reality once in a while."

"You're hopeless."

"Thank you."

"Can we go now?"

I smile. "Yes. Where's Nico?"

She hops off the stool. "In the studio working on some new tracks. He probably won't be done until late, so we have hours and hours to smother little Abby in auntie love."

"A-smothering we shall go!" I link my arm through hers and we head back out to the car.

The drive from Kat and Nico's in Hollywood to Chloe and A.J.'s in Laurel Canyon takes about thirty minutes in traffic. By the time we get there, it's dark and my stomach is grumbling. I skipped breakfast and only had a salad for lunch.

"We should've brought food," I say, pulling into the driveway. The house is much more modest than Kat's, but still sprawling in comparison to the average home.

Kat says, "No need. A.J. said Chloe's mother has brought so much food over there's not enough space for it."

I shut the car off and turn to look at Kat. "Chloe's mother doesn't cook."

She waves a hand at me. "When I say Chloe's mother you know I mean their housekeeper. Same thing."

"Chloe's mother isn't anywhere *near* the same thing as their housekeeper."

"You're right," Kat says, getting out of the car. "Their housekeeper has a soul."

Chuckling, I follow her to the front door. "You're in fine form tonight. Everything okay?"

"Yep," she answers, a little too quickly. Avoiding my eyes, she knocks on the front door.

Chloe opens it before I can force Kat to tell me the truth.

"Girls!" Chloe throws her arms around both of us. When she pulls away she's beaming. Even in a ratty T-shirt and sweats, with no makeup and her blonde hair pulled into a sloppy ponytail, she looks stunning. "How are you?"

"I'm fine." I look pointedly at Kat. "But this one is only pretending she is."

Kat snaps, "Hello pot, meet kettle!" and barges past Chloe into the house.

Chloe and I look at each other. "Uh-oh," says Chloe.

I lower my voice. "Do you think she and Nico had a fight?"

"She hasn't said anything to me. You?"

"Not a word. We'll get it out of her, though." In a normal tone, I say, "Now where's that gorgeous baby of yours?"

Chloe giggles. "With her daddy, of course. Where she always is. C'mon in."

I step inside the house. Warmth and a profusion of scents hit me, baked bread and baby powder and fresh flowers, a pleasant mélange of homey goodness. Chloe shuts the door, and then leads me through the entryway into the living room, where we find Kat standing silently in front of the rocking chair A.J. is sitting in.

More correctly, the rocking chair A.J. is stuffed into. His huge frame overflows from all sides, threatening to crush the thing. His eyes are closed. His head lolls to one side. His mouth is slightly open, and he's softly snoring.

His sleeping daughter is cradled in his big, tattooed arms.

Kat turns to us. Her eyes are bright with tears. She makes a motion with her open hands—*Look at this, would you!*—and turns and heads for the kitchen.

Chloe and I share a smile.

We tiptoe past A.J. and the baby, careful not to wake them. Thankfully the kitchen is on the other side of the house, separated from the living room by the dining room and the den, so we can talk without disturbing the two sleeping beauties.

When we walk into the kitchen, Kat already has her head stuck inside the fridge. "Do you have any white wine?"

"No, I have something better." Chloe reaches past Kat and pulls out a frosty pitcher full of pale yellow liquid. "I made margaritas!"

"Oh, thank God," moans Kat. "You're an angel. Gimme, gimme!"

"Go sit, both of you." Chloe motions with her chin to the kitchen table. "I'll get us set up."

"Honey, you should be resting, not waiting on us!" I protest, trying to take the pitcher from Chloe's hands.

She lightly smacks my hands away, laughing. "I had a baby, Grandma, not a heart transplant! I feel fine!"

"I'm pretty sure you're abnormal, though." I watch her with narrowed eyes to make sure she's not overextending herself as she gets glasses from the cupboard and pours two drinks. She sets the pitcher on the table, empties a bag of tortilla chips into a big bowl, and puts that out along with some freshly made guacamole.

"Ta da!" she says, grinning like a maniac. "It's just like we're at Lula's!"

"Except there's no hideous mariachi music and you're not drinking," notes Kat. Not wasting any time, she slurps her margarita.

"Yeah, I've gotta figure out the whole breastfeeding versus alcohol consumption thing. I can't have a drink if Abby needs to eat within a few hours, and considering she *always* needs to eat within a few hours, I'm pretty much out of luck." Chloe smiles. "Not that I mind. I'd make that trade-off any day."

I take a seat at the round wooden kitchen table and reach for my drink. "How are you not even tired? You look like you just got back from vacation!"

Chloe's smile grows soft. Her blue eyes glow with warmth. "Turns out the drummer from Bad Habit is a natural-born baby whisperer. Believe it or not, I'm sleeping almost all the way through the night because every time Abby makes the slightest peep, he picks her up and she goes quiet. Even when I'm breastfeeding she always looks right at him, and has to be holding his finger. He's doing everything from changing diapers to giving her a bath. He's been amazing."

I'm a little surprised by this information. "He can do all that?"

Chloe nods. "The mobility and independence training he's been getting since the operation has been incredible. He's taken to it like a duck to water. I honestly think there isn't anything he couldn't also do when he was sighted." She smiles. "Except drive. Though as far as he's concerned, the jury's still out on that."

"Oh, sweetie," I say softly, reaching out to squeeze her hand. "I'm so happy for you."

"Me, too."

There's something strange in Kat's voice that makes Chloe and me look at her. She inhales a long, trembling breath, and then guzzles the rest of her margarita.

"Kat?" says Chloe, reaching for her hand. "What's wrong?"

"No." She shakes her head. "I'm not raining on your parade."

"My parade is your parade," says Chloe. "Talk."

"It's really not a big deal."

"Don't make me beat it out of you."

"I'm fine, honestly—"

"Cut the crap," interrupts Chloe. "We're family. *Talk.*"

Her hands shaking, Kat pours herself another margarita. Then she blows out a hard breath, sweeps her hair off her face, and looks at us.

"Nico and I have been trying to get pregnant. And it's not happening. I got my period today. And I'm . . . because of what happened before . . . I'm afraid . . . there might be something wrong with me." She looks at the tabletop. In a quieter voice she says, "I'm afraid I won't be able to give Nico the family he wants, and then . . ."

She trails off into silence. Her face is pale and somber. I feel every ounce of her pain, exactly as if it were my own.

"And then you'll adopt," I say gently.

She looks up and meets my eyes. She whispers, "That's what he said. But—"

"No buts. If he's on board with that idea, there's no problem. Have you seen a doctor yet?"

Kat shakes her head. "I've been too freaked out to go. I know it's stupid, but I'm worried what I might find out."

"We'll make an appointment for next week and go with you," Chloe declares.

"I agree. Denial isn't the way to deal with this, sweetie."

Kat looks at me. Her big green eyes flash with sudden anger. "Excuse me, but you're in no position to be talking to me about denial, Grace!"

I'm taken aback by the force in her tone. "What do you mean?"

"I mean this whole Brody situation you're so determined to pretend isn't happening!"

Enunciating every word, I say calmly, "There is nothing happening between me and Brody."

"You can deny it all you want, but I've never seen you look at a man like that."

I can't resist. I have to know. Even though this is dangerous territory, I'm going in. "Like what?"

*"Hopefully."*

I laugh. "Honey, the only time I've *ever* looked at a man hopefully is right before I unzip his pants for the first time and I'm praying he's packing more than five inches."

Kat shakes her head. "Fine. Don't admit it. But it doesn't change what I saw."

"Maybe you need to get your eyes checked."

In a flat, no-nonsense tone, Chloe says, "You realize we know you too well for you to get away with this tough-chick act you try to pull, right?"

Kat and I look at her in surprise. Chloe rarely calls anyone out on their shit, and when she does, she feels so guilty afterward she always apologizes and says she didn't mean it.

Right now she doesn't look guilty. She actually looks a little mad.

Maybe being a mother is bringing out the tiger in her.

"It's not an act, Chloe. I actually am very tough."

She retorts, "Only on the outside."

Impressed, Kat blinks at her. "Go on, girl. Preach."

Encouraged by the traitor, Chloe leans forward. "I've seen the way you look at Brody, too. And not only that, but I saw the way you looked at Abby when you first held her. And the way you looked at her when you just came in."

She stares at me with a challenge in her blue eyes.

I say drily, "Your large, beast-like child is uncommonly pretty, Chloe. I like pretty things. That's all."

Chloe scoops up a handful of chips and chucks them at me. They smack me on the chest before I can duck out of the way. "Hey!"

"Take that back!"

I brush the crumbs off my shirt. "You're right. That was unnecessary. She isn't beast-like, she's beautiful—"

"Not that, you nincompoop!"

Even though Chloe is trying to fry me with her eyeballs, I can't help myself. I break into a grin and look at Kat. "*Nincompoop*? Oh boy, now she's breaking out the big guns."

Chloe—aggravated to the point that she pounds her fist on the table, making the silverware clatter—growls, "Stop trying to pretend you *don't have a heart*!"

That stops me cold.

I sit back against my chair and exhale. Blood pounds in my temples. "I'm happy, Chloe—"

"You're not happy. You're safe. They're two different things. You said that to me once, and it was totally true. So now I'm saying it to you, and I'm going to say something else that you're not going to like but you really need to hear. Are you ready?"

"Absolutely *not.*"

Chloe ignores that. She leans even farther over the table and looks deep into my eyes.

"You didn't die in that car crash with your parents, Grace. You just stopped living."

# Chapter 6

Sucker punch to the gut. My throat closes. I swallow, but I can't find any air.

Every once in a while Princess Buttercup pulls a gem like that one out of the clouds and knocks me flat on my ass.

I look back and forth between her and Kat. "You two have already talked about this, haven't you?"

Kat remains silent. Chloe lifts a shoulder.

*Houston, we have a problem.*

"Well I *don't* want to talk about this."

"Tough shit," says Chloe softly, holding my gaze. "We've let you get away with hiding for way too long. You're my friend and I love you, and I'm sick of watching you use sex as a shield. You distract men with your friendly vagina so they don't have a chance to get to know you, so you don't have a chance to get attached, so you'll always be alone because you think you should be. Well I've got news for you. That's a shitty, empty, pointless way to spend a life. And you're better than that, Grace. *You. Deserve. Happiness.* But the only way you're ever going to get it is if you let someone in."

Kat leans toward me so now I've got *two* meddling harpies up in my grill.

"Like Brody, for instance. Or Marcus. Hell, even Barney seems to have the hots for you!"

I spread my hands flat on the table. I inhale a slow, deep breath, contemplating what I've just heard, and how much I should tell them.

Finally I realize I have to tell them the truth. The whole, ugly truth. They want something for me that I can never have, and until I tell them everything, they won't stop pestering me. Not since they both found their happily-ever-afters and decided I should get one, too.

So . . . here goes. I take another breath and begin.

"I love you guys. I love that you're worried about me. I hear what you're saying, I do. And now I'm going to tell you both to *mind your own business* because neither of you will ever—*could* ever—possibly understand what it's like to wake up one day with no family, no memory, and no idea who you are or where you are or even what your own goddamn name is."

Kat says softly, "Honey—"

I hold up a hand to stop her. "No. This is the last thing I'll say, and then we're not going to ever mention this topic again. It took me years after the accident to not want to kill myself. I lived through hell. And I made it out alive. But I could go back there any minute."

Chloe blinks. "Go back? What do you mean by that?"

I blow out a hard breath. "With the kind of amnesia I have and the damage to my hippocampus, I could lose all my memories again. My new memories, the ones I've made since the accident. I could wake up one day and it would all be gone, like that"—I snap my fingers—"*again.*"

Horrified, Chloe and Kat gasp.

"Oh my God," chokes Kat. "You never told us that!"

"Well for obvious reasons it's not something I really want to discuss. It's just . . . no one has a guarantee they'll get a tomorrow. Anyone could die at any moment. People know that on an intellectual level, but unless you're old the odds of death on any one day are low. But for me, there's a good chance every day I could wake up in the morning and have no idea who or where I am. *Every day*, literally, could be my last."

Chloe and Kat are white, silent, gaping at me in shock.

"So to fall in love . . ."

I have to take another deep breath because I'm getting so choked up. "To fall in love would not only be pointless, but also possibly the cruelest thing I could ever do to someone." I look at Chloe. "Imagine if A.J. woke up tomorrow morning and had no memory of who you are. No memory of Abby, or your life together, or even being in love with you. What if you were nothing to him but a stranger? How would you feel?"

Her eyes well with water. She whispers, "I'd want to die."

"Yes," I say quietly, holding her gaze. "Welcome to my world."

There's a long, tense silence. Then, at the same time, Chloe and Kat burst into tears.

Kat jumps up, throws her arms around my neck, and starts to sob all over me. Hugging me tightly, she wails, "Why didn't you ever fucking tell us this before, you fucking selfish goddamn twat?"

I have to smile. When Kat gets emotional her paper-thin logical side flies out the window and she starts to curse like a drunken sailor and emote all over the place.

"Gee, I don't know," I say, my face smashed into her boobs. "Couldn't be anything to do with the reaction I knew I'd get."

"Oh, Gracie. Oh, honey, I'm so sorry."

Now I've got Chloe on my other side, hugging me and crying into my hair.

I feel like someone should be filming this for a PMS commercial.

"Oh, stop you two. You're ruining my silk blouse." I gently push them away. They sit, their wet faces and big, weepy eyes so depressing I have to down the contents of my glass in one gulp.

Jesus, women are high maintenance.

"My point of telling you this isn't to make you feel sorry for me, but to try to get you to accept that the house in the suburbs and the two point five babies and the man of my dreams isn't in the cards for me. And that's okay. I have a full life. I have a job I love." I glance at them sourly. "And I have you two dimwits. Quite frankly, I think I'm luckier than most."

Silence.

Then Kat bursts into tears again. Which of course makes Chloe join in.

"Oh for fuck's sake." I sigh, and pour myself another drink.

By the time I get back to my condo, I'm mentally, physically, and emotionally exhausted. All I want to do is take a bath and a Xanax and crawl into bed. I drop my purse and keys on the console inside the door, flip on the lights, and go into my bedroom, where I notice the red light blinking on the answering machine. It's a message from the concierge downstairs, saying they have a package waiting for me. I call down and tell them to send it up.

Five minutes later I'm staring at an enormous bouquet of white orchids in a crystal vase.

"What the hell?" I mutter, standing at the open door in my bare feet.

"Would you like me to put it anywhere in particular?" asks Sheridan, the night concierge, from behind the flowers. He's a big guy, but the bouquet is even bigger. I can't see his upper body.

"Sure, how about the dining room table?" I swing the door open wider and let him in.

Sheridan walks carefully forward, peering through the flowers, trying not to trip on any stray objects.

"Chair on your left," I warn, just as he's about to stumble into it.

"Thanks. This sucker's huge." He manages to get it to the dining room without breaking any body parts or furniture, and sets it down on the table with a grunt. Then he stands back and examines the flowers with his hands propped on his hips.

"Looks like you made a big impression on somebody, Miss Grace."

"Or someone heard I died."

Startled, Sheridan looks over at me.

"Only kidding." My gallows humor doesn't always go over.

I hand him five bucks and show him to the door. Once he's gone, I open the white envelope attached to the flowers. It reads:

*Grace,*

*Bring your date to my housewarming on Saturday. I need to get a look at the competition.*

*Yours,*

*Brody*

*PS – I've made a list of rebuttals to your arguments of why we shouldn't date. It's pretty detailed but I'll give you a little preview of #17, in response to your assertion that it would be awkward if it didn't work out between us due to the inevitability we'd be forced to see each other because of the relationships of our mutual friends:*

*No one has to know.*

*PPS – I can't stop thinking about you. I might need to seek therapy. Know any good therapists?*

*PPPS – I know you can't stop thinking about me, either. If it feels like this now . . .*

He leaves the rest unwritten, but the meaning is clear. If it feels like this now, before we've even touched—except for a brief, closed-mouthed kiss that I quickly ended—what would it feel like if I actually gave in and we got together?

"Like trouble," I say aloud to the empty room.

Cocky son of a bitch.

He signed it with a scribble, his phone number beneath. I hesitate for a moment, thinking, but then decide to call, thank him for the flowers, and offer another firm, polite refusal so this doesn't go any further.

I mentally don my strongest, steeliest armor and dial his number from my cell.

He answers after two rings with a sleepy, "Hello?"

"Hello, Brody," I say briskly, all business. "This is Grace. I'm calling to say thank—"

"Grace. Do I know a Grace?" he muses, his voice low, scratchy, and full of mischief. "Lemme think. Describe what you look like."

"Ha-ha. You know exactly what I look like. As I was saying, I'm calling to—"

"Are you the Grace with the hump back and the hairy wart on the end of her nose?"

"What? No! Of course not!"

"Hmm." He pretends to think. "The short one with the extra toe on her left foot?"

"Oh my God. This is ridiculous. You know *exactly* who I am—"

"Oh yes," he sighs dreamily. "You're the one with skin like fresh cream and hair the color of autumn and eyes like thunderclouds over the sea."

After a moment I ask, "Have you been drinking?"

I feel his chuckle all the way down to my toes. "No. I've actually been napping. And having seriously dirty and wonderful dreams of you. Come over, I'm still in bed."

I put the phone to my chest, close my eyes, and inhale a big, calming breath.

"Hello?"

I put the phone back up to my ear. "I'm here."

"Did you drop the phone?"

"No. Sort of. It doesn't matter. Listen, what I've been trying to say is—"

"I just want to get to know you better," he interrupts with sudden intensity. "No strings. No expectations. No pressure. Don't blow me off yet. Okay?"

*Dear God. This man is going to be the death of me.*

I turn my back on the flowers and walk slowly down the hallway into my bedroom. I go into the bathroom and stare at myself in the mirror.

"You're not saying anything," he prompts. "What're you doing right now?"

I answer honestly. "Looking at myself in the mirror and trying to decide if I should hang up or not."

"Please don't," he softly begs.

Something in the center of my chest melts. Warmth spreads throughout my body.

*Fuck.*

I whisper, "I have this really awful feeling that you're going to be my Kryptonite."

"So you have a Superman complex. Interesting."

His tone has switched from pleading to teasing, lightning fast. I wonder if it's because he could sense I was about to not only hang up on him because it was getting too intense, but erase his number forever, move to the Amazon jungle, and join an all-female cult that worships cats and carbohydrates as divinities.

But because we've moved to safer ground, I ditch that plan and stay on the line.

"Actually Batman was always my favorite."

"Really? Why?"

He sounds genuinely interested, so I tell him. "Because he's not really a superhero. He doesn't have superhuman strength, or amazing powers, or really any advantages other than money and technology. He's just a man with a fucked-up past trying to do the right thing."

The silence that follows throbs with something I can't describe. Then, in a husky voice that cracks more than once, Brody says, "On a scale of one to ten, how weird would it be if I told you I just fell in love with you?"

I don't know why, but that makes me laugh out loud. "Eleventy-seven."

He laughs, too. "Oh good. No worries, then."

After our laughter dies down, he says, "Moving on—you haven't yet thanked me for the flowers."

I roll my eyes. "What do you think I've been trying to do this entire call?"

"Pretend you're not as into me as I am into you. Your usual MO. But that's beside the point. Did the florist send the big drapey white orchids like I asked?"

"They did."

"And are they as amazing as they promised me they'd be?"

"They are."

He sounds smug. "Good. You can go ahead then."

"Go ahead and what?"

"Thank me! *Tsk.* Where are your manners, Slick?"

"Slick? Did you just call me *Slick*?"

His voice turns practical. "I figure you've probably been called every variation of red, in honor of your hair color, so I thought I'd go with the general, overall impression you made the first time I saw you."

I'm not sure if that's a compliment or not. "You thought I looked . . . slick."

Without hesitation or artifice, he quietly replies, "I thought you looked like the most beautiful thing I'd ever seen."

Blood rushes into my face. A dull, hot throb in my cheeks quickly spreads to my ears and neck.

"Uh-oh," says Brody. "She's gone radio silent again."

"Normally I'm not this easily rattled, but I must admit, Mr. Scott, you really know how to throw me for a loop."

The smug tone makes a reappearance. "Aha! So you know my last name! You've been stalking me on the internet, haven't you?"

I say drily, "Let's not get carried away."

"Speaking of getting carried away, what're you wearing to my party on Saturday?"

In spite of myself, I chuckle. "Number one, that was the absolute worst segue I've ever heard. And number two, I never said I was coming to your party."

"You are, though, right? The flowers totally worked?"

He still sounds playful, but I hear the undertone of seriousness. I sigh, rubbing a hand over my burning cheek. "No."

"You know what that tells me?"

I look at the ceiling, hoping for a stray asteroid to demolish my building so I won't have to continue this conversation. "I can hardly wait to know."

"That you're afraid."

"I'm not *afraid*, Egosaurus, I'm just otherwise engaged."

"So be otherwise unengaged. I told you: bring him."

"Are you always like this?"

"Like what?" he asks innocently.

"Like a friggin' goat."

"A *goat*?" He sounds insulted.

"You know, because they're so stubborn."

"No. No, that's an absolutely terrible comparison. C'mon, seriously, a goat?"

"What would be better, a dog?"

"A *dog*?" he shouts. "You're *terrible* at this! Dogs are like *the* most obedient animals on the planet!"

"Okay. I give up. What animal would you like me to compare you to?"

His voice turns reflective. "Well, cats are really stubborn, but they're also mostly assholes, too, so we can't go with a cat. I would say mule, but there's absolutely nothing sexy about a mule—"

"God forbid he doesn't get a sexy animal," I mutter.

"—and birds are just dumb. A panther is super cool and probably totally stubborn, lone hunter and all that, but also technically a cat and therefore I'm sure it has all that cat assholiness."

I start to giggle and can't stop. This is alarming, not only because I'm not a person who *giggles*, but also because I'm enjoying this conversation way too much for my own good.

When Brody starts to talk again, I can hear in his voice that he's trying to stifle his own laughter. "Okay, so we've gone through canines, felines, aves—"

"Aves?"

"That means birds—keep up, Slick—bovidae, and equidae—"

"Did you want to be a zoologist when you were growing up or something?"

"And we've gotten nowhere fast, so I'm thinking we should maybe move on to *fictional* animals."

There's an invitation in his pause. "Apes!" I declare.

"Can you be more specific?"

"King Kong. He was *super* stubborn."

"Also big. I approve of this comparison! He probably had a *huge*—"

"Brain?" I say sweetly.

"Appetite, I was going to say. Imagine the amount of vegetation a one-hundred-foot-tall ape would consume in a day."

"Imagine the size of his ape-y turds."

Brody makes a disgusted sound. "No. I'd rather not, thank you. God, now that you mention it, that jungle probably stunk like a port-a-potty at Woodstock."

That does it. My giggles turn into full-on, uncontrollable hoots of laughter. I even snort a time or two, I'm so out of control.

"And she's snorting! Do you snore, too, you delicate flower?" Brody teases.

Still laughing, I say, "Probably. Although I couldn't say for sure."

"What, none of your boy toys ever told you?"

"None of them have ever spent the night." It's out of my mouth before I can censor myself. Instantly, my laughter dies.

Brody senses my sudden distress. He says gently, "Easy, Slick. I won't ask."

Relieved, I release a slow breath.

He adds, "Unless you feel the need to, you know, unburden yourself or something. I hear confessions can be quite cathartic."

"No, thanks. And I think that's bullshit, by the way."

"What is?"

"That confessions are cathartic. I think it's the coward's way out."

His silence burns. He says softly, "How do you mean?"

"I mean if you did something bad and the guilt is eating you up, find a way to handle it yourself, in a constructive way. Don't go blathering your guilt all over the place for everyone else to deal with. I see it all the time in my practice. A couple comes in because out of the blue the husband couldn't take the guilt of some one-night stand he had and confesses it to his wife to make himself feel better. Only now *she's* devastated. They would've both been better off if he'd just kept his mouth shut and dedicated himself to being the best husband he could be in the future."

After a while, he says cryptically, "Well. That answers that."

I frown. "Please don't tell me you have something terrible you need to confess."

His pause is so brief I think I imagined it. "Well, I *was* going to confess that I'm sitting here with my dick in my hand because your voice is so fucking sexy it gets me hard, but geez, after that little speech I'll just keep my mouth shut and deal with it myself." He chuckles.

"Constructively." He chuckles again. "If you hear any odd moans or groans, just ignore them."

The heat comes back into my cheeks. "Are you trying to have phone sex with me, Mr. Scott?"

He groans. "God, it's hot when you call me that in that stern librarian tone. It totally gets my sexy teacher fantasy going."

"Hmm. Perhaps I'll have to spank you with a ruler."

He sucks in a low breath. "Oh, you're an evil, evil woman."

"And you, Mr. Scott, are a bad, bad boy."

"Fuck. I'm gonna ruin these new sheets," he mutters.

"I'll leave you to it, then," I say evenly, trying to keep the tremor running through my body out of my voice.

"Wait!"

I hesitate. "What."

"Say you'll come to the party."

I don't respond.

He says, "Please."

I still don't respond.

He says, "Pretty please?"

"I can't trust myself around you!" I blurt, and instantly want to punch myself in the face.

His tone gets all growly and gruff. "Because . . . ?"

I sit on the edge of the bathtub, close my eyes, and sigh. "Because I'm too attracted to you."

Even his silence sounds confused. "You realize that makes zero sense, right?"

"It does to me. I don't expect you to understand."

"I would if you explained it."

"No."

"Gee, hesitate a little, why don't you?"

"Stop being cute, it's aggravating!"

"Sorry, Slick, cute is my middle name."

"Argh."

"Is this a bad time to ask you what you're wearing?"

"Oh. My. *God.* I'm going to strangle you when I see you next!"

His voice brightens. "So you *are* coming to the party!"

"Good-bye, Brody!"

He says quickly, "How about this—think about this whole situation over the next few days—"

"Which whole situation, specifically?"

"Us. Me wanting you. You wanting me. You being a big wuss and not giving me a chance because I'm so scorching hot your panties melt off every time you look at me."

"Dear God," I grumble. "I've created a monster."

"Ahem. As I was saying. Think about what you want to do here. Then come to the party, and we can talk about it."

When I make a dangerous noise in the back of my throat, he quickly adds, "Okay, we don't have to talk about it . . . you can wear something that will tell me what your decision is."

"I think you were right when you said you needed therapy. Seriously, Brody, you're crazy."

He completely ignores that. "A green dress for 'Go.' A red dress for 'No go.' Whaddya say?"

"I say you're nuts."

"Good," he says, sounding as if I've just agreed to his terms. "See you Saturday then, Slick." His voice drops. "And please don't break my heart—wear a green fucking dress."

Then the bastard hangs up on me.

I open my eyes, stand, and stare at myself in the mirror. "We're *not* going to that party," I say firmly to my reflection.

She doesn't look convinced.

# Chapter 7

The next few days pass quickly. I'm busy at work, and exhausted by the time I get home because I'm not sleeping well. I've been eating dinner and going to bed early.

And getting up early, screaming and covered in sweat.

It's a good thing my condo building has excellent soundproofing, because I'd be giving poor old Mr. Liebowitz upstairs a nightly heart attack if he could hear me.

On Friday I have a date with Marcus. By "date" I mean rough, animalistic sex at my place. I come more times than I can count, primarily because the entire time I'm fantasizing about—guess who?

Yes, that's right. The panty-melting, guitar-slinging, King Kong–channeling, velvet-voiced lusciousness that is Brody Scott.

I'm so screwed.

Lying next to me on his back—sweating and panting, the bedcovers demolished beneath us—Marcus starts to laugh. "Holy *hell*, Grace. You almost broke my dick off. That was *epic*."

I smile drowsily at the ceiling. "I know. I'm a goddess."

"You taking new vitamins or something?"

*Yep. Vitamin B.*

When I chuckle at my own inside joke, Marcus rolls to his side and gazes down at me, his eyes warm. He pulls the sheets down to my stomach and begins to languidly trace a finger over my breasts. He says casually, "So . . ."

I look at him sharply, already knowing where this is going. "The answer is no."

His finger falls still beneath my left nipple. "You don't even know what I was going to say."

"You were going to ask whether or not I'd thought about extending our one-month stand. And the answer is no."

He looks confused. "No, you haven't thought about it, or no, you don't want to extend it?"

"Both."

He blinks. "Ouch."

I sit up, sighing, and push my hair off my face. I prop my elbows on my knees and look at him over my shoulder. "You'll find someone else within a week."

"Yeah, probably. That's not the point."

"That *is* the point. We're both tramps. It's what we do."

"And we're good at what we do—together."

I groan.

Marcus sits up and slides his big, warm hand up my back, under my hair. "All I'm saying is that a thirty-day limit seems arbitrary."

"It isn't. Believe me. It isn't."

He studies my face for a while in silence. Then he quietly asks, "Does this have to do with that big binder you keep on your kitchen counter?"

Immediately I'm in uber-defensive mode, hackles up and hissing. "That's none of your business!"

It's as if he takes that as a challenge, because he bulldozes straight ahead. "The binder that contains pictures of your friends and work associates with their names on labels and descriptions of how long you've known them, and detailed lists of your bank accounts, insurance policies, credit cards and mortgages, and a letter to yourself explaining that if you wake up and don't know where you are—"

I jump out of bed and stand livid at the side, my hands clenched to fists, my pulse thundering in my ears, glaring daggers at him. "Get out," I say, deadly soft, "*right* now."

"Grace—"

"You had no right. No *fucking* right to look at that."

His eyes are big, dark, and full of something I'm horrified to recognize as pity.

He says, "I get it. Why you do what you do. Keeping people out, pushing them away. It's a defense mechanism. It's self-preservation—"

"So help me God, if you say one more word I'll pick up that letter opener on my dresser and stab you to death with it."

"Grace," he says softly, his eyes pleading with me. "I know what it's like to always be alone."

"You don't know anything, Marcus," I say bitterly. A hot prick of tears stings my eyes. "Now get dressed and get out of my house."

He purses his lips, looks at me for a while, and then declares, "No." He leans back against the headboard, his arms behind his head.

I almost scream I'm so frustrated and furious.

I whirl around, stick my hands into my hair, close my eyes, and count to ten. Then I count to ten again. Finally when I'm more calm, I cross my arms over my chest and say, "All right. Go ahead and say your piece. But at the end I'm still going to throw you out."

There's a long pause, as if he's carefully choosing his words. "I saw that binder the first time I came over here, a month ago."

*Mother. Fucker.*

"I didn't say anything because I knew it wasn't my business. I hoped you'd eventually talk about it, thought maybe . . . after we'd been together a few times and had such a connection, I guess I hoped you might feel safe with me. We're, like, *exactly* the same person, Grace. Except I have a dick."

My voice is hollow when I answer. "We met at a sex club, Marcus. There is zero chance of this ever becoming anything other than what it is: meaningless sex."

"It isn't meaningless," he protests.

I turn to look at him, letting him see the truth in my eyes. "It is to me."

His nostrils flare. "You're only saying that because you're angry with me."

Suddenly I feel so tired I just want to lie down on the floor, go to sleep, and never wake up.

I sit on the edge of the mattress and take Marcus's hand. "No. I'm sorry, but it's the truth. It's not you. And I know that sounds like a total cliché, but it isn't you. I can't have that kind of connection with anyone."

He pulls me against him, tucks my head into his shoulder, and winds his arms around my body. Against my hair he says, "You *could* have that kind of connection with someone. And he's right here."

"Oh God," I groan. "You have a bigger vagina than I do, buddy."

My head jiggles up and down as his chest moves with his laughter. "Are you calling me a girl?"

"No, I'm calling you a cab."

His arms tighten around me. He whispers, "Are you sure? *For sure* for sure?"

When I answer, "Yes," without hesitation, Marcus sighs.

"You're shit for my ego, lady."

"You'll survive."

We lie together for long moments, just breathing. The room is warm and quiet. Beyond the bedroom windows, I hear a dog barking somewhere outside.

I don't think I've ever heard anything as lonely in my entire life.

Finally Marcus stirs. I look up into his face. He says, "Technically we still have one night left."

"Oh."

He chuckles. "Try not to sound so enthused."

"It's just . . . it sort of feels like we already broke up. Adding one more night so we can just break up again seems redundant."

Still chuckling, he kisses me on the forehead. "You're a real piece of work, you know that?"

*Yes. More than anything else, that I do know.*

He suggests, "Maybe we could go to the movies. Or something that feels not like a breakup but like an 'ex-fuckbuddy who got friendzoned' outing. No sex, just hanging out, for our last night together. What do you think?"

A light bulb blinks on over my head. "Like a housewarming party?"

"Sure. That works. Maybe you could introduce me to some of your single girlfriends," he teases, but I'm too distracted to reply.

Brody *did* say I should bring Marcus to his party. He also said I should wear something that would let him know, definitively, one way or the other, what I'd decided to do about us.

Us. Like that's a thing.

I start to get excited. This could be a perfect solution all the way around! I'll bring Marcus on our last date to the party of a rock star, where there will undoubtedly be several hundred hot, single women milling around like piranha, ready to bite, and I'll wear a red dress which will signal to Brody in no uncertain terms that there is not and never will be anything between us, *and* I won't have to talk about it with him.

*Well, isn't that all wrapped with a pretty bow.*

Feeling much better, I sit up and look at Marcus.

"Okay. Housewarming party it is. Pick me up at three thirty. And wear something hot, I want to make sure we pick out a good replacement girl for you."

As I trot off into the bathroom to take a shower, I hear Marcus's amused laugh behind me.

He's going to be just fine.

## Brody

"Check. One, two. Check, check, checkeroo."

"You're good!" calls SpongeBob from behind the amp. He pops his square blond head around the big black amp box, grinning, showing off the space where his tooth went missing when he took a drunken header into a curb on our Eurotrash tour in Germany last year. He was so fucked-up he didn't feel a thing. I haven't asked him why he hasn't gotten it fixed, because he'd probably answer with some supremely SpongeBob-y thing like, "Dude, I've got, like, two dozen others."

Some of my best friends are roadies, but they're generally not the sharpest tools in the shed.

"Cool, man. Thanks."

I jump down off the stage and survey the setup. My backyard is fucking huge—you could land a jumbo jet out here—and has an amazing view of the Pacific. It also has a private beach, two swimming pools, a separate guest house, and an enormous stand of king palm trees that have been growing on the property since it was first developed back in the forties.

They're the perfect backdrop for a beach rock 'n' roll show.

"Hey! Asshole!"

A grinning Nico is headed toward me from the open patio doors. Beside him, Kat smacks his arm and appears to be scolding him as they get closer.

Chicks don't get how much we guys enjoy giving each other shit.

"What's up, dickface?" I say, giving him a hug.

"Not much, ballsack."

"Better to be a ballsack than a taint, like you. Ballsacks are very useful. No real use for a taint."

Nico grins. "Unless you're a taint-licker. Like you."

Kat throws her hands in the air. "For God's sake, you two! Can you find some friendly insults that don't involve the four inches between your balls and your butthole?"

Nico and I look at each other. At the same time we say, "No."

"Ugh. Typical." Kat gives me a hug. When she pulls back, she looks at my flip-flops, my board shorts, and my T-shirt and says, "You look like you just got back from swimming."

"Surfing." I run a hand through my wet hair. "Do it every chance I can. The private beach is mainly the reason I bought this place."

"Right," says Nico, looking around. "Couldn't have anything to do with the view."

"Or the fifty-thousand-square-foot house," adds Kat, lifting her hand to shade her eyes from the bright afternoon sun.

"It's only eighty-five hundred square feet."

"Oh, *excuse* me." She rolls her eyes. "Eighty-five hundred square feet on about four million acres."

"*Two* acres. You're incredibly bad at judging the size of things, you know that?" I smile at Nico. "She probably thinks your tiny Johnson is like, ten inches long, am I right?"

Kat spreads her hands about two feet wide. She says with a straight face, "I don't know, is this ten inches?"

Nico smirks at me.

*Touché. Moving on.* "So did Grace come with you guys?"

Kat uncomfortably shifts her weight from one foot to the other. "Um. No. Have you talked to her?"

I look between her and Nico, who only shrugs. "Not for a few days. Why?"

"Well . . . she's coming. But she's bringing Marcus. She said you told her to."

I'm thrilled she's coming, because I've spent days obsessing over whether or not she would, what she would wear, and my approach when she showed up in a red dress, but then I stop short, pulled up by the second part of that statement. "She's bringing Marcus."

*So the competition's name is Marcus. Cool name. Sounds . . . concerning.*

"Oh yeah, I told her to bring him," I say casually, dragging my hand through my hair again. I squint off into the distance. "She, uh . . . she likes this guy, huh?"

Nico makes a noise like a snort, only way more caustic. "Yeah, the way a cat likes a mouse."

Kat sends him a death glare the likes of which I've never seen, and which, if I were on the receiving end, would shrivel my balls to the size of raisins. She hisses, "One more word, superstar, and you're sleeping on the couch tonight."

Unperturbed by this outburst, Nico gazes down at her. A slow, cocky smile spreads across his face. "Yeah? You think you could sleep without me, baby?"

Her cheeks turn pink. She looks primly down at her shoes. He laughs out loud, drags her against his chest, and gives her an embarrassingly intimate kiss.

"Get a room for fuck's sake," I mutter, looking away.

I'm not mad. Just jealous as fuck.

I know something like what Nico and Kat have isn't in the cards for a guy like me. I might not believe in God anymore, but I do believe in karma because she's been kicking me in the teeth in the relationship department for years. A good woman falling in love with me is about as likely as seeing a flock of pigs fly overhead.

I'm not complaining, though. It's not as if I deserve to be happy. I'm just really good at pretending I am.

I ask, "Do you guys know if A.J. and Chloe are gonna make it? I texted him this morning but he didn't get back to me."

Kat reluctantly extricates herself from Nico's greedy embrace. Smiling now, she says, "Chloe wanted to come but A.J. put the kibosh on it. Said it was too soon for the baby to be at a party."

"Too soon!" I repeat in disbelief. "She's the offspring of a *rock star*! She's got parties in her blood! She had a party in her room ten minutes after she was born! Jesus, he's turning into an old woman. Next thing you know he'll be knitting baby booties and hitting up the local bingo parlor."

Nico says, "He's a father now. Your priorities shift." He looks at Kat. "Personally I can't wait for it to happen to me."

Then he tucks Kat underneath his arm and gives her a smile that leaves her starry-eyed.

Uncomfortable, I look away again. "Dude."

Nico chuckles. "You just wait, brother. One of these days you're gonna meet someone that blows your whole fuckin' world apart, and then you'll get what I'm talkin' about."

Then, as if it were scripted in a fucking romance movie, a flash of red appears in my peripheral vision.

There stands Grace at the open glass patio doors of my new house, her hands lifted to shade her eyes from the glare of the sun as she scans the backyard. My eyes drink her in. Those long legs and those dangerous curves and that amazing hair waving past her shoulders, shiny and thick, the color of persimmons. And that sexy little dress she's wearing—

Oh my God. The fucking dress!

I start to laugh, because really there's nothing else to do.

"Why are you laughing?" asks Kat.

"Inside joke," I say, my gaze still on Grace. "Your friend's a goddamn firecracker, you know that?"

"Actually," Kat answers quietly, "I think she might be the bravest person I've ever met."

I'm just about to ask her what she means when a black dude the size of a skyscraper appears by Grace's side and slings a giant arm around her shoulders.

His head is shaved. His shoulders are like boulders. His clothes—a white dress shirt and tan slacks—were obviously custom made to fit his enormous frame. He's wearing dark sunglasses and a confident, easy smile, like he's used to having all eyes on him, and loves it.

Enter the competition.

"Whoa," says Nico. "Is that Grace's flavor of the month?"

"Marcus," Kat affirms. "He's a talent agent at CAA. Reps a bunch of huge names. Cruise, Damon, Statham. Specializes in action heroes."

"He's very . . . large." Nico coughs into his hand.

Large doesn't even cover it. The dude is *massive*. He gives A.J. a run for his money in the size department.

I glance down at myself. I'm no shrimp, and I've got pretty good muscle definition from all the surfing I do, but if I had to arm wrestle this Marcus character there's a strong chance I'd end up in the emergency room with a team of surgeons trying to reattach the bloody stump of my biceps to my shoulder.

And if his *arms* are that big . . .

Fuck.

The angry toddler inside my head starts howling and breaking shit in frustration.

Nico bursts out laughing. "I'd pay a million bucks for a picture of your face right now, my friend!"

"Suck it, Nyx," I growl, my hungry gaze still on Grace.

Kat suggests, "Maybe he has small feet. You know, because if he has small feet . . ."

Nico and I look at her with our brows raised. She shrugs. "Just trying to be helpful."

Grace catches my eye again. She waves, says something to Marcus, and the two of them start to walk down the winding stone pathway toward us on the lower lawn.

As they get closer, Nico drily observes, "Yeah, that theory just went out the window."

We all look at Marcus's feet, clad in a pair of seriously expensive-looking brown leather dress shoes. And *holy—*

In a low, impressed voice, Kat says, "Oh my. Do you think he could use those as skis?"

*I hate my fucking life.*

"Hi, kids!" says Grace brightly, stopping beside us. She gives Kat and Nico hugs, and then turns to look at me. With a totally serene, unruffled expression, she says sweetly, "Kong."

"Slick," I reply, holding her gaze. "Nice dress."

It's sleeveless, short enough to show off her long, bare legs, with a belted waist and little gold buttons all the way down the front. But that's not what makes it so interesting. What makes it so interesting is the color.

It's red.

*And* green.

It's fucking *polka dot.* Big green and red polka dots on a background of white. If she's trying to drive me completely insane, it's working.

Grace looks down at herself. "Oh, this old thing?" When she looks up at me, her smile is brilliant. "Well, I couldn't decide what to wear, so . . ."

"So she dressed up in Christmas colors," says the giant, Marcus, in this smooth baritone that would make the late, great Barry White gnash his teeth in jealousy.

The guy is huge, good-looking, dresses well, has enormous feet, a job that chicks probably think is super glamorous, and a voice I bet Nico would trade his Ferrari collection for, and I'm standing here in flip-flops and wet hair like I'm the fucking pool boy.

"Hi, I'm Brody." I extend my hand to Marcus.

Because fuck if I'm gonna be intimidated by him—*she wore polka dots.*

"Marcus. Nice to meet you."

Marcus shakes my hand. It's like trying to shake hands with a catcher's mitt. We give each other a manly, serious nod.

I try really hard not to puff out my chest the way my inner toddler is demanding I do.

"And I'm Nico. Nice to meet you, man."

Nico and Marcus shake hands, too, and then Grace introduces Kat.

"And this is one of my best friends, Kat. Don't let her size fool you, she's savage in reverse proportion to her height."

I watch Kat's hand disappear into the monster that is Marcus's hand. He says to her, "It's a pleasure, Kat. I would say I've heard all about you, but . . ." He throws an easy smile at Grace. "That'd be a lie."

Grace smiles back at him and shrugs.

My heart leaps. What does that mean? Why wouldn't Grace have told him anything about her best friend? Does Grace not tell him anything about anything? Does Grace not really like him that much?

*Don't get too excited, bonehead. Just look at the size of his shoes and calm the fuck down.*

"Amazing place you've got here, man." Marcus addresses me, his voice sincere. "Used to be Spielberg's if I'm not mistaken?"

"Yeah. That's right. Thanks."

"I'm really digging the open-plan living room with the peg-and-groove hardwood floors."

I have no ideà what peg-and-groove hardwood floors are. I only know that the floors are brown and made of dead trees. "Oh. Yeah. The peg and groove. Right."

Grace cocks a brow at me. She obviously knows I have no idea what Marcus is talking about, but she doesn't give me away. She turns the conversation to another topic before he can really do a number on what's left of my shredded manhood and ask me what the roof is made of, to which I'd have to respond, "Roof stuff?"

"Are we early? I thought you said four o'clock, but it looks like we're the first ones here. The valet guys were barely even awake out front."

"Nope, you're right on time."

Grace looks confused. "Then where is everyone?"

Nico and I chuckle. I say, "The sun's still up."

"So . . . your friends only come out after dark? You close with a bunch of vampires or something?"

I shrug. "Musicians aren't exactly known for their love of daylight and exemplary timeliness. I figure most people will start to show around six, which is when I wanted them here, which is why I told everyone four."

Grace looks appalled. She turns to Marcus. "Are actors like that, too?"

He says, "Only the addicts. Most actors are so anal-retentive they show up two hours *early*."

Grace pronounces, "Then I like actors better than musicians," and I think my head will explode.

Nico glances at my face, tries not to smirk, fails miserably, and coughs into his hand again to hide his laugh.

Marcus gestures at the stage to our right. "You guys doing a private show tonight?"

"We were, but A.J. bailed so we don't have a drummer, so I think we'll probably just end up—"

"I can play drums," says Marcus, full of confidence. "Been playing since I was a little kid. Had a music scholarship for college, too, but I took the football scholarship instead."

When no one says anything because we're all too mind-fucked over this new piece of news, he adds, "I mean, it's cool if you don't want me to. I'm actually really good, but no worries. I get it, band cohesiveness and everything. And no one could ever fill A.J.'s shoes anyway."

Kat looks at Marcus's feet, looks at me, and then pulls her lips between her teeth because she's trying not to laugh.

"Would you all excuse me for a moment?" I say, smiling. "I just have to go inside and hang myself."

# Chapter 9

Grace finds me in the kitchen just as I'm about to down my third shot of tequila.

"Hey, Kong," she says casually, gliding in with that ballerina's walk of hers. "That was a pretty fast exit you made back there."

"Yeah, well, it was either run away or fling myself facedown in the sand and throw a tantrum, so I decided to go with running away. Plus, there's tequila in here."

"Oh? Needed something to steady your nerves?"

"Ha. No, your boyfriend ate my nerves for lunch. This is just to get me through the next few hours until I can pass out at a respectable time. Hopefully *black* out so I won't have to relive the joyous moment when I was completely emasculated in front of this girl that I've kinda sorta had a huge crush on since the dawn of time."

I raise the shot glass in a toast to her, and then swallow its contents.

Smiling, she moves closer to where I'm standing at the sink. "He's not my boyfriend."

My eyes bulge. "If you say, 'He's just a stud that services me sexually with his enormous *talent*,' you'll have to deal with a grown man sobbing at your feet."

She leans her hip against the counter, folds her arms over her chest, and levels me with her eyes.

I wasn't kidding when I told her they were the color of thunderclouds over the sea. I've never seen eyes like hers, flinty one moment, soft and playful the next, every possible shade of gray depending on the light, from pearl to iron to dove to steel. They're fascinating.

*She's* fascinating.

Fuck. I'm toast.

"Not a pretty picture," she muses, straight-faced. She pauses for a moment, and then says, "If it makes you feel any better, this is our last date. We broke up yesterday."

I keep my expression neutral, but inside my head there's a stadium of fans who just leapt to their feet and started screaming because a batter hit a home run out of the park.

"Would you like to elaborate?"

She moistens her lips. My dick takes that as some kind of Morse code for fellatio because he springs to life behind my zipper the way Cookie Monster springs to life when he catches the scent of chocolate chips.

She says, "It's complicated."

Without breaking eye contact, I ask, "As complicated as that dress you're wearing?"

She pulls her full lower lip between her teeth, and I swear to God my dick almost explodes with the amount of blood that rushes into it.

*This is ridiculous. Get a grip!*

"Do you have any idea," she says softly, "how difficult it is to find a red-and-green polka dot dress on short notice?"

I am all boner. I have zero brain cells left. There is no blood circulating anywhere else in my body. Someone stick a fork in me, because I am fucking *done.*

Our eyes still glued together, I say, "You do realize there's a big green polka dot right over your crotch, right?"

"Oh," she answers, all Bambi-eyed innocence. "There is?"

We stare at each other. The moment stretches out. Finally, when I can't take it anymore I whisper gruffly, "Grace."

It's like hearing me say her name does something to her, because her eyes flutter closed and she inhales a sharp breath. "Wait," she says quickly. "Don't say anything else yet."

I stand there and watch her breathe with her eyes closed, fighting every instinct inside me that's screaming *touch her kiss her take her in your arms!*

I have to do something. I reach out and, very softly, touch her cheek.

And she shudders.

She fucking *shudders*.

I've never felt anything like the bolt of need and longing that crashes through me, hot as fire, dark as midnight. My hands shake with it. My heart pounds with it. It takes every ounce of self-control I have not to crush my mouth against hers, yank up her dress, pull down her panties, and fuck her right here, bent over the kitchen counter, fast and hard.

Because I know she wants it just as badly as I do.

"Open your eyes," I demand.

When I see what's reflected in her eyes when her lashes slowly lift—the desire and ambivalence, the raw emotion—I groan. "I have to kiss you," I whisper, stepping closer and taking her face in my hands.

"Brody. Please. Wait."

She flattens her hands over my chest. I groan again, my lips inches from hers.

"I'm—I—I can't . . ."

I look into her eyes. "You can. I know you want to."

"I don't—"

"Don't fucking lie to me," I growl, pressing up against her. When our bodies meet, she inhales the sexiest little gasp that manages to make me feel like a Viking warrior who just conquered a new continent. Thrilled by the sound of it, I put my lips next to her ear and say, "My cock is so hard it hurts and your nipples are so hard I can see them right through your clothes and I bet if I put my hand inside your panties right now it would come away soaking wet. Am I right?"

Her only answer is a shaky exhalation.

"Yes," I growl. "I'm right. And you said you broke up with Marcus. So give me one good reason why I shouldn't kiss you, Grace. Just one."

Her whole body is trembling. Her breath comes in short, soft pants.

Fuck it. This is happening. Right. *Now.*

The moment my lips touch hers, Grace blurts, "Because I don't want to hurt you!"

I freeze, and open my eyes. She's staring back at me with this wild look, like she might bolt at any second. I stay perfectly still.

"Do you have venomous saliva?"

It's meant as a joke, something to lighten the moment, but it doesn't work. She looks away, as if she's ashamed.

"Talk to me." When she doesn't respond, I gently turn her face back to mine. We look into each other's eyes.

I have the strangest sense of falling, like I've just stepped off a tall building and am headed at top speed for the ground.

She takes a breath, gathering her strength. "I have memory problems. Most people don't know about it but . . ."

But I do, because Chloe told me.

It was the day Abby was born, before Chloe went into labor. We were sitting around the kitchen table at Nico's house. I'll never forget that moment, or Chloe's words.

*When she was eighteen, Grace was involved in a bad car accident. Her parents were killed . . . she lost her memory. She can't recall anything from before the crash. She had to relearn who she was when she woke up; she didn't recognize anyone, she didn't remember anything about her life. So now she has this whole 'live for the moment' philosophy. Especially with relationships. If she thinks someone she's dating is getting serious, that's it. It's over.*

*It doesn't help that they never found the bastard that ran into them. It was a hit-and-run.*

It was the last part that made my blood run cold and bile rise up in my throat, hot and choking. Even after Chloe's water broke and everyone rushed to the hospital, I sat frozen at the kitchen table, fighting the urge to vomit, blinded by horrible memories and wondering what the odds were that the woman I felt so drawn to had suffered that particular tragedy.

That old bitch karma again, stabbing me in the heart and laughing in my face.

A strong feeling of protectiveness comes over me. All I want to do is put my arms around Grace and tell her everything is going to be okay, but she's not done talking yet.

She looks into my eyes. In a small voice, she says, "I could not remember you one day. We could start something and then . . . I could lose any recollection of it. You'd be a stranger. Do you understand?"

Like fingers interlacing, several things slowly come together and fit into place.

"You could fall in love with me and not remember it?" I whisper.

She swallows and nods.

Dumbfounded, I stare at her. "Holy fuck."

Looking miserable, she nods again. She tries to pull away but I don't let her. I put my arms around her and squeeze.

She resists for what feels like forever, stiff and uncomfortable in my arms, but then slowly she gives in. She melts against me with a sigh, tucks her face into the space between my neck and shoulder, and winds her arms around my waist.

We stand like that for a while, not talking, feeling the chaotic beating of each other's hearts. Her hair smells like sunshine. She's soft and warm against me, lush and feminine. My dick is still wrestling for control with my brain, which is in a state of shock and is just sitting there lifelessly inside my skull like a big lump of cheese.

And suddenly I realize what a gift I'm being offered.

I can never right the wrongs of the past, no matter how desperately I might want to. But maybe those wrongs aren't the end of the story. Maybe they're only a new beginning.

If I'm going to do good by her, this is a fucking fantastic place to start.

My voice gruff, I say, "I'm in."

She pulls away and looks at me, a little furrow between her brows. "What?"

"I said I'm in. Fuck it. If I can make you fall in love with me once, I can make you fall in love with me again and again. Every day if I have to."

Grace blanches. "The Egosaurus rides again. I'm *not* in love with you!"

"But you will be," I vow, looking at her dead-on. "Because I'm not gonna leave you any other choice."

I plunge my hands into her hair, grip her head, pull her toward me, and fit my mouth against hers.

It's like the Fourth of July and New Year's Eve and Christmas morning, all rolled into one.

Heat. Color. Noise. Fireworks behind my eyes. She moans into my mouth, digs her nails into my back, arches against me. I moan, too, fucking her luscious mouth with my tongue, one hand behind her neck and the other roaming all over her body, learning her shape, the dip of her waist, the full, tight curve of her ass.

It's greedy.

It's scorching.

It's *everything.*

If there were a Guinness World Record for the most amazing, mind-blowing, cock-stiffening, heart-pounding, panty-melting, burn-down-the-house kiss, we'd win that motherfucker hands down.

We're both breathing hard, desperate, mindless, lost. The kiss goes on and on, until I'm drunk on her. I'm flying. I'm melting. I'm—

Someone loudly clears his throat.

Stunned and reeling, Grace and I break apart.

Nico stands in the kitchen doorway with his hands on his hips, grinning like an idiot. "Hiya, kids," he drawls. "What're you two squirrels up to?"

Flushed and trembling, Grace lifts a hand to her lips. She lets out a short, astonished laugh and cuts her gaze to me.

I can't talk, either. My mouth can't form any coherent words. I just stand there, dumb as a rock, my mind blank, my shorts tented, staring at Grace like I've spent my entire life up to this point living in a dark cave, surviving on worms and insects, and she just walked in with candles and flowers and a big fucking steak on a hot plate.

"Uh . . ."

Nico bursts out laughing.

"I'll just go see what Kat's up to." Grace's voice is high and shaky. She bolts from the room.

"Just wanted to let you know a few people are starting to show up." Nico glances at the front of my shorts and chuckles. "So, uh, you might want to pull yourself together, brother."

Shaken to my core, I sag against the counter, gripping it hard for support, and let out a ragged breath. "Jesus. Is that what it's like for you with Kat? That feeling like you're . . ."

"Free-falling?" Nico supplies when I can't find the right word. "High flying? Completely out of control?"

When I look up at him, he nods. "Yeah, brother. It is. At the beginning. And then it gets so much deeper and so much better, there aren't any words for it at all." His eyes—bright, cobalt-blue eyes that made him famous—pierce me. "But be careful. Because once you get on that speeding train, you can't get off. Even if it jumps the tracks, crashes into a nuclear power plant, and burns the whole world to the ground."

He gives me one long, last look and then turns around and leaves.

From somewhere very far off, I hear the sound of my demon laughing.

## Grace

I hide behind a palm tree on the side of the house for the better part of ten minutes, trying desperately to get my bodily functions under control so I can appear in public without people thinking I'm on the verge of collapse.

Because I am. I so am. It's taking every bit of my willpower just to stand upright with my back against this tree. My knees are Jell-O. My blood pressure is volcanic. My hands are leaves shaking in a hurricane wind.

That kiss was thermofuckingnuclear. I've had more men than the Milky Way has stars and I've never experienced anything even remotely close to the sensation I felt when Brody fitted my mouth to his.

I couldn't have known it would be that intense, that overwhelming, that *passionate*. No, "passionate" is too weak a word. But whatever—I could never have guessed.

If I had I never would've let it happen.

"This is bad," I confess to the little green lizard sunning himself on a rock next to my tree. "This is really bad. This is bad like when the girl goes swimming at the beginning of *Jaws* and that creepy dun-dun, dun-dun, duh-na-*NAH!* music starts."

The lizard thinks I'm an idiot. He closes his eyes and falls asleep. Or maybe he's just pretending to be asleep so he doesn't have to deal with the stupid human having a nervous breakdown next to his rock.

I drop my face into my hands and groan.

The way Brody tasted—heaven. The way he smelled—heaven. The way he felt against me, his surprising strength, his heat, the feel of his heart hammering against mine—*heaven.* For a few short moments I was transported to a place I didn't know existed, had never guessed could be real, and now I'm back here on earth with all my walls lying in smoking piles of rubble around me.

I built those walls over years, painfully, brick by brick, stone by stone, with a thick layer of mortar to hold it all together, and Brody Scott just tore them all down with a single kiss.

If I slept with that man he'd ruin me for all other men forever.

Which obviously means I'm never sleeping with him.

Which also obviously means I can never kiss him again, because if Nico hadn't walked in at that precise moment I *know* I would've turned into the cock-gobbler Kat accused me of being and been down on my knees within ten seconds putting my considerable oral skills to good use.

I lower my hands to my sides. I pull a deep, cleansing breath into my lungs. I recite the mantra I say to myself every morning when I wake up and still know my name.

Looking out at the sea, I whisper fiercely, "You are a lion. You are a tiger. You were given this life because you're strong enough to live it. Now get out there and let them hear your motherfucking roar!"

Then I stumble off in search of a drink because, let's face it, self-affirmations can only get you so far.

By seven o'clock, the sun has long since set over the Pacific, the party is in full swing, and I have a fine buzz going, courtesy of the newly friendzoned Marcus, who took one look at me when I came walking pale faced and stiff limbed down the pathway from the house like a zombie and steered me toward the bar set up opposite the stage.

He handed me an ice-cold glass of champagne and hasn't left my side since.

"So . . . you want to talk about it yet?" he says now, looking with interest at a trio of girls across the pool. They're standing close to one another, giggling behind their drinks, glancing in his direction every few seconds, being as subtle about their interest in him as a murder scene in a Tarantino movie.

"Nope." I finish off the rest of my current glass of champagne and smack my lips. "But I think you should go over there and show those three little piggies what the big bad wolf is packing under his furry pelt before they finally bat their fake eyelashes clear off."

A burp escapes me, quite robust in its volume. "Seriously, have you ever *seen* such vigorous fluttering? I bet they could power a twin-engine plane with all that kinetic energy. I think the one on the right in the black miniskirt is about to lift off."

Marcus chuckles. "I'd ask if you were jealous but I know the answer is no."

I wave a hand vaguely in the air in agreement. "Steer clear of that busty blonde, though. She looks insane. Or is she cross-eyed? I can't tell from here. The brunette looks like she could suck the chrome off a trailer hitch—look at those lips! I'd go for her."

Marcus looks at me from the corner of his eye. "I know it has to be something to do with Brody. He looked at you like you'd just descended from a cloud and started playing harp music. Never seen a man look at a woman with so much . . ."

My breath held, I look over at him.

When he pronounces, "Hope," I'm not sure whether to laugh, cry, or tie a big rock around my neck and jump into the pool.

"Hope is for fools."

Marcus heaves a sigh. "You know what your problem is, Grace?"

I snort, closing one eye because the yard has, just slightly, begun to spin. "How much time do you have?"

He takes my empty glass from my hand. "You think that because something terrible happened to you once, it's bound to happen to you again. And that's just not the reality of how life works."

When I glare at him, he doesn't back down. "Hey, I'm your friend now. I can speak the truth without worrying it'll cost me sex."

"I would never withhold sex as a punishment!" I say, offended.

He ignores me. "The odds are exactly as good that you could fall in love and get married—"

"Married!" I exclaim, laughing.

"—as they are that you could get shot in a convenience store holdup, or win the lottery, or trip and hit your head on a rock and die, or find out you were adopted, or become president, or be the first person to cure cancer."

I blink. "I think that's completely wrong. Where are you getting these statistics?"

"My point is that life is random. The universe didn't pick you out specifically for a tragedy, like, 'Oh, it's Tuesday the twenty-fourth, time to fuck with Grace Stanton.' Bad shit happens. Good shit happens. *Life* happens. You can't take any one thing and point to it as proof that life is any one way or the other. Life just is. And it keeps going."

He leans closer and drops his voice. "Until you're dead, and then you don't have any more chances to see what might happen with a man who looks at you like the sun is shining right out of your damn head."

He kisses me on the temple and strolls away, heading toward the three girls on the opposite side of the pool.

"Dick," I mutter, because I really hate it when other people are right.

"Lovey! Omigod, what're you doing standing here all by your lonesome?"

Kenji appears out of nowhere in a purple sequined unitard, white platform boots, and a long feathered cape, screeching and frantically waving his arms at me like a night owl protecting her nest. I put a hand to my forehead and wince.

"Oh, nothing. Just having my ass handed to me by someone who knows me well enough to make it hurt."

"Ugh. Don't you hate that?" He stands on his tiptoes and kisses me on both cheeks. When he pulls back and looks at my expression, he cries, "Who died?"

"No one died."

"Then what the hell happened to your face, girlfriend, because you look like you just found out your mama was married to her brother!"

When all else fails, Kenji can always be relied upon to add a dose of humor to the situation.

"Someone just told me some really harsh life truths that I'm wishing I could unhear."

Kenji lifts a hand to his mouth. His eyes go wide. "Oh my God. Did One Direction break up?"

"Please go away now."

"There you are!" Kat comes up and pinches my arm. "I've been looking all over for you!"

"I was just here." I gesture morosely to nothing in particular. "Hanging out. Dealing with life's vagaries the only way a reasonable person can: with alcohol."

Kat and Kenji share a look. "Where's Marcus?" asks Kat.

"Off in search of greener pastures." I nod in the direction of the three little piggies. Marcus has joined their clique across the pool. From the looks of things, he'll be having a foursome tonight.

Looking at them, Kenji says, "Sweet baby Jesus. That blonde is frightening. Is she cross-eyed?"

"As a Siamese cat!" I say cheerfully, then grab Kat's drink from her hand, down it, and cough. She's drinking whiskey, straight.

More correctly, *I'm* drinking whiskey straight.

"Wait—why is he over there with those girls and you're over here with a face like Trojan discontinued their line of ribbed-for-her-pleasure condoms?" Kat asks.

Smug as shit, Kenji says to me, "Told you."

"The next person who tells me what anyone's face looks like will be losing his head!" I glare at Kat. "Or hers!"

Then Barney walks up with his slight limp that somehow manages to make him look sexy and mysterious and says, "Ladies." He looks at Kenji. "Oh. I didn't realize it was a costume party."

Kenji smiles. "Every party is a costume party, lovey. Every day is a stage. Every time you walk out your front door you're choosing what to tell the world with what you wear."

Barney looks him up and down. "And today you chose to tell the world you're starring in the remake of *The Rocky Horror Picture Show*?"

Kenji smacks him on his arm. "You beast! I'm wearing Alexander McQueen! You wouldn't know fashion if it hit you upside the head with a brick!"

"Lucky me," quips Barney, and then turns his gaze to me. "Angelface. Good to see you."

"Barney. It's good to be seen."

He squints at me.

I sigh. "Please don't say it."

"Say what?"

Kenji explains, "She's having some kind of existential crisis which evidently took a shit all over her face."

Barney's expression turns worried. He steps closer and touches my arm. "You okay?"

I don't miss the look Kat and Kenji exchange, all arched eyebrows and pursed lips, but I'm way past caring. "Define 'okay.'"

"Sweetie, we're gonna get you another drink." Kat grabs my empty glass and pulls Kenji away by his arm. She winks at me, looks at Barney, and wiggles her eyebrows up and down. "Be back soon!"

God, my friends are hopeless.

When they're gone, Barney murmurs, "What's up, Angelface?"

"Life. Life is up."

"You wanna talk about it?"

He's wearing some kind of spicy cologne. It's light, sexy, and smells expensive. I stare at him for a long time, trying to decide if it would be a good idea to tell him the truth or not, when out of my mouth comes something so unexpected it takes us both by surprise.

"Have you ever been in love?"

He cocks his head. A roguish dimple appears in his cheek. "Close to it right now, as a matter of fact."

I roll my eyes. "I'm being serious, Barney. I need advice."

He studies me in silence for a moment, and then moves next to me so we're standing shoulder to shoulder, staring out together at the party from our spot in the long shadows of a thicket of scarlet bougainvillea cascading over a wall.

In a low voice that I can barely hear over the music and the sounds of laughter and people talking, he says, "Once."

In those four letters I hear an ocean of pain. I know that whatever happened, it wasn't good.

"So you wouldn't recommend it then."

Surprised, he looks at me. "Yes, I definitely would."

I meet his eyes. "But . . . maybe I have it wrong, but it sounded like, um, it didn't end well."

Barney swallows. With a tight jaw, he says, "It didn't. She died."

"Oh God, Barney," I breathe, devastated. "I'm so sorry. I'm such an idiot. I apologize for bringing it up—"

"You couldn't have known. And don't be sorry. I don't regret it. Not for a minute. Before she died, I was the happiest I've ever been in my life."

I stare at him, dumbfounded, a wreck of warring emotions. "And now?"

He looks off into the distance. His profile is handsome and incredibly sad. He says softly, "And now I have amazing memories. And now I still think I was lucky." He inhales a slow breath, lets it out, briefly closes his eyes. "And now I'm a better man for having loved her."

He's killing me. I'm going to drop dead right here on this perfect patch of lawn and they'll have to cart my corpse off on a stretcher.

He looks over at me, sees the expression on my face, and sighs. "Love isn't something you choose, Angelface. It chooses you. And even if it only lasts a little while, it's worth it. Even if it ends in flames, it's worth it. Even if it cuts out your heart and leaves you a bruised, bloody mess, it's worth it."

My voice cracks when I ask, "Why?"

He lifts a shoulder and sends me a small, pained smile. "Because it's love. Love is the only thing that really matters in this life. Love is everything."

I moan and cover my face with my hands.

"Hey." Barney puts his arms around me and pulls me against his chest. It's not romantic, it's friendly, and I'm grateful for the support. He asks quietly, "Who you trying not to fall in love with, Angelface?"

Then—because life has decided kicking me when I'm down would be good for shits and giggles—Brody's tense voice comes from behind us.

"Grace."

Barney and I break apart.

Brody has changed from the shorts and T-shirt he was wearing before into a black button-down shirt and a pair of tight black jeans.

The shirt is rolled up his forearms and open halfway down his chest, exposing an intricate tattoo, angel's wings and something written in script I can't make out because the light is behind him.

He looks at me, looks at Barney, then looks back at me. I can't tell where Barney is looking because I'm too busy being floored by the expression on Brody's face, which hovers somewhere between horror and despair, with a side order of bitter jealousy.

Brody says, "I just wanted to let you know we're gonna play a set, if you wanted to come stand up front . . ." He looks at Barney again. A muscle in his jaw flexes. "Or not."

"Yes!" I blurt. "I do want!"

They both look at me. No one says anything. Heat scorches a path up my neck to my face.

Holding Brody's gaze, I add with more composure, "I mean, I would love to. Yes. Thank you for asking."

Barney scratches his head. "Right. Well, uh, I think I see Nico over there waving at me." He walks off abruptly without another word.

Brody folds his arms over his chest. Then he drags a hand through his hair. Then he scrubs his hands over his face and groans.

*You are a tiger. You are a lion. You were given this life because you're strong enough to live it.*

I gather all my courage and decide to jump off that cliff that's right in front of me.

In a quiet voice I say, "It's not Barney. It's not Marcus. It's not anyone else, either. It's you."

Brody's head snaps up. He stares at me, his lips parted, his body tensed, his gorgeous green eyes shining with need.

I take a steadying breath and continue. "You were right when you said I was afraid. I've gone skydiving and hang gliding and bungee jumping and climbed the highest summit of Mount fucking Kilimanjaro during an ice storm with a guide named Rooster who was drunk the entire time, and I've never been as scared of anything as I am of this thing I feel for you.

"I'm not ready to start . . . whatever this is. I'm not trying to be a cock tease, or lead you on, or send mixed messages. This dress was a stupid idea, but it's honest. I want you and I don't want you. I don't *want* to want you as much as I do. But mostly I don't want anyone to get hurt. I don't want *you* to get hurt."

I swallow around the rock in my throat. "I couldn't bear it if I hurt you."

There's so much tension in Brody's body he's practically vibrating with it. He steps closer to me. His nostrils are flared. His eyes are blazing. His breathing is irregular. When he speaks, his voice is rough.

"Thank you for being honest. I know that couldn't have been easy for you. And now I'm gonna tell you that I'm a big boy and I can make my own decisions."

I groan. "Brody—"

"No, Grace," he whispers with quiet intensity, closing the distance between us. "I don't care. I don't care if we only get one amazing night together and you don't remember a fucking thing tomorrow because *I'll* remember." He grabs my arm and drags me against him. "And I know it'll be worth it."

He crushes his mouth to mine.

It's everything it was the first time, and more, because now it's all out there between us, my heart as exposed and fragile as a naked baby tossed out into the snow. He holds my head and kisses me with a depth of passion that leaves me dizzy, gasping against his mouth.

I'm on fire.

I *am* fire.

And he's the fuel that makes me burn.

"Fuck," he whispers, dragging in a breath against my lips. "Fuck, Grace. Tell me you feel that, too."

All I can do is softly moan and cling to him.

He kisses me again. Just when I think my knees will give out for good, Brody breaks it off. He grins down at me, his cheeks flushed with color.

"You climbed Mount Kilimanjaro?"

"I'm sort of an adrenaline junkie," I admit sheepishly.

His grin grows wider. "Good," he says gruffly. "'Cause I have a feeling this is gonna be one *hell* of a wild ride."

# Chapter 11

Rock 'n' roll. Whoever coined that phrase was a goddam genius.

Standing two feet in front of the temporary stage set up in Brody's backyard, I stare with an open mouth as Nico leads the band into their fourth song. Even missing A.J. on percussion, they sound amazing—primarily because Marcus is on the drum kit, playing his balls off.

He wasn't kidding when he said he was good. He's better than good. He's awesome. And he knows all of Bad Habit's songs.

Funny the conversations we missed because we were too busy knocking boots.

The music is eardrum-shattering loud. Everyone around me is jumping up and down and screaming. Kat stands next to me, laughing like a lunatic, singing along to all the lyrics in her terrible voice. Marcus's three little piggies are on my other side, shaking their moneymakers for all they've got. Behind me are a few hundred of Brody's friends. The night air is crisp, the salty sea breeze is invigorating, and the energy of the crowd is incredible. I literally feel the ground rolling under my feet.

Whoa. The ground is rolling under my feet!

I stumble against Kat, who then stumbles against a guy next to her, and then it's like a line of bowling pins as we all topple sideways, staggering, trying to stay upright. Luckily there are so many people pressed so close together we're eventually pushed back the way we came.

Only I end up swaying like one of those egg-shaped Weeble dolls, snorting with laughter as the sky tilts sideways and all the stars slide off the edge.

I'm exceedingly drunk.

Kat yells over the music, "You okay?"

I give her two thumbs up. Then I burp, which makes me laugh and makes Kat's eyes widen in alarm.

"How much have you had to drink?" she yells, steadying me with a hand gripped around my arm.

I make a sloppy gesture that's supposed to mean "a lot" but looks more like I'm describing the gargantuan breasts on the cross-eyed blonde next to me.

Kat—normally the first to get shitfaced at a party and fall into a random shrub—takes it upon herself to adopt my usual role of mother. She grasps me firmly by the hand, turns, and clears a path through the crowd by shouting, "She's going to puke!"

"Thanks a million, girlfriend," I say drily as people leap out of the way in horror.

She drags me across the wide lower lawn to the winding stone path. Then she drags me up the stone path. When she drags me into the house, I protest, "You're bruising my arm!"

It comes out as, "Yerbruthinmaarrm!"

I sound like an inebriated pirate with a lisp.

Kat marches me into the kitchen, where she retrieves a bottle of cold water from the big stainless fridge. She props me up against the counter, opens the bottle, and shoves it into my face.

"How many times," she scolds, "have you told me you have to stay hydrated when you're drinking?"

I reach for the water bottle. For some inane reason, she moves it out of the way. "Hey! Quit that!"

Kat looks at the ceiling. "I'm holding my hand steady, lushy. It's you that's moving."

She helps me get a grip on the bottle. When I've got both hands around it, I lift it to my mouth and drink. Most of it goes down the right pipe. Some of it goes down the wrong pipe. I cough, spraying water into Kat's face.

Which, because I'm a terrible, terrible friend, makes me laugh.

"Oh my God, you're so lit." She sighs, wiping her face with the back of her hand. She gingerly takes the water bottle from me like it's a Molotov cocktail I'm about to toss into a crowd, and looks around. "Let's go into the living room. Lie down on the sofa until I can get Marcus to drive you home—"

"I'm not going home with him! He's going home with the three little piggies! And I don't crash on people's sofas like somebody's unemployed pothead uncle!"

The look she gives me indicates that my indignation is ridiculous for someone so drunk. "Ookay, then. A bed. We'll find you a nice, quiet room where you can sleep for a bit."

Two minutes or two hours later—my concept of time is completely shot—we're standing in the doorway of a guest bedroom. There's a king-sized bed, a matching modern dresser and chest of drawers set, and not much else. Everything is rocking in the most lovely, soothing way, like we're on a boat.

Kat sits me on the edge of the bed. She takes off my shoes. She lifts my legs up, forcing me to lie on my back. She smooths my hair off my forehead with a cool hand and smiles down at me. "I've never seen you drunk," she muses.

"I'm not drunk," I slur, smiling dreamily. "I'm wasted."

"I left the bottle of water on the nightstand right next to the bed, okay, sweetie?"

I nod obediently. She leans down and kisses my forehead, and then turns for the door. She shuts off the lights. Just as she's about to close the door behind her I say, "Kat?"

The door opens wider. "Yeah, sweetie?"

Thinking of Brody's beautiful face, I smile into the darkness. "I'm a tiger."

She laughs softly. "I know you are, hon. Go to sleep."

She closes the door and I promptly follow her instructions.

"How did she get so drunk?"

"She drank a lot."

"Yeah, but *who* was giving her so much to drink?"

An amused chuckle, in a deep baritone that sounds like rolling thunder. "If you think anyone could make Grace do anything she didn't want to do, you don't know her very well."

"What's that supposed to mean?"

"Guys—"

"It means, Brody, that you'd have an easier time convincing the sky to rain money than you'd have convincing her to *not* drink if she wanted to drink, or drink if she didn't want to."

"Guys—"

"My point is that you should've been watching her—"

*"Me!"* Another deep, amused chuckle. "*I* should've been watching her?"

"Why is that so funny?"

*"Guys!"*

I recognize Kat's voice. It's the shrill, angry one.

"What?" respond two male voices in unison.

*Brody. And Marcus. Yes, I recognize them, too. What are all these voices doing in my head? I'm trying to sleep here, people!*

"She's an adult. She had too much to drink. It's happened to all of us. She's safe, and she's sleeping. She'll be fine in the morning. Can we please move on?"

"No. No, we can't move on, Kat, because she could've been hurt! What if she wandered away on her own and fell off a cliff?"

Marcus sighs. "There are no cliffs on your property, dude—"

"Or broke her ankle by stepping in a gopher hole and had to lie there in agony all night with a busted leg until someone found her in the morning?"

"You've got a pretty advanced sense of drama, Brody, you know that?"

"This isn't fucking funny!"

"Jesus," Kat mutters, "please take me. Just take me now."

"What's all the hubbub?"

Another voice joins in. Male, strong, controlled. I recognize it instantly: Barney.

Kat says, "Nothing. Grace is sleeping, that's all—"

"Sleeping? It's not even nine o'clock. Why is she sleeping?"

"Because she's drunk!" exclaims Brody. "Because this bozo was feeding her booze all day!"

"Now wait just a fucking minute—"

"You got Grace drunk?" growls Barney, his voice low and dangerous. *"Intentionally?"*

"That's it!" exclaims Kat. "I will *not* have a cockfight on my hands, do you understand me? Marcus, go get the assfuck triplets and go home! Barney, butt out, this doesn't concern you! And Brody, calm the fuck down, Grace is *fine*—because *I* made sure she was!"

That shuts them all up. I hear some grumbling and grousing, and then heavy footsteps receding down the hallway.

Finally, I hear Kat's heavy sigh. "Fucking men are such fucking *babies*."

And then I don't hear anything more because I drift back down into darkness.

Pain. Blood. Flashing lights. The smell of things burning: rubber, plastic, oil.

Hair.

A broken moan. It's coming from me. The pain is everywhere, all over me, inside and out, devouring me. I can't move. I can't speak. I can barely open my eyes. When I do, everything is upside down. I'm buckled into a car seat. My left arm is pinned against something metal. Something hot.

Something getting hotter.

I turn my head and see stars, hear a crunching noise in my neck. When the stars recede, I don't understand what I'm looking at. The sky is made of black asphalt and yellow lines, broken pieces of plastic, sheared off hunks of metal . . .

Body parts.

A lone finger, torn from the root. A foot, still clad in a red high-heeled shoe. A bloody hand, outstretched to nothing, attached to nothing, all alone.

I hear screaming. Hoarse, frantic screaming. In the distance, sirens wail. Then a hand wraps around my wrist.

Someone is pulling on my wrist.

It hurts. God how it hurts. The sirens grow closer. The grip on my wrist grows tighter. My body jerks forward as the hand pulls hard. I groan. The pain is excruciating.

"You have to get out! I have to get you out! You need to release your belt buckle *now*!"

A man is frantically screaming at me. No—a boy. A dark-haired boy, his head stuck inside the shattered window, his eyes huge and terrified, his features obscured by blood gushing from a nasty gash on his forehead.

*I was in a car crash. We were driving . . . my parents were driving . . .*

An atomic blast of horror hits me the same time a loud pop like an explosion erupts nearby my head.

The hand. The foot. My parents.

*My parents!*

Blistering hot, a ball of fire explodes around me.

I open my mouth and scream.

## Brody

The sound is one I've never heard before. It's a piercing, primal wail of pure anguish that sends a chill like death straight down to my bones.

My heart thundering, I jerk upright in bed. For a moment I'm disoriented. Bright sunlight streams through my bedroom windows. Birds chirp in the hibiscus bush outside. It's early Sunday morning, and everything is quiet and still.

Except that scream. It comes again, louder and even more terrifying than before.

I leap from bed and almost fall when my legs tangle in the covers. Stumbling over the hardwood floor to the door, I crack my knee against the dresser. I curse and hop on one foot until I get my balance back, and then I tear through the house toward the sound of that awful scream.

It's coming from the room where Grace is sleeping.

My heart takes off like a rocket. My legs carry me toward her faster than they've ever moved before.

Without slowing, I slam into the door. It crashes open and hits the wall with a thunderous bang.

On the bed is Grace, thrashing in the covers, screaming bloody murder to wake the dead.

"Grace!" Terrified, I fall onto her. I grab her wrists, hold them down against the pillow above her head. She fights me, howling like a banshee, her hair flying everywhere, her body bucking beneath me. "Grace! Wake up! Wake up! For God's sake *wake up*!"

I shout the last part into her face. She falls still. For a moment there's nothing, just the sound of my harsh breathing and the tremors of her body shaking the bed. Then she opens her eyes and looks up at me through the wild mess of her hair.

Her gaze is full of horror and darkness.

I say her name. She slowly blinks. For an awful, bottomless moment, I think she doesn't have any idea who I am.

Then she whispers, "B-Brody?"

The relief that washes over me is so intense I'm momentarily speechless. I nod, trying not to let my panic show on my face. "You were dreaming. You had a bad dream."

Her face is ashen. "I . . . the . . . blood . . . the blood was everywhere . . . and the fire . . . and the . . . *parts* . . ."

Hearing her describe her dream makes the tiny hairs on my body stand on end. My sense of déjà vu is crushing, as is my self-loathing.

I have to swallow several times before I can talk again.

"You're safe. I'm here. Nothing can hurt you," I vow. I release her wrists and drag her against me. She's trembling so violently it shakes us both. The back of her dress is damp with sweat. Burrowing against me, she hides her face in my chest.

"Oh God. Oh God."

Her voice is choked, a half whisper.

"I'm here," I murmur, smoothing her hair and rocking her. *I'll always be here*, I don't say. *I swear on my worthless life I'll always do everything I can to make you feel safe.*

After a while her trembling slows, and then stops. She lifts her head and looks at me. Damp strands of hair cling to her cheeks. Her eyes are huge, so dark gray they're almost black.

"Usually I don't give a woman nightmares until *after* she's slept with me," I say with a straight face.

She moistens her lips, swallows. The faintest of smiles curves her mouth. "Not during?"

I'm relieved to see a glimmer of humor. This is good. "I'll have you know I'm told those thirty seconds are incredible. It's everything else about me that sucks."

Now her smile really comes on. She sits up straighter and pushes her hair off her face. "Thirty seconds, huh? You stud."

Adopting a smug expression, I puff out my chest. "Oh yeah. I'm so studly I probably just got you pregnant from my hug. With *twins*."

She chuckles. It's a little shaky, but she's definitely feeling better than she was just moments ago, which oddly makes me want to do a Tarzan-style chest thump.

"Yes, I think I can feel my uterus throwing a fertilization party. You're very talented, Mr. Scott."

"You know what it does to me when you call me Mr. Scott," I tease, lowering my head and looking at her pointedly from beneath my brows. "The sexy librarian fantasy, remember?"

She laughs. The sound of it unspools something tight in my chest.

"How could I forget?" She glances around the room and muses, "Now if only I could find a ruler . . ."

Then we're smiling at each other. Her eyes have brightened, and her face is no longer such a deathly shade of white.

I wonder if this is what Neil Armstrong felt like when he first stepped onto the moon. I feel slaphappy. I feel invincible. I feel like doing a crazy dance around the room, all because I helped, in some small way, to make her feel better.

I grab the water bottle on the nightstand and hand it to her. After she drinks half of it down, I ask, "How do you feel? You tied one on pretty good last night."

She thinks for a moment, squinting her eyes. "You're only a little bit fuzzy around the edges."

"Are you hungry? I could make eggs."

Her face turns faintly green.

"Right. No eggs. Drink more water."

She obeys without hesitation, something that makes me feel like pounding my chest again.

I've seen sexy Grace, and fierce Grace, and confident, sophisticated Grace, but I've never seen obedient Grace.

I could get used to obedient Grace.

A startlingly vivid image of her, naked, bound at her wrists and ankles on my bed, pops into my mind. I achieve an instant erection.

Even when distraught, this woman makes me produce testosterone by the gallon. *Think of something else, dickhead! Baseball. Baseball. Base—*

I'm hit with inspiration. "You know what we need?"

"What?"

"We need to go to church."

Grace stares at me as if I've just told her she has terminal cancer. "No. We definitely *don't*."

I arch a brow. "Not a big churchgoer, huh?"

She says emphatically, "No. Are you?"

I shrug. "Used to be when I was a kid. My parents went every Sunday, dragged me along. But not anymore. God and me . . . we have our differences."

She cocks her head and considers me. "You can't dangle such a juicy morsel out there like that and expect me not to bite."

Our fingers are threaded together. I don't know when that happened. "I . . . I was in an accident once, a long time ago. It pretty much changed the way I looked at everything else afterward."

Grace falls still. "An accident?"

I nod.

"Was it bad?"

After a moment of letting my stomach settle from the onslaught of memories, I say quietly, "The worst kind of bad there is."

We stare at each other. Finally she whispers, "I was in an accident, too."

I'm not sure if I should tell her I already know, but decide to keep it to myself. "Was it bad?"

"The worst kind of bad there is."

I stroke a stray lock of hair off her cheek. "Is that what the memory problems are from?"

She nods.

"And the nightmares?"

Her eyes briefly close. Then she nods again.

"I had them for years, too."

Her eyes widen. "Really? Do you still have them?"

"Hardly ever anymore. I found something that really helps."

Astonished, she blinks. "What is it?"

When I say, "Church," she visibly deflates.

I reassuringly squeeze her hands. "No, Grace. This isn't like any kind of church you've ever been to before. This is the kind of church where you really can see God."

She says sarcastically, "Yeah, I'm sure that's what Jim Jones told everyone before they moved to Jonestown. Next you'll be asking me to drink poisoned Kool-Aid."

I stand, gently pulling her up with me. When she's on her feet I ask, "Do you know how to swim?"

She stares at me for a long time. "You're a very strange person."

I grin. "But super hot, right? I can tell you're totally trying not to jump my bones because I'm so unbearably hot."

"Oh, totally." She looks at the ceiling and shakes her head.

Then I tuck her arm under mine and lead her toward salvation.

I'm digging through boxes in the garage, muttering to myself in frustration, when from behind me Grace says, "I don't understand what's happening."

"I can't find it!" I tear through yet another cardboard box of clothes. Still not finding what I want, I lift my head and shout at the top of my lungs, "Magda!"

"The plot thickens," muses Grace with a chuckle. "Is Magda your imaginary friend?"

"Ugh!" I throw down an armful of clothes in disgust. Why do I have so many still-packed clothes? More to the point, why do I have so many clothes in the first place?

Oh right. Because I'm a clothes whore. Hoarding clothes is what we do.

I stalk across the garage to the intercom on the wall next to the door that leads inside. I stab my finger on the round black button. "Magda! I need you in the garage!"

A loud crackle of static answers back.

"Magda! *Magda*!"

The crackle clears. A rough female voice answers with a flat "*Si*."

Because I know her so well, I know the interpretation of those two letters is basically "What the fuck do you want *now*, you spoiled, annoying, helpless child."

I adore Magda, but I swear the woman makes the Grinch look like Mother Teresa.

I say into the intercom, "Where's the box with the extra wetsuits?"

Grace says in surprise, "Wetsuits?"

Magda's sigh sounds like she's been waiting for a thousand years for the mother ship to come back to earth and rescue her from all the morons on this planet. Then there's nothing but more static. She disconnected.

"Fuck." I turn to Grace. "Well, I guess you can just wear mine and I'll wear the spring suit—"

The garage door swings open with an ominous creak of metal hinges.

In the doorway that leads to the kitchen stands Magda, all four foot nine of her, hands on her stout hips, glowering at me from beneath thick brows that have never seen a strip of wax or made even a passing acquaintance with a pair of tweezers.

As always, she's dressed entirely in black, with the exception of the spotless white apron tied at her waist. Her silver-threaded dark hair is scraped severely away from her scalp into two thick plaits and pinned to the top of her head in an elaborate coiled style that makes Princess Leia's hairdo look amateur. If you put your hand into it, you'd never be able to get it out.

She has skin like leather, hands like a bricklayer's, eyes like knives, and a heart the size of a Raisinette.

And I love her as if she were my own mother.

Who I also love, by the way. That wasn't sarcasm, just an accurate comparison.

I say brightly, "Good morning, sunshine!"

Magda answers back in aggrieved Spanish, punctuating every other word with a stabby gesture of her finger pointed toward my chest.

I smile broadly at her. "I love you, too. And may I say you look especially beautiful today. Done something new with your hair?"

More irritated Spanish. I have no idea what she's saying because I don't speak the language, but I think the gist of it is that I'm lazy, stupid, and an embarrassment to all people with testicles everywhere.

Grumbling, she walks past me, waving me out of the way. She makes a beeline toward one of the three or four dozen unmarked boxes I still haven't unpacked since moving in last month. She drags it away from its companions, turns to me, points to it, and says with withering disdain, *"Aquí."*

"Oh, great! Thanks!"

Then she notices Grace and freezes.

"Oh, sorry. Magda, this is my friend Grace. Grace, Magda. My housekeeper. She basically runs my life. Like a jail warden. Only not as cuddly."

Grace says pleasantly, "Hello, Magda. It's nice to meet you."

With slitted eyes, Magda gives Grace a searing once-over.

"Uh, Magda. This is my guest. Don't bite."

"It's okay, Brody," says Grace, smiling. Then she says something to Magda—*in Spanish*.

"Haha*ha*!" cackles Magda loudly. Her leathery face creases into a grin.

"Wait—was that a *laugh*?" I'm astonished because in over a decade of knowing her, I've never heard her make that particular sound.

Magda fires something back at Grace, who answers with an equally rapid-fire response, and then the two of them are cackling like they've been besties since forever.

I have no idea what the fuck is going on.

Magda walks past me again, bumping me out of her way with her shoulder. She goes to Grace, takes her hand, and gently pats it. Then she turns it over and inspects her palm. After a moment she pronounces in perfect English, "Don't take the coast highway at night."

She turns and exits the garage.

"Are you kidding me?" I shout after her. "You speak ENGLISH? All these years you've been speaking only Spanish to me but you speak ENGLISH?"

A faint cackle comes from inside the house.

Grace says warmly, "What a darling woman. Except that last bit was a little cryptic, don't you think?"

I turn and stare at her. "Did we smoke a bowl that I forgot about or something?"

Grace's smile is angelic.

"No, seriously. I've gotta be on drugs. *Magda speaks English*!"

"Did she say she didn't?"

"No, but it's not like I could ask her—I don't speak Spanish!"

"Why on earth would you hire a Spanish-only housekeeper if you can't speak the language?"

"She was my family's housekeeper from when I was a kid. She moved with me when I came to California to pursue a career in music after high school."

Grace's brows lift. "Mommy and Daddy didn't trust their baby boy to survive on his own?"

"It's a long story. Never mind." I turn back to the box with the wetsuits in it.

Grace says sharply, "Stop."

Arrested by the tone of her voice, I glance at her over my shoulder. "What?"

Her expression is severe. Fraught, even. Surprised, I turn all the way around. "What's wrong?"

Slowly, holding my gaze, she says, "I'm going to ask you something, and I want you to tell me the complete truth. Everything depends on you being *totally* honest."

This sounds bad. I'm scared already. "Uh . . . okay?"

She drills me with those steely eyes of hers. "Do you have a terrible secret?"

My blood crystallizes to ice. "A secret?"

Grace takes a threatening step toward me. "Yeah. A secret. Like, the person everyone thinks is your girlfriend is really your sister, or you have a brain tumor and only have so long to live?"

She's referring to Nico and A.J., respectively, and the whoppers they were hiding from Kat and Chloe. I only have seconds to decide on an answer, but I already know there's no force in the world that could ever convince me to hurt this woman, so really it's no decision at all.

"Oh. A *secret* secret. No, I don't."

Grace narrows her eyes at me. They were a nice dove gray a second ago, soft as a cashmere sweater, but now they're stormy. "So you have *no* secrets."

*Stay cool, Brody. Don't blink. Don't look away. What happened to you has nothing to do with what happened to her. You've already realized there's no need for a confession.*

I spread my hands in the air. "I mean, I guess *technically* speaking, how many times a day I masturbate to the thought of you is a secret."

Now her eyes narrow to slits. A hurricane is brewing.

She asks, "Are your parents related by blood?"

I blink in surprise. *"What?"*

"Are you actually a woman?"

That one makes me laugh out loud. "I wish! I'd spend all day fondling myself! By the way, you're lucky I'm secure in my manhood because that little doozy could really fuck a guy up."

"I'm being serious, Brody. Are you bankrupt?"

"No."

"Do you have twelve illegitimate children?"

"Twelve? Why, thank you! Such confidence in my fertility! No. And before you ask, I don't even have *one*."

"Are you addicted to porn?"

"Define 'addicted.'" When she glares at me, I laugh again, shaking my head. "That would also be a no, Slick."

"To drugs?"

"No."

"To the shopping network?"

"No."

"Food? Alcohol? Sex with anonymous strangers you met on Snapchat?"

"No, no, and no. This is getting a little depressing, by the way."

She crosses her arms over her chest and taps her toe against the floor. "I'm trying to discover your awful, dark, hidden side! Help me out!"

My dark, hidden side taps me on my shoulder, but I push him back and plaster a fake grin on my face.

"I'm *normal*," I insist, my arms now wrapped around her. "I mean, as normal as a guy who plays guitar for one of the most famous rock bands on the planet could possibly be."

She gives me a really wicked stinky side-eye. "You don't seem very normal."

"Are you calling me *ab*normal?"

"Abby Normal," she quips drily.

"Oh my God, did you just make a *Young Frankenstein* reference?"

"Maybe. Why?"

"Why? Because it's only, like, my all-time favorite fucking movie, that's why!"

"Really?" she asks, blinking rapidly. "That's *my* all-time favorite movie! I think Mel Brooks is a—"

"Genius!" I finish before she can. "Me, too!"

After we stare at each other for a while, starry-eyed and breathless, Grace laughs. "I think we should probably go do something else before my twins turn into triplets."

I give her a quick, hard kiss. "Oh, sweetheart, you've already got quintuplets goin' on up in that bun factory."

She grimaces. "Bun factory? Jesus. How do you ever get a date?"

I whisper into her ear, "Those thirty seconds are *legendary*."

Grace laughs, pulls away, and smacks me on the arm. "Yeah, I bet. Let's hope this church of yours is as legendary or this affair will be over before it's even started."

*Affair.*

Be still my fucking beating heart.

How have I achieved the ripe old age of twenty-nine without ever feeling this alive?

# Chapter 13

## Grace

As it turns out, Brody was right. This church of his is *amazing*.

Straddling a longboard bobbing gently up and down with each swell headed for shore, I've got my legs dangling in the ocean, my face turned to the sun, and my ears filled with the sharp, lonesome cries of seagulls. Waves crash onto wet sand far behind me. The fresh sea breeze teases my hair into floating tendrils around my face. The sun is warm, the water is cold, my heart is as wide open as the endless blue horizon. I don't even feel hungover anymore. I feel . . .

Peaceful.

For the first time in a long time, I feel totally at ease.

"I could *really* get used to this," I say, smiling. "I wonder if I should prescribe water therapy for my patients?"

Brody chuckles. "Any time you want to tell me what a genius I am, I'm all ears."

He's straddling his own board a few feet away and grinning at me.

A water baby for sure, he's as confident on his surfboard as he is on dry land. He showed me how to paddle out through the breakers, how to balance my body, trusting the buoyancy of the board to keep me afloat without fighting it, how to cut through the top of a cresting wave by throwing all my weight forward onto my chest. He even showed me how to leap onto my feet in one swift motion so I could try to catch a wave, but I ended up nose-diving into the water every time, so we took a break from that.

Now we're out past the "takeoff zone," floating peacefully. I'm learning the rhythm of the ocean, its sets and lulls, the restless motion of it beneath me, vast and beautiful and dangerous. I could be riding the back of an enormous dragon, gliding through the air.

"How long have you been doing this?" I ask.

He shrugs. "Ever since I moved here. I've been obsessed with the ocean since the first time I saw it. Topeka, Kansas, is about as far away from any ocean as you can get."

"Homegrown in a fly-over state, hmm?"

He cuts a sharp gaze to me. "Are you serious? I can't *believe* you haven't Googled me! We've been eye-fucking each other for two years!"

"A year and a half."

He grins. "I know it's a year and a half. I just wanted to see if you did."

I smile mysteriously. "That was a lucky guess, actually. I have no idea when we first met. I just didn't want you to feel bad that I've never bothered to Google you."

He splashes me with water. I scream—because for whatever bizarre biological reason, that's what girls do when boys splash us with water—and then laugh. I splash him back. Then we're in a water fight, dousing each other with big handfuls of cold salt water, kicking it at each other, laughing like mad, playing like a couple of schoolyard kids on recess.

It's then that I spot the fin.

Dark and triangular, it's about fifty feet away from us on my side, cutting through the surface of the water as easily as a knife cuts through butter. It's moving fast in our direction.

This time when I scream it's for real.

"Sharksharksharkshark*shaaarrrk*!"

I whip my legs up out of the water. That causes me to lose my balance, which then causes me to topple over sideways—into the shark-infested ocean.

I come up kicking and screaming, panicked, gasping for air. Salt water stings my eyes. Inhaling a mouthful of water, I cough, my arms flailing for the safety of the board. Brody's calling to me. I can't make out what he's saying, I'm shrieking and splashing too loudly, but when I manage to drag myself halfway onto the surfboard I can finally hear him.

And the bastard is laughing.

*Laughing.*

"It's only a dolphin, Grace! Look!"

A pale gray body whips past us in the water, not ten feet away. Then like a rocket it blasts through the surface and flies glinting into the air. It hangs there for a moment, sleek and shining, raining drops, and then angles down and slices back into the ocean, leaving barely a splash in its wake.

"Here's another one!" shouts Brody, pointing behind me.

Breathless, my heart hammering, I spot another fin headed toward us. There are four more behind it, flared out in a V formation. They fly past us and then break the surface as the first one did and leap high into the air.

My mouth drops open. A circus act couldn't be more perfectly timed.

"They're playing!" Brody slides off his board and paddles the few feet that separate us. He hangs onto the edges of both of our boards, making us a little flotilla. His smile is brighter than the sun as he faces me, bobbing in the water only a foot away. "They're playing with us!"

I can't speak because I'm still too traumatized by the thought that I was about to become a tasty hors d'oeuvre for a great white. Half a dozen more dolphins speed past, jumping and blowing, splashing and jostling, having as much fun as a bunch of unleashed dogs in a doggie park.

Curious, they circle back and fly past us again, and I swear as each one surfaces from the water they *look* at us with their merry little eyes, like, *"Hey, there, ungainly land creature! You sure are strange looking but you're welcome here!"*

When they finally go, disappearing into the deep blue without a trace as quickly as they came, the ache in my chest tells me I've witnessed something special.

Something sacred.

Brody sees how moved I am. He swims closer and plants a wet, salty kiss on my cheek. "Yeah," he says, his voice husky. "There are still miracles in the world, Grace. You just have to know where to find them."

As we float in the water, smiling into each other's eyes, I can't help but wonder if Fate is finally extending me a long-overdue olive branch.

Or setting me up for a soul-shattering fall.

Side by side, our surfboards under our arms, we trudge silently up the beach through the sun-warmed white sand to the path that leads to the lawn. The path eventually meets up with the stone walkway that takes us through Brody's yard to the large patio, shaded by swaying palm trees, their stiff fronds glinting in the light. I'm physically exhausted but feel high, buzzed, as if I've been drinking, but my mind is sharp.

Everything around me is crystalline sharp, painfully bright, saturated with brilliant color. Every crack on the pavers beneath my feet seems made by design. Every drop of water falling from my hair is a tiny, perfect reminder of one of the most wonderful mornings of my life.

Something powerful and mysterious is moving in me. A kind of seismic shift is taking place, and it's all because of the man walking in quiet contemplation by my side.

I don't want to examine too closely what's happening. For now, it's enough to just feel.

And God, do I.

Everything from awe to terror to glee, along with a strange sort of friction, like my skin has grown too tight. Like at any moment I might crack open the shell of my body, shed it like a cocoon, and take flight in a riotous burst of color.

I wonder if he's feeling this, too. This . . . change. This electricity. All my senses crackle with the anticipation of what will happen when we get back to the house.

It doesn't help that I'm naked under my wetsuit, and I know he is, too.

"We can rinse off over there, get the sand off our feet before we go inside." Brody points to an outdoor shower on the side of the house. It's open on three sides, with a smooth bed of stones underfoot and a removable showerhead above.

He leans his board against the side of the house. He takes mine from me and does the same, standing them so close together they're touching. I know I'm a fool but it feels symbolic.

Purposeful.

"They're making out," jokes Brody, seeing where my gaze lingers.

"Must be awkward, making out with no lips," I joke back, hoping he'll attribute the color in my cheeks to our time spent in the sun.

He flashes me a smile. "There are all kinds of ways to make out."

My stomach flips. I can't wait for him to show me what that means.

He turns the shower on for me. I rinse off my feet first, then rinse the salt water from my hair and face. I'm aware of his gaze on me the entire time, warmer than sunlight.

When I'm finished, he quickly rinses off, too, shaking his head under the spray like a dog. Then he turns off the spigot, reaches behind him for the long tether on the zipper at the back of his wetsuit, yanks it down, and peels the wetsuit off his arms and chest. He lets it hang at his waist so his entire upper body is bare.

A wave of intense heat flashes over me.

I once read an article about spontaneous human combustion. It's an extremely rare phenomenon, but there are documented cases of people igniting out of the blue from no visible cause. Apparently the fire starts *within* the body due to some bizarre combination of factors, and the person is consumed within minutes. There's even a Wikipedia page dedicated to the subject.

A picture of the smoking pile of ash that used to be me will soon be featured on that Wikipedia page.

Brody's body is, in a word, stunning.

He's not bulky in the least, but he's beautifully muscled, with the definition of a long-distance runner, all sculpted planes and breathtaking angles, an incredibly poetic symmetry of form. The muscles in his biceps bulge as he raises his hands to rake them through his wet hair. Water runs in glistening rivulets down his chest and over the six-pack of his abs, channeling into the V below his waist that leads down to his pelvis.

His shoulders are wide, his waist is narrow, his skin is a gorgeous golden hue, burnished from all the time he obviously spends in the sun.

The tattoo that spans the breadth of his chest is a pair of angel's wings, flared wide, with something written in black ink just below his collarbone, in a language that looks like cursive hieroglyphics.

I have no idea how long I stand there stupidly staring, but at some point I become aware that Brody is saying my name.

"What? No. I mean yes. I'm listening."

His eyes sparkle with amusement. "How you doing there, Slick?"

"Uh—good. Fine. I'm great." I toss my wet hair out of my face and attempt a nonchalant expression, like he didn't just catch me ogling him with drool running down my chin.

"You sure? You look a little . . . flushed."

He grins. I've never seen a man's smile look so goddamn smug.

*Turnabout is fair play, Kong.*

"To tell the truth, Mr. Scott, I was just admiring your breasts."

His brows shoot up. He glances down at himself, and then back up at me. "My . . . breasts."

"Yes. They're quite spectacular."

He shakes his head slowly, still grinning. "Just out of curiosity, how many men's fragile egos have you crushed in your life? Because honestly, Slick, you're the worst at giving compliments. You're, like, the anticompliment queen."

Feeling cheeky and emboldened because I've narrowly escaped death by instantaneous combustion, I ask, "Does that mean you don't want me to touch them?"

He stares at me. "Do you want to touch them?"

I think he was aiming for casual, but there's a telling edge to his voice, a rough little growl beneath the lighthearted delivery. It gives me a thrill.

"I would very much like to touch them, yes." I step closer.

He doesn't move, but the pulse in the base of his neck quickens. I take another step closer, and another, and then we're standing only inches apart.

Holding perfectly still, he gazes down at me. His green eyes are half-lidded. A drop of water glistens on his chin. I resist the urge to stand up on my toes and lick it off.

"Well, go ahead then," he says gruffly. "Touch them."

The pulse in his neck throbs.

I reach out and touch his arm. The muscle in his biceps tenses. I slide my finger up to his shoulder. His nostrils flare. I trace the elegant line of his collarbone down to the hollow of his throat, where I let my finger rest for a moment on that wildly throbbing vein.

He's holding so still. His eyes are so hot. I feel like we're on the cusp of nuclear fusion.

I flatten my hand over the center of his chest. I feel the heat of his body, the clamor of his heart, and that crackle of electricity passing back and forth between us on a fast, repeating loop.

With a crack in his voice he says, "You're trembling."

"So are you."

"Those are shivers. I'm just cold from being wet. And the wind."

I let my hand drift down his chest until I feel a small, peaked nub under my thumb. "Is that why your nipples are so hard?"

He swallows. "Yep."

As he struggles to remain still, I slowly circle his wet, hard nipple with my thumb. I whisper, "You must be *very* cold, Mr. Scott."

"Not everywhere."

It's a husky, needy rasp, and I love the sound of it.

"No?" My hand drifts lower.

His breathing grows irregular. The muscles of his stomach contract under my touch. Just beneath his belly button there's a fine down of hair. I stroke it, moving my finger languidly lower.

He licks his lips. His entire body tenses. At his sides, his hands curl into fists.

I ask, "Are you trying not to touch me?"

"Yes."

"Why?"

He exhales a small, shaky breath. "Because if I start I won't be able to stop."

I tilt my head up, daring him with my eyes. My hand drifts lower. "And that's bad because . . ."

He grabs my wrist and winds my arm behind my back. He pulls me against his chest, bunches a hand into my wet hair, and rasps, "Because the first time I fuck you, Grace, it'll be the last time either of us fucks anyone else, and you're not ready for that yet."

To punctuate this shocking statement with an exclamation point, he angles my head toward his and kisses me, deeply, greedily, feeding on my mouth like he's starving and the key to his survival is the taste of my lips.

I kiss him back just as hungrily.

I can't get enough of this—of him. I thread my fingers into his wet hair and pull his head down harder, greedy for every possessive little growl he's making in his throat, desperate for there to be no space between us. I want, so badly, to feel him inside me. I want to feel him everywhere.

"*Señorita* Grace!"

With a groan, Brody breaks off the kiss. He glares at Magda, standing at the open patio doors. She's holding my handbag in her hand. On my way into the party yesterday, I'd stashed it in a covered basket beneath a table in the entry.

Magda holds out the bag. *"Esta es tuya?"*

I answer in Spanish, "Yes, Magda. That's mine."

She tells me the handbag has been ringing for an hour.

Brody demands, "English, devil women!"

"Apparently my phone's been ringing nonstop while we were out."

Brody drops his forehead to mine. He chuckles. "Saved by the bell."

"I don't need saving, Kong."

His smile is devastating. "I wasn't talking about *you*, Slick."

On cue, my phone—buried inside my handbag—begins to ring again.

I sigh and pull away from Brody. As much as I'd like to continue this lovely moment, I'll need to deal with whoever is on the other end of that phone first.

I take the bag from Magda, dig my phone out, and frown at the caller ID. It's the main office at my condo building.

"Hello?"

"Ms. Stanton?"

It's the building manager, Linda Conley. She sounds panicked, but the woman is as high-strung as an overbred Chihuahua, so I don't give it a second thought.

"Hi, Linda. How are you?"

When she exhales an anguished cry, a twinge of alarm zings through my stomach.

"Oh thank God! You're safe!"

The twinge of alarm balloons into fear. "What're you talking about? What's happened?"

Brody looks at me sharply. Magda turns around and wanders back inside the house.

Linda breathes, "Oh, Miss Stanton—Grace—there's been . . . there's been a terrible accident."

Everything inside me freezes. My blood stops circulating. My lungs refuse to contract.

"Accident?"

In a few long strides, Brody's at my side, his hand on my shoulder, his worried gaze on my face. Linda tells me the news, her words all running together.

"Yes, there was a terrible accident, Mr. Liebowitz in unit 1302, you know he was on oxygen for his emphysema, he wasn't supposed to be smoking, all the doctors told him not to smoke but he was a stubborn man—God forgive me for saying that—and you know how volatile those oxygen tanks are—what *could* he have been thinking? Everyone's in a panic, the fire department is here, so many paramedics and fire trucks, it's absolute pandemonium! And the *mess*! It's such a terrible mess, I don't know *how* long it will take to clean everything up, it's like 9/11 over here—"

"Linda!" I shout. *"Tell me what happened!"*

There's a short pause. Then Linda says quietly, "Mr. Liebowitz blew himself up."

He lived in the unit directly above me.

I close my eyes, already knowing what Linda's going to say next.

"I'm so sorry, Grace, but . . . your home was also destroyed in the explosion. There's nothing left. It's gone."

# Chapter 14

I can't move. I can't speak, even when Brody desperately begs me to talk to him, to tell him what happened, to tell him if I'm all right.

I'm not all right.

I'm homeless.

"Grace, you're scaring me. Please. Look at me."

The freeze abruptly thaws and all my bodily functions slam into high alert at once. I start to shake, sweat, and hyperventilate.

Brody grips my arms. "Is it Kat? Chloe? Did someone get hurt?"

I moisten my dry lips, swallow the bile rising in my throat. "My condo . . . the man who lived above me had these big tanks of oxygen delivered every Saturday. He was a smoker. There was an explosion. My . . . my home is gone."

My voice is surprisingly steady, but that's all I can manage to say in one breath.

"Gone? What do you mean?"

"Destroyed," I say. "Blown up. All my things . . ."

I have extra copies of my bible at work—that's what I call the binder where I keep everything pertinent to my life in case I wake up one day a blank slate—so at least I have *something* left.

I have paperwork left.

Thank God I didn't own a pet, because it would be dead. If I hadn't slept at Brody's house last night, *I'd* be dead.

*Getting drunk saved my life.*

*Kat saved my life.*

*Brody's housewarming party saved my life.*

*Brody saved my life.*

My mind is a soup of chaotic thoughts, swimming in stress hormones, churning with what-ifs. Only one thing's for certain: I've escaped death twice. That's two more times than most people get.

Which gives the phrase "third time's a charm" a whole new meaning. That warped thought makes me laugh, only it sounds more like I'm choking.

Brody's brow wrinkles with worry. "Let's go inside."

He gently guides me into the house. I'm dripping wet, doing my best impression of a leaf in gale-force winds. The brain floods the body with the hormone cortisol when under stress, and I'm pretty sure my brain just opened the floodgates and let loose its entire store.

"Sit on the sofa."

"I'll ruin the leather."

"Fuck the leather. Sit."

I follow his command and sink to the sofa, immediately grateful I'm no longer standing because the room has started to narrow and fade.

"You're hyperventilating, Grace. Put your head between your knees and take deep breaths."

Dizzy, I bend over my legs, close my eyes, and suck air into my lungs. Brody puts his hand on my back and begins to rub circles, the movements slow and steadying.

Steadying for my pulse, not for my mind.

*Maybe this is some kind of twisted sign.*

*Maybe Marcus was wrong when he said the universe doesn't pick people out for misfortune. Maybe I'm one of those people who bad luck shadows all their lives.*

*Maybe I'm cursed.*

"Give me your phone."

My knuckles are white around the phone I'm still clutching in my hand. Inhaling another shaky breath, I allow Brody to gently peel my fingers away and take it from me.

"Magda! We need towels!" he calls out.

She must have anticipated this request, because no sooner has he made it than she appears from around the corner of the living room with a bundle of bright beach towels in her arms. She takes one look at me hunched over on the couch and exclaims, "*Ai! Mija! Estas blanca como un fantasma!*"

You're as white as a ghost.

Brody impatiently takes the towels from her, wraps one around my shoulders, and gently wipes the water from my face. "Just sit here quietly for a minute, Grace. I think you're in shock. Sit here until you catch your breath, then we'll get you out of this wetsuit and into dry clothes. And then we'll figure out what to do next. Okay?"

Numb, I nod.

Brody murmurs some instructions to Magda. I don't pay attention to the words, only to the cadence of his voice, the strong, soothing tone of it. Flashbacks hit me with vivid intensity, memories of another time I sat white and numb in an unfamiliar place while a soothing male voice whispered words of instruction to others, the smell of antiseptic and death sharp in my nose.

Brody's home is far more beautiful and comfortable than the emergency room at a hospital, but at the moment they feel like exactly the same thing.

# Chapter 15

## Brody

Helpless isn't a feeling that sits well with me.

Only once before have I ever felt anything close to this level of uselessness, when things were so fucked there was absolutely nothing I could do about it. Now, as it was then, my first instinct is to try to fix it.

I hope I get better results this time.

My firecracker sits still and pale on the sofa, all the life drained from her eyes. For a woman so vibrant, she looks unnervingly like a corpse.

"Magda, will you please make Grace a cup of tea?"

*"Claro."* She hustles off into the kitchen, moving faster than I've seen her move in years.

I gently kiss Grace's forehead, and then stride into the dining room where I can make a quiet phone call while still keeping her in my sight. Tense and pacing, I dial Nico's number from Grace's phone.

He picks up with a sleepy, "Yo."

Keeping my voice low, I say, "Nico, it's Brody."

"Oh hey, bro. I didn't recognize the number." There's rustling and a murmur in the background. A female voice asks who it is.

"Shit, man, did I wake you guys up?"

"Yeah, you did, and it better be good 'cause my beautiful fuckin' wife's naked next to me in bed and I've got some serious morning wood."

"Jesus, dude. TMI."

Nico chuckles. "What time is it? You okay?"

"No. Listen—turn on the local news for me."

"The news? What's wrong?"

I glance into the living room. Grace still sits unmoving on the sofa, staring blankly at the floor. "Grace got a call from someone at her building saying her condo blew up."

"Blew up! What the fuck?"

"What happened? Is he okay?" In the background Kat's voice is no longer sleepy. It's sharp and loud.

Nico instructs her to turn on the television and find a news station. Kat says he can forget about his morning wood until he tells her what's going on. Nico laughs, Kat squeals . . . and then there's a suspicious silence.

"Nico! For fuck's sake!" I hiss under my breath, trying not to let Grace hear me.

"Sorry, bro. TV's comin' on."

After a moment the blare of a news station crackles over the line. "Local news, baby," Nico says to Kat. Then to me, "Your power out over there?"

"Just trying to avoid traumatizing Grace any more than she already is."

"Wait, baby—stop on that one!" Nico is quiet a moment, and then he murmurs, "Holy shit."

In the background Kat shouts, "Oh my God! That's Grace's building!"

I demand, "Tell me."

"Looks like whoever called Grace was tellin' the truth. That fancy high-rise she lives in has a big hole right in the middle of it. Smoke's pourin' out. Got fire trucks and paramedics all over the place. Looks like a bomb went off—"

Fumbling noises, muffled cursing. Then a panicked Kat commandeers the phone. "Brody! Is Grace okay? Is she still there?"

"Yes, she's here—"

"Has she seen the news? It's a fucking disaster!"

"Kat—"

"Thank *God* she spent the night at your place! Put her on, I need to talk to her!"

"Kat, calm down—"

*"Put her on the phone right now!"*

Wincing, I jerk the phone away from my head. When no more eardrum-piercing sounds emit from the speaker, I put the phone back to my ear. "You being out of control emotionally isn't going to help her, Kat."

The silence bristles. There's an aggravated snarl like a bear rudely awoken from its winter hibernation, and then a sigh. "Okay. You're right. I'm calm. Ish."

"Good. Thank you. What I need you to do is get some clothes together for her—anything you or Chloe have that would fit—and some cosmetics. Hair stuff, girl stuff, I'll leave it to you. You know what she needs. Anything you don't have I'll get from the store. I'll have a driver pick it up from your place later, or you guys can come over and—"

"Wait a minute. She's *staying* with you?"

"Yes."

"For how long?"

I glance over at Grace. A powerful feeling washes over me. It's a feeling I'm unfamiliar with, but one I want—more than anything else I've ever wanted—to dive deeper into.

I say softly, "I haven't asked her yet, but . . . for as long as she wants. Hopefully forever."

Kat's gasp tells me her emotions are about to spiral out of control again, even before she says with hysterical urgency, "Are you guys a thing now? Oh please, *please* tell me you're a thing!"

"Kat. Focus. Clothes."

"Yes, okay, yes, I'll get the stuff together. I'll be over there as soon as I can."

She stops speaking abruptly. After a moment, her voice lowered, she says, "I've always liked you, Brody. I think you're a great guy. But if you ever hurt my girl, if you ever so much as make her *frown*, I'll rain down a shit storm of such Biblical proportions on your head you won't know what hit you. I will rip off both your arms and beat you to death with them. Literally."

I can't help but smile at that. "I know you will, Rocky."

"No—listen. She's not as tough as she seems."

"I know. She told me about her memory situation. I know what I'm getting into. And I'm a thousand percent on board. She's not like anyone else I've met before, I've never felt like this before, and there's nothing on the face of this fucking earth I'd rather do than take care of her. I'll never hurt her, Kat. Never. I swear on my mother's life."

Kat's exhalation has a religious fervor to it. She sounds like she's making the sign of the cross over her chest.

"And now I'm gonna hang up and go take care of our girl, okay?"

Kat sniffles. She says a choked, "Okay," and gives the phone to Nico.

He barks, "What did you just say to make my wife cry, asshole?"

"I kinda told her . . . in so many words . . . that I'm falling in love with her girlfriend."

After a brief silence, Nico chuckles. "Yeah, that'd do it."

In the living room, Magda hands Grace a mug of tea, sits down on the sofa beside her, and gives her a hug.

I almost drop the phone.

Magda doesn't give hugs. She gives tongue-lashings. She gives the evil eye. She does *not* give hugs.

Unless I'm hallucinating, which is a definite possibility.

"I gotta go, Nico."

"Yep. Let us know if you need anything."

"Will do. Thanks, man."

I hang up and head straight back to Grace. The moment I stop in front of the sofa, Magda launches into an unintelligible rant accompanied by a lot of choppy hand gestures that seems to indicate I'm doing everything wrong and am not competent enough to deal with a soaking wet, distraught woman.

"Magda, I have no idea what you just said, but I need to talk to—"

Magda throws up a hand. She turns to Grace and, very gently, says something to her in Spanish.

Grace takes a sip of her tea. She whispers, "Thank you, Magda. That's very kind."

Magda pats her back, nodding. Then she says something else in Spanish to Grace.

"Oh, no. I . . ." Grace glances up at me, then quickly looks away. "I couldn't impose like that. I'll get a hotel, my insurance will cover it—"

"Yes," I interrupt, guessing what Magda has said from the context of Grace's denial. "You should stay here. We want you to. *I* want you to."

Magda throws me a killer glare that's supposed to shut me up but doesn't, because I've been on the receiving end of so many of them I'm immune.

I sink to a knee in front of Grace and take her hand. "If you don't feel comfortable staying with me in the main house because we're not . . . uh . . . because we haven't . . ."

Grace's brows lift. Magda growls at me.

I blurt, "The guest house is three thousand square feet! It has its own pool! And its own private entrance! You could come and go anytime, it would be like your own place!"

Shaking her head, Magda exhales through her nose and looks at the ceiling.

Ignoring her, I squeeze Grace's hand. "At least for tonight. Or a few days, until you get settled with whatever other arrangements you need to make. You can stay however long you need."

Grace drops her gaze to our hands. She chews her lower lip for a moment, thinking.

"Please."

She doesn't say anything.

"I promise I won't be weird or anything."

Grace looks up at me with a furrow between her brows.

"I mean . . . more weird."

Finally she cracks a smile.

"Is that a yes?" I press, excited.

Magda says, "Ach. *Patetico.*" Then she explains something to Grace in Spanish.

Grace listens. She takes another sip of her tea. When Magda stops speaking, Grace looks at her for a long while, and then at me. She says, "Whatever you're paying her, this woman deserves a raise."

Then she and Magda stand, so I do, too.

Sounding more steady, Grace says, "I'd like to take a shower and get into some dry clothes."

"Yes, of course. Take a shower and I'll find you something of mine to wear—sweats and a T-shirt okay?"

Grace nods.

"I called Kat. She's gonna bring some clothes over for you later. I'll get the guest house ready, and then . . ."

I trail off into silence, because I don't know what's supposed to happen then.

But Grace lives up to her name, because she gives me a sweet, soft smile, and kisses me on the cheek. "And then we'll talk."

My heart starts pounding. "Yes. Then we'll talk."

Is it wrong that I'm hoping she meant to say a different four-letter word that ends with a K?

Yes. It's wrong. I'm a perv. I know. I can't help myself. I've been lusting after this woman for so long now the inside of my brain is wall-papered with images of her naked body.

Then it hits me that what Grace needs right now isn't another dude waving his dick in her face. What she needs, more than anything, is a friend.

If I really want to do right by her, I need to be her friend, not the guy who's trying his hardest to get into her panties when she's most vulnerable.

Which means I need to back off.

*Damn* it's inconvenient having a conscience.

She turns and walks away, down the hall toward the guest bedroom she spent the night in. I watch her go, Magda by my side. When Grace closes the bedroom door behind her, Magda looks up at me. She says in English, "You're welcome. Don't fuck it up."

Exasperated, I throw my hands in the air. "Magda! Why have I never heard you speak English before today?"

She shrugs. Then, with a gleam in her dark eyes, she answers in Spanish.

I glare at her. "You've *got* to be kidding me."

She smiles, pats me on the arm, and then turns and walks away.

I call out, "If I didn't love you so much you'd be so fired right now!"

I hear her cackling long after she's disappeared from sight.

# Chapter 16

I'm lying on my back in my bed, staring at the ceiling while I listen to my mom gripe about my younger brother, Branson, who still lives at home, when Grace walks in.

Her face is bare. Her damp hair is combed straight. She's wearing my gray sweatpants and Neil Diamond T-shirt I left out for her on the bed in the guest bedroom while she was taking a shower. Seeing me on the phone, she hesitates in the doorway, her hand resting on the frame.

Neil's face has two perky points jutting out from the middle of it.

Trying to nonchalantly adjust my thickening cock beneath the sweats I'm wearing, I sit up. "Uh, Mom. I have to go."

"Go? We've been on the phone for two minutes! I haven't talked to you since last week!"

"I have company."

My mother's silences are so rich and nuanced they're like symphonies. This one has a top note of curiosity and a healthy baseline of irritation, because there's nothing more she loves to do than complain to me about my brother. Luckily I only have to hear about it once a week.

"From your tone, Brody, I take it this company is of the female variety?"

I can't look away from Grace. It's like my eyeballs are superglued to her. A horde of zombies could crash through the window and start to eat my face off and I'd still be sitting here staring at her, stunning as a Caravaggio painting in my doorway, looking at me with her lower lip pulled between her teeth and her gray eyes soft and needy.

*Be a friend. Be a friend. Be a friend, you fucking selfish asshole.*

"Yes," I tell my mother. "Very."

She laughs. "Oh my. That sounds serious."

"It is."

After another deafening pause, she says sternly, "I expect you to be responsible and wear condoms, son."

"Christ, Mom! I'm twenty-nine years old, not twelve! Also—gross!"

"Condoms aren't gross, honey, they're practical."

"You telling me to wear one is gross! This conversation is gross!"

"Well, I've seen pictures in my entertainment magazines of some of those 'ladies' you date, and quite frankly I'm surprised you haven't yet been diagnosed with some incurable venereal disease." She gasps. "Or have you and you're just not telling me?"

"I'm hanging up on you now."

"On a related topic, the pill isn't always one hundred percent reliable, you know—"

"Oh my God! Dude!"

"I am not a 'dude,' I'm your mother, and I'm ready for more grandchildren, Brody, but not by some floozy named Iguana Azalea or Bone Chyna or Rainbow Trout or whatever. We are not the Kardashians."

"Good-bye, Mother."

"One final thought: antiviral lubricant is very effective at killing a wide variety of—"

I hang up before she can succeed in making me puke.

Grace stares at me with one elegant brow cocked. "That sounded interesting."

"You really don't want to know."

"That was your mom?"

"Yeah."

"Did I hear the word 'condom' mentioned?"

I drop my head into my hands and groan.

Grace walks over to the bed and perches on the edge of the mattress. I open two fingers and peek at her.

She asks, "So you're close with your family?"

"Unfortunately."

When Grace blinks, I feel like the hugest asshole in the world. She doesn't have a family and here I am being completely insensitive.

I backtrack as fast as I can. "No! I mean—yes, we're close. That came out wrong. I love them, and I'm grateful to have them—"

"It's okay," she says, smiling. "I know what you meant."

I blow out a relieved breath. "Sorry. I'm an idiot."

She looks down and thoughtfully picks at the comforter. "I guess one of the girls told you about my parents, huh?"

*Oh shit. Could I fuck this up any more perfectly?*

I try to be as diplomatic as I can while still being honest. "Only because I kinda forced the subject. And they wouldn't say much. They love you, you know. I don't think I've ever seen closer friends than you three."

She nods. "Yeah." Her voice grows softer. "I would never have made it this far without them."

There are so many questions I want to ask her, so many things I want to say, but the timing is fucked. Anything I say would probably only make things worse, so I end up nodding mutely.

She saves us from the awkward silence when she says, "I made a bunch of calls. Some of my friends in the building. My insurance company. A colleague at work who covers for me when I'm out of the office.

I'll have to reschedule all my clients for the next few weeks, I doubt I'll be helpful to anyone right now. Then I made the mistake of turning on the television to watch the news."

The waver in her voice stirs that protective instinct in me again. I touch her arm.

She looks up at me with big eyes. She whispers, "Would it be okay if . . . could I maybe ask for a hug?"

Without thinking I say, "You could ask for anything you want and I'd give it to you."

We stare at each other for a beat, electricity sparking between us, and then she smiles. "In that case, I'd like to request a tropical island—"

"An *island*! Geez, go big or go home, Slick!"

"Just one of the little ones! In the South Pacific maybe? C'mon, you're rich!"

Grinning, I take her by the arm, gently pull her next to me, lie back, and tuck her under my arm so we're lying side by side. She rests her cheek on my shoulder, slides one bare foot under my calf, and bends her other leg so it's resting over my thigh. She spreads her hand flat on my chest, and sighs in contentment.

It feels incredible. We're a perfect fit. Even our breathing seems to fit, synchronizing so our chests rise and fall in the same slow rhythm.

Now if only my dick would behave, everything would be just peachy.

Grace clears her throat. "Um. Should I move?"

"No. Ignore it. The thing has a one-track mind."

We're quiet for a minute, just breathing. Then, with a smile in her voice, she says, "Are you doing that on purpose?"

"Doing what?"

"That . . . twitching."

I cover my red face with my hand. "You're supposed to be ignoring it."

Her body shakes with suppressed laughter. "How could I ignore, it, Brody, it has its own heartbeat!"

"Ugh. Sorry. It's not normally so obnoxious."

"Yeah, right."

"I'm not kidding. Being around you gives me perma-wood. I feel like a teenager again."

"Or a dirty old man."

"Who you calling old, woman? I'm not the one on this bed who's on the dark side of thirty."

She chuckles. "Oh, that's right. I'm robbing the cradle."

"Excuse me—twenty-nine is hardly in a *cradle*. God, between you and my mother . . ."

She replies in a baby voice, "Does widdle Bwody need his ba-ba?"

I exhale slowly, smothering the violent urge to flip her onto her back and show her just how much of a ba-ba I need. "You're lucky I'm trying to be your friend right now, Slick. That's all I'm gonna say."

"My 'friend'? That sounds ominous."

When I don't answer, she muses, "I've never had a male friend."

"Exactly."

"I didn't mean it as a good thing."

"Well, it is."

She props herself up on her elbow and looks down at me. "Is this your way of telling me you don't want to have sex with me?"

"I want to have sex with you more than I want to survive to see another day. More than I want Ben Affleck to stop making superhero movies. More than I want flying cars to be a real thing. That's not the point."

Her forehead wrinkles. "What is the point?"

My dick is throbbing so hard I actually don't know what the point is. I have to use all my willpower to focus and try to get some blood back up into my brain. "I think the point is that . . ."

She waits, her brows lifted.

"The point is that I already told you the point. I don't want to fuck you—*yet*. I mean, I do, desperately, but I won't."

Her brows return to their normal position. "Hmm."

"Okay, *that* sounded ominous."

"I'm trying to decide if that's romantic or just dumb."

"Gee, thanks."

She lays her head on my chest again and snuggles up against me. Then she starts to toy with the hem of my T-shirt.

It seems absentminded, the way her fingers accidentally skim my bare skin just above the waistband of my sweatpants, but this is Grace Stanton we're dealing with here. Nothing she does is by chance.

When she draws a series of slow circles around my belly button, I warn gruffly, "Grace."

"I know," she whispers. "I felt that, too. Do you think he'll chew a hole clean through your sweats?"

"I can't believe we're talking about my cock like he's an inmate about to make a prison break."

She slides her thumb under the elastic of my sweats, and my dick bucks like a rodeo bull right before the bell sounds and the gate flies open.

I feel her smile on my chest. "It's a good analogy, though."

She presses a kiss to the side of my neck, just under my ear. A bolt of lust surges through me, so strong it steals my breath.

Grace says, "Whoa. Even *I* felt that."

I wrap my hand carefully around her wrist. My voice comes out raw. "It would be probably *the* most selfish thing I could do to fuck you right now. I'd feel like a total asshole after. We're not going there."

The tone of my voice or my hand restraining her from moving does something to her, because a little tremor runs through her body and her breathing goes all ragged.

She whispers, "What if I told you it's exactly what I need, though?"

Something in her voice brings back Chloe's words like cold water splashed on my face. *Grace isn't the girl who wants the roses and the love poems and the happily-ever-after.* She told me that the day Abby was born, the same time she told me Grace's parents had been killed in an accident.

But now I have another piece of the puzzle, because I know the reason *why* Grace doesn't want the happily-ever-after, why she's chosen to live every day as if it's her last.

She doesn't think she'll remember any of it.

And she doesn't want to hurt anyone her memories might leave behind.

I roll her onto her back, take both her wrists in my hands, and press them into the pillow so she can't randomly fondle me and weaken my resolve. We're chest-to-chest, nose-to-nose, crotch-to-crotch, staring into each other's eyes, breathing each other's breath.

If there's anything more perfect in this world, I've never found it.

"I don't want this to be like anything else either one of us has had," I say. "I don't want it to be casual. I don't want it to be only about the sex. I don't want to jump into a physical relationship before we get to know each other. I want it to be special, because it *is* special. I've never . . . with you I feel this weird . . . there's a connection. I don't know why, there just is. And I don't want to fuck it up.

"I meant what I said outside. Whatever this is between us, it's real, Grace. It's fucking *real*, and I'm gonna respect it by giving it a little room to breathe and grow before I go sticking my dick in it."

Grace's eyes are wide and unblinking. I can't tell if she's horrified, surprised, or about to bolt from the room and never look back.

She says flatly, "Oh. My. God. You're totally in love with me."

It's only after the mischievous smile flits over her face—there then instantly gone—that I realize she's messing with me.

Naturally I can't let *that* stand.

With a straight face I answer, "How could I be in love with you? You're probably the most hideous woman alive."

Her lips twitch. She's trying not to laugh.

"It's not funny, Grace. You're revolting. I don't know how you don't get arrested for public indecency when you leave the house. It's like you fell out of the ugly tree and hit every branch on the way down."

"At least I don't have a sex-obsessed gherkin living in my pants."

I snort. "Don't you?"

"Oh. Yeah, you might have me there. Let me try again."

"Sure. Have at it. Witch face."

"I might have a witch face but at least I'm not a mama's boy."

I grin. Smart chicks are the best. And smart-*mouthed* chicks . . . if I were Kenji, this is where I'd heave a dreamy sigh and faint into a pile of lavender-scented pillows.

Instead I ask, "If I throw a stick, will you chase it?"

Grace laughs. "Oh, I get it, because I'm a dog! That's called a metaphor. I'd explain it to you, but I don't have any crayons."

I press a soft kiss to her lips and whisper, "The last time I saw a face like yours, I fed it a banana."

She giggles. "Excuse me, Kong, we've already established that *you're* the ape in this relationship."

I'm trying really hard not to laugh. "I love what you've done with your nostril hair. How did you braid it like that?"

"Hey!" She playfully kicks me in the shin.

"Sorry, have I gone too far? Nose hair is where you draw the line?"

We grin at each other, until finally she sighs. "Okay. Obviously I'm not going to be able to convince you to have sex with me. Which, by the way, has never happened to me before. So."

"So feel special?"

"Exactly."

I roll to my back, taking her along, and settle her on top of me. "Funny, but somehow that doesn't make me feel so special."

Gazing down at me with her hair curtained around her face, Grace smiles. "It should, Kong. Because if it were anyone else but you, I'd already have kicked his ass to the curb."

"You wanton little trollop." I cup her face and kiss her again, deeper this time, exploring her sweet mouth with my tongue.

Against my lips, she says breathlessly, "*Your* wanton little trollop."

My heart stalls out before taking off like a rocket. "I'm gonna hold you to that, Slick."

This time the kiss is serious. It lasts for what feels like forever. Her body is a soft, delicious weight on top of mine. She smells like shampoo and clean skin. An animalistic urge to tear off all her clothes, bury my face between her thighs, and find out what her pussy tastes like rips through me. She flexes her hips, rubbing her pelvis against my stiff cock, and I groan.

"I'm sorry. That was an accident."

I growl, "You're a shitty liar."

I have her breasts in my hands. How did that happen? They're full and heavy in my palms, a lush weight covered by the barest layer of soft cotton. I rub my thumbs over the taut peaks of her nipples and she gasps.

Acting purely on instinct, I lift my head and suck on one rigid nub, right through the T-shirt.

Her moan is so erotic I almost come in my pants.

I bite down gently and am rewarded by another moan, this one even more sensual than the last. Shuddering, she arches into my hands, into my mouth. Her hair spills down her back.

"More," she begs, rocking on top of me. "Brody. More."

Fuck. Fuck fuck *fuck*.

"Grace."

"Please? Just a little bit more?"

There's no man on earth who could resist the beautiful woman that he's completely insane over begging him to keep playing with her tits.

If there is, he's a better man than I am.

I slide my hands under her shirt. Her skin is hot, silky. My hands almost span her waist. Moving slowly, loving the sound of her ragged breathing, the hazy, lust-filled look in her eyes, I move my hands up, tracing her skin with the tips of my fingers.

When I cup her breasts, squeezing the fullness of the globes, she groans. I pinch both her nipples and her eyes slide shut.

"Your mouth," she rasps. "I need your mouth."

I'm starting to sweat. My heart thinks it's a jackhammer. I have no idea how much longer I'll be able to keep up this little game before I have to go jerk off in the shower, but I decide to find out.

I push up her T-shirt and latch on to a rigid pink nipple with my mouth.

She moans my name.

I'm a warrior. I'm a king. I'm a fucking *god.*

I go back and forth between her breasts, sucking and gently biting, stroking and pinching the nipple that isn't in my mouth. Her tits are gorgeous, rosy and flushed, incredibly sensitive to my every touch. My dick is a steel pipe.

A throbbing steel pipe.

Grace rocks faster against it, dry humping me as I fondle her.

Against her breast I whisper, "Are you trying to get yourself off, sweetheart?"

Her only answer is a low, ragged moan.

I know a "yes" when I hear one.

I flip her to her back, straddle her, drag the T-shirt over her head and up her arms, and tie it in a knot around her wrists.

Blinking and breathless, she stares up at me. Her cheeks are pink, her lips are parted, her hair is damp and wild all over the pillow.

She's the single most gorgeous thing I've ever seen.

"Did you just handcuff me with your shirt?"

Breathing hard, I answer, "Fuck yes I did. Can you come just from having your nipples sucked?"

She whispers, "I— I don't know. I've never tried it."

My grin is savage. "Until now. And for the record, this isn't sex. This is just foreplay."

I lower my head and begin the experiment.

# Chapter 17

## Grace

With every pull of Brody's lips on my nipples, a wave of hot, pure pleasure pulses between my legs. I writhe and moan beneath him, desperate for more.

"God, the sounds she makes," he mutters to himself, before diving back in for another mouthful of flesh.

He's straddling me, his legs on either side of my hips, so I have nothing to rub against, nothing but the pressure of my thighs pressed together to answer the growing ache between my legs. It's not enough. I need more.

I need *him*.

"Take out your cock," I whisper breathlessly.

He glances up at me, his cheeks flushed, fire in his eyes. His big hands cup both my breasts. His skin is golden against my paleness. His lips are wet around one hard nipple.

He sucks it so strongly his cheeks hollow. I arch and moan again. The sound is broken. "Please, just let me see it."

"I'm *not* gonna fuck you, Grace."

Why does hearing him say those words in that gruff, almost angry tone drive me right to the edge of sanity?

"I need to see it. I need to see how hard you are for me," I pant, rocking my hips like the wanton little trollop he teasingly called me. Against his sweats, his cock bobs, and I whimper.

He moves to my other nipple. Looking up at me, he slowly circles his tongue around it, and then takes it between his teeth.

When he gently bites down, my lids slide shut. I groan, arching into his mouth.

"Tell me how wet your pussy is," he demands, squeezing my breasts.

"Soaking. I'm soaked, I need you to touch me, I need your fingers, please Brody, I need your tongue—"

"You have my tongue, sweetheart," he whispers. He bites me beneath my nipple in the full part of my breast. I gasp in pleasure. Then he licks the sting away, and I start to plead with him again.

"Between my legs. If you won't give me your cock, I need your tongue between my legs oh God *please*—" I break off with a cry as he pinches both my nipples. Heat pulses in my core.

"You want me to lick your pussy, Grace? You need my tongue on your sweet little clit?"

When I open my eyes, there's a different Brody on top of me, staring down with startling intensity at my face. This isn't the boyish Brody, the adorable surfer with the cocky swagger and the even cockier grin.

This is Brody the *man*, with a wolf's hungry eyes and dangerous growl, ready to pounce and tear me to shreds.

My voice comes out small. "Yes. Please."

That low, animal growl rumbles through his chest.

Goose bumps erupt all over my body.

He watches me for a moment, his eyes glittering, his chest rapidly rising and falling with his breath. Finally he makes a decision on whatever argument is going on inside his head. He commands, "Don't move."

He sits up, crosses to the door, closes and locks it, and then turns back to me. He pulls his shirt off over his head and drops it to the floor, so he's standing there bare chested and barefoot, wearing only the sweats with the big pole tenting the front, staring at me with wild eyes and a hard jaw, his pulse throbbing hard in his neck.

His gaze on mine, he crosses back to the bed and slowly crawls up the mattress.

My heart beats so frantically I can't catch my breath.

When his head is level with my stomach, he stops. His hands are planted on either side of my hips, his arms braced so all the muscles bulge. He moistens his lips. He leans his weight onto one hand, and with the other brushes his thumb in the damp seam between my legs.

When I make a soft cry he shushes me. I bite my lip.

Every part of me is trembling. My nipples and pussy are aching. I've never felt such profound physical *need*.

Watching my face, Brody slowly strokes his thumb up and down, rubbing my pussy through the fabric that covers it. The pressure is light—too light. I flex my hips up, wanting more.

"Move again and I'll stop," he warns, in this dark, dominant voice that gives me another rash of goose bumps.

I fall so still I might as well be playing dead. If I could somehow stop breathing, I would.

Still lightly stroking me, he lowers his head and presses a gentle kiss to my belly. His lips part, he traces his tongue around my belly button, and then dips it in.

The barest moan breaks from my lips.

Right through the fabric, he lightly pinches my clit. I jerk, gasping. He growls, "No moving, no noise, no exceptions. Understood?"

*Sweet Ryan Gosling on a unicorn, dominant Brody is sexy as FUCK.*

I don't dare answer. I close my eyes and lie there, incandescent with desire, wishing I believed in God so I could pray to Him to help me be still and quiet without being a complete hypocrite.

Brody praises me with a murmured, "Good girl."

His mouth is hot on my skin, soft and wet. He kisses and licks me, nips me with just enough pressure to sting, all over my belly and across to my hip, taking his time, making a meal of it. He adjusts his weight so he's balanced on his knees, and then inches the waistband of my sweats down, agonizingly slowly, pulling it past my hips until he stops with a low chuckle that sends a tingle right through me.

"No panties, hmm?"

*Sue me.*

That thought is tossed out the window when Brody blows a breath of air over my exposed flesh.

I catch myself before the groan leaves my lips, and lie there with my hands clenched to fists, bunched in his T-shirt over my head, every nerve in my body singing.

"Look at this beautiful pussy. *Look* at you. Fuck."

His words are whispered and reverent, like a prayer.

With infinite gentleness, almost chastely, lips closed like you would kiss someone's cheek, Brody kisses me between my legs.

I'm going to burst into flames. I'm going to be one of those bizarre cases of spontaneous human combustion and explode in a giant ball of fire, all from the touch of this man's lips on my skin.

Inhaling, he nuzzles the fold between my thigh and pussy. He softly groans. The sound is so carnal, so purely sexual and masculine, my clit throbs in response.

His tongue—oh God his tongue. Hot and soft. Seeking. *There.*

The shudder that runs through me is involuntary. I couldn't stop it if I tried.

"Easy, sweetheart," he whispers. "You're doing so good."

I swallow a whimper.

He cups my ass and squeezes. He drags my sweats farther down, his fingers digging into my flesh like he loves the feel of it, like he wants to bruise me, leave his mark. He bites my hip, then my upper thigh, and I begin to shake.

Not tremble. Shake.

"Oh, she likes it," he breathes. "She likes my love bites. Will she like it when I do this?"

His teeth scrape over my clit.

I almost pass out.

His groan vibrates through me. "Your pussy is throbbing, Grace." More softly, to himself, "Fucking *throbbing*."

With a soft moan, he lifts me to his face with both hands under my ass and shoves his tongue deep inside me.

I bite my lip so hard I taste blood.

He feasts on me, licking and sucking and fucking me with his tongue. I try desperately to stay still, to stay silent, to do nothing that would make him stop, until I open my eyes and see him reaching into his sweats.

His face buried between my thighs, making animal noises low in his throat, Brody pulls out his beautiful stiff cock and starts to stroke it.

I've done everything. I've seen everything. I've had so much sex in my life I could write the preeminent instruction manual on the subject. Yet I've never seen anything as downright *sexy* as this.

As him, worshipping me with his mouth, helpless not to touch himself as he does it.

His eyes drift open. Our gazes lock. Time slips away, reason follows, and then there's only my heartbeat like thunder in my ears and the smell of lemon furniture polish and sex in my nose and a hot wave of pleasure cresting over me, rising and rising and rising, burning my skin, expanding inside me until I'm sure I'll shatter into a million tiny pieces and disappear.

My back bows from the bed.

"Wait!" he commands hoarsely, breathing hard. "*With me.*"

A sound—fractured and incoherent—escapes me.

"With me, Grace, not before," he growls, his erection jutting from his fist.

He sees the "*yes*" in my eyes, because he drops his head again. He sucks my clit into his mouth. He strokes his cock from base to tip, squeezing the head, thumbing over the slit to spread the bead of moisture around, and then back down to the base. He watches me the whole time, his dark green eyes aflame with possession.

The rhythm of his hand increases. He starts to rock into the pumps of his fist, his ass flexing, all the veins standing out on his arm.

His eyes close. The stubble on his jaw scrapes my flesh, enflaming my already exquisitely sensitive pussy. I inhale a sharp breath through my nose, biting my tongue to keep from crying out.

Then, shuddering and jerking, he moans into me, a deep, guttural sound that I recognize at once.

He's there.

I close my eyes, spread my legs wider, and let go.

My scream is long, loud, and wavering. I come and come and come, convulsing around his mouth, my thighs shaking, my neck arched, my fingernails digging into my palms, the world red and spinning under my eyelids.

"Brody! God—Brody!"

Pushing down, he flattens his hand over the center of my chest and keeps eating me as my orgasm rocks me, keeps licking me even as he's bucking, his own orgasm tearing through him, his grunts of pleasure muffled in my sex.

*The best the best the best best best best best—*

One after another, wave after wave, pulses so violent I'm helpless to do anything but let them slam into me. Every muscle in my vagina contracts and releases, hard, again and again. My clitoris is the center of the galaxy. A supernova exploding into space. My entire body is flushed with heat. My nipples tingle, as does every inch of my skin. The intensity of it all makes me lose my breath.

Finally I'm a noodle. A panting, sweating noodle, unsure whether I'm on the cusp of laughter or tears.

I open my eyes. Brody is watching me, his eyes half-lidded, his mouth still buried in my flesh. His hand and cock are both glistening. So is his expensive silk duvet cover, and a good part of my abdomen and upper thighs.

And he calls *me* Slick? The man is a human fire hose!

I dissolve into laughter.

In a husky voice, Brody says, "That is *so* not the reaction I was hoping for."

I laugh harder. Between gasps of air I manage to say, "You—you *glazed* me. And your hand. And the bed! Ba ha ha ha!"

"Excuse me, comedian, but *you* glazed *me*." He lifts his head and smiles at me.

His cheeks and chin are wet.

I groan. "Oh my God, this is the least sexy after-sex conversation I've *ever* had!"

Brody turns his head and bites my thigh. Then he looks up at me, grinning. "But the best, right? Because it's me, so . . . obviously."

I try really hard not to laugh, only I fail spectacularly.

This feeling of euphoria is new. Normally after sex I'm jumping hurdles to get to the front door, but right now I'm floating somewhere way above cloud nine.

"And not to correct you or anything, because it's indelicate to correct a lady so soon after such an eardrum-shattering orgasm, but that *wasn't* sex."

"Well it certainly wasn't a turnip."

"I told you, Grace. That was just foreplay."

"Foreplay my ass. That was the sun and the stars and the entire known universe."

Brody's chuckle is low and satisfied. "Now *that's* a compliment. Much better, Slick."

I sigh. My entire body feels like Jell-O. "You deserve it, Kong. That was spectacular."

He crawls up to me, takes my face in his hands, and gives me a deep, heartfelt kiss. "*You're* spectacular," he whispers, gazing down at me. "And you taste even better. I'm already addicted." He kisses me again.

"Maybe you just have an addictive personality," I tease, loving his intensity, his playfulness, the rough edge in his voice and the happy light in his eyes. Loving all of this. The way he sounds and feels and touches me. How it all just seems so right.

"No," he says seriously, looking into my eyes. "It's because it's like someone asked me for a list of all the things that would make up my ideal woman and then created you in a lab for me. It's because you're funny and smart and sexy and independent and strong and can have any man you want, but you look at me like I'm a Christmas present. Like I'm a kept promise. Like I'm your favorite song."

His voice drops. "It's because you're perfect, but you make me feel like *I* am."

My throat closes. An invisible hand squeezes my chest. I stare into Brody's beautiful green eyes and think, *Oh.*

*Oh.*

*So this is what it's like.*

Instead of admitting I'm feeling emotional, I make a joke. "I'm not perfect."

His brows lift.

"My left foot is half a size bigger than my right."

A grin spreads over his face.

"Also one of my ears is slightly higher than the other. You can only tell when I wear sunglasses, but still. My ears aren't level."

Brody kisses the tip of my nose, my forehead, both my cheeks. "I've been telling you this, sweetheart. You're hideous."

"I'm also covered in, uh . . ." I glance down at my stomach.

Brody follows my gaze. "Oh. Right." He pauses a moment, and then says, "Would it be gross to tell you that I have this really primal urge to smear it all over you and not let you take a shower for days?"

I laugh. "Yes. That would be gross. Caveman."

He glances up at me and grins. "You bring out the Neanderthal in me, witch face." He kisses me quickly, then pops up from the bed. "Stay there for a second. Help is on the way."

He disappears into the bathroom. After running a washcloth under the faucet and squeezing it out, he returns to me with it, and a hand towel.

I start to sit up, but he barks, "No!" He waves his hand, indicating I should stay as I am.

I settle back against the pillows. "You're incredibly bossy, you know that?"

"Don't act like you don't like it," he murmurs, running the washcloth over my skin. He cleans me gently and diligently, smiling this hilariously smug smile the entire time. Then he dries me with the hand towel, pulls my sweats up to my waist, and unties the T-shirt from around my wrists.

He helps me sit up, helps me put the shirt on, and then tackles me, taking us both back down to the mattress.

"Hey!"

"Hugs," he says, his words muffled against my neck. "You need hugs, remember?"

He squeezes his arms around me, curls his legs around me, and engulfs me.

He's hugging me with his entire body.

I close my eyes and snuggle into him, as close as I can get. His heart thuds loud and strong beneath my cheek. He's warm and heavy, gently kissing my neck and shoulder, sighing quietly as if he's feeling the same things I am.

Contented. Euphoric. Joyful.

Home.

*God*, I think, drifting off to sleep. *Maybe I was wrong about you after all.*

# Chapter 18

I awaken in stages, first aware of birds chirping somewhere outside, and then the delicious scent of baking bread. My body feels light, as if it's floating. So does my spirit when I see how the sun has changed direction, slanting low through the windows in the west.

It's late afternoon. I've been asleep for hours.

I didn't have bad dreams.

When I lift my head and look around, I'm alone. I yawn, sit up, stretch my arms overhead, and catch sight of the folded note on lined yellow paper on the pillow next to me. Smiling, I unfold it and read.

*Most Hideous Female Who Ever Lived,*

*Watching you sleep is like watching one of those foreign art-house movies that win all the awards for cinematography and production design because they're so ravishingly beautiful and moving, even though no one has any idea what they're actually about.*

*If that makes me sound like I've ingested some incredibly potent drugs, it's because I have: you.*

*I'm high on you.*

*(I know you know that's the title of a Survivor song, but for the sake of romance, we'll both pretend we don't. I'm working on some better material. These things take a minute.)*

*You were sleeping so soundly I didn't want to wake you. Also my dick decided it was time to start throwing his weight around again so I had to leave before he could bully me into sneaking in a few rubs against your criminally sexy bottom. Because hello, gross creeper.*

*You see, chivalry isn't dead!*

*On a more serious note, I REALLY, REALLY hope you don't wake up feeling any kind of regret or ickiness about what happened because it was hands down the most incredible experience I've had as a human since I was born. Also because you feeling bad about it would make me want to kill myself.*

*So, no pressure.*

*Not liking your ugly mug at all,*

*Brody*

*PS – Dude, get a nose job. Do you even own a mirror?*

*PPS – I think you said my name in your sleep. #giddy*

*PPPS – I looked at your feet. You were totally lying. They're like TWO sizes different, Sasquatch.*

When I set the note back on the nightstand, I'm smiling so widely it hurts. I can't remember the last time I felt this . . . excited? No— giddy. Brody found the perfect word. I'm as giddy as a schoolgirl with her first crush.

Even though my condo blew up this morning.

Even though tomorrow morning I might have no idea who or where I am.

Even though everything.

*Wow, this oxytocin is some powerful shit.*

Energized, I fling back the light blanket I'm covered with and leap from the bed. I use the bathroom, splash water on my face, comb my fingers through my tangled hair, and smile at myself in the mirror.

"Well, hello, gorgeous," I say to my reflection. "Don't you look like a million bucks!"

I definitely feel like I do. I'm a homeless millionaire.

I'd better not repeat that to Brody or he'll start calling me Slum Dog.

I make my way from his room, down the hallway, and into the kitchen, following that amazing smell of baking bread. Magda is at the big gourmet stove with pot holders, pulling a golden brown loaf from the oven.

"Hi, Magda. Do you need help with that?"

Her back to me, she cackles and replies in Spanish, "The day I need help with my cooking is the day I find a nice, high ledge to jump from." She waves a hand toward the open patio doors. "Go on. He's in the guest house, probably making a mess."

"Okay. Thanks!"

She turns and peers at me. Then she nods, as if satisfied, and turns back to the stove.

I don't even want to ask.

Barefoot, I cross the patio and then head across the huge lawn toward the structure behind the stand of giant palm trees. It's about a five-minute walk. The sun is warm on my shoulders. The ocean breeze plays with my hair. I wonder if the house has a name, as many of these grand homes do. If not, I'm going to suggest to Brody that he christen it Shangri-La, because it's truly an earthly paradise.

When I round the thicket of palms, I come to an abrupt halt, staring. Then I start to laugh.

The "guest house," like the main house, is something straight out of *Lifestyles of the Rich and Famous*. It's a sprawling Mediterranean with saffron-hued walls and a red tiled roof, surrounded with lush, landscaped gardens, mature trees, a koi pond with a waterfall, and a wraparound balcony that looks straight out to the sea.

A kidney-shaped pool with a black rock bottom is shaded by palm trees. A fountain in the shape of a mermaid rising from a wave burbles in the middle of the lawn. A private driveway, lined with blooming jasmine bushes, winds out of sight over a low hill at the far end of the yard.

It's magical. It's utterly charming.

And, for tonight at least, it's mine.

Admiring the general splendor, I walk slowly toward the front door. It's half wood, half beveled glass, and it's open. I go inside and find myself standing in a cool, quiet entryway. Mirrors and polished marble glisten everywhere.

"Hello? Brody?"

His faint call of "In here!" comes from the back of the house.

I move slowly through the rooms, touching a sculpture here, admiring an oil painting there, wondering what it must be like to have this kind of money. My parents were solidly middle class, by no means wealthy. I know this not because I remember my upbringing, but because of the meeting I had with their attorney a week after their deaths, wherein he informed me I was lucky they both had life insurance policies.

"Lucky." That's not the word I would have chosen to describe my situation.

I find Brody in the master bedroom, arranging birds of paradise in a vase on the glass table by the open windows. He turns to me, smiling.

"You're up!"

"I am. And you're . . . arranging flowers?"

He glances at the flowers and the clippers on the table like he's just been caught doing something naughty. He shoves his hands into the front pockets of his jeans, shrugs, and looks bashfully at his feet. "Uh, yeah. I thought you might, you know, like some flowers in your room. I cut them from the yard."

My heart melts into a puddle.

When I don't say anything, Brody looks up at me. He misinterprets the expression on my face, because his brow crinkles. "Oh—are you allergic? Shit, I'm sorry, I never asked—"

I cross to him and throw my arms around his neck.

"I love flowers," I say hoarsely, standing on my toes to hug him. "And that you thought I might want some in my room. That is so sweet. You're so sweet, Brody. And silly. And romantic. And funny. And completely unexpected."

I have to stop because my voice is getting high. My throat is too tight to continue.

Brody winds his arms around my back and pulls me against his body so there are no gaps between us. He nuzzles my neck, inhaling into my hair. "And manly. Don't forget manly."

"Right. My bad. Manly should've been the first thing I said."

He chuckles. "I mean, I know it goes without saying since you're already pregnant with octuplets—"

"Octuplets!" I pull back and smile up at him.

Pushing a strand of hair off my cheek, he grins. "Oh yeah, baby. I've got your bun factory workin' overtime. I've got some *powerful* spooge in these loins."

I wrinkle my nose. "Spooge? Ew."

"Oh, I'm sorry, the *word* offends you but having it sprayed all over your body doesn't?"

"Fortunately for you, pal!"

He beams at me. "True. How 'bout if I try another word? Like . . . jizz?"

"Ugh."

"Spunk?"

"More ugh!"

"Man milk? Baby batter? Homemade yogurt?"

"You're disturbed. Stop talking before I take back all that nice stuff I just said about you."

"Just trying to show off my awesome vocabulary, sweetheart."

"Oh yes. Your intellect is truly dizzying, my friend."

"Aha! You just quoted the Man in Black from *The Princess Bride*, didn't you?"

"I don't know, did I?" I ask, testing him.

He nods. "But you got it wrong. The actual quote is 'Truly, you have a dizzying intellect.'"

We grin at each other like a pair of lunatics. Then Brody takes my face in his hands and gives me a soft kiss.

"So . . ." He sweeps his thumbs over my cheekbones, looking at me from beneath his lashes. "How are you feeling? About . . . you know."

"Your jizz?" I tease.

He kisses the tip of my nose. "Seriously. Are we good? You're not regretting it, are you?"

This man is impossibly sweet. Wonderful, thoughtful, and sweet. He's worried that I'll regret it, when it was *me* throwing myself at *him.*

I rest my cheek on his chest and sigh in happiness. "Frankly I'm only regretting that you wouldn't give me access to your man-milk maker itself."

"About that."

I look up at him sharply. "Uh-oh. That doesn't sound good."

Brody unwinds my arms from around his waist. He leads me by the hand to the bed, a massive four-post affair with enough pillows to start a wholesale pillow outlet. We sit on the end, facing each other.

"So, here's the deal," he says, looking at our hands, our fingers threaded together. "I know you just broke up with Marcus a few days ago."

He glances up at me for confirmation. When I nod, he looks back at our hands.

"And I also know you're kind of . . . you're sort of a . . . serial dater."

My brows shoot up. "If you're about to slut shame me, princess, I'm about to give you a black eye."

Brody sits up ramrod straight, his eyes wide. "No! God no, I'd never do that! I'm totally guilty of the same thing!"

When I narrow my eyes at him, he slaps a hand over his mouth. "Not 'guilty'! I didn't mean it like that! I only meant that I sleep around a lot, too." He winces. "That *so* didn't come out right."

I fold my arms over my chest. "If you *dare* ask me how many men I've slept with, I'll cut a bitch."

He groans and scrubs his hands over his face. "I'm fucking this up. Just hear me out, I have a point."

"I can hardly wait," I say drily. "I'm sure your enormous vocabulary will be a big help."

He blows out a breath, and then, as if he's gathered his courage, looks me square in the eyes. "I think we shouldn't have sex for a month."

To say I'm stunned would be an epic understatement. I stare at him, waiting for an explanation that makes any kind of sense. When he just sits there gazing at me with the earnestness of a Labradoodle, I demand, "Please tell me you're not a virgin."

"Of course not." He laughs, but his laughter dies as quickly as it appeared and he looks horrified. "Oh God—do I seem like one? Like, inexperienced in bed?"

"Honestly?"

His face pales. He nods.

"That thing you call 'foreplay' was the best sex I've ever had."

He sags with relief. "Jesus. Fuck. You scared the hell out of me!"

"Are you Amish?"

He makes a face. "Do you see me driving a horse and buggy and churning my own butter?"

"Then why are you saying we shouldn't have sex for thirty days?"

"Because I like you," he answers simply. "I like you . . . a lot."

We stare at each other. Then I say, "Okay. I get it. You're respecting me. You're showing me respect. Right?"

"Right."

"Respect noted. Now I think we should bang."

He makes another face. "*Bang*? And you have a problem with *my* vocabulary? You sound like a teenage boy!"

A terrible thought hits me. I cover my mouth with my hands.

Brody asks, "What?"

I whisper, "Do you have herpes? Do you need time for the sores to clear up?"

He looks at the ceiling and sighs. "Grace. No. I do not have herpes. Or any other STD, thank you very much."

Out of options for this ridiculous conversation and at my wit's end with how to get him to change his mind, I throw my hands in the air. "I haven't gone without sex for a month since I was eighteen years old!"

He grins at me. "Trollop. Knew it."

"Can't you find some other way to respect me that doesn't involve denying me my favorite thing in the world?"

He cocks his head. "Sex is your favorite thing in the world?"

Now *that* sounded bad. I try to backtrack, only it gets worse.

"Dick is my favorite thing in the world."

Brody's grin reappears. "Can I just take a moment here to say that you're my dream woman?"

I pinch the bridge of my nose between two fingers. "This isn't going in the direction I'd hoped."

"Seriously, the fact that those words would even leave your mouth makes me so happy you don't even know."

"Brody—"

"Nope."

"Nope what?"

"Nope, we're not having sex for a month, and we're not negotiating. I told you before: I want to get to know you before we do it."

"May I remind you, Kong, we already *did* it?"

"Not all the way," he says, sounding very reasonable. "There was no penetration. No outie in the innie. So technically we *didn't* do it. Why are you looking at me like that?"

"I'm just wondering what planet you lived on before you came to earth."

He pulls me onto his lap and kisses my cheek. "Uranus."

I dissolve into laughter. I collapse against his chest and laugh until I'm hoarse, and then I laugh some more.

Brody falls back onto the bed, taking me with him. He rolls on top of me. Then—bastard!—he starts to tickle me.

"Nooo!" I scream, writhing helplessly. "No tickling! I hate tickling!"

"Say 'we're not having sex for a month,' and I'll stop," he says, digging his fingers into my ribs.

"That's blackmail!"

He wiggles his fingers into my belly. I scream again, trying to roll out from under him but he's too heavy.

"Say it, Slick, or you get the tickle treatment forever."

"I'm going to kill you!"

Wiggling fingers poke into my side.

"Okay, I give! Uncle! No sex for a month!"

Smiling, his hair falling into his eyes, Brody gazes down at me. "Deal. The clock starts now. One month, no boning."

I ask breathlessly, "But we can still do the foreplay thingy, right?"

He purses his lips like he's thinking, and I groan. "Brody!"

He grins. "Only kidding. Yes, we can still do the foreplay thingy. I'm not a total masochist."

"No, you're a total sadist!"

"Speaking of which . . ." He wraps a hand firmly around my wrist and presses it to the bed. Ducking his head, he whispers into my ear, "You like being restrained, don't you?"

His voice has that dark, dominant tone that makes my pulse quicken.

"Do you want total honesty here?"

"Yes," he answers instantly.

"Like, radical honesty?"

"Yes. That's exactly what I want from you from now on: radical honesty. Go."

"I've always been the one doing the restraining."

Brody lifts his head and considers me with his brows pulled together. "You mean you like to be on top or something?"

"No, Brody. I like to be *the* top."

Understanding crosses his face. His smile comes on slow and sultry. "So you're not only a wanton little trollop, you're a wanton little *dominatrix* trollop."

"It's not like I'm dressing up in latex corsets and beating anybody with a riding crop. I just like being the one in control, sexually and otherwise." I hesitate for only a second before deciding our new policy of radical honesty should be honored. "I mean, I did. Up to now. Before you. But now I think losing control might be even more exciting . . . because I think I might be able to trust you to catch me when I fall."

He examines me in silence, his eyes burning with intensity. Then he says quietly, "You have no idea how good that makes me feel."

My heartbeat goes haywire. "You have no idea how good you make *me* feel. But if I'm wrong about you catching me, I'll sic Marcus on you."

Brody pretends to be shot in the heart with an arrow and flops onto his back, clutching his chest. I jump on top of him and pepper kisses all over his face as he makes a dramatic show of expiring.

"You're a terrible actor," I tell him. "It's a good thing you went into music."

He rolls atop me again and commences with more tickle torture. Luckily it doesn't last long, because the sound of an old-fashioned car horn pulls us apart.

I ask, "Is that coming from your butt?"

"Yep. Incoming text." From his back pocket he pulls out his cell phone. He looks at the screen, and then at me. "The cavalry's here. It's Nico and Kat."

I sigh. "So the first meeting of the Mutual Admiration Society comes to an end. Bummer."

Brody rolls off me, pops up from the bed, takes my hands, and pulls me up. He squeezes my hands and grins at me. "Yeah, but we're gonna have meetings every day for the next month, so don't sweat it, Slick."

Following behind him, I let him lead me by the hand from the room. "And then we're going to have daily meetings of the Horizontal Mambo Society."

I feel his husky chuckle all the way to my toes. "Daily? If I know you at all, it's gonna be hourly."

My smile is wide and happy. "Damn straight. Better get your beauty rest this month, because at the end of next month you're going to be chapped, dehydrated, and totally exhausted."

Looking at me over his shoulder, he laughs. "I can hardly wait."

I say drily, "That makes two of us."

# Chapter 19

The first thing Kat does when she sees me is throws her arms around me and bursts into tears, complete with hysterical sobbing.

Nico, Barney, and Brody stand in the foyer of the main house, watching us. Not even three seconds have passed since we let them in the front door, and I've got Ms. Drama Queen 2016 having a breakdown all over my Neil Diamond T-shirt.

I haven't yet told Brody I'm claiming it for my own, but I've literally had some of the happiest hours in recent memory in this stupid old shirt, and there's no way I'm parting with it now.

Over Kat's shoulder I look at Nico with my brows raised.

He shrugs. "She's worried about you."

Barney says, "We all are. You doing okay, Angelface?"

Beside him, Brody stiffens.

Barney has about fifty pounds on Brody, is trained in martial arts, used to be in the military before he worked as a bodyguard, and is armed with a handgun, yet I have no doubt Brody would go toe-to-toe with Barney if the man so much as looks at me sideways again.

In the name of radical honesty, we'll have a talk about that later. Jealousy is a deal breaker for me.

"I'm good, Barney, thank you." I smile at Brody. "I'm being very well taken care of."

As if a faucet has been turned off, Kat stops crying. She pulls away and looks at me, then at Brody—who's no longer bristling but grinning—then back at me. "You're good?"

I nod.

She wipes her face with her fingers. "Are you sure?"

I give her hand a squeeze. "Honestly, Kat, I'm really lucky I wasn't home. All that stuff that blew up is just that—stuff. It can be replaced."

She groans. "But your beautiful clothes . . . all your jewelry!"

A spike of pain pierces my heart. I don't really care about the clothes, and the insurance will pay for the jewelry, but there were a few things that can never be replaced.

Like the engagement ring my grandfather gave to my grandmother.

Like the small gold locket my mother used to wear around her neck that had a picture of me as a baby inside.

Like my parents' wedding rings—returned to me in a little plastic bag from the morgue.

My smile fades as my stomach sours. "Well, what doesn't kill you . . ."

"Makes you stronger." Brody steps up beside me. He clasps an arm around my shoulder, pulls me against him, and kisses me on the temple. He gazes into my eyes. "And you're a tough cookie, Slick," he murmurs, looking at me as if there's no one else in the room. "You're gonna make it through this just fine." His lips curve upward. "Plus, you've got the octuplets to focus on now, so there's really no time for feeling bad."

Kat barks, "What? Octuplets? What did you just say?"

Brody grins at her. "Oh, Grace didn't tell you yet? She's pregnant with—"

I elbow him in the side.

"Ow!"

Judging by the look of distress on Kat's face, I should have elbowed him harder. I have a feeling her emotional outburst when she came in has more to do with her than me.

"He's joking, Kat," I reassure her. "Nobody's pregnant." I shoot Brody a sharp sideways glare. "Nobody's *getting* pregnant, either."

Brody mock pouts. "Is this your subtle way of telling me you don't want kids? Because my mother just told me today that she's ready to be a grandma again, and I was thinking after our thirty days are up we could—"

"One more word," I interrupt him calmly, "and you won't be able to get *anyone* pregnant because you'll be missing the proper equipment."

All this talk of pregnancy is making Kat ghostly pale. I'm not the only one who notices.

Nico takes her by the arm, pulls her toward him so her back is against his chest, wraps his arms around her, ducks his head, and whispers something into her ear.

Eyes closed, lips pressed together, she nods.

*Shit.*

Barney drawls, "Thirty days? What's that all about?"

He and Brody lock eyes.

*Double shit.*

Before Brody can answer, I jump in. "So Brody said you guys were going to put together a little care package for me, Kat? Clothes or whatever?"

"Oh. Yes, sorry, sweetie." Kat sends me a shaky smile. "I've got bags and bags of stuff for you in the car. Chloe and I tore through our closets. The only thing we didn't give you was underwear, for obvious reasons."

Brody quips, "She won't be needing underwear anyway."

He and Barney are still glaring at each other.

*Wonderful. Looks like we'll be having that cockfight after all.*

Nico, ever the conciliator, says to Barney, "Hey man, would you get the bags from the car for Grace, please?"

"Sure," he says, holding Brody's gaze. "Anything for Grace." For several long moments, he doesn't move, he simply stands there giving Brody a level, challenging look, but then finally he turns on his heel and stalks out the door.

"Ookay," says Kat, watching him go. "That was awkward."

Irritated, Brody asks Nico, "You gonna talk to him about his attitude, bro?"

"*His* attitude?" repeats Nico. "You know that shit's a two-way street, right?"

"That dude is way out of line—"

"That *dude* has saved your ass more times than I can count—"

"He's your fucking employee, man!"

"—and has been a friend for years. Not only mine, but yours, too."

"Yeah, he has. And now he's acting like a dick and I'm not gonna put up with it. Would you, if the shoe were on the other foot?"

Nico's gaze cuts to me. "You on board with this, Grace? You think I should have a talk with Barney, tell him to back off?"

"No." I take a step away from Brody, cross my arms over my chest, and meet his eyes. "And since you brought it up, here's some radical honesty for you, Brody: jealousy is petty, immature, and has no place in a healthy relationship. I won't tolerate it. Either we trust each other or we don't. If we do, it doesn't matter how many other people flirt with us. If we don't . . . well, we might as well just quit while we're ahead and save ourselves the aggravation."

Brody looks as if I've slapped him.

"Be right back," he says, and bolts out the front door after Barney.

Watching him tear off across the driveway, Nico mutters, "What the hell have you done to him?"

Kat peers out the open door. "Apparently she's hypnotized him with her magical vagina. I've never seen anyone do such a one-eighty!"

I don't want to stand there and gape at him in the doorway, so I take a few steps back and ask, "What do you mean? What's he doing?"

After a while, Nico chuckles. "Looks like he's eating a big ass bucket of crow."

"Kat, a little help here?"

She smiles. "Brody and Barney are standing next to the Escalade. Barney has his arms crossed over his chest and his legs spread, in badass mode, and Brody is doing all the talking." She pauses. "Now Barney is nodding his head." Another pause. "Now they're shaking hands." She laughs. "Now they're doing that macho guy, hug-it-out thing, lots of back thumping and play shoving." She looks at me, grinning. "Looks like your boy just went and apologized."

*He can't be for real. He has to be too good to be true. No one is this perfect.*

"Nico?"

He glances at me.

"You know Brody better than anyone, right?"

"Yeah. Like a brother."

"I need to ask you something."

Nico lifts his brows. "Shoot."

"Is he a good guy? I mean, everyone has faults, but bottom line—is he good?"

Nico grins, showcasing his dimples. His blue eyes twinkle with mischief. "Why? You like him or something?"

I exhale a shaky breath. "Please don't fuck with me. I need an honest, unbiased opinion."

Kat and Nico stare at me with new expressions, like I'm someone they've never met before, some body snatcher who's murdered the real Grace and is now walking around wearing her skin.

Nico says softly, "You really *do* like him."

Chewing my lip, I nod.

Unsmiling, Nico nods, too. "Okay. Then I'll tell you the truth, Grace. Yes, he's a good guy. He's reliable and honest, he's considerate and unselfish, and he's generous to a fault. He's not one to wear his heart on his sleeve and I know sometimes things bother him that he'd never admit to, but he's definitely good."

His gaze grows penetrating. "And since we're truth telling, as far as I'm concerned, he's the one who needs to worry about getting hurt in this scenario."

"Nico!" snaps Kat. "That's not fair!"

But I'm not insulted in the least. If I were looking at things from Nico's perspective, I'd think the same thing.

"Yes, it is, Kat. It's totally fair. If you judged things by my dating history, that is." My voice grows softer. "But if you judged things by the way he makes me feel, you'd know you wouldn't have anything to worry about."

Nico doesn't look convinced. "Yeah? So how does he make you feel?"

It falls from my tongue without even a thought, as simple and true as an exhaled breath. "Like everything bad that's ever happened to me was worth it, because it was all leading up to him."

After I speak those words there's total, stunned silence.

Until a loud *thunk* comes from the doorway.

When I see what made the sound, my heart stops.

Barney stands there, two large suitcases clutched in his meaty fists. Brody is right behind him, staring at me with blazing eyes and two spots of color high on his cheeks. A large duffel bag sits at his feet, where he dropped it.

*He dropped it because he heard me.*

For a second I'm panicked. But then I decide, screw it. I'm already this far down the rabbit hole. Might as well go ahead and eat the cake.

"Your timing's impeccable, Mr. Scott," I say softly, meeting his eyes.

His voice thick, he replies, "And thank fuck for that."

I glance at Barney. "Did you two kiss and make up?"

He lifts a shoulder. "Hard to stay mad at a guy who says he's sorry ten times in a row—and means it." He purses his lips, adding, "Not sure he's good enough for you, though."

Brody rasps, "I'm definitely not. No one is. She's a fucking goddess."

The way he's looking at me definitely makes me feel like one. I bet if I concentrated, I could fly.

Brody makes a beeline for me. When he's an arm's length away, he grabs me and throws his arms around me. He squeezes me so tight it leaves me breathless. Into my ear he whispers gruffly, "Goddamn, witch face, you sure know how to knock a guy off his feet."

"We'll be in the kitchen raiding your liquor cabinet," says Nico with a chuckle. "C'mon, baby. Barney."

Their footsteps recede. When we're alone, I say into Brody's neck, "Radical honesty?"

"Yes."

I lift my head and look into his blazing eyes. "I'm totally going to use this to try to get you to have sex with me before thirty days."

He bursts into laughter.

"And thank you for apologizing to Barney. I know he appreciated it."

Smiling down at me with wonderful warmth, Brody cups my face in his hands. "I didn't do it for him, sunshine. You know I didn't do it for him."

When he kisses me, I'm smiling against his lips.

# Chapter 20

## Brody

Kat, Nico, and Barney stay for about an hour. We talk. We drink. We hang out like we always have, but this time it's completely different, because this time *I'm* different.

No one ever told me it could be like this. Like you finally understand who you are and why you're here, and all your broken pieces don't even matter because there's something so much more important to think about.

Namely, doing everything in your power to make the goddess suddenly in your life feel as amazing as she is.

And she is amazing. Way more than that. We've joked about my incredible vocabulary, but I don't think there's a word in any language that could accurately describe how balls-out *fantastic* this girl is.

Not girl—woman. She's all woman, the kind who knows how to turn a boy into a man, and a man into a slave. Putty, that's what she's turned me into. Putty in the palms of her elegant, manicured hands.

I'm sitting next to her at the kitchen table listening to her talk and marveling at how fucking smart she is—seriously, she gives my brain a hard-on, I didn't even know that was a thing—when Barney says, "You think A.J.'s okay, though? Chloe seemed worried."

My head snaps around. "A.J.? What do you mean?"

Kat fidgets in her chair. Tapping her nails against her glass of wine, she says, "When we went by Chloe and A.J.'s to pick up the clothes, A.J. was sleeping."

Grace repeats, "Sleeping? What's wrong with that?"

Kat and Nico share a look. "Chloe said he had another headache and had to lie down."

A chill runs down my spine. "*Another* headache. Oh fuck."

"Yeah. We managed to pry it out of her that over the past two weeks he's been getting them every few days. This one was so bad he took two Tylenol with codeine." Kat pauses. "And when that didn't work, he took two more."

We stare at each other in silence.

Grace absently reaches for my hand. I squeeze it between both of mine as she sits forward in her chair.

"Has he gone to the doctor?"

Kat shakes her head. "He won't go."

"*What?*" shout Grace and I, horrified.

Nico finishes his whiskey in one swallow, and then sets the glass down with a shake of his head. "Chloe didn't confirm this and I didn't want to get into it with her today, but I think it has to do with what the doctors told A.J. to anticipate after his brain surgery."

Grace's brow furrows. "You mean these headaches are normal?"

For a moment, Nico stares down at his glass. When he raises his gaze to Grace's, all the tiny hairs on the back of my neck stand on end.

"I mean that if he started to get headaches it was a symptom that the tumor had invaded the temporal lobe."

Grace gasps. "No!"

Nico nods. "They weren't able to get the whole tumor during his surgery, we know that. And with any remaining tumor tissue there's always the possibility it will continue to grow—"

"But he could do radiation! Or chemo!" interrupts Grace, distraught.

"And kill healthy brain tissue as well as the tumor," says Nico gently. "With side effects ranging from memory loss, speech impairment, changes in judgment-making capability, even changes in personality."

I'm feeling a little queasy. "Changes in personality? Like what?"

Nico's somber gaze cuts to mine. "Primarily . . . aggressiveness."

Grace covers her face with her hands. She whispers, "Oh God. Chloe. *The baby.*"

"Yeah," sighs Nico, raking a hand through his hair.

"But we don't know this for sure, right?" I ask, desperate for some kind of hope.

"Not for sure, no. But I gotta be honest, man. A.J. told me right after he came home from the hospital that he was living on borrowed time. He knew even though the surgery was successful at removing most of the tumor it wasn't a home run, that most likely he'd only bought himself another few years. And he was determined those years would be good, not spent hooked up to machines or sick from chemo drugs. If the tumor's back . . . he's gonna let it run its course and enjoy every last minute he can with his family."

Grace slaps her hands on the table. Everyone jumps.

"God*damn* it!" She jolts to her feet, knocking her chair back. She glares at us, each in turn. "We are *not*," she says, breathing heavily, "allowing him to give up!"

Wow. Angry Grace is kind of terrifying.

"I don't think we really have a choice. If this is A.J.'s decision—"

"No," she says flatly, cutting me off. "This isn't only about him. This is about his family, too, and his friends, and everyone who loves him. He can't just unilaterally decide he's not getting any more treatment without even finding out definitively what the problem is. No," she says again, stiffening her back and squaring her shoulders. "*That* isn't happening."

Nico leans back in his chair and folds his arms over his chest. It looks like he's trying not to smile. Kat is worrying her lower lip. Barney, meanwhile, is grinning up at Grace with this big, dumb smile, like a happy farm animal.

I'd like to kick his leg under the table, but Grace wants me to be mature and not jealous, so instead I briefly allow myself to imagine him being trampled to death by a herd of stampeding bulls, and then I let it go.

But not before feeling the tiniest bit better.

"So what are you saying we should do?" I ask. "Go over there and confront him?"

Grace thinks for a moment. Then she sinks back into her chair. "No. No, I don't want to upset Chloe, or embarrass him. I'll figure something out."

Kat reaches for her hand. The two of them exchange a fierce, determined Amazon warrior look that I really hope I'm never the subject of.

I'm starting to get the feeling I'd better keep all my ducks in a row or I'll get my ass kicked six ways to Sunday by three best girlfriends.

Which is *all kinds* of awesome.

Nico catches my eye and grins.

I duck my head and hide my smile by rubbing my hand over my jaw.

"All right. We've loitered long enough, we'll let you two squirrels get back to collecting nuts." Nico stands, and so do the rest of us.

"Dude. What is it with you and the squirrel comparisons? Do we look like a couple of rodents?"

Grace says, "It's because they're so cute, right?"

Kat wrinkles her nose. "They carry the plague!"

Nico says, "Really? I thought rats carried the plague."

Barney chimes in helpfully. "They do, and so do squirrels, rabbits, and camels."

Everyone looks at him.

He shrugs, tapping his temple. "Got a lot of useless trivia up here. If you ever need to know which product was the first to have a bar code, I'm your man."

Grace says, "That's easy. Wrigley's gum."

Barney looks surprised. "Correct. How'd you know that?"

She answers, "The same way I know how many cars and lampposts are on the back of a ten-dollar bill."

Barney replies instantly, "Four, and eleven."

Grace grins. "Winston Churchill was born in a ladies' room, during a dance."

Super cocky, Barney shoots back, "A cat has thirty-two muscles in each ear."

Now I'm starting to get nervous. I blurt, "Al Capone's business card said he was a used furniture dealer!"

Grace turns to me, grinning even wider. "Oh yeah? Well, elephants are the only land mammals that can't jump."

"I thought white men were the only land mammals that couldn't jump," says Kat, and everyone starts to laugh.

Thank God, because I'm only just beginning to get my feet wet with this whole "no jealousy" exercise, and listening to Grace and Barney play trivial pursuit almost gave me a heart attack.

I know she wouldn't like it, but the possessiveness I feel for her tells me unequivocally how serious I am. She's mine. I mean, I know she's not *mine* mine, I'm a liberated guy, she's her own person, nobody *owns* anyone, that's not what I'm saying.

Oh fuck it, who am I kidding? I'm saying she's mine and I'll pound any motherfucker who tries to get between us.

Grace looks at me. "You okay?"

"Yep. Why?"

"Because you just let out this weird little grunt."

My cheeks go hot. *Jesus. I'm falling apart over here. Get it together, Brody!* Embarrassed because everyone is now staring at me, I ask sheepishly, "Is it okay if we talk about it later?"

She gets it. I can tell by the way her eyes go all soft and how she smiles at me, secretly pleased. "Sure." She reaches out and clasps my hand.

I raise her hand to my lips and kiss it.

Nico says, "Anything else you need, darlin', just let us know, yeah?"

"Thank you, Nico." Grace turns her warm gaze to Kat. Her voice lowered, she says, "You, too, Dramarama. Thanks for always being there for me. I love you."

Barney, Nico, and I watch as Kat and Grace silently embrace. They stand like that for several long moments with their arms around each other, supporting each other, and honestly, I'm not a weepy dude, but it kinda brings a tear to my eye.

It doesn't help that I'm imagining those three words leaving Grace's lips while she's looking at *me*, but that's neither here nor there.

Grace glances at me. "You just made that weird noise again."

Barney claps me on the shoulder. "He's all right." He sends me a conspiratorial wink. "Go easy on him, it takes a while to get your sea legs."

Kat and Grace do this confused head-cocking thing, like, *What the hell are you talking about?* but Nico and I know exactly what he's talking about.

He's talking about falling in love.

"Fuck you, man," I say gruffly, and Barney laughs.

Chuckling, Nico says, "Remember to tack when the wind changes, bro. Don't want any slack in your sail."

"Fuck you, too, Nyx."

Barney adds, "And you gotta ride those monster waves, buddy, head straight into that storm, because a secret island paradise lies on the other side, but only for the sailor with balls big enough to ride it out."

"Excuse me, but when did this get-together become a scene from *Moby Dick*?" says Kat, exasperated.

I look at Nico. "So. Many. Jokes."

He and Barney burst into laughter.

Kat comes over and gives me a kiss on the cheek. She whispers into my ear, "I'm so happy for you guys."

"Thanks, Kat."

"Also I'll kill you if you fuck this up."

I sigh. "I know, Kat. Get in line."

She pulls away, smiles at me, and follows Nico from the kitchen. I walk everyone to the front door, Grace at my side.

Everyone says their good-byes. If Barney hugs Grace a little too long, I pretend to ignore it and keep my shit-eating grin plastered on my face, because that's what my girl wants me to do.

She rewards me with a swift kiss on the lips as soon as she breaks away from Barney.

He and I nod to each other, and then they're off.

Grace and I stand at the door and watch them drive away in the Escalade, Barney behind the wheel. Once they're out of sight, she turns to me.

"I'm proud of you, Kong," she says softly, going up on her toes to kiss me again.

I wrap my arms around her waist and drag her against me. "I have no idea what you're talking about."

She whispers, "Oh, you're *good*."

I nuzzle her neck, inhaling the soft, warm scent of her skin. "Do you want me to tuck you in now?"

"If this 'tucking' involves your outie and my innie, definitely yes."

"I'm talking about getting you settled for bed, horndog!"

She smiles up at me, eyes shining. "Me, too."

Is it normal to feel so happy it seems like you could float right off the floor? "You've got a mind like a fourteen-year-old virgin who just discovered internet porn," I say sternly, trying my best to scowl, but when she takes my lower lip between her teeth all thoughts of scowling are toast.

"What can I say," she whispers, rubbing her breasts against my chest. "You give me a giant lady boner."

I groan as she licks and nips my mouth, playfully touching her tongue to mine but immediately withdrawing, only to slide her hand between my legs and grip my thickening dick.

She purrs, "And speaking of giant boners."

I gather her hair in my hand and wrap it around my wrist. Then I use it like a leash to pull her head back. "You're gonna be the death of me, you know that?" I growl against her arched neck, cupping her breast in my other hand.

She answers breathlessly, "Maybe. But you'll die a happy man."

She can't see it, but my smile is ruthless. In one swift move I bend and throw her over my shoulder.

"Hey!" she shouts, hitting me on the butt with her fists. "Put me down!"

"No can do, sunshine." I saunter out the front door, balancing her body with one hand on her hip and another spread across her ass. I head toward the guest house, enjoying the feel of her, listening to her grumbly protests and watching her feet kick in front of me as I walk barefoot over the grass.

After a few minutes she says, "I'm getting light-headed," so I stop and set her on her feet.

She wobbles a little, finding her balance. "You're strong. I'm not exactly light as a feather."

I make like a bodybuilder and flex my biceps, growling.

"Oh shit. We forgot the bags."

"I'll get 'em," I say, taking her hand and walking again. "Why don't you take a bath or something, get settled? I'll open a bottle of wine, and we can chill for a bit before you go to bed."

We walk for a minute, not saying anything, until Grace exhales a soft, wistful sigh.

"Uh-oh. What was that sigh? I don't know that sigh yet. Is that bad?"

"No. That was my pinch-me-because-this-can't-be-real sigh."

My chest puffs out all on its own. Didn't know it could do that. I squeeze her hand, smiling. "In that case, I suppose I should make one, too."

Thoughtfully, she says, "It's funny, isn't it?"

"What is?"

"Life."

"Funny ha-ha, or funny strange?"

She shrugs, looking out toward the restless ocean, glinting in the pale moonlight. "Both. If anyone had told me last week that my condo would explode in a fireball and I'd be left homeless but wouldn't particularly care, I'd have written him a prescription for an antipsychotic."

I stop abruptly and pull her into my arms. Looking down into her eyes I vow, "You'll never be homeless, Grace. Not while I'm around. You'll always have a place to stay—with me."

She shakes her head a little, as if she can't believe it. "I know," she whispers, gazing at me. "Which is just so . . . weird. Don't you think this is a little weird? Us—this?"

She makes a motion with her finger, pointing between our chests.

"No," I answer honestly. "I think it's amazing. To me it just feels right."

She nods. "That's what I'm saying! How can this feel so right, when everything else seems to be so wrong? Kat wanting to get pregnant, A.J.'s tumor, all my worldly possessions are destroyed, and yet I'm . . . this is terrible to say, but I'm really . . ."

"Happy," I say softly, finishing for her.

When she nods silently, her eyes wide and full of wonder, my heart swells so big I think it will explode.

But I don't want to get too sappy on her because it might scare her away, so I say matter-of-factly, "I told you, Slick—*powerful spooge*."

She groans in disgust and pushes on my chest. "You're hopeless, you know that?"

*Hopelessly in love*, I think.

My heart stops dead.

Grace mistakes my sudden stillness and laughs. "You make the best faces! Seriously, you look like you're having a stroke!"

I open my mouth to answer, but nothing comes out. I've lost the power of speech.

Love has literally rendered me speechless.

"C'mon, Kong," says Grace, pulling at my hand. "Tuck me in and tell me a bedtime story."

She pulls me toward the guest house. All I can do is stumble along blindly behind her, dazed with joy, thinking, *Once upon a time, a boy fell in love with a beautiful princess . . .*

Looking back, *that's* the moment I should've known it was too good to last. Because in fairy tales with beautiful princesses, there's always an evil wizard to contend with, a witch casting a curse, a dangerous dragon to be slain.

But I never could have guessed that all those terrible things would turn out to be me.

# Chapter 21

## Grace

After showing me where everything is in the guest house, Brody brings me the bags of clothes from Kat and Chloe, runs me a bath, and opens a bottle of wine.

"I could get used to this," I say, contentedly up to my neck in bubbles. Brody, sitting cross-legged on the floor beside the bathtub, pours me another glass of Cabernet.

"Your wish is my command, my lady." He lifts his glass in a toast, and we both drink.

It turns out swallowing a mouthful of wine while grinning is pretty tricky.

Brody laughs at the liquid dribbling down both sides of my chin. "How's that drinking problem of yours coming along, Slick?"

"Hole in my lip," I say, licking all around my mouth. He watches my tongue with the focused concentration of a lion hunkering down to stalk a meal.

"Well," he says after a moment, his voice husky, "I should let you get to sleep." He stands, finishes off his wine in one big gulp, leans over the tub, and kisses me brusquely on the forehead. As he turns to go,

I ask bemusedly, "Is the sight of me immersed in bubbles offensive to you, Kong?"

Halfway to the door, he stops. Over his shoulder, he says, "Yes. You're so hideous I think I'm going to be sick." He adjusts his crotch. "And now I need to go rub one out to make myself feel better." Without looking back, he salutes. In a moment the front door closes, and then I'm alone.

I'm wet, naked, slippery with bubbles, and well on my way to tipsy, and the man just *walked out on me*.

Either I'm losing my mojo or Brody Scott is one hell of a gentleman.

I soak until I'm pruned, and then dry off and wander naked into the bedroom with my glass of wine. I stand in the middle of the room, looking around at the elegant furnishings, fretting over all the to-do lists I should be making, all the things I'll need to deal with in the morning, but finally decide that tonight there's nothing I can do but try to get some sleep.

So I finish my wine, crawl under the covers, turn out the lights, and lie in the dark listening to the muffled sound of waves crashing on the shore below and the wind whispering in the willows.

Half an hour later, still wide awake, I get out of bed and retrieve my cell phone from my handbag on the dresser.

Snuggled back under the covers, I dial Brody's number. He picks up on the first ring.

"If you're calling for video of me stroking my cock, I'm not sending it," he says with a smile in his voice. "You've had enough of that, missy."

"Not that I owe you an explanation, but just so you know, I deleted that."

His voice turns apologetic. "I wasn't trying to make you feel bad, I was only teasing. It's none of my business what you did before we were together."

We're quiet for a minute, just breathing, until I say, "So we're together. But not having sex. And you can't stand to be in the same room with me when I'm naked. It's like we're married!"

He exhalation is ragged. "You're relentless, you know that?"

"I'm relentless with everything I want badly."

"You want me . . . badly?"

I smile. "I want you more than I want to survive to see another day. Oh, wait—that sounds familiar. Where've I heard that before?"

His voice sours. "Har har."

I hear some rustling in the background. "What're you doing?"

"Sitting up."

"Are you in bed?"

"Yep."

I stretch my legs beneath the covers. "Me, too. And still naked, in case you were wondering."

It goes quiet on the other end of the line. "You sleep naked?"

"Always."

He softly groans. "Evil temptress."

I whisper, "Are *you* naked?"

His chuckle is deep and amused. "I don't want to ruin a beautiful fantasy for you, but I'm sitting here in my boxer briefs and socks, watching TV."

"Take off the socks," I command, and he chuckles again.

"My feet are cold."

"They won't be in a minute."

"Why, you gonna get me so worked up my toes will be on fire?"

"Along with every other part of you, yes."

"Meh. I feel lazy. What if I just *tell* you I'm taking them off, will that work?"

"No! Off!"

He grumbles, "Bossy friggin' princess," but there's more rustling, and then he says, "There. Satisfied?"

"Don't even get me started asking if I'm *satisfied*, Mr. Scott. I am most definitely not *satisfied*. Wait—did you just call me a princess?"

"Yeah, but not in a derogatory, you're-so-spoiled way. Like in a you're-a-beautiful-fairy-tale way."

Why that should please me so much, I have no idea. "So I suppose you're the frog in this story?"

Brody laughs. "Definitely."

"So then I need to kiss you. A lot."

His laughter turns into a low sigh. "Hopefully. *A lot* a lot."

The longing in that sigh makes me bite my lip. I say softly, "You're adorable, you know that?"

When he answers, "Yeah, I do," I burst out laughing.

"And also *very* humble."

"Speaking of humble, turn on channel 518."

"What's on channel 518?"

"If you turn it on you'll find out, won't you?"

I roll my eyes, flick on the light on the nightstand, prop myself up against the pillows, and grab the remote. "How the fuck does this thing work? There's about four thousand buttons on it."

He snorts. "In your clinical opinion, is it estrogen that makes women unable to operate a television remote? I've always been curious."

"Careful there, Kong. Those are fightin' words."

"Hmm. Probably the same hormone that makes it impossible for you people to parallel park."

"Ha! You're lucky I just found the power button or I'd be headed over to your place with a shotgun, my friend."

"Channel 518." He pauses. "You can get there by pushing the little buttons with the numbers—"

"I've got it!" I shout into the phone.

Muffled laughter.

Grousing under my breath, I punch in the channel. Now I'm watching Harrison Ford and Annette Bening sharing a hug.

I recognize the movie instantly. My heart starts thumping like mad. "It's *Regarding Henry*. This is my favorite part."

Brody and I watch together in silence as Harrison and Annette retrieve their daughter from the elite boarding school they enlisted her in before her father's accident. A narcissistic, unethical attorney in Manhattan, he interrupted a robbery one night and was shot, leaving him with retrograde amnesia, his entire memory wiped clean.

He had to learn who he was all over again, who his real friends were, what his relationship with his family used to be like.

He didn't like what he found.

"You were watching this before I called?"

Brody pauses for a moment before he answers. "This is the third time I've watched it in the past three days."

My eyes sting. "Because?"

"Because it's the closest I can get to understanding what it might've been like for you. I've been doing web searches about memory loss, too. And I ordered some books from Amazon."

I close my eyes and release the breath I didn't know I was holding.

"I'm sorry," he says quietly. "I shouldn't have mentioned anything."

"No. I'm not upset with you, I'm just . . . a little blown away, to be honest."

"I know you probably don't want to talk about it—"

"You can ask me anything, Brody."

He must hear the raw emotion in my voice, because he says gently, "Not if it hurts you. I'd rather stab out my own eyes than do anything to hurt you. And radical honesty, that's like ninety-nine point nine percent true."

My hands are trembling. I swallow around the lump in my throat. "I want you to know me," I whisper, my voice quaking.

His slow exhalation is full of deliberation. Then he says, "This accident you were in."

I wait, staring at the ceiling, my stomach in knots.

As he wrestles to find the right words, I suffer a pang of empathy for how hard this must be for *him*, dealing with a woman who may or may not remember him in the morning.

Quite frankly, I wouldn't be up for it if the situation were reversed. Why expose yourself to that kind of possible trauma? Why volunteer to have your heart ripped out?

"I don't know where to start," he says finally, sounding miserable, so I take pity on him and help him out.

"I can't remember the actual accident itself. I dream about it—well, you know. The dreams are always violent. Dark. But when I wake up there are only snippets left. Fractured pieces, like a puzzle, different parts but nothing fits into a whole that makes sense. Mainly what I remember are the feelings the dream evokes. The terror."

I pause to moisten my lips, allow my heartbeat to find a slower, more even rhythm.

"When I woke up in the hospital, no one knew who I was. My parents . . . their remains . . . there was a fire. A bad fire. It took a while for their bodies to be identified. Even the license plates on the car were melted beyond recognition. For three days I laid in a hospital bed wondering what my name was. I didn't recognize my own face in the mirror. I didn't know my age or where I lived, if I had siblings or a boyfriend or a dog or allergies or was a virgin or knew how to drive. It was like waking up on an alien planet in a body that wasn't mine, with no knowledge of how I ended up there. I was just . . . blank."

Brody breathes out. "Fuck."

I produce a shaky laugh. "Yeah, fuck is right. It scares me now to think of it. But the brain is a funny thing. I *thought* I was blank, but I did have knowledge. It was just locked away. The pathways to access things had changed. Kind of like Jason Bourne in the *Bourne Identity* movies."

Brody makes a joke. "So you can kill people with your bare hands and make bombs out of toilet paper rolls but you're not sure how you know how to do it?"

"Maybe. I haven't tried either of those things, now that you mention it. But the idea is the same. For instance, math."

"Math?"

"Yeah, math. That's how the doctors first started testing my memory. If certain areas of your brain are destroyed or affected by severe trauma, your ability to problem solve, like long division as an example, can be destroyed. In my case, I could easily complete an algebraic equation, I just didn't know *how* I knew how to do it. The memory of learning math was gone, the knowledge of understanding math was gone, but the ability itself remained. Put a piece of paper with a mathematical formula in front of me, I could correctly solve it. Ask me to describe what I'd solved, I'd have no clue."

Brody's "*Dude*" sounds so deeply impressed I have to chuckle.

"I know, it's a little esoteric. But that's how it was for me with a lot of things. As it turned out, I *did* know how to do math, and drive, and most other things I'd learned by rote or with muscle memory, like swimming. I just couldn't remember what I knew and didn't know! It was so frustrating I can't even describe it. Everything had to be relearned, rediscovered, reintroduced. But some things refused to come back. Some parts of my brain are still locked away to me, even now. Most likely they always will be."

There's a moment of fraught silence as Brody digests what I've said. Then he asks, "Which parts?"

I chew a little piece of skin on the inside of my cheek. "My parents. I don't remember them at all. Or my childhood. School. Friends. Growing up in San Francisco. The life I remember started when I was eighteen, when I opened my eyes in a strange bed in a strange room wearing an ugly blue gown that tied in the back, hooked up to beeping machines, with an old nurse with kind brown eyes leaning over me and asking if I could hear her."

"Don't move," says Brody, his voice tight. "I'm coming over."

He hangs up before I can say another word. In two minutes, the front door flies open. I'm already sitting up in bed.

"You didn't even put a shirt on," I manage to get out before he's on me.

He takes me flat to the mattress and crushes me to his chest, the covers smashed between our bodies. "Baby," he says, choked, his face pressed to my neck. "Oh God, baby."

He's called me Slick. He's called me sweetheart. He's called me sunshine and princess and witch face and who knows what else, but hearing him call me "baby" in that wrecked tone of voice, his big, strong body trembling with emotion, rips down any barrier I might have tried to erect between us.

I cling to him and let the tears come, hot and silent on my cheeks.

"I'm so sorry. I'm so sorry." He keeps saying it over and over, a litany of regret that seems so genuine it's almost like he feels at fault.

I press my cheek to his and whisper into his ear, "It's better now. You make it better." I hug him hard, my arms thrown around his shoulders. "*This* makes it better."

When he lifts his head and gazes down at me, his eyes are wet.

Seeing his emotion moves me so much it hurts my chest. I skim a fingertip over the fringe of his lower lashes. He squeezes his eyes shut, almost as if he's hiding.

"What is it?" I ask, because I know it's something more.

He rests his forehead against mine. It's hot, like he has a fever.

His voice a cracking whisper, he says, "You don't believe in confessions, remember?"

"But I do believe in radical honesty."

He blinks open his eyes. They're dark and full of pain. Tortured.

My heart beats faster. "Brody, what is it?"

His lips part. Staring down at me with an anguished expression, he blurts, "I'm crazy about you, Grace. I'm just . . . fucking . . . *gone*."

Heat suffuses me, flushing my face, my chest, the tips of my fingers. I stare at him, knowing he's telling me the truth, knowing, too, that this unexpected admission is tied inextricably to what I've told him about the accident, that somehow the two things are bound together, a knot I can sense but don't understand.

"Please don't let that turn you off, but I can't not say it. It's what's in my heart. I know it's fast—"

"Someone I love once told me that when these things are real, they happen fast," I interrupt softly, stroking his face.

He inhales a ragged breath. "Really? Who?"

I smile. "Kat. And besides, it's not that fast. We've known each other for a year and a half, as you keep reminding me. Honestly I'm surprised you didn't tell me this like seventeen months ago, you've been making moon eyes at me the whole time. You big sap."

He threads his fingers into my hair and kisses me, a deep, hot kiss that leaves us both panting softly. His erection is trapped between us, insistently poking into my hip.

"I am a sap," he says huskily. "I'm a big, drippy ball of goo—for you."

I smile. "That sounds unhygienic."

He doesn't smile back at my joke. Nuzzling my neck he whispers, "If I said I wanted to spend the night over here, would you be able to keep your hands to yourself?"

"No."

"Well, tough. 'Cause I'm staying. I don't want you to have to sleep by yourself tonight."

I exhale a ragged breath. "I always spend the night alone, Brody."

He kisses my neck, my shoulder, my jaw. Then he softly kisses me on the lips again, but this time it's tender instead of passionate. "There's a first time for everything, Slick."

He reaches across me and turns out the light. Then he rolls to his side, taking me with him. Lying on top of the covers, he pulls me to his chest so we're back to front with the sheets between us, spooning, his legs drawn up behind mine, his arm under my head, the other arm wrapped around my middle.

Into my hair he murmurs, "Look on the bright side. You'll finally find out if you snore."

"I don't snore," I whisper, smiling.

He snuggles into me, burrowing his face deeper into my hair, and makes a low, masculine sound in his throat. He finds my hand and threads his fingers through mine. Then he sighs, deeply and quietly, his body warm and heavy, relaxing against me.

Just as I'm about to drift off into sleep, Brody whispers, "Thank you."

"For what?" I ask groggily.

A gentle kiss on the back of my neck, the barest brush of his lips against my skin. "I wasn't talking to you, baby. Go to sleep."

And so, lulled by the deep, even sound of his breathing, I do.

Waking up the next morning feels like being reborn.

It's early. So early the birds aren't even up yet. The barest wash of color is lifting the sky beyond the windows from deep sapphire to pearl gray. I inhale, smelling the warm, pleasant musk of sleepy male.

Brody is lying on his back beside me, his arm under my neck. I'm draped over him like another blanket, one leg thrown over his body, my arm across his chest.

His bare, beautiful chest.

In sleep he's somehow even more gorgeous, all tousled hair and golden skin, his square jaw shadowed with stubble. When I touch my fingertip to the cursive letters tattooed across his chest he shifts drowsily, mumbles something unintelligible, and then with a soft exhalation falls still.

Beneath his boxer briefs, he's hard.

Looking at his erection, I bite my lip. It's just sitting there like a dare, bold and beautiful, taunting me.

I have to touch it. I literally cannot *not* touch it, my fingers are already creeping downward over his chest of their own will.

Using the barest possible pressure, I trace the outline of the head.

Brody makes a soft sound, but doesn't stir. His breathing doesn't change.

*Is this wrong?* I think, stroking the head of his cock through the cotton. When his cock reacts with a welcoming jerk against my fingers I decide his penis has a mind of its own, rights of its own, and if Brody is too busy sleeping, Mr. Throbby and I are going to take this opportunity to become better acquainted.

I lightly wrap my hand around his erection. Eager to become friends, it pulses against my palm. Sleeping Beauty doesn't move. Emboldened, I slowly stroke my hand down the length of him, all the way to the base, careful not to make any sudden moves.

His cock is thick, and as hard as steel. He could knock over a building with it. At least a multiunit apartment complex anyway. And it's *frisky*—no sooner have I gently moved my hand to cup his balls than I get another pulse from it, this one stronger.

*You want my mouth, don't you, big boy?*

Slowly, with minute movements of my body, I lift my leg from over Brody's. Then I inch down the mattress, holding my breath and keeping an eye on Brody's face.

He's still blissfully in la-la land, so I keep heading south.

When I'm eye-to-eye with his crotch, I lean over and softly kiss his cock through the cotton. Straining against the fabric, the vein on the underside throbs. I kiss the head, the shaft, nuzzling my nose along the length of him.

"Mmm."

Brody turns his head on the pillow. I freeze.

After a moment when nothing happens, I slip my fingers through the opening in the front of his briefs.

Warm skin, the softest anywhere on his body. With tiny movements and light pressure, I stroke my fingers over it.

Brody shifts his legs, but doesn't wake.

His cock insistently pulses against my fingers, begging for my tongue.

So I have to oblige. It's the polite thing to do.

I lean over again, spread the opening in his briefs farther apart, and close my lips over the throbbing vein just beneath the head of his cock.

Brody makes a sound, something like a moan or a plea. Whatever it is, it makes my heart take off at a gallop.

I want to hear that sound again.

I slip the engorged head into my mouth. Reflexively Brody's hips move, pushing him deeper.

The moan I'm rewarded with this time is lower in register, longer, and so fucking sexy my nipples harden. I'm getting wet between my legs.

I slide his cock farther into my mouth, sucking on the shaft. He's hot against my tongue. He tastes like the ocean.

Then a hand fists into my hair.

"Grace."

Brody's voice is thick with sleep and desire. I glance up. He's staring down at me, his head lifted off the pillow, a flush creeping up his neck.

Slowly and deliberately, I swirl my tongue around the head of his cock.

His eyes flare. His lips part, but no sound comes out. His hand tightens in my hair.

I close my fingers around the thickness of his shaft at the base, and then, looking up at him, take his cock all the way down my throat.

"Oh fuck," he whispers, shuddering.

*Good morning, Mr. Scott.*

When I slide my mouth up toward the head again, he fists his other hand in my hair and makes a noise like a growl.

*It's a fine morning, isn't it?*

Sucking on the head of his cock, I stroke my hand up and down the shaft. Wet from my mouth, hard and pulsing, it slips through my fingers.

He sucks in a sharp breath. All the muscles in his abdomen stand out. He says my name again, this time followed by a husky command.

"Faster."

I'm nothing if not accommodating, so as I continue to suck and lick the head of his cock, I stroke my hand faster up and down, squeezing, my fingers curled tight.

Brody starts to fuck my mouth, flexing his pelvis in time with my strokes, watching me. Watching my mouth. The movements of my tongue.

"Yes, baby," he whispers, straining against my lips. "Exactly like that. That's so fucking good. Your mouth feels amazing."

When I moan around his cock because I'm so turned on, he demands harshly, "Let me see that beautiful pussy."

Using my free hand, I shove the covers off me, exposing my naked breasts and body. He hisses in a breath.

"Show me how wet you are, baby. Touch yourself. Let me taste you."

I've officially died and gone to heaven.

I slip my fingers between my legs. I'm soaked. My clit is swollen, so exquisitely sensitive I whine when my fingers brush over it.

"Give it to me," Brody demands.

When I lift my hand from between my legs, Brody grabs my wrist, sits up a few inches, and hungrily sucks my wet fingers into his mouth.

We both moan.

He licks my fingers, greedy for my taste, which is so erotic I moan again. When he's finished licking my fingers clean, he puts his hand around my throat.

His other hand still fisted in my hair, rhythmically fucking my mouth, he lightly squeezes my neck.

"So beautiful," he whispers when I shiver, aroused out of my mind by that small gesture of dominance. "You're so beautiful, sweetheart. Look at you. Look how perfect you are." His expression is fierce, concentrated, hard. His hand tightens around my throat.

I slip my fingers back between my legs and frantically stroke my throbbing clit.

"Don't you dare come yet," he says softly. "If you come before me I'll punish you."

*Oh god yes please yes punish me I'm very bad you should punish me NOW.*

Brody's husky chuckle sends a thrill through my body. "You want that, don't you?"

I close my eyes and moan around his cock, building fast toward climax.

His voice gets gruffer. Lower. Darker. "You want me to restrain you, Grace? You want me to tie you up?"

My nipples are so hard, so sensitive. My pulse is a wild, thundering roar in my ears.

In one sudden move, Brody sits up, flips me onto my back, and straddles my chest. Hard and wet from my mouth, his cock rests between my breasts. He wraps his hands around my wrists and stares down at me with a look of lust so unleashed it steals my breath.

"Answer me."

I whisper, "Yes."

"Stay here."

I swallow, nod, and stay perfectly still as he crawls off me and goes into the other room.

Not daring to even lift my head from the pillow, I lie there and breathe through the waves of heat washing over me. It seems as if I can feel every nerve in my body, all my muscles and bones, the air being sucked from my lungs to feed all the tiny capillaries.

Brody returns. He stands in the doorway looking at me. He's removed his briefs. A length of rope dangles from one hand.

When he hears my soft moan, he smiles.

Dragging the rope through his hands, he walks slowly to the edge of the bed, never taking his gaze from mine. "What are we gonna do with you?" he muses. "Waking me up like that when you knew you were supposed to behave?"

My chest rises and falls in quick, uneven bursts. He strolls toward the bed, watching my face, gauging my reaction to his approach. Then he stops beside the bed, his erection jutting out, straining toward me.

"Up and on your knees, facing me."

In one whip-crack motion, I do exactly as he commands and kneel on the mattress in front of him.

"So eager," he whispers, brushing my hair over my shoulder. His hand lingers a moment, steadying me. The pause is excruciating. My heartbeat is like a hummingbird's.

Brody leans down and kisses my neck. "Are you gonna be quiet?"

I nod vigorously.

He kisses the wildly fluttering pulse at the base of my throat. "Good. Because your little noises will make me come too fast." He reaches around me, bends my arms so they're crossed over my back at my waist, and winds the rope around my wrists. He gives the rope a little tug to tighten the knot, and I gasp.

He tilts his head and looks at me in warning from the corner of his eye.

Biting my lip, I look down.

Moving agonizingly slowly, he winds the rope back around my torso, just under my breasts, looping it around his hands. It's a soft rope, the color of straw, about a quarter inch thick, perfectly suited to the task. He passes it around my body and crisscrosses it between my breasts, so they're lifted and separated, blatantly on display. Then he ties another knot just above my belly button, and I'm bound.

His expression is intensely focused. I can tell he loves what he sees, and also notice his concern that he hasn't bound me too tightly as he runs his finger under the rope, testing the tautness against my skin.

"Okay?" he asks, whisper soft.

I moisten my lips and nod.

"If it gets uncomfortable, tell me right away."

I nod again, my pulse flying, tension rising and rising under my skin. Brody pushes me gently down against the mattress and stares down at me with this incredible combination of passion, possession, and protectiveness in his eyes, and it's all I can do not to groan aloud.

No one has ever looked at me the way he does. No one has ever made me feel the way he does. I know we're crossing over into new territory, that this kind of emotional intimacy never goes hand in hand with physical intimacy for either of us, and it scares the shit out of me but also makes me so elated I feel drugged. Adrenaline crashes through me until I'm trembling all over, quaking with need and emotion.

"It's all right," says Brody, watching me with soft eyes. "I'm here. You're safe. Just breathe." He settles a hand low on my belly. "Spread your legs for me, baby."

I part my knees. He runs his hands slowly up my thighs, and nudges my legs wider apart. Then he stands there looking down at the most private part of me, his cock twitching.

He gently pinches my folds between two fingers.

I close my eyes, arching into his hand.

"Sweet, beautiful girl," he rasps, stroking the rough pad of his thumb over my clit, dipping it down lower to press inside me. "You're so pink and sweet here. So soft. So wet."

I'm starting to sweat. The combination of his words, the husky tone of his voice, the rope chafing my skin, and how gentle he's being all combine to make me desperately hot. I'm burning up.

He drags me by my hips to the edge of the bed so my bottom is hanging over by a few inches. He kneels between my legs, digs his hands into the flesh of my ass, and licks my pussy.

My sucked-in breath is loud, but it must not count because Brody ignores it.

He kisses me there as he would my mouth, a gently swirling motion and constant suction, a deliberate sweep of his tongue over the swollen bud of my clit. I strain against my bindings, panting, my head thrown back, my trembling legs thrown over his shoulders, listening to all the noises he's making, the wet sucking sounds and deep, pleased grumbles, trying to hold back the scream building inside my chest.

Then he presses two fingers inside me and lightly scrapes his teeth against my clit.

I jerk. A ragged moan tears from my lips before I can stop it.

Brody reaches up and pinches my nipple—hard.

"Please," I whisper, desperate for release.

His fingers gentler, he strokes his thumb back and forth over my throbbing nipple. Suckling my clit, he presses his fingers deeper inside me.

I helplessly rock against his mouth. He grabs on to the knot above my belly button and uses the rope to pull me even closer. He reaches up with both hands and squeezes my breasts, rhythmically pinching my nipples. Losing it, I begin to buck against his mouth.

"I'll spank this pussy so hard if you come before you're told!"

He goes right back to eating me as soon as those words are spoken, but it's too late. I'm there.

With a loud, wavering scream, I come.

Brody rears up and shoves his hard cock deep inside me.

I convulse around it, thrashing and moaning like a madwoman, my thighs drawn up around his waist. I hear him cursing, feel his hands on my neck and breasts, holding me down, but I'm barely aware of anything else because he feels so goddamn good it's unreal.

"That's *your* cock, baby," he growls into my ear. *"Come on it."*

I do, over and over, crying out his name, until my legs are jelly and the pulsing in my core finally slows, and then stops.

I float for a while, almost disconnected from my body, somewhere peaceful inside my head. When I come back to myself, Brody is still on top of me—still *in* me—his arms tensed and his heart pounding hard against mine. I blink up at him.

He mutters, "Oops."

I turn my head to his arm and weakly start to laugh.

"You're gonna need to give me a mulligan here, Slick. That was an accident."

I laugh harder.

"It's kinda funny how every time we do this you end up laughing."

I kiss his arm. "Funny ha-ha, or funny strange?"

He starts to withdraw from my body, and I groan. "No!"

"Yes."

"It's too late! The thirty-day thing is toast! You already screwed the pooch!"

"You should never refer to yourself as a pooch, beautiful. You're anything but."

With a regretful grunt, he pulls out of me.

"Oh God, I hate you right now."

He tsks. "Careful, Slick. I still haven't punished you for coming yet."

I freeze. "What?"

He stands, beautiful and naked, legs spread, at the edge of the bed. Gazing down at me with heated eyes and a mysterious smile, he pulls me up by the knot on my stomach. "We'll get to that later. Open your mouth."

With one hand on his erection and the other around my jaw, Brody guides my lips to his cock, still wet from being inside me.

"Clean me off," he whispers. "Every drop."

I lap at him like an obedient puppy as he watches me, his breathing erratic. I lick him base to tip, swallowing every so often, tasting myself.

"The rope still okay, sweetheart?"

"Yes."

He digs his hands into my hair. "Good. Now suck."

When the head of his cock nudges the back of my throat, I make a little noise that sends a shiver through Brody's body. His eyes drift halfway shut.

"I want to come in your mouth. If you don't want that tell me now so we can do something else."

I suck harder.

"That's my girl," he whispers, flexing his hips.

My toes dig into the carpet as he starts a slow, repetitive thrusting, slightly deeper with each push. I love how he holds my head motionless, how helpless I am to use my hands or even move. All I can do is submit to him as he sets the pace and uses my mouth for his own pleasure.

"I'm close," he says, breathing hard. "God, sweetheart, you're so fucking—"

He cuts off with a fractured groan. He pumps hard into my mouth several more times, his fingers digging into my scalp, and then, with a shout, throws his head back and comes.

And comes.

And comes.

He starts to lose his balance or the strength in his legs, because his knees buckle. He curses. Without releasing my head, he takes a knee on the mattress so he's supporting all the weight of my upper body with his hands behind my head. He stares down at me, his face red, his lips parted, his eyes dazed.

I swallow, breathing through my nose. Brody moans as the muscles in my throat contract around him.

"Grace," he gasps, shuddering. "Grace."

I swallow again.

He plants a hand on the mattress and eases me down, keeping his cock in my mouth and a hand under my neck, until finally I'm flat on my back and he's balanced over me, stroking my throat and softly groaning as I continue to suck and swallow everything he's giving me.

I'm bound, helpless, completely at his mercy, yet, because of what I see in his eyes, I've never felt more powerful in my life.

When his body is no longer racked with tremors and his breathing has slowed, he carefully pulls out of my mouth. He releases the knot on my stomach, unwinds the rope from around my body, rolls me to my side so he can untie the knot at my wrists, and then tosses the rope to the floor.

"Come here, baby." He gathers me in his arms. He rolls us around so I'm on top of him, my head resting on his chest, and then starts to massage my neck, shoulders, and arms. "Are you okay?"

*"Mrpf."*

He chuckles. The sound reverberates through my head. "I'll take that as a yes."

He gently rubs one wrist, and then the other. I let him handle me with no resistance, my muscles limp. He presses a kiss to the center of my palm.

We're quiet for a while. I drift, physically and mentally drained, taking support from the heat and strength of his body beneath me. The rhythm of his breath soothes me on a deep, visceral level, so in a few short minutes I'm almost asleep.

Until Brody whispers, "Time for church, sweetheart."

I lift my head and blink up at him, and he smiles.

"I know you've already seen God once this morning, but a second time never hurts."

"Your ego is only matched by your terrible sense of humor, Mr. Scott."

"And your beauty is only matched by your gymnastic tongue, Slick."

"Yes, I'm a very cunning linguist."

Eyes wide, Brody asks, "Did you just misquote a line from *Tomorrow Never Dies*?"

I lift my brows. "If you're about to tell me that's another one of your favorite movies, I'm about to start believing in Fate."

"You like James Bond?"

"Like? No. I don't like James Bond. I *love* James Bond."

He considers me seriously for a moment. Then he narrows his eyes. "I'm not gonna get too excited because next you'll probably say you like Daniel Craig best in the role."

I scoff. "Sean Connery all the way, baby! That time when he was dancing with the girl in *Thunderball* and he spun her around so the bad guy would shoot her in the back instead of him—classic asshole move! I actually clapped at that part!"

Brody drops his head back against the mattress. He starts to laugh, softly at first, and then with more volume when I add sourly, "But don't even get me started on Timothy Dalton."

"No," he says, squeezing me, his voice husky, his embrace tight. "I wouldn't dare."

# Chapter 23

"And *then* what happened?"

"Then we went surfing again. It was as cold as Christmas in Antarctica. I kept expecting an iceberg to float by with some polar bears on it. After that, he made me breakfast. And when I say 'he' I mean Magda, his housekeeper, who should have her own cooking show, she's that good. Then he drove me into town so I could go look at the building and get my car."

On the other end of the phone, Kat moans. "Oh God. How bad was it? Was there anything left?"

Standing at the window of my office in Beverly Hills, I look out into the February sky. It's crystal blue, not a cloud in sight, cheerfully refusing to admit we're in the middle of winter.

"Security wouldn't let me up to the floor. My floor and the two above have both been completely evacuated. All the elevators have been shut down due to safety concerns—it's not known yet if the blast affected the lift mechanisms. So a lot of folks are displaced. And where my and Mr. Liebowitz's condos used to be there's a gigantic black hole. There's debris everywhere that the investigators are going through." I sigh. "I'm sure they'll find my vibrator collection scattered in a million little pieces over the doggie walk."

"Or worse, totally intact."

I smile at the image of Linda Conley, the high-strung building manager, having a fainting spell when confronted by my XXL hot pink dildo protruding from a shrub somewhere on the grounds. Then I think of poor Mr. Liebowitz and feel bad. He was a nice old man. Exploding in an oxygen-fueled fireball isn't the ideal way to go. I bet those investigators will be finding bits of him all over the place along with my vibrators.

But he's also a dick for blowing up my condo. I hope wherever he is right now he's feeling really bad about it.

Kat asks, "So what's next?"

I turn from the windows and walk back to my desk, where I've spent the last several hours making calls. Everyone who had an appointment this week had to be rescheduled, which was about as fun as getting a root canal. High-powered people in the midst of marital counseling aren't generally the most understanding lot. More than one demanded that I come over to their home instead of inconveniencing them, and hollered at me when I declined.

Because yes, I'm so sorry my life blew up and your session will be delayed a week. How rude of me.

"Next I have to find a place to live, sign a bunch of paperwork with the insurance company, and buy a new wardrobe, along with furniture, dishes, flatware, and whatever else. *Everything* else. Thanks again for the clothes, by the way. I'm wearing a blouse I know must be yours because it's all stretched out over my tits."

"That could be Chloe's! She just had a baby, her boobs got totally bigger!"

"She went from an A cup to a B cup, honey, that's not exactly getting bigger."

Kat grumbles, "I'm sure A.J. would disagree." She pauses for a second, and then says, "Speaking of Chloe, I talked to her this morning."

I have my coffee cup in hand, halfway to my mouth, but stop short at the tone in Kat's voice. "And?"

She exhales a worried breath. "Annnd . . . A.J. was taking another nap."

"Oh shit." I sink into the captain's chair behind my desk.

"I know. I'm really worried, too. What do you think we should do?"

"Talk to her about it, definitely, before we try to do anything else, like force him to go see a doctor." Now it's my turn to pause. "Which reminds me."

Kat knows what I'm going to say before I utter another word. "I made the appointment with a fertility specialist this morning. It's this Friday at three."

Her voice is subdued. She's trying to be strong because I'm neck deep in my own pile of shit, but I know her. On the inside she's having a meltdown.

"I'm going with you," I say promptly. When she doesn't respond, I demand, "What?"

She says quietly, "I haven't told Nico."

"Oh, honey." My heart goes out to her. She tells Nico everything, so for her to withhold this, she must really be terrified.

"Don't say anything to Brody, okay?" she pleads. "I'll tell Nico, I promise, I just . . . I just don't want . . ."

"You don't want him to worry unnecessarily if there's nothing wrong," I finish gently.

A little sniffle comes through the other end of the phone. "Yes."

"Sweetie, everything's going to be fine. I promise. I double promise, okay? Not knowing is the worst part. Once you know what you're dealing with, one way or another, you can figure out a plan how to move forward." My voice turns wry. "Trust me, I know."

Kat huffs out a breath. "Oh fucksicles. I'm such a twat."

"What've you done now?"

"St. Patrick's Day is only a few weeks away and I haven't even started to plan for our annual movie night."

Every year since we became friends, Kat, Chloe, and I spend St. Patrick's Day together, watching old movies, eating ice cream, and drinking too many margaritas. It's basically the exact same thing we do every year on Kat's birthday, but instead of trying to cheer Kat up because it's the anniversary of the day her father left, we're trying to cheer me up because it's the anniversary of my parents' deaths.

We really need to get happier reasons for annual get-togethers.

"If I'm still crashing at Brody's, we should have it there. You should see the size of the TV in the living room. I think it can be seen from outer space."

"You think you'll still be crashing at Brody's in three weeks?"

I sigh, gazing out the window again. "We'll see."

"Whoa. *Whoa*! Was that a swoony sigh? Did Grace 'Titanium' Stanton just make a super swoony sigh?"

"Get a grip on yourself, Katherine. I don't swoony anything."

"You *totally did*," she breathes, a thrill in her voice.

I warn, "Kat."

She goes all practical on me. "Oh, okay, so you're saying he's just another random pony ride for you?"

I roll my eyes. "You know very well I'm not saying anything of the sort."

"Of course you're not, because *I was there* when you said—and I quote—'he makes me feel like everything bad that's ever happened to me was worth it because it was all leading up to him.'"

I say drily, "So now you have a photographic memory. Congratulations. That would've been very convenient when you were trying to find the Hermès scarf I lent you last year that you lost."

After a short pause, she asks, "You know he's in love with you, right?"

The flush starts in my chest, creeps up my neck, and invades my cheeks, where it starts to burn. "He did mention something to that effect."

She gasps. "He told you he loves you?"

"Not those three words, but the general idea."

"Did you say it back?"

She sounds overly excited, like I've just told her she's won a cruise to the Bahamas. "Of course not."

"Why of course not?"

"Well, for one thing, it's way too soon."

Her voice sours. "It's never too soon to tell someone how you feel, dumbass."

I recline in my chair and close my eyes. "Okay, I'm not saying the L word, but he is amazing. Everything I could possibly want in a man: kind, funny, smart, good-looking, successful, passionate . . . good God is he passionate. For someone who looks like the boy next door he fucks like the devil."

"Wait. I thought you said he was 'respecting' you and refused to give you the D?"

"There might have been a little slippage."

Kat laughs. "What, like you tripped and fell on his erection?"

"Something like that."

"Well, if I know you, he'll be giving you the D on the regular within twenty-four hours. I don't know if you sprinkle pixie dust on your cooch or what, sister, but I've never seen anyone with such power to produce boners in the male population."

Now it's my turn to laugh. "Oh yes, didn't you know? That's my superpower. My boner-inducing supercooch. I'm saving the world with it, one man at a time."

"You should be almost there by now!"

"Ha."

"Which brings me to my next question: Barney."

My stomach tightens at the odd tone in her voice. "That wasn't a question."

"Yeah, well, you should know that even though he was acting like everything was fine when we left yesterday, he spent the entire drive home white-knuckled, looking like he was about to go on a murder spree. I've never seen him so agitated."

When I don't say anything because I'm mulling over that tidbit of information, Kat prompts, "Did Brody tell you what he said to him at the car?"

"No. Did Barney tell you?"

"No. But I got the distinct feeling from Barney's stabby vibe that he wasn't happy about it."

The last thing I can add to my worry list right now is Barney. The worry list is already too full. "He's a big boy. He'll be fine."

Kat's tone turns hesitant. "Was there . . . anything going on between you guys?"

"Nothing other than a little harmless flirting," I answer truthfully.

"Somehow I don't think he took it as harmless."

My office phone rings. "Sweetie, I've got to get back to work. Can I call you later?"

"Of course! And let me know if you want me to come shopping with you, I need some new lingerie."

"New lingerie? You have more lingerie than any woman I know!"

"The baby-making efforts require a lot of costume changes."

I laugh out loud. "Will do. Talk to you later."

"Love you, Gracie."

"Love you, too, Kat."

When we hang up, I'm smiling. I answer my office phone with a brisk "Grace Stanton speaking."

"Hello, beautiful. Am I interrupting?"

Low and sexy, Brody's voice sends a rash of goose bumps up my spine.

"Hey, you. Why aren't you calling on my cell? Not that I mind, it's nice to hear your voice either way."

"Because it's been so long since you heard it," he jokes, though I can tell he's pleased.

I lean back in my chair and put my feet up on the edge of my desk. "Well, you know what they say. Parting is such sweet sorrow."

"And now she's quoting Shakespeare! Awesome. Good thing I paid attention in my English Lit classes."

I'm grinning, feeling stupidly happy all of a sudden. "It's impossible for me to picture you sitting behind a desk in class. I bet you were the teacher's pet."

"Let's just say I got a lot of A's for no good reason."

"Being cute has its perks, hmm?"

"Cute?" he repeats, offended. "Excuse me, Slick, but kittens are cute. Babies are cute. *I* am devastatingly handsome."

"It's hard for me to tell one way or the other with that giant ego obscuring my view."

He chuckles. "Is ego your code word for 'penis'?"

"Of course it is, Kong. You're much too intelligent for me to slip these things past."

"Speaking of penises, what time do you think you'll be finished at the office?"

I make a face at the phone. "Has anyone ever told you that you're the absolute worst at changing subjects?"

He breezes right past that, saying, "Because I want to take you out on a date."

"A date?"

"You sound like you've never heard of the practice. Let me inform you. So a guy likes a girl, right, and he wants to impress her. So he goes, 'Hey, girl, let's go get some food or something—'"

I snort. "Yes, that's *very* impressive."

"And she goes, 'I'd love to! You manly, manly man!' And then he picks her up in his car and takes her to a fancy restaurant and spends a lot of money on dinner and wine and tries to be really cool with his conversation so she's all impressed with him—"

"Is this story going anywhere except Crazy Town?"

"—and then they go back to his place and he tries out all his super slick manly moves on her until she's dizzy with passion, and then they do it."

"Right. Except in our version of a date, we *wouldn't* do it, because the guy is so busy respecting the girl he's all discombobulated and thinks he can't possibly treat her with consideration and regard while also humping her into blissful oblivion. Which is what the girl wants more than anything, so actually the guy is *dis*respecting her by not allowing her to get her freak on with him."

"Geez, when you put it that way I sound like a selfish prick."

"Hey, if the shoe fits . . ."

His voice drops. "Allow me to correct you about something, however. I *did* let you get your freak on."

The blatantly sexual tone of his voice makes me squirm. In a good way. "Well. Maybe a little."

"Only a little, hmm? We'll have to do something about that."

*Dear George Carlin in heaven I certainly hope so.*

I turn the conversation to a safer topic before I stick my hand in my pants and start frantically grinding on it. "I should be done here in about an hour, but I need to start house-hunting—"

"That's last on the to-do list," says Brody confidently. "Since you already have a place to stay. With amazing views. And a fantastic landlord. Rent free."

"Rent free? No. I'm not comfortable staying there without paying you anything."

Brody's pause is unnaturally loud. "If you ever say anything so stupid to me again, I'll take you over my knee. *Not in a good way*, before you get too excited."

I can tell by his tone that he's dead serious. But what he doesn't know is that I'm dead serious, too. I pay my own way. I always have and I always will. Nobody's giving me a handout, even if I do happen to be shagging him.

Or whatever it is we're doing.

"We'll talk about this on our date."

His tone turns from stern to playful. "So you accept?"

"You're right, I shouldn't be so hasty. Where are you taking me?"

"Where do you want to go?"

"No, that's not how this works! You're the guy, I'm the girl, you just told me you're supposed to pick me up in your car and take me out to wine me and dine me! I shouldn't have to decide where we're going!"

"You're high maintenance, aren't you? Like super, ultra, mega high maintenance."

I smile. "I can afford to be high maintenance, Kong. I'm the one paying the bills."

"Not with me you're not, Slick."

"I can tell this is going to be a sticking point," I say, chewing on the end of a pencil. "What if we compromise?"

"Sure. We'll compromise by having me pay for everything."

I throw the pencil down. "That's not a compromise, that's a dictatorship!"

"No, a dictatorship is when I don't let you have a say in *anything*. I'm just not letting you have a say in this *one* thing." His voice drops. "And by the way, can I take a moment to say that when you're tied up you're the sexiest, most beautiful, arousing, tantalizing, cock-stiffening woman ever in the history of mankind? You should see your eyes, Grace. You should see your face. The way you look at me makes me feel like a sex god. Fuck, I'm hard just thinking about it."

My heart starts to beat faster. My mouth is suddenly dry. "Another random topic change, but thank you." Feeling something like shyness, I add, "I like the way you look at me, too."

"Yeah? What else do you like?"

His voice has gained that gravelly edge it gets when he's aroused. Hearing it sends a ripple of pleasure down between my legs.

"I like the way you touch me."

"How do I touch you?"

I close my eyes, remembering. "Like . . . you're trying to memorize my body with your hands."

"I am. With my hands, and my mouth."

I nearly groan aloud. His mouth, oh *yes,* his mouth.

"Your pussy is the sweetest thing I've ever tasted, Grace," he whispers. "You're so fucking sweet."

My nipples tingle under my blouse. "I like the way you taste, too. And the way you feel in my mouth. You were so hard for me."

"I'm hard for you right now, too. If I were there I'd get you on your knees and show you just how hard I am."

The memory of his hands around my head as he thrust his cock into my mouth makes me inhale a shaky breath.

He hears it, and makes that sexy growly noise I love so much.

"How do you want me to fuck you, sweetheart? The first time, for real—how should I fuck you? From behind, on your knees, your wrists tied behind your back?"

The sound that comes out of my throat is one I'm almost certain I've never made before. It doesn't even really sound human, but more animal, guttural and low.

"Yes, you like that idea." He chuckles. "Or how about I tie you to one of the posts on the bed in your room and fuck you that way, standing up, your legs wrapped around my waist?"

I lick my lips. There's an ache between my legs, growing hotter.

When I don't say anything, Brody's voice gets harder, somehow even sexier.

"Or how about if I make you suck my hard cock while I punish your perfect ass for coming before you were told, and then I tie you up, and then I lick your sweet little clit until you're begging me for release, and then I spank you some more until your ass is pink with my handprints and you're dripping wet all down your thighs, and *then* I fuck you, nice and slow and deep, sucking and biting your nipples as my cock drives into your throbbing pussy, until you can't take it anymore and you come so hard all the neighbors will hear you screaming my name."

I'm panting. Literally panting, like I just ran a sprint. My nipples throb. The ache between my legs has turned into a pulse. I restlessly press my thighs together, and feel how wet I am.

"Yes."

"Yes, what?"

"Yes, that. I want it that way, the first official time."

"Say please."

*Holy fuck*, the way he says those words. The power, the confidence, the absolute dominance in his tone. It makes me whimper with want.

"I'm waiting, Grace."

I whisper, "Please."

There's a moment where we just breathe at each other. Then Brody asks, "Are you there alone?"

"Yes. I mean, the main door outside is unlocked so anyone could come in—"

"Go lock it."

He doesn't have to ask me twice. I jump to my feet and hustle my ass across the office so fast I practically leave burn marks in the carpet. I lock the outer door to the waiting room, and then I close and lock my office door as well, for good measure. When I sit back down at my desk, I'm breathless with anticipation.

"Okay. Done."

"Do you have a mirror in your office? A big one, like a wall mirror?"

I slowly swivel in my chair and look at the full-length mirror I installed on the back of my office door so I could check my appearance before meeting with clients. Reflected in it, I'm bright red, my cheeks burning. Barely breathing, I say, "Yes."

"Tell me what you see."

I know what he wants, so I give it to him. "I see me . . . all flushed and excited, with red cheeks, sitting in my office chair."

He makes a sound of approval. "Describe what you're wearing."

He already knows because he spent the morning with me, but I'll be damned if I'm going to point that out.

"A white blouse that doesn't fit too well across the chest, a black pencil skirt, and a pair of nude heels that are a size too big. They're Chloe's, because Kat's feet are smaller."

I'm flustered so I'm adding unimportant details, but Brody doesn't seem to care. He says, "A blouse that doesn't fit? We can't have that. Unbutton it."

With shaking fingers, I unhook the small white buttons down the front of the blouse. Beneath it I'm braless.

"Tell me," Brody demands.

"I've unbuttoned it, down to the top of my skirt. I'm not wearing anything underneath. I can see my skin. My cleavage."

His voice caressing, he says, "Open it wider. Tell me what you see."

I use my free hand to open the shirt wider, lifting it back until both my breasts are exposed. I've never really looked at myself like this, when I'm aroused. I look . . . different.

I whisper, "There's a flush all over my chest. My nipples are hard. They're pink against my pale skin, dark pink. The pulse is pounding in my neck."

Brody softly groans. "God, I love your nipples. Touch them."

I cup a breast in my hand, rubbing my thumb back and forth over the taut nub of my nipple, and then do the same to the other one. Sparks fly along all my nerve endings, headed in a fiery path straight down to my pussy. I shift restlessly in the chair.

"It feels good," I whisper, panting softly. "Tingly. I can feel it between my legs when I touch my nipples, like there's a current connecting them."

"Pull up your skirt."

His tone is tense, focused, almost harsh. I obey him without hesitation, sliding my skirt up my thighs until I see the shadowed cleft between them, reflected in the mirror like a secret waiting to be discovered. I whisper, "I'm not wearing panties."

"I know you're not, baby. You have one pair at my house, the pair you wore under the polka-dot dress, but you didn't want to wear those today, did you?"

"No."

"Why not?" The question is so gentle, yet so full of dark laughter it makes me shiver.

He knows why I didn't wear panties today.

He knows exactly why.

"For you," I whisper.

I'm mesmerized by the rapid rise and fall of my chest, the way the sunlight from the windows spills across my bare thighs, trembling ever so slightly, how dark my eyes look with the pupils dilated so wide. In the afternoon light my hair is the color of blood.

I've been told I'm pretty by enough men to believe it must be true, but now, sitting in my comfortable leather office chair with my legs spread and my breasts exposed, staring at myself in a state of full arousal in a mirror I've only ever used to brush a stray wrinkle from a suit jacket, I feel that "pretty" is too anemic, too dainty a word for the savage creature staring back at me.

I'm not pretty. I've never been *less* pretty in my life, or felt more fucking beautiful.

"You make me feel so beautiful," I say, my voice breaking.

"Because you are, Grace. You are."

My heart is beating like a hammer. I can't catch my breath. My hands are damp and shaky.

"You know what I want you to do," says Brody softly.

As if I'm a spectator, I watch as my hand drifts from the arm of the chair, over my thigh, and dips slowly between my legs. I suck in a breath when I feel how ready I am.

"Tell me."

"I'm very wet, and sensitive. It feels . . . swollen. Hot."

He growls, "Stroke your hot little pussy, Grace. Let me hear you stroke it."

The moment my fingers glide over my engorged clitoris, I moan.

Brody mutters an oath under his breath. "Tonight I'm gonna spank you while you play with yourself."

"Yes," I whisper, my fingers moving faster. "Yes, please."

"Spread your legs wider, baby. Watch yourself in the mirror."

I can't get closer to the mirror because of the phone cord, so instead of scooting the chair over to the upholstered ottoman a few feet away, I simply raise my leg and rest it on the edge of the desk. The view is disturbingly intimate, and undeniably sexy.

Listening to my ragged breaths, Brody softly warns, "Don't make me ask you again to tell me what you see."

"I'm so wet I'm glistening. My pussy lips are plump, pink, and very . . ."

"Very what, baby?"

"Voluptuous? Provocative? I don't know the right word. They just look . . ."

He hisses, *"Like they need to be fucked."*

"Oh." It's hardly a sound from my mouth, just a little breath of startled air, forced out by the sudden, violent urge to feel him inside me, to have his cock and mouth and hands possessing me, bending me to his will.

"Stroke your clit, Grace. Pinch it between your fingers and stroke it."

My fingers glide through my wetness. I pinch my clit as he instructed, moaning because it feels so good. My hips start to rock in time with the strokes of my fingertips.

"Faster," he says, his voice tense and hot.

"Yes," I whisper, watching myself in the mirror. "Oh God, Brody. I'm so wet. I'm getting it all over my hand, the inside of my thighs. It's slipping down to my ass."

A snarl of frustration comes through the phone. "My cock is throbbing so hard for you right now. I'm standing in a conference room with glass windows in the middle of the record label's offices, and I'm half a second away from taking out my dick and coming all over this big polished oak table. Fuck, Grace. Fuck."

I say breathlessly, "My thigh muscles are all tensed. My hips are rocking back and forth. My breasts are bouncing I'm rocking so hard. I'm riding my hand and wishing it was you and oh—oh—"

*"Come for me, Grace,"* commands Brody in a throaty rasp.

Instantly, I do.

It hits me so hard I can't make any noise at first. My back arches. My eyes snap shut. My head slams against the headrest. In Chloe's too-big shoes, my toes curl.

The first clench is an entire body clench, every muscle tensed to full capacity. Then come the contractions, waves of pulsing that radiate violently from my core. They shake my body, one after another. I slide my fingers inside myself, desperate to be filled, and cry out.

In my ear Brody is whispering, *"Yes baby come for me God you're so beautiful you're a fucking dream my gorgeous fucking girl. Come—come!"*

I sob, climaxing around my fingers, lost to the strong, rhythmic tightening and releasing of my inner muscles, lost to the sensation, to the pleasure, to him.

I'm lost to him. Brought to orgasm by the simple magic of Brody's words in my ear, I'm completely lost.

And I'm terrified.

This—*this*—is what I've been so careful to avoid all along. This loss of boundaries. This opening of the gates.

This love bullshit, which ruins more lives than it saves, and now has me so unexpectedly in its clutches. *Me*, the tiger! *Me*, the lion! *Me*, the biggest disbeliever of them all!

Panting, sweating, shaking helplessly, I open my eyes and look at myself in the mirror once more.

I'm a mess. A satisfied, terrified mess.

When Brody asks me to tell him what I see, I can't answer.

There aren't any words for when a woman discovers every fear she's ever had are all starting to come true.

# Chapter 25

## Brody

After the phone call with Grace, I have another hour of meetings with the execs at my label, but all I can think about is her.

Why can't I keep my promise that we're going to be friends for the next month?

Every time she touches me I fall apart. She doesn't even have to touch me, just hearing her voice makes me fall apart. All the willpower in the world couldn't save me from this reckless drive to have her.

I hate myself for being so fucking selfish. Her life is in upheaval, everything she owned except her car and the clothes on her back is gone, and all I can think about is getting her naked.

I'm a dick. A dick with no self-control, the worst kind.

And here I was, so convinced after I saw the priest that day on the way to the hospital that I could do the right thing. That I could do good. That by doing good by her somehow I could make restitution for the time I'd been so bad.

I give myself a stern talking-to on the drive from Hollywood back to Malibu. Traffic is shitty, as usual, so it's a long talk. I make a stop to pick up a gift for Grace, and get home just as it's getting dark.

She isn't there yet. It doesn't surprise me how disappointed I am by that.

Magda gives me a lifted eyebrow when I walk in the door, but I'm too lost in my own thoughts to pay much attention. I pour myself a Scotch, go outside to the back patio, and stand looking out at the ocean as I nurse my drink, listening to my demon chuckle darkly in my ear.

# Chapter 26

## Grace

Twenty minutes. That's how long it takes to file a claim with my insurance company for the loss of everything I own. I've had manicures that lasted longer.

Luckily I kept extremely detailed records of all my belongings, right down to photographs, purchase receipts, and written value estimates from my jeweler for each piece of jewelry in my collection. I'm no Elizabeth Taylor, but I did have some beautiful things.

It says a lot about me that I almost mourn my lost vibrator collection more.

It feels so strange to drive to Malibu instead of Century City when I head "home." I'm putting quotes around the word in my head, because I refuse to allow myself to start thinking about Brody's place as anything other than a temporary pit stop. That would be putting the cart *waay* before the horse. Even after shopping for three hours for new clothes, I'm still rattled by what happened today on the phone with him. I still feel like I'm walking around missing a layer of skin.

If I thought I was a goner before, now my armor has been completely stripped away. I'm just a bundle of exposed nerves, feeling everything too strongly.

I pass a hotel on Pacific Coast Highway and almost turn in the drive, but at the last second I convince myself not to be such a coward. A few more nights at Brody's until I find a place won't kill me. And he deserves, at the very least, to be kept informed of my plans.

Not that I have plans, per se, it's more of a general sense of panic that I should be doing something more to keep myself safe.

How do people walk around like this, so soft and open, experiencing everything in such glaring color, such jarring volume? I feel so . . . *naked*, like an egg peeled out of its shell.

The first time I jumped out of a plane at twenty thousand feet I had the exact same sensation, only this time I'm not wearing a parachute.

About a mile out from Brody's on PCH, my phone rings. I pick it up with the hands-free button on the steering wheel.

"Grace Stanton speaking."

A deep baritone rumbles through the car. "Grace."

"Marcus! How are you? Worn out from the three little piggies yet?"

"I just saw the news."

About my building, he means. It's been all over the local newspaper and news station.

His voice is full of concern when he asks, "You all right?"

I think about how to answer that. "I'm coping. It's not the end of the world." I laugh feebly. "Honestly, ex-fuckbuddy who's been friend-zoned, it's not my demolished condo that's the real problem."

After a beat he makes a gentle noise of understanding. "It's your demolished view of your heart as untouchable."

My eyes widen. "You're spooky, you know that? Seriously, how would you even know I was talking about Brody from what I said?"

"Not to be crass, but I've spent a lot of time inside you, Grace. I know you better than you think I do."

I groan. "God, you make me sound like a bus station."

He chuckles. "At least you're an upscale bus station. I spent the remainder of the weekend at the Greyhound depot on skid row."

"I told you to watch out for that cross-eyed blonde."

"Well, a man can't eat filet mignon every night. Every once in a while a greasy burger from a street truck hits the spot just right."

I can't help but laugh. "So in a ten-second phone call we've gone from comparing vaginas to public transportation and cuts of meat. I'm not sure how much lower this conversation can go. If you make a joke about beef curtains I'll never speak to you again."

"Oh," he says, sounding interested. "You were planning on speaking to me again? Even though you tossed my ass in the trash like yesterday's newspaper?"

I roll my eyes. "You're probably just being so pissy because the blonde stole your wallet, right?"

"I'm just worried about you," he replies. "I know you hate being out of control, and between your new boy and your house blowing up, I'm thinking you're feeling about as out of control as it gets."

Fine. So he's insightful. So I might not have been as concrete and untouchable as I thought. If he knows me so well, maybe he can help me get a better grip on things, help me see things from a different perspective.

I ask, "You're a man, right?"

Marcus makes this disbelieving, offended snort. I imagine him sitting at his desk, staring at the phone, wondering who the crazy person is on the other end that he accidentally called.

"Last time I checked. Great to know I made such a lasting impression."

"What I meant to say was that I need a man's opinion."

He sounds interested again. "*You* need a male opinion? Since when?"

"Since right now. And don't make me out like such a raging feminist, I take male opinions into consideration all the time when I'm making decisions."

"Really? Name once."

I try to think of an example, but all I can come up with is when I asked Nico for his opinion about Brody. And if I'm being honest, if Nico had replied that Brody was a major asshole and I should absolutely stay away from him, I doubt that would have made a difference.

I've been quiet too long, because Marcus says, "I already know you can't so you can stop trying to think now. What's the question?"

"Okay fine. If you told a woman who you were very attracted to that you wanted to be friends for a period of time to get to know her better before having sex, what would the reason be?"

Without a single breath of hesitation Marcus says, "Guilt."

I blink. *"Guilt?"*

"Yes. Because I did something wrong and I'm trying to make it right by denying myself the thing I really want from her. You told me this once yourself when we were talking about how fucked-up most people's relationships are. When a man exhibits sexual ambivalence toward his partner, it usually comes down to one of three things: a Madonna-whore complex, confusion related to his sexual orientation, or guilt."

He pauses. "Just a totally uneducated guess because I don't know the guy, but your boy doesn't seem the type for a Madonna-whore hang-up, and he doesn't seem confused about which gender he prefers. So my money's on guilt."

"I was asking about *you*, not him!"

His tone turns dry. "Sure you were. Because you know how often I tell women I want to fuck that I'd like to be friends to get to know them better first."

"Couldn't he just be being a gentleman?"

Marcus pauses before answering. "That was a joke, right?"

I'm hit with a memory. In the hospital on Valentine's Day as we were all waiting for Chloe to have the baby, listening to Nico ask Brody about the stop he'd said he made on the way to the hospital, and watching Brody squirm over the answer.

Strange. It was strange.

But this whole friends first proposal of his only happened after the condo situation. He was gung ho for me before. Wasn't he? Or did I sense some ambivalence before that?

I can't recall.

"You're not talking, Grace. It scares me when you're not talking."

"I'm thinking."

"I know. That's what scares me."

Flanked by a pair of towering palm trees, the large iron gate that opens to the driveway to Brody's guest house appears around the curve in the highway ahead. "Marcus, I have to go. But thank you. You've given me something to think about."

"More thinking," he mutters. "Poor Brody."

"Hey! Whose side are you on?"

"Yours, lady. Always yours. You know where to find me if you need a friend."

Before he hangs up on me, he adds, "A friend who'll *never* have guilt about fucking you, by the way. Something to keep in mind."

When I pull into the driveway and turn off the car, I'm surprised to see rows of white votive candles flickering down both sides of the pathway that lead to the front door of the house. Brody must have lit them in anticipation of my arrival.

*How sweet*, I think, only to hear Marcus in my head shouting, *Guilty!*

"Shut up, Marcus," I mutter. I grab as many bags as I can from the backseat and head inside.

The front door is unlocked. More votive candles line the baseboards in the foyer, bathing the walls in a warm, romantic glow. "Hello?" I call out.

No answer.

I drop the bags on the floor and head into the living room, where the pathway of votives leads. They flare out and surround the large L-shaped leather sofa and glass coffee table in a circle.

On the coffee table are two wrapped presents, tied with red bows.

I'm touched. It's obvious Brody put a lot of thought and care into this. I glance around, expecting him to be peeking around a corner, watching me with that roguish grin, but I'm alone. I sit on the sofa and tear into the first gift.

It's a Polaroid camera.

"I haven't seen one of these in years," I muse, balling up the wrapping paper and tossing it aside. My first thought is that Brody must want to take pictures of me naked, without leaving digital files on his phone. Celebrities get their private email and phone accounts hacked all the time.

This is smart of him. I approve.

When I open the other gift I understand what the camera is really for.

It's a large, rectangular book, bound in brown leather, thick with creamy parchment pages. Embossed in fancy cursive script on the front cover are the words "Making Beautiful Memories."

It's a scrapbook.

A memory book.

For me.

With trembling hands, I open the cover and flip to the first page.

In gold stickers attached to the top of the page are the words "A Look Back." A cutout newspaper story about me opening my practice in the famous Two Rodeo building in Beverly Hills is glued to the page, along with my black-and-white photo, fierce and unsmiling at twenty-five, that accompanied the article.

I wrinkle my nose. I always thought that picture made me look like Nurse Ratched from *One Flew Over the Cuckoo's Nest*. There isn't any life in my eyes.

Next to the article is a picture of my graduating class at Stanford. It must be a printout from the internet. There's a URL in the white part in the upper left corner.

I look at my scowling self, third from the left in the second row. "Jesus," I whisper. "Did you even *know* how to smile?"

I trace my finger over the grainy picture of my face, one of nearly identical hundreds in cap and gown. The commencement ceremony was held outdoors in the stadium on a blisteringly hot Sunday in May. I was sweating and unhappy in that black polyester gown. I got a sunburn that made my nose peel for weeks. Unlike my classmates, none of my family attended the ceremony.

The dead aren't really good for that kind of thing.

After the ceremony I went straight back to my apartment and finished packing for my move to L.A. I left that night and never looked back. I didn't keep in touch with any of my classmates. I didn't leave a forwarding address. I haven't thought about college since.

That ruthless lack of sentimentality I developed after the accident has served me well.

Until now.

I flip to the next page.

More gold stickers at the top of the page declare "Besties Forever!" Beneath is a collage of photos of Kat, Chloe, and me, taken in various places over the years. The pictures are cut in different whimsical shapes: hearts, ovals, squares with scalloped edges.

He must have asked the girls for these. When? I pull my lips between my teeth and blink hard several times.

On the next page is a single picture of Brody. It's a selfie. A Polaroid. He's lying in bed, smiling gently, his eyes heartbreakingly soft. The gold stickers at the top of the page are what finally cause the water in my eyes to crest my lower lids and slide down my cheeks.

They read "My Knight in Shining Denim."

His eyes in this picture . . . it's all right there in his eyes.

The rest of the pages in the book are blank. The Polaroid camera is already loaded with film, ready to make more beautiful memories for me.

Bowing my head, I hug the book tightly to my chest. I've never received a gift like this, one so full of hope and kindness. One so full of love.

I don't know how long I sit there like that before my phone chimes with an incoming text. I swipe at my eyes with my fingertips, set the book carefully on the coffee table, and retrieve my phone from my handbag where I left it near the door.

It's a text from Brody.

*Magda asked if you're coming over here for dinner or if she should bring it over there. What voodoo magic spell have you cast, Slick?? The woman hates everyone but you've got her waiting on you hand and foot. I must know your secret.*

I text back. *What happened to our date? Wining and dining? Picking me up in your car?*

His reply is swift. *You try telling Magda you're going to a restaurant after she made a seventeen-course meal.*

I smile. It's so adorable that he's this big shot rock star but his life is run by his ironfisted housekeeper.

I approve of this, too. Every man needs a strong woman to keep him in line, no matter how powerful he is.

I text him that I'll be there in fifteen minutes. Then I change into a dress I bought this afternoon, a sexy green sleeveless number with a belted waist and a flowy skirt that hits just above my knees, and head over to the main house.

By the time I get there, I'm shivering with cold. February at the beach is different than February in the city. I should've bought a jacket today. Item number four thousand to go on the to-buy list.

When Brody opens the front door, my eyes devour him. He's more dressed up than I've seen him, with the exception of Kat and Nico's wedding. He's in a fitted pale gray button-down shirt, open at the throat to reveal his golden skin and rolled halfway up his forearms, a pair of beautifully cut charcoal-gray slacks, and black leather dress shoes. His normally air-dried and finger-combed hair is damp, slicked back from his face, perfectly neat. Contrasting these polished details are the hint of tattoo peeking from below the second button of his shirt, the small silver earring in his ear, and that leather cuff he likes to wear around his wrist in lieu of a watch.

He looks partly like a king of Wall Street, and partly like a bad boy with a dominant streak.

In other words, panty-melting hot.

The first thing he says is, "You don't have to ring my doorbell, Grace. Just walk in." He reaches for me, pulls me over the threshold, and takes me into his arms. "You're freezing cold!"

Shivering, I burrow against the heat of his chest. "I know. I forgot to buy a coat today."

Brody closes the door behind us with a kick of his foot. Rubbing his hands up and down my bare, goose-pimpled arms to warm them, he grins down at me, eying my dress. "I see you went shopping. Nice."

Smiling, I wind my arms around his neck. "You'll think it's even nicer when you see what's underneath."

His green eyes bright, he raises his brows. "I can hardly wait," he murmurs. Then he looks at my face more closely. "Are you okay?"

My smile wavers. I whisper, "Radical honesty?"

Tension invades his body. His arms tighten around me. "Yes. Always. What's wrong?"

I hide my face in his neck. "The present you got me . . ."

"You didn't like it?" He sounds devastated, which makes my heart throb.

"I loved it. Brody, it's amazing. I've never had anyone do something like that for me. It's so . . . romantic. It's so *you.*"

He exhales a relieved breath. After a moment he says, "I didn't do anything majorly stalkerish for the first part, I just searched your name on the internet to see what I could find to include about your past. There wasn't much except the pic from your graduating class at Stanford and that newspaper article."

When I don't respond, because there's a very good reason there's not much to be found about me on the internet, Brody continues.

"I got the idea from the movie *The Notebook*. I started a journal, too. I'm calling it 'The Story of Us.'" His voice falters, gets quieter. "In case, you know. There comes a time when I have to remind you who I am."

*Fuck.*

I keep my eyes closed, my face pressed to Brody's neck, and just breathe.

"Hey," he whispers, kissing my temple.

"I'm okay," I lie. Then I blow out a hard breath and tell the truth. "Actually, Brody, I'm not okay." I lift my head and stare into his eyes. "I'm terrified."

His gaze burning into mine, he cradles my face in his hands. "Sweetheart. Why?"

I can't find the right words. I stare at him for a moment, my heart pounding, my stomach in knots, until finally I do the only thing I can think of to make him understand.

I take his hand and press it flat over my chest so he can feel the chaos inside. "Because of this. Because I've never felt this. Because before you I had nothing to lose."

With a soft groan, he takes my face in his hands again and kisses me. It's hard and desperate, a kiss like a promise. A kiss like a vow, which his next words repeat.

"I'm never gonna hurt you, Grace. *Never.* I swear to you. All I want to do is spend every day making you happy."

"And if something happens with my memory?" I ask, searching his face.

"You said you could wake up one day and not remember me."

He says it like a statement, but there's a question behind it. I nod, waiting for the rest.

"Have you had any problems since your accident with losing new memories?"

"No," I admit. "But the doctors told me I could—"

"But you haven't," he interrupts firmly. "And I've been thinking. When was the last time you saw a doctor about your memory?"

"Ten years," I answer immediately. I remember the exact date.

Brody repeats slowly, "*Ten years*. You know what? It's time to get another opinion."

I shake my head, wanting him to understand how little hope there is. "Nothing will have changed—"

"Or maybe everything will have. Maybe there's new technology. Maybe there's even something that could be done to help with regaining your old memories. A decade is a long time in the medical world, Grace. A decade is forever."

He makes it sound so reasonable. He makes it sound so possible. He makes it sound like it could be a storybook ending, that my knight in shining denim will be able to make everything right inside my head when no other force in the universe has been able to up to now.

But he's trying. He's hoping. He's not giving up, which is more than I can say for myself.

I gaze at him in wonder. "How are you so perfect? How do you not have one single flaw I can find?"

Darkness crosses his face. It's like a curtain being drawn across a window, or a storm cloud passing over the sun. In a voice I've never heard him use, a terrible voice choked with self-loathing and regret, Brody says, "I have flaws. I just haven't told you what they are yet."

Something about those words makes me go stone cold. My thoughts fly back to the day in the hospital, to the strange way he acted when Nico asked what had delayed him, his odd, shifting gaze and red face.

My pulse picking up its pace, I say, "If we're really practicing radical honesty, now would be a good time to prove it."

Briefly, his eyes close. When they open again they're filled with darkness to match his voice. "Which do you want to hear first? The worst, or the least worst?"

"The worst," I demand, pulling away so I can get a better look at his expression.

Brody stares at me in silence so long I think he might not answer at all. But finally, in a harsh, bitter whisper, he says, "I'm a coward."

Everything inside me rebels against this judgment. "No. That's not true. That's not true at all."

A muscle in his jaw flexes. He swallows, hard. His eyes shine like he has a fever. With horror I realize it's because they're full of tears.

I touch his face. He looks away, ashamed.

"Brody. I want you to tell me what you mean."

He closes his eyes and inhales a deep breath through his nose. His hands drift to my shoulders. He gives them a squeeze. "I will. I promise I will. Just . . . not tonight. I want tonight to be about you, not about me."

"You said you didn't have any secrets!"

His headshake is full of sorrow, like his eyes when he opens them again and focuses his gaze on my face. "Not like you meant. I don't have a secret life, illegitimate kids, a hidden drug problem, any of that. But . . . I . . ."

He trails off. This is excruciating for him to talk about, that much is obvious. Which makes my curiosity and my growing panic all the worse.

Blinking rapidly, he takes another breath. "I once did something, when I was very young. Something stupid."

My relief is huge, like a wave of water breaking over me. "Oh, Brody," I whisper. "Everyone did stupid shit when they were young."

"Not like this."

The way he says that, the flat, absolute certainty of it, convinces me that he believes whatever he did is unpardonable. I can also tell he's punished himself for it a thousand times over, in a thousand different ways.

*Guilty*, whispers Marcus inside my head.

I say slowly, "Okay. We'll talk about this later, when you're ready. But I do have one question for you now."

Brody stands in tense silence, watching me, waiting.

"Are you sorry?"

He answers without hesitation, his voice breaking over the words. "Every minute of every day."

He's telling me the truth. It's in every tortured look, every tremor in his body, every telling crack in his voice.

I frame his face in my hands. Deliberately, looking deep into his eyes, I say, "Then I forgive you."

He stops breathing. His face drains of color. He stammers, "W-what?"

"Life goes on, Brody. We can't take back mistakes we've made, we can only try to do better in the future. If there's a way to make reparations, we do, but if there's not, the only thing to be done is to learn and walk forward with new understanding, new kindness, new humility, and try to do good. All we can do is try our best to be good. If you're doing that, then no matter what might have happened in the past, you're a good person. Nothing is unforgiveable if you're truly sorry. Let your sins be your teachers instead of the cross you hang yourself on."

I gently kiss his lips. His eyes are fierce with unshed tears.

I whisper, "Whatever you did, it's past. It's done. You're sorry, and you're a good person, and I forgive you."

A sob breaks from Brody's chest. Shaking, he sinks to his knees, wraps his arms around my thighs, and hides his face in my dress. Shoulders shaking, he starts to cry.

For a moment I'm stunned speechless, frozen in shock. Whatever it is that's been gnawing at his conscience, he's been holding it in for so long, hating himself for so long, that the simple act of hearing me say it's okay has literally brought him to his knees.

I'm flooded with emotion. My hands shake with it. I rest them on his shoulders, unsure what to do, and stand witness as he cries his guilt out at my feet, washing his soul clean.

Dinner is eaten almost entirely in silence.

Brody and I sit side by side, holding hands under the dining room table, both of us too wrung out yet simultaneously wound too taut to speak. Magda serves us, moving with quiet efficiency to bring courses and clear plates. Her gaze darts between us, taking in our state of fragility, two naked, frightened creatures washed up on unfamiliar shores.

Brody drinks too much wine. He's pale, sweaty, disheveled, looking like he just fell off a cliff and smashed every bone in his body.

As for me? I can only judge by Magda's eyes when she looks at me, by her vigilant, hawk-like expression, as if she's every moment on the verge of calling 9-1-1.

"Have more," she urges me gently in Spanish, gesturing with a serving spoon to the casserole dish in her hand. It's chicken enchiladas with a verde sauce, deliciously succulent, one of at least five other things she's urged me to take a second helping of in the last ten minutes.

Brody was only slightly exaggerating about how many courses she made. Several platters await on the kitchen counter, steaming under aluminum foil, and there's some kind of pastry baking in the oven for dessert, but I know it will all go uneaten tonight.

We're only sitting here out of courtesy and respect for Magda. The only place we both want to be right now is naked in each other's arms.

I feel like we've got a Vulcan mind meld thing going on. As if every emotion he's having, I'm having, as if every thought inside his head is echoed inside mine. It's the most surreal experience. I'm not entirely convinced I'm not on the verge of a mental break.

"PTSD," says Brody suddenly, gazing in wonder at a blob of refried beans on his plate like he's seeing an image of Christ in it. He slowly lifts his head and turns his gaze to me. His eyes are dazed, a little unfocused. "I was diagnosed with PTSD after . . ."

After *it*, he doesn't say. Whatever it is.

My feeling of unreality growing, I whisper, "Me, too."

He looks like I've just told him I found his lost puppy. "Really? That's . . . oh. Wow. So the nightmares—"

I nod. "And the hypervigilance—"

"And the avoidance—"

"Triggers—"

"Anxiety—"

"Depression—"

"Claustrophobia."

I wrinkle my brow. "No. Not for me. Claustrophobia? That's awful."

He nods woodenly, looking back at the refried beans. "Yeah. I have trouble in enclosed spaces. Like planes. Even the big ones make me freak out." His laugh sounds a little unhinged. "Which makes touring with the band super fun."

*So this is why his house is so big and open*, I think, looking around. With the exception of the bedrooms, the entire floor plan is basically that of a loft, all yawning spaces and high ceilings. And you don't get much more wide open than an endless, empty horizon looking out to the sea.

"You don't seem to me like the kind of man with any of those problems," I say softly.

His laugh is without humor. "Some people are better at pretending they're fine than others."

I think, *I know. Like me.*

He and I are so alike, especially in how well we've both perfected our masks. Mine is one of toughness. His is one of lightheartedness.

But inside, we're both battered in all the same ways. Perhaps this is why he feels so familiar, why, as he said, there's a weird connection between us. Because our broken pieces match.

I squeeze his hand. He looks up at me. My eyes pleading, I whisper his name.

That's all it takes.

He jolts to his feet, bringing me along with him. "Magda," he says, his voice husky. "Thank you. And good night."

He turns abruptly, pulling me away by my hand. My last look at Magda is of her standing startled by the end of the dining room table, an oven mitt held in the air in confused farewell.

We stumble down the long hallway toward Brody's bedroom like two toddlers getting used to their new feet. He slams into his bedroom door with a shoulder, throwing it open. He turns to me, his eyes wild.

"Grace," he chokes out. "Grace."

My name is a prayer on his lips. I fall on him, kissing him hungrily, desperately. He swings me up into his arms, kicks the door shut, and takes us down to the bed where we crash against each other, our mouths seeking, our hands grasping, our hearts unfettered, finally breaking free.

*Free free free*, I think, spinning. *I'm like a bird set free.*

When he hears my garbled laugh, Brody stills, panting above me. "What is it?"

"Sia," I answer, reaching up to pull his head down toward me. "I've got a Sia song in my head."

"At least it's not Taylor Swift. I'd be worried we're breaking up."

"Never," I hear myself whisper, as if I'm outside my own body. I kiss him, and say the word again, against his lips, this time as a promise. *"Never."*

Brody softly groans. "I want—I want—"

"I know, honey," I say breathlessly, pressing my pelvis to his. He's already hard.

He groans again, hiding his face in my neck, fighting his instinct to tear off my clothes and bury himself in my body. I feel how hard he's fighting himself, but we need to be done with this. We're past this now. I turn my face to his ear.

"I want you to make love to me. I want you to show me how you feel about me, and I want to show you how I feel about you. With my body, and my hands, and my mouth, and my heart, I want to show you how I feel. I want to bare myself to you. I don't want any more walls between us."

I press my lips to that place on his neck just beneath his ear that makes his entire body shudder. "Make love to me, Brody," I whisper urgently, rocking my hips against him. *"Make love to me and make me yours."*

It's as if my words are a key that unlocks the cage to the dark, animal part of him. An animal I've seen glimpses of, prowling around me, growling and sniffing, hackles raised as I run my fingers through its fur. But now the animal is unleashed. It pounces in all its full, bristling fury, and devours me.

With a snarl, Brody crushes his mouth to mine.

This is no gentle lover's kiss, no sweet, sentimental meeting of lips. This is hard, hungry, and possessive, a claim that sends a thrill straight through me and leaves me gasping for breath. I kiss him back, desperate for the connection, for his taste and the wave of adrenaline sizzling over my skin.

My thigh is drawn up beside his hip. He shoves the hem of my dress up my leg, his fingers digging into my flesh, and breaks the kiss with a growl when he feels the elastic of my stocking against my thigh. He lifts his head, stares at the black garter attached to the stocking, and mutters an oath.

He rears up to his knees and pushes my dress all the way up to my waist.

"Garter belt and stockings," he whispers, breathing hard as he stares down at my spread legs. "And no fucking panties." His eyes, glittering, flash up to meet mine.

Like a rabbit caught in a cobra's hypnotic gaze, I lie still, panting softly, frozen except for the rapid rising and falling of my chest.

We stare at each other as he unbuttons his shirt. It divides between his fingers, falling open to reveal his beautiful skin, the angel's wings tattoo spanning his chest, the hard, bunched muscles of his abdomen. He discards the shirt to the floor.

"There's no running away after this, Grace. There's no going back. You're mine, and I'm yours. And that's it. Understood?"

I want to moan in anticipation but can't find the breath, so I simply nod, never looking away from his face.

He plants his hands on the mattress beside my head and leans down until we're nose-to-nose. "Say yes or no, sweetheart."

I whisper, "Yes."

He takes the plunging neckline of my dress in his hands and rips it wide open.

I gasp, shocked at the sound of tearing fabric, at how quickly he moved, and gasp again as he cups my breasts in his hands, squeezes them together, and falls on me, sucking a nipple into his mouth so strongly I arch off the bed and cry out.

"No bra, either," he whispers, moving to my other nipple. "Such a bad girl. My perfect, bad, beautiful girl."

I'm delirious. The way he praises me with words as he worships me with his mouth—I never knew I could love something so much, that it could feel so natural, so good. I'm a flower, opening her petals to the sun.

He sucks and licks my nipples until I'm squirming beneath him, and then he gives me his teeth. He knows exactly how I like it, how much pressure will make it sting without really hurting, how to make me breathlessly beg for more.

"Please, Brody," I whimper, my hands dug into his thick hair, pulling him closer because I can't get him close enough.

"Don't worry, baby. I'll take care of you." One of his hands finds my thigh, drifts downward as he circles his tongue around a nipple. "You know I'll take care of you."

Very lightly, he slaps me between my spread legs.

I jerk and yelp. He presses his palm over my sex. He lifts his head and gazes into my eyes. His own are hot and half-lidded, dark with lust.

"Which gets punished first, sweetheart?" he softly asks. "Your ass or your pussy?"

I think I might faint from desire. I softly moan.

"I love you like this," he breathes, lightly rubbing his thumb back and forth over my clit, watching me with those predator's eyes. "So soft for me. So unguarded. You're never this vulnerable with anyone, are you, sweetheart?"

"No Brody only for you only *ever* for you."

It's a breathless, incoherent rush, and it makes his jaw harden.

"I think I fell in love with you the first time I saw you, Grace. That badass attitude and those long legs and all this beautiful fucking hair." He bunches his hand in my hair and makes a fist. "I just wanted to bury my face in it. I wanted to drown in it. I wanted to drown in *you*. And now I'm going to, and I'm never gonna come up for air again."

He takes my mouth, pulling my hair so my head arches back. My hips bucking against his other hand, my pulse flying and my body on fire, I dig my nails into his scalp.

"Ass or pussy, love," he growls, nipping my lower lip. "Decide."

I've always believed that actions speak louder than words. So in one swift motion, I roll over beneath him, look at him over my shoulder, and wiggle my behind.

His chuckle is darkly satisfied. "Ass it is."

He stands at the side of the bed, kicks off his shoes, removes my heels and tosses them to the floor. Then he unzips his fly and takes his erection in his fist. He whispers, "On your knees, Grace."

Trembling all over, my mouth dry, I get on my hands and knees. My dress is hiked up over my hips, exposing my bare bottom.

"Come over here."

He holds out his hand. I crawl to the edge of the bed. He steps closer and gently cups my jaw. Looking down at me, he says, "I'm not into pain. Giving it or receiving it. For me this is all about pleasure, both yours and mine."

He waits for me to respond. I whisper, "Same."

"Good. Now, if you want it, ask me to spank you."

I look up at him, letting him see what's in my eyes. All the desire and the need, the permission he's seeking. My voice wavering, I say, "Brody, please spank me."

He nods, satisfied. Moving slowly, he reaches out and caresses my bottom, one cheek at a time, a gentle gliding slide of skin on skin that makes me shiver. He firmly pinches my flesh, and I moan.

His hand tightens around my jaw. His voice comes out raspy with desire. "You'll never know how much I fucking love that sound, Grace. But you have to be quiet. Those little moans of yours make me lose control."

I bite my lip and hold my breath, my entire body primed to his touch. He stares down at me, his face flushed with color, his chest heaving, his jaw hard.

His hand flashes up and down. It cracks across my flesh. I jump and shudder but remain silent.

"Perfect," he whispers. Then he asks, "Harder or softer?"

I choke out, "Harder."

"I'll do three and ask you again. Okay?"

I nod. Between my legs, I'm soaked. I can't ever remember feeling like this, this extraordinary combination of lost and found, of shattered but whole, of finally being safe, and *seen*.

He spanks me three more times in quick succession on the same cheek, his hand firm and sure, his other hand still gripping my jaw, steadying me. When he stops I release a pent-up breath in a noisy rush, then gasp for air.

"More, more, don't stop now!"

"You know what I need to hear."

I whimper. "Please."

He leans down and kisses me. "Play with yourself as I spank you, baby, but *don't come*. I want you to come with my cock inside you, not before."

He straightens. I put my hand between my legs, gasping again when I feel just how soaked I really am, how sensitive under my fingers.

"Tell me."

I groan. "I'm so wet, Brody, I'm so wet for you—"

Crack!

At the first blow, my pussy clenches. I rock my hips into each successive blow, my eyes closed and my mouth open, everything else blotted out of my consciousness except my hand between my legs and Brody's on my ass, claiming me.

When he stops he says gruffly, "I need your mouth, beautiful."

The head of his cock nudges my lips. I open my mouth, greedy for his taste, and suck it in.

His hand tight around my jaw, he inhales a sharp breath. I take him deeper.

His moan is low and ragged, and the sexiest thing I've ever heard.

Softly panting, he says, "Suck me as I spank you, sweetheart, and keep playing with yourself. You get ten more strokes and remember—*don't come.*"

I moan around his cock, and am rewarded with a sharp, stinging slap on my behind.

"I know you did that on purpose," he growls, stroking his hand over my tender flesh to soothe it.

I open my throat and take his hard cock all the way to the base. The zipper of his trousers is cold and sharp on my chin.

He grunts. "So. Fucking. *Good.*"

Crack! Crack! Crack!

I lose count after three. I sink down into myself, past the noise in my head and the sound of the blood screaming through my veins, past all thought and memory. I exist on a plane of pure sensation, untethered from time, untouched from all worries. Each stroke of my fingers over my clit, each swirl of my tongue around his cock, each blow of his hand that rocks my body, making my breasts swing and heat bloom over my ass, takes me deeper.

Finally I become aware of Brody moaning my name. "Not yet, Grace, don't make me come yet!" He moves his hand to my throat and lightly squeezes.

I'm so close to orgasm it takes an enormous effort of will to remove my hand from between my legs and wrap it around the base of Brody's cock. I open my eyes and gaze up at him, only to find him staring down at me with a look of utter adoration.

He swallows and moistens his lips. "You okay?"

I slide his cock out of my mouth, furling my tongue around the head. "More than okay."

His laugh is husky. "You look a little blissed out. You sure you didn't come?"

I shake my head.

"Good." He pushes me back by my shoulders. "Let's see how well you can obey me when I've got my mouth between your legs."

I fall flat to the mattress. Brody whips off the belt of my dress, a soft length of fabric tied in a bow at one side of my waist, and wraps it around his hands. He commands, "Put your arms over your head."

*Oh God. He's going to tie me up. He's going to do exactly what he said he'd do on the phone and tie me up and—*

"That's right," he says softly, watching my face. "Now do as you're told."

Trembling, I lift my arms overhead and rest them against the pillow. Brody leans over me and binds my wrists together, wrapping the belt around and between them. He takes the two loose ends and ties them into a loop, which he then pulls under the edge of the mattress to the right side of my head and ties off around the leg of the headboard. He then steps out of his slacks and briefs, peels off his socks, and stands there gazing down at me, stroking his erection.

I bend my knees so my dress slides up my thighs, exposing me, and watch his expression transform.

The wolf is on the prowl again.

He kneels on the bed between my spread legs. Sliding his hands along my thighs, he pinches the tender flesh here and there, testing it first with his hands and then his teeth as he leans in to draw it into his mouth. The feel of his tongue on my flesh, so soft and warm, sucking, makes my pulse go haywire all over again. He blows a breath of air between my legs, chuckling when I start to rock my hips, eager for his mouth.

He whispers a warning. "Make any noise and I won't let you come."

Then he lowers his head and gives me what I need.

I arch sharply off the mattress, biting my tongue to stay quiet, straining against the bindings around my wrists, my eyes squeezed shut. Brody slides two thick fingers inside me and presses them deep, making gentle circles as he swirls his tongue around my clit. With his free hand he reaches up and cups my breast, and then pinches my aching nipple between his thumb and forefinger.

Pleasure builds and builds and builds, coiling hotly around that bright center of Brody's clever tongue, until I'm panting hard and loud and my legs are quivering.

"God, you're beautiful," comes the reverent whisper from between my legs. "You're close, aren't you?"

"Yes." The word is gritted out through clenched teeth. I'm right *there*, right at the edge, teetering.

Brody flips me onto my belly, presses a hand flat to the small of my back to hold me in place, and then starts to spank my behind again, lighter than before but faster, back and forth from side to side, creating a rhythm that sends shockwaves pulsing through my lower body. He keeps it up until my ass is burning and I'm grinding my pelvis against the bed.

I cry out his name. He stops abruptly and leans over me.

"Talk to me."

I sob, "I'm so close I'm so fucking close, please Brody, please *please*!"

His breathing is as rough as mine. He smooths a hand over my stinging behind, and then slides his fingers down between my thighs.

"Fuck," he whispers. "You're drenched, sweetheart. You loved that, didn't you?"

My only answer is a broken, pleading sob.

His fingers slide over my pulsing clit. I jerk, crying out again.

Brody whispers, "Shhh. Baby, hush."

I whimper into the pillow. "I need to come so bad. Please make me come."

He bites me softly on the shoulder, and then nuzzles my ear, nosing aside my hair. His hand is still between my legs, gently stroking, keeping me right on the razor's edge.

"Let me get a condom."

"I'm clean," I say immediately.

"Me, too. But—"

"And I'm on the pill."

Brody's exhalation is half growl, half groan. "You want me to fuck you bare, sweetheart?"

I open my eyes and look at him. In a harsh whisper I demand, "Make me yours. Come inside me and make me yours."

Brody takes my head in his hands and kisses me so hard I can't breathe.

Then he rolls me over again and hooks my leg over his arm so I'm spread open wide. He guides the head of his throbbing cock to my wet entrance, takes one of my nipples into his mouth, and begins to suckle it, holding himself still, not pushing forward inside me.

I groan, pulling hard against the ties around my wrists and rocking my hips so the head of his cock is sliding up and down, slipping through my folds. It's friction, but it's not enough. I'm out of my mind with need.

Brody eases forward an inch. I moan brokenly, calling his name.

Then I start to beg.

"Please fuck me. I need you to fuck me. I need it *now*, Brody, *now*, please—"

"So demanding," he whispers, and flexes his hips. It takes him another inch inside.

I moan in frustration, loud and long. Into my ear Brody breathes, "Oh, sweetheart, you know what I said about that."

He curls his fingers around the stocking on my left leg and rips it right off the garter by pulling it sharply down my thigh. The delicate nylon tears apart like gossamer. The garter springs back. He bends my leg, yanks the stocking all the way off, and then balls it up and shoves it in my mouth.

Then, with one hand gripping my ass and one cradling my head, he thrusts inside me.

My sob of pleasure and relief is muffled by the stocking.

Brody puts his mouth next to my ear. Whispering how much he adores me, how good I feel, how he'd do anything for me, he starts to fuck me as he said he would on the phone, deep and slow. His breath is uneven, his body is heavy, hot and shaking on top of mine.

I come fast and hard, convulsing beneath him, crying out against the stocking, feeling the slap of his balls against my ass as he fucks me with firm, rhythmic strokes of his cock. He kisses my breasts and neck and face, his big hands roaming all over my body.

"Grace," he gasps, thrusting faster. He grips my head in both hands and stares down at me, so I see the exact moment it happens. His eyes close. A sound comes from his throat, deep inside him, a guttural noise of pleasure. Then he comes, jerking and groaning, gasping for air.

"Grace," he rasps, shuddering on top of me. "My saving Grace. My angel."

Still moving inside me, he presses his cheek to mine.

I don't know if the wetness I feel there is from his tears or mine, but I do know, with every wild, painful beat of my heart, in all the dark, abandoned parts of my soul, that he's got it wrong. It isn't me who's saved him.

It's him who's saved me.

*Hallelujah.*

# Chapter 28

We sleep. I awaken sometime in the night, whimpering from a bad dream, but Brody is there, shushing me gently, stroking my back, cradling me against him. Soon I'm quiet and fall back into slumber in his arms.

When the day breaks gray and still outside, he makes love to me again, but this time slower, softer, and silently. There are no words or bindings or spankings. There are only our bodies and shared breaths, a mutual sense of wonder reflected in our eyes.

We sleep again.

When next I awaken it's to a brilliant blue sky and the smell of frying bacon.

Brody is gone. On his pillow are three Polaroid pictures of us, taken while I was sleeping, my head tucked into his neck. He's looking into the camera with the expression of a man who's converted to a new religion.

With the pictures is a note.

*Grace,*

*I don't know who I am today. Yesterday I was someone else, someone smaller. Today I looked in the mirror and it's like I grew a foot taller and understand things I didn't understand before. I feel like a new man. A better man.*

*Because of you.*

*I didn't want to wake you because you looked so peaceful. I went surfing. Will be back by 8. I hope you don't think it's creepy that I took pictures while you were sleeping, but I wanted to capture the moment for the memory book. The moment we first became Us.*

*Yours,*

*Brody*

*PS – I'm crazy about you.*

*PPS – I absolutely adore you.*

*PPPS – I'm so fucking insane over you. I'm out of my mind.*

The sheet of paper trembles in my hand. I realize my cheeks are wet, and start to laugh. How is it possible for the human body to hold so much emotion? How is it possible that I'm not splitting wide open with all the hope and terror and joy I'm feeling?

I don't know. I don't care.

Right now I really just need some bacon.

I leap out of bed. My new dress is on the floor, demolished. I pick it up, laughing again, and hug it to my chest. I spin around in the middle of the room with my arms flung wide like Julie Andrews in the mountain meadow when she played the nun in *The Sound of Music*. Except naked.

And I'm no nun.

I take a shower, singing show tunes at the top of my lungs.

When I'm done with the shower, I rifle through Brody's drawers and steal another T-shirt, this one advertising Bad Habit, how apropos, and a pair of his sweats, which I have to roll up at the ankles and fold over at the waist. Then I head out to the kitchen and the delicious scent of breakfast.

"Magda!" I shout when I see her at the stove, cooking.

She jumps and turns to look at me.

I spread my arms and smile. *"BUENOS DÍAS!"*

She snorts, rolls her eyes, and turns back to the stove, shaking her head. I go up behind her and give her a hug.

Poking at sizzling bacon with a metal spatula, she says to me in Spanish, "He's a slob, you know. A terrible slob, worse than a pig. You think this house is so clean because of him? No. Also, he doesn't call his mother enough. And he uses a pore-reducing facial mask. What kind of a man does this? Ech. He's too pretty for his own good. But if you can get past all these character flaws, I think you will be happy with him. He's trainable," she says with a shrug, like that's the most we women can hope for in a life partner.

"You've done a good job with him," I say.

She pauses her stirring to contemplate the bacon. "He was a wild thing when he was a boy. I worried that he'd turn out bad. But he learns from his mistakes. Like I said," she begins to stir again, "trainable."

Eager to hear stories of Brody as a boy, I'm just about to pepper Magda with questions when the man himself walks in through the patio doors.

He's barefoot and dripping, still in his wetsuit, smiling a smile that would put the sun to shame. "My two favorite girls in the kitchen," he says, his gaze trained on me, green eyes alight.

Magda barks something at him in Spanish that I don't bother to translate. I run over to him and fling my arms around his neck.

He laughs, staggering back a few steps. "Whoa. Did someone have a Red Bull this morning?"

I smile up at him, not caring at all that the front of my T-shirt is getting wet. I whisper, "Someone had a raging bull last night."

Grinning, he lowers his head and kisses me. He tastes like the ocean, sweet and salty. "You're getting better at those compliments, Slick. Keep 'em coming."

"Yes, sir!" I reply. He lifts an eyebrow.

*Looks like I'm trainable, too.*

Pointing with her spatula at the towels she left for him on a little table by the patio doors, Magda shouts at Brody to dry off before coming in the house. Though it's spoken in Spanish, he gets the idea.

"As you command, evil overlord," he says seriously. He bows.

Magda and I share a look. She turns back to the stove, smiling.

Brody dries off and goes to change while I help Magda set the table. Though she protests we should have our privacy, I insist she have breakfast with us. When Brody reappears and sees the two of us getting ready to sit down, he smiles.

"You're looking a little misty-eyed over there, Kong," I observe, watching him pull out his chair. When he sits down, I pass him the bowl of seasoned home-fried potatoes.

He takes it from me and scoops some onto his plate. "Honestly? I feel like I won the lottery or something."

Magda yells at him that he did and he better not fuck it up. Brody looks to me for help.

I try not to laugh when I say, "She said she really loves you. That's all."

His lips twist. "Hmm. I see I'm outnumbered."

Magda brings over a plate of bacon on paper towels and a bigger plate piled with scrambled eggs and dusted with Mexican *cotija* cheese. She pours glasses of fresh-squeezed orange juice from a pitcher, sits down at the table with us, folds her hands under her chin, and closes her eyes.

When Brody and I just sit there looking at her, she opens her eyes. "Grace!" she barks.

She doesn't mean my name.

Though I'm as religious as a garbanzo bean, I obediently fold my hands together and bow my head. Sitting across from me, Brody does the same, hiding his smile behind his clasped hands.

"Good morning, God," begins Magda, sounding like they're business partners. She's praying in English, which means she wants Brody to understand what's being said. "We thank you for this food, and for this day, and for this family. We thank you for the blessings of our health, and our friends, and the many bounties of this life you have given us."

*I was given this life because I'm strong enough to live it.*

Given by whom? I never thought to ask myself before now. I listen with my heart beating harder as Magda continues.

"We thank you for the lessons you teach us, even when they're hard, and for loving us, even when we don't deserve it. We thank you for forgiving us all our many sins, and we promise to always do the same for each other. No matter what. Amen."

There's a moment of silence so stark I'm sure I can hear my fingernails growing. Then Magda makes the sign of the cross over her chest, and happily begins to eat.

Brody and I stare at each other across the table. He swallows, his Adam's apple bobbing up and down. He reaches out for my hand. When I grasp it, his fingers are trembling. He squeezes. I squeeze back.

And just like that, over bacon and eggs and a morning prayer, a pact is sealed between us.

Forgiveness, no matter what.

From the corner of my eye, I see Magda smile.

Brody has a taping for Jimmy Kimmel's late-night talk show with the band today, so after breakfast I'm left to my own devices.

My "devices" include floating through the air as if on clouds, dreamily unpacking the clothes I bought yesterday and hanging them in the closet in the guest house bedroom, and calling Kat, only to forget what I wanted to say by the time she picks up.

"What's the matter with you, space cadet?" she asks when it becomes apparent I have no idea why I'm calling. When I don't answer quickly enough, she gasps.

"You got the D!" she screams gleefully.

*Boy, did I ever.*

"I . . . oh, Kat. Why didn't you warn me it would be like this?" I ask feebly, staring at myself in the bathroom mirrors. My cheeks are red. My eyes are wild. I look like I just snorted a line of heroin.

The laughter on the other end of the phone is raucous, and lasts a ridiculously long time.

"I hate you," I say, only that sounds dreamy, too.

"The bigger they are, the harder they fall!" she crows. In the background I hear a voice asking her what's going on. She covers the phone with her hand, but not tightly enough, so I hear her muffled response.

"Brody has entranced Grace with his enchanted penis and now she's in love!"

"I can hear you, idiot! And who are you talking to?"

She comes back on the line. "Chloe and Abby are over. What're you up to today?" She giggles. "Besides being dick dazzled."

I run my hand through my hair, watching it sift through my fingers, fascinated for some strange reason by the fiery color of it, the way it drifts down to my shoulder like feathers on a breath of air. "Nothing. I . . . I'm off this week. I need to go house hunting, and shopping, and . . ."

When I trail off, distracted by the weird glowing light behind my eyes, Kat starts to laugh again.

I say, "Kat."

"Yes, Gracie?"

"I owe you an apology."

"An apology?" she repeats, confused. "What for?"

I touch my cheek, feeling the burn. "For any time I didn't support you about what you felt for Nico. For any time I mocked it or said something insensitive or was a horrible, cynical bitch. I just didn't . . ." I inhale a shaky breath. "I just didn't understand."

After a short pause, Kat whistles. "Wow. You've got it bad, don't you?"

I close my eyes, nodding. "Yes. The worst. And to be completely honest, I'm so happy I could die and so scared I could piss myself. I have no idea what to do."

Kat says gently, "Join the club, Titanium."

I groan, covering my eyes with my hand. Kat hurries to add, "But don't worry, it gets better. The terror recedes. I mean, a little. And if you're together long enough you'll get bored of him and won't want to have sex with him anymore and he'll start to irritate you and it will get easier."

My eyes widen. "Is that true?"

She laughs. "No. I was just trying to be helpful. If it's true love, it doesn't change. Ever. Every time he walks into a room you'll still feel those butterflies. Every time he smiles at you you'll still feel like you're home. Did you think all those books and songs and plays about love that have been written over thousands of years were bullshit?"

I think about it for a minute. "Well . . . yes."

She sighs. "I kinda feel sorry for your patients right now."

My patients. Holy shit, my patients! How will I ever face the wife who admitted she's only staying married because her husband is filthy rich but she's in love with the gardener, or the husband with five children who thinks he might be in love with his secretary—his *male* secretary?

Everything is so much more complicated *when you understand.*

Love isn't a problem to be parsed out on a spreadsheet with columns of pros and cons. Love isn't something you weigh against money, or duty, or convenience. Barney was right: love is everything.

Love is the only fucking thing that matters, the only really *real* thing there is.

I burst into tears.

"Grace!" Kat cries. "Oh my God! Are you—are you *crying*?"

"The worst part is that I can't *unknow* it!" I sob, my shoulders shaking, tears streaming down my face. "Now that I *know*, I can't go back to the way I was before!"

Kat's sigh is soft. "Oh, sweetie. Welcome to the human race." She pauses. "You'll like it here. There's a lot of weeping and stupid fights, but we have really good make-up sex."

In between my tears, I start to laugh.

"Atta girl. Now you've got the idea," Kat says. "Just keep that up for the next few months straight and you'll have a glimmer of understanding of what the rest of us have been going through since birth."

"That sounds exhausting."

"It is. You'll live. So are you coming over or what?"

"I am. And I love you, Kat. I love you so much."

She mutters, "Holy Christmas, now she's so nurturing she's practically a womb."

"I'll be there in an hour."

"We'll be waiting with bells on. And Grace?"

"What?"

I can feel Kat's smile over the phone. "I love you, too."

On the drive to Kat's, my insurance company calls to say that if I can sign all the claim paperwork today, the settlement for my condo and temporary living expenses will be in my bank account within seven business days. I make a detour to their offices, and arrive at Kat's feeling like I have a new lease on life.

Because I learned from my parents to have everything I own insured to the teeth, I'm looking at a substantial chunk of cash. I had no idea my condo had gone up in value so much since I bought it, and had forgotten about the annual inflation clause in the insurance policy that increased the value of things like my jewelry from their actual purchase price.

For obvious reasons, I did *not* include my cherished vibrator collection in the policy.

I'll have to ask Brody if he thinks I'll require replacements. That's a conversation I'm very much looking forward to.

By the time I ring Kat's doorbell, I'm grinning like a maniac.

She opens the door and blinks at me. "I'm sorry, we don't allow solicitors here."

"Solicitors?"

"Yes. Judging by that zealous smile, you're obviously with some crackpot religious outfit and are here to discuss my relationship with God. And when I tell you I'm in tight with the man upstairs, you're going to ask me for money. Go sell crazy somewhere else."

She slams the door in my face.

Two seconds later it opens to reveal Chloe, laughing.

I say, "Is she getting weirder in her old age?"

Chloe replies, "She's a total whack job. And she's talking about getting *cats*, so we might want to arrange an intervention. Come in."

She pulls me over the threshold, closes the door behind me, and gives me a hug. Looking effortlessly gorgeous in a simple white shirt and blue jeans, ballet flats on her feet, her long blonde hair in a ponytail and not a speck of makeup on her face, she sets her hands on my shoulders.

"I hear you're in love."

I purse my lips. "Is that what you call it when you feel like you have been electrocuted and injected with mind-altering chemicals, are deliriously happy but also constantly on the verge of panic, and are so horny you could be a case study for a book on nymphomania?"

Chloe says, "Yes."

"Shit. I was hoping it was the stomach flu."

With an expression you'd wear to a funeral, she says, "Congratulations."

I raise my brows. "I'm sorry, what have you done with my friend Chloe? The bright and shiny one with the Day-Glo smile and the My Little Pony obsession who still believes in Santa Claus?"

She ignores that. "Have you had your first fight yet?"

"We just had sex for the first time last night. If we're fighting already, there's trouble in paradise."

Her smile is knowing, and a little sad. "Oh, there's always trouble in paradise, girlfriend. And it'll catch up to you when you least expect it. So I'm going to give you a piece of advice I learned the hard way to save you some pain when trouble finally shows up: Don't. Run. Away."

I look around for help from some other, more sane person. I call out, "Are there any normal people at home today?"

Chloe gives my shoulders a shake. "I'm not kidding, Grace."

I look more closely at her. "Chloe, is everything all right?"

She inhales a long breath through her nose, and then drops her hands to her sides. "Actually," she says, her lower lip trembling, "I think A.J. is dying."

She might as well have just reached into my chest, grabbed my heart, and ripped it out. I gasp, horrified. "*No*! Chloe, tell me you're not serious!"

"You know I would never joke about that."

I throw my arms around her and hug her as hard as I can. Into my hair, she whispers, "I don't think I can live without him, Grace. I don't think I'm strong enough to go on if he—"

"Don't you *dare* say that!" I pull back and grip her by her upper arms. "You have Abby to think about now! You can't indulge in that kind of nonsense, not even for a second!"

Her face crumples. "I know," she whispers, shaking. "I know. But the thought of being without him . . ."

She can't say anything more, because she dissolves into tears.

I hug her again, more gently this time. My heart feels like it might explode with all the pain inside it. I can't even imagine what Chloe must be feeling right now. "What does his doctor say?"

She sniffles. "I finally got him to make an appointment. It's in a few weeks. That's the soonest they could fit him in."

"Wait." I pull away again, searching her face. "So this is just a feeling of yours? You don't have any evidence?"

"He's getting these terrible headaches! And he's tired all the time!"

That's all she offers as proof of A.J.'s impending demise. I'm so relieved I could faint. "Sweetie, you're doing this thing called 'awfulizing.' It's when you overestimate the potential consequences of a perceived threat—"

"He's not himself," she protests. "He's sick, I can tell!"

"Okay," I say, keeping my voice soothing. "I believe you. But until he sees the doctor, let's keep our thoughts positive, all right? It could be something serious, but it also could be something simple. For both A.J. and Abby's sake, you need to try to focus on good thoughts. For your sake, too. You're the glue holding your family together, Chloe. You have to be Super Glue. And Kat and I are here to be *your* Super Glue, okay?"

I cup her wet face in my hands. "No matter what happens, we've got your back. Always. In all ways. You will never, ever have to go through anything alone. Nod if you believe me."

She nods, sniffling, her eyes red and her face blotchy. I blow out a breath, straighten my spine, and say, "Good. Now let's have a drink."

"It's eleven o'clock in the morning."

"Yeah, well, it's 10:00 p.m. in Tanzania."

Chloe looks confused. "What the hell is in Tanzania?"

"Mount Kilimanjaro."

Her face brightens. "Oh yeah, I remember when you went there. Do you ever hear from that guide—what was his name? The one who was so in love with you and kept emailing all that terrible poetry? Chicken?"

"Rooster. And no, the last I heard he moved to Indonesia and became a Trappist monk."

"Wow, Grace. Way to ruin a guy's life."

"It's not *my* fault he decided to retreat from society and live with a bunch of guys in robes on the side of some desolate mountain!"

Wiping away her tears, Chloe smiles at me. "Sure it's not."

I return her smile. "You're a terrible friend."

"Yet you love me. Now let's go get that drink."

"I thought you'd never ask."

We link arms and walk toward the kitchen, where we can hear Kat and Abby having a spirited back-and-forth about the ideal temperature for reheated breast milk in a bottle.

Kat's doing Abby's voice as Darth Vader.

I love my friends.

I end up spending the rest of the day at Kat's. We eat, and swim, and play with Abby, who is the world's most adorable infant. She has her mother's innate happiness, smiling at everything, cooing and gurgling like an advertisement for the joys of motherhood.

"I love this kid," I say more than once, staring at her. "How awesome is this kid?"

Kat and Chloe share one too many secret smiles when I say that, and I have to tell them to shut up.

After we make plans to go with Kat to the fertility clinic on Friday, I drive back to Malibu in the late afternoon, into the setting sun, listening to Frank Sinatra at full blast, feeling like a million bucks. A Jeep full of teenage boys pulls up alongside me at a light on PCH. They start to catcall and yell sexually aggressive things, rambunctious as a bunch of dumb puppies. I smile, blow them a kiss, and leave them in the dust when the light changes.

Brody isn't home yet when I get back to the house, so I pour myself a glass of wine and take a bubble bath. I must doze off because the next thing I know I'm hearing the mechanical pop and whirr of a Polaroid camera.

I open my eyes and find Brody standing at the edge of the bathtub, grinning at me.

"Is it wrong that I keep taking pictures of you when you're unconscious?"

I smile up at him. He's sexy as hell in what I think of as his rich-bad-boy-musician attire, lots of tight denim and black leather, motorcycle boots, and bohemian silver jewelry, with incongruously perfect hair and a chunky platinum diamond-encrusted watch.

He's so L.A., and I love it.

"Technically I think it's illegal, but I hereby give you permission to photograph me in any state of consciousness. Or undress." I bat my eyelashes at him and float up a few inches, so my boobs, rimmed in bubbles, poke out above the water. "After all, it's for posterity."

Brody stares at my wet, bubble-slicked breasts. His voice husky, he says, "Posterity. I forgot what that word means."

I giggle. "Just take a picture, Kong."

He does. Then he sets the camera and the undeveloped print on the sink counter, kneels, and plunges his arms into the bathwater. I squeal as he grabs me and lifts me out of the tub, dripping wet.

"Brody!"

"Grace," he answers calmly, standing. He turns and heads into the bedroom. We leave a trail of bubbles behind us, floating to the floor.

I cling to him, laughing in disbelief. "What the hell are you doing?"

"Taking my woman to bed."

We reach the bed in just a few strides of his long legs. He drops me on the mattress so I bounce, still laughing, and before I can do or say anything else he's on his elbows and knees with his fingers digging into my hips and his mouth, hot and greedy, between my legs.

I arch instinctively, my laughter swallowed by a groan.

"Thought about this beautiful fucking pussy all goddamn day," he mutters, sliding a finger inside me. "I can't get enough of you, Grace. I'll never have enough."

He goes right back to sucking, his tongue lashing my clit, his finger pressing deep. I cup my breasts and pinch my hard nipples, feeling his approving groan right in the center of my body, vibrating through me.

I whisper breathlessly, "I missed you, too."

He straightens, rips down the zipper of his jeans, frees his hard cock, and, without removing any of his clothes, shoves it inside me.

I cry out. He starts to fuck me, hard, with no preliminaries.

"Look at you," he whispers, his eyes devouring me, thrusting into me so my breasts are bouncing and the whole bed is shaking. He lifts my legs, hooks my ankles over his shoulders, and grips my ass, lifting my pelvis off the bed so when he thrusts into me again the angle has changed. Deepened. I cry out once more, this time louder.

Bubbles are flying everywhere. I'm completely wet, he's mostly wet from the plunge into the bathtub and carrying me, and we're both frantic.

When I'm gasping, on the verge of orgasm, Brody abruptly pulls out of my body, flips me over, puts an arm under my waist, and hikes my ass in the air so my face is buried in the pillow. Then he starts to spank me.

I close my eyes and grip the bedcovers in my fists, biting back my moans of pleasure.

"All day I dreamed of this," he growls through a clenched jaw. "This gorgeous ass pink from my hand and your little sounds as I fucked you and you tried so hard not to come. You fucking own me, Grace. *You own me.*"

The spanking ends, replaced by the hot, hard slide of his cock deep inside me.

He bends over my body so his chest is pressed to my bare back, fists a hand in my hair, and flexes his pelvis, pumping into me again and again.

My bottom stings. My nipples ache. I'm dripping between my legs, throbbing there, every shove of his thick cock inside me pushing moisture down my thighs. It's somehow hotter because I'm nude and he's fully clothed, hotter still because he couldn't wait to have me long enough to get undressed, or let me dry off, or even take off his boots.

He reaches around and pinches my clit between his fingers, and I come.

"Oh fuck yes let me hear you scream, love," he breathes as I wail through my orgasm. He rubs his fingers back and forth over my engorged clit, faster and faster, until I'm convulsing, mindless, lost to the enormity of the pleasure he's giving me.

I sob his name.

He grunts, thrusting into me with forceful jerks of his pelvis. "God," he gasps. "Fuck oh God Grace *Grace—*"

He stills, and then shudders. A long, low moan breaks from his chest. Then he spills inside me, his hand wrapped around the place our bodies are joined, stroking both of us as he gasps through his orgasm, my own orgasm still rocking me so I'm clenching around him as he's pulsing into me.

*Forever*, I think, riding a wave of pure bliss.

*I want this to last forever and ever amen.*

Stupid.

I knew, even at that moment some part of me knew, but, overwhelmed by my feelings of euphoria, of being like the lyric from that song—a bird set free—I ignored the one truth I'd seen over and over again in my years of counseling couples.

Love can set you free, but it can also kill you.

And what a cold death mine would turn out to be.

# Chapter 30

The next few days pass in a blur. Bad Habit is recording their next album, so Brody spends the mornings with me, making love at dawn followed by an hour or two of surfing, and his days in the studio. I hire a realtor and begin the hunt for new digs, which is more challenging than I thought it would be, partly because I have more money to spend than I did last time I was in the market.

"Boo hoo," says Kat without the slightest hint of sympathy when I tell her my plight. "You poor, sad rich person. Talk about first-world problems. You're like the poster child for the one percent!"

It's Friday. We're driving with Chloe to Kat's appointment at the fertility clinic. Her mood is Terminator meets Predator, with a healthy dash of hangry Godzilla thrown in.

"And why are you even looking for a new place to live anyway, when you've got the absolute *most* perfect situation right now?"

Ignoring that obvious lure, I chastise her instead. "One percent? If I may correct you, Katherine, I was *not* born with a silver spoon in my mouth. I worked my ass off to get where I am now, I saved every penny I made, and I made a few smart investments along the way. And I'm comfortable, *not* rich." I send her a pointed stare.

"I'm not rich, either!" she protests.

"Excuse me," pipes in Chloe from the backseat, "but California is a community property state. Nico's rich, and you're married to him, which means *you're* rich."

I glance at Chloe in the rearview mirror. "Same goes for you, Goldilocks. When you and A.J. get married, that is."

They'd planned on getting married after the baby was born because Chloe didn't want to do an aisle march with a baby bump, but I haven't heard any news of late. I'm hoping she'll spontaneously provide some information, but she just shrugs, looking out the window.

"The money doesn't matter to me."

Kat swivels around in her seat to glare at her. "It doesn't matter to me, either!"

"Honey, I wasn't saying it does—"

"And how do you know I didn't sign a prenup that prevents me from getting anything if we divorce?"

I'm so surprised I almost drive off the road. "Nico made you sign a prenup?"

Kat turns back to look out the windshield, slouches down in her seat, and crosses her arms over her chest. "No," she admits churlishly. "But he could have. I would've signed one, too. It's his money, not mine."

Chloe sits forward and squeezes Kat's shoulder. "Kat. Cut it out."

Kat turns her head a quarter of an inch. "Cut what out?"

"You know what."

"No, I don't."

Chloe looks at me. "Grace will tell you. It's called awfulizing."

Kat blows out a noisy breath through her lips and slouches down farther in her seat.

I reach over and squeeze her arm. "He's not going to divorce you if—and this is a *big* if—you can't have kids."

Kat grumbles, "I never said he would."

Chloe winds her arms around Kat's shoulders from behind and gives her a hug. They sit in silence like that for the rest of the trip to the doctor's office. Every once in a while I look over and see Kat swallowing hard, blinking back tears.

She really wants to have Nico's baby.

*I wonder if Brody wants kids. He said his mother wanted more grandchildren, and he's always joking about getting me pregnant . . .*

As I'm pulling into a parking space in the medical building's lot, Kat asks, "You okay, Gracie?"

"Sure. Why do you ask?"

"You're looking a little pale over there."

I put the car in park, turn it off, and sit staring blankly at the steering wheel. My mind has started to spin.

Chloe says, "Earth to Grace. Come in, Grace."

Gathering my thoughts, I listen to the engine tick as it cools. I look up to find Chloe and Kat staring at me with identical looks of worry. I open my mouth, close it, open it again, and say, "I've never, not once in my entire adult life, thought about having children. Until right now."

They watch me, eyes wide, waiting.

"Motherhood is something I never contemplated, because why torture myself with thoughts of the impossible? It was something I couldn't have and didn't want. Period. But . . ." I draw a breath. "What if the real reason I never wanted children is because I never met a man whose children I wanted to have?"

Stunned silence.

I understand why they're so shocked. I'm shocking myself, too.

"And following that thought to its logical conclusion," I continue, "what if I met a man whose children I *wanted* to have? What if *he* wanted to have children? What the hell would I do then? Because I can't . . . I couldn't . . ."

I look back and forth between them. "What kind of a monster would want a child she might forget she ever had?"

Kat's eyes well with water. She whispers, "Oh, sweetie. Oh fuck."

I turn my gaze to the view outside the windshield to avoid the look of pity in their eyes.

Chloe's hand on my shoulder is warm. She leaves it there a moment, reassuring, and then says quietly, "For what it's worth, I think you'd be an incredible mother."

I close my eyes against the anguish that explodes like a bomb in my chest.

At that moment, a text comes through from Brody. I dig my phone out of my handbag and read it, biting my lip.

*Date nite 2nite!! Pick you up at 8 for an evening of wining and dining. Wear something you won't mind being ripped off your body. PS – I miss your smiling face. Even tho it's hideous.*

"Let's go in," I say, and open the door to escape the sudden claustrophobia of the car.

Kat is in with the doctor for two hours. Chloe and I sit in the waiting room and read women's magazines, which are completely depressing. Every article seems to be about what to do if your man is cheating, how to lose weight, or how to make a killer dinner to impress the in-laws or your husband's new boss. I suppose the clinic couldn't put out *New Parent* magazine for risk of traumatizing their patients, but every one of those women's magazines is like an episode of *Mad Men*, like the women's movement never happened and the best we can hope for in life is to get married and learn how to make a perfect Bundt cake.

If I'd known, I'd have snuck in a few copies of *BDSM for Beginners* to scatter around.

When Kat comes out, she looks tired but she's smiling, which immediately makes Chloe and me feel better.

"You okay, superstar?" I murmur, giving her a hug.

"Yeah," she says, nodding. She sounds relieved. "The test where they injected radioactive iodine into my uterus wasn't a walk in the park, but the doctor said she didn't see anything abnormal from the physical exam, the X-rays, or the ultrasound, so that's good. The blood work will take a while to process, and there's a few other tests she might order based on the results of those, but for now all I can do is wait."

When she stops and chews on her lip, Chloe and I prompt, "What?"

She sighs. "She wants to check Nico's sperm."

I burst out laughing. "I'll bet she does! The old-fashioned way?"

Chloe elbows me in the side, but Kat waves her hand in the air like she'd expect nothing less. "Under a microscope, pervert. To see if his swimmers are strong or lazy."

The thought of Nico Nyx with lazy sperm is too much for Chloe, who goes beet red and puts her hands up in surrender. "Discussing the state of your husband's semen is where I draw the line, my friend."

I say to Kat, "I guess this means you're going to have to tell him sooner rather than later." I link my arm through hers, Chloe does the same on Kat's other side, and we head toward the clinic doors.

"Yep," says Kat, wearing a brave smile. "As soon as I get home. And then I'll do a little sperm testing of my own, if you know what I mean."

She makes lip-smacking noises at Chloe, who makes a face and mutters, "Gross."

Kat and I grin at each other.

Some things never change.

By the time eight o'clock rolls around, my nerves are wound so tight I might snap. I've spent all afternoon thinking about the future, a dangerous proposition I rarely allow myself to indulge in. When the doorbell rings, I jump, sloshing the wine in my glass. Fortunately it doesn't spill. I down it in one big gulp and go answer the door.

Brody stands there, freshly shaved, with perfect hair and a smile that could bring world peace.

"Hello, beautiful," he murmurs, letting his warm gaze travel over me.

"Hello, beautiful, yourself," I reply, wowed by the incredible dark blue suit he's wearing, perfectly cut, obviously custom made. He looks like a duke. "Is that Cifonelli you're wearing?"

Brody cocks his head. "How could you possibly know that?"

I don't bother to tell him that I once had a torrid affair with a famous architect who was so obsessed with the bespoke Paris suit maker that he owned over three hundred Cifonellis and built his entire house around his closet. Instead I say breezily, "It's in the cut of the shoulder."

"Hmm." Brody's smile quirks up on one side. "Well, whoever he was I hope you broke his heart."

I grin at him. "That is what heartbreakers do, darling."

He steps over the threshold and takes me in his arms. "Darling, is it?" he murmurs, gazing down at me with fire in his eyes. "I like. So formal. Very James Bondy. And may I say you look like a Bond girl in this dress. *Muy sexito.*"

I tilt my head to give him better access as he brushes his mouth down my throat. His lips skim my skin, leaving a trail of sparks behind. "If Magda hears you butchering her language like that, she'll probably poison your breakfast."

His arms tightening around me, he inhales against my neck. "I've been expecting it for years. You smell incredible."

"Thank you. It's Clive Christian."

Brody chuckles, kisses my collarbone, and looks at me. "Of course you'd wear the world's most expensive perfume."

Now it's my turn for lifted brows. "And how could you possibly know that?"

Grinning now, he quips, "It's in the cut of the shoulder."

"Ah. Well, whoever she was I hope she broke your heart. Although it doesn't appear that way, since your ego seems perfectly intact."

Brody looks deep into my eyes. His smile fades. "No one's ever broken my heart, because no one's ever had it. Until now."

My heart thumping, I wind my arms around his neck and kiss him.

When we finally break apart, we're both breathing hard. Brody says, "If we're gonna do dinner, we'd better go now because I'm about two seconds away from turning this beautiful dress of yours into a pile of shreds."

"You already did that with one of my dresses, Kong. If you keep it up I'll be buying a new dress every day."

He grins at me. "Or you could just walk around naked all the time and save me the trouble."

I kiss him lightly on the lips and smile. "You wish, buster. Let's go eat, I'm looking forward to this wining and dining you've promised me."

He kisses my hand and leads me out the door. His car, a sleek black Tesla, is parked in the driveway of the guest house. He opens the passenger door for me, lends me a gentlemanly hand as I settle in, and then jogs around to the driver's side and hops in, slamming the door behind him.

"Seat belt," he directs sternly when he sees I haven't fastened it.

"Yes, sir." I offer him a solemn salute and then do as he's instructed. When he's satisfied I'm all belted up, he clips in his own seat belt and starts the car.

The electric engine's utter silence makes me laugh. "Now that's a really unsatisfying lack of noise. I thought all you bad boy musician types liked some macho rumble under the hood."

Brody's smile is bright in the dim interior. "Oh, I've got some macho rumble under my hood, Slick, and you know it." He winks.

Laughing, I roll my eyes. "You're unbelievable."

"No, I'm adorable. And charming. And completely irresistible. Stop me if I'm wrong."

I go all clinical psychiatrist on him. "Oh, no, please continue! As a case study in derangement, you're fascinating. Your state of delusion is unusually acute. If I write a paper on your particular pathology, I'll probably get famous. But don't worry, I'll only refer to you as patient B so you can continue living in Crazy Town in total anonymity."

Grinning wider, Brody drives past the gate and out onto PCH, and guides the car into traffic. "Just admit it, Slick. You're madly in love with me and you want to marry me and raise the octuplets on a ranch somewhere in Montana where I'll be a farmer and you'll dress the kids in hideous matching outfits you sewed yourself."

Heat flashes over me first, followed by a chill. He just worked the words "love," "marry," and "kids" into one sentence.

I try to form a pithy response, but can't because my nervous system is too busy having a meltdown.

When I don't respond, Brody glances over at me. "Oh," he says. "I see I've hit a nerve. I won't joke about that stuff if you're uncomfortable—"

"It's just that I don't sew," I say, staring straight ahead.

After a few moments, I chance a look at him. He's staring back at me with an expression of surprise, hope, and fierce devotion.

His voice husky, he asks, "What about the rest?"

My pulse is flying. It feels as if I'm on the verge of a heart attack. "You should probably keep your eyes on the road."

He sends a cursory glance at the highway in front of us, and then looks back at me. "Answer the question."

*Don't answer the question. You're smarter than this. Love is a myth, Grace! Love is just hormones! Love is the root of most of the misery in the world! You can still save yourself!*

Then the memory of Barney's solemn, soulful words at the housewarming party inconveniently pops in.

*Love is the only thing that matters. Love is everything.*

Goddamn it.

I hate being this conflicted. Life was a helluva lot simpler before this gorgeous complication named Brody Scott showed up.

My heart and my brain warring, I finally say, "I can't really see you as a farmer."

Brody warns, "Grace," in a low, throaty growl. He reaches over and squeezes my hand.

*Don't be such a fucking mouse. You're a lion! You're a tiger! You were given this life because you're strong enough to live it, remember? So why don't you prove it for once?*

Well, hell. Leaping off cliffs seems to be what this relationship is all about.

"I . . . I think eight kids is about six too many."

Brody pulls off onto the side of the highway so fast I gasp in surprise. When we're stopped on the shoulder with a cloud of dust settling around the car, he yanks up the parking brake, turns to me, and takes my face in his hands.

"You're in love with me. You want to marry me. You want to have my kids."

He says it like a demand for confirmation, staring right at me, nose-to-nose.

Instantly regretting what I've done, I shake my head. "No. That would be insane."

"No, that would be beautiful."

"It's impossible."

"And yet it's what we both want."

My heart stalls out, and then takes off again like a rocket. "You . . . ?"

"You know I do. You know how I feel. I'm yours, if you'll have me." He kisses me, his grip on my face caressing.

*Oh God. This is crazy. What am I doing? I need to put the brakes on this. I can't do this to him.*

I groan his name against his mouth. "My memory . . . you need a woman . . . someone normal—"

"I need *you,*" he interrupts in a tone of finality. "And I talked to someone about the memory thing. A guy I know, he's a specialist—"

"You talked to someone about me?" I say, horrified.

"I didn't mention any names, I just said I had a friend," Brody replies gently, stroking his thumbs over my cheeks. "This guy is the best, Grace. I want you to look up his background, you'll see he's legit. I want you to see him. I think he could help us."

Us, he says.

Not you. Us.

I put my face into the shoulder of Brody's perfectly tailored, monstrously expensive suit, and concentrate on breathing in and out.

Brody says softly, "You're everything I've ever wanted, Grace Stanton, and I'm not gonna let a little thing like your glitchy goddamn brain get in my way."

Gripping his lapels, caught up in a wave of intense emotion, I produce a shaky laugh. "My brain isn't little."

Then Brody laughs, too. "I know. I can tell by the size of your head. You can never find a hat that fits, can you, Sputnik?"

We sit in his silently running car on the side of Pacific Coast Highway, holding each other and laughing, the girl with the glitchy memory and the boy with an unnamed guilt, thrown together by chance, now held fast in the clutches of the ruthless terrorist that so perfectly blinds young and old, rich and poor alike:

Hope.

# Chapter 31

## Brody

Dinner is dinner. It's food. The restaurant is in Malibu, so celebrities are crawling all over the place like cockroaches, but I couldn't tell you who was there or what they wore or anything.

All I can tell you is that I'm in love.

*I'm in love.*

And I flat out don't deserve her, which is probably obvious to anyone who gives us even a passing glance.

Yeah, okay, I'm not a bad-looking guy, I've got money, and I'm in this band that's kind of a big deal, but none of that means shit compared to who she is. The reality of who and what Grace Stanton is would melt the heart of even the most zombified, frostbitten White Walker George R.R. Martin could ever conceive.

Everyone in the restaurant stared at her when we walked in. And I mean *everyone*, from the giraffe-necked hostess to the people crowded three deep around the bar to the toy Yorkie sitting on the lap of some overly tan socialite and eating off her plate. Grace just has this thing where she walks into a room and instantly owns it. There are a lot of stunning women in L.A., but I've never met one who can silence a dozen conversations just by entering the same air space. She's a magnet, drawing every eye, stealing all the light, sucking every molecule into her orbit.

She glows. She glows so bright she outshines everything else in sight.

And I stand beside her, a fool in a five-thousand-dollar suit, basking in the warmth of her light like a reptile soaking up the sun so it doesn't freeze to death from its cold, cold blood.

Unfortunately, the dark residue of my guilt is the one thing that can't be lightened by Grace's beautiful shine, but at least it doesn't tarnish her. After half a lifetime of perfecting my sunny mask, my stains are only ever seen by me.

"You're quiet," she observes.

We're at a table in a corner of the elegant dining room. I've ordered wine and the waitress has poured it, but neither of us has touched our glasses. I think we're both in a mild state of shock at what happened in the car.

In my mind, there's really only one thing that can happen next.

I take her hand across the table and look into her eyes. "I have a proposal."

First her face pales. Then two spots of color bloom over her cheeks.

"No," I chuckle, squeezing her hand. "Not *that* proposal." It stings when she looks relieved. "You don't have to look like you just got a pardon from the parole board!"

In what appears to be a stalling move, she sips from her water glass. She slowly sets the glass down, strokes her thumb up and down the stem, and, looking at our joined hands, quietly says, "You'll be gratified to hear it wasn't relief I was feeling."

I can't describe the emotion that grips me. It's like a giant invisible hand just reached into my chest and clenched into a fist. I lean closer to her and lower my voice. "No? What was it then?"

She shoots me a look from under her lashes, her eyes sparkling. "That ego of yours certainly needs a lot of stroking, Mr. Scott."

I ignore that and inch my chair closer to hers. "Then stroke away, baby," I murmur. "I'm all ears."

She looks down at my crotch. "Well. Not *all* ears." When she looks up at me her cheeks have pinkened again.

"Goddamn," I say gruffly. "Do you have any idea how perfect you are?"

She wrinkles her nose. "You keep saying that word. And I keep trying to tell you all my imperfections—"

"You're perfect for *me.*"

That silences her. She starts to chew on her lower lip, and my heart begins to thump like crazy.

*She's almost there. I can make this happen. I can make her happy, forever, and we can both be free.*

I say, "I want you to move in with me."

When her mouth drops open in astonishment, I press on before she can protest.

"Now. Tonight. Forget about trying to find a place to live. Let's move your things into the main house and just do this. For real."

There's a vein in her temple that goes haywire whenever she's feeling strong emotion. I doubt she's aware of it, because she'd probably have had it removed years ago. Right now it's giving me some very clear insight into what's happening inside her body.

As if her trembling hand and shallow, rapid breathing weren't enough.

"I . . ."

"Say yes."

Her laugh is disbelieving. "Wow. This 'dating' business is intense. No wonder I've always avoided it."

I can see she's feeling overwhelmed, so I sit back in my chair to give her some breathing room. The last thing I want to do is scare her off when I'm so close to having everything I've ever dreamed of.

To lighten the moment, I say, "It was really Magda's idea. I think she sees her chance to double the Brody Beatdown Team and isn't gonna let it get away from her."

The waitress arrives to take our meal orders. I watch Grace carefully as she turns her attention to the menu, probing the waitress for recommendations, asking questions on this or that dish, knowing full well she's buying herself time before we return to the subject at hand.

She finally decides on a dish. I give the waitress my order, too, and then we're alone again.

I lean forward. Before I can speak, Grace says, "Before you repeat your incredibly flattering, incredibly stunning, and overall mind-bending offer, can we maybe just . . . talk?"

"Talk?" I repeat, staring at her. Worry gnaws a hole in my stomach.

"Yes, Brody. Talk. Like people do. On a *date*."

Our gazes hold. The sounds of the restaurant seem suddenly loud in my ears, silverware clanging and people laughing and the music playing on hidden speakers, delicate guitar chords and faraway violins.

Throwing caution to the wind, I say quietly, "Okay. Let's talk. I'll go first. Move in with me."

She sighs. "Oy."

I make a sound like a buzzer. "Wrong response. Try again."

She pins me in one of her no-nonsense stares. "Why are you trying so hard to make this happen?"

"Because it *is* happening, whether you're comfortable with it or not. Whether we put the brakes on it or not. Whether we let our fears get the better of us or not, we want each other, we make each other happy, we're two people who've sown a shit ton of wild oats between us, and there's no reason we shouldn't at least give it a try."

She looks down at the knife beside her plate and begins to stroke it in contemplation. "Okay. That's fair. It's just sudden."

"When you realize you want to spend the rest of your life with somebody, you want the rest of your life to start as soon as possible."

The look she sends me could cut steel. "I know that's a line from *When Harry Met Sally.*"

Holding her lethal gaze, I reply, "Why do you think I said it, sweetheart?"

After a long time, she says quietly, "Because you knew I'd know."

"Correct. This is true love. You think this happens every day?"

She closes her eyes, smiling. "And now he's quoting *The Princess Bride.*"

"I'm irresistible, I keep telling you this. Also, the fact that you recognize every single quote I throw out there is proof that we were made for each other. Say yes."

She opens her eyes, tilts her head back, and stares at me with a challenge in her gaze. "Not to be a killjoy, but I recognize all the quotes Barney throws my way, too."

I chuckle. "Keeping me on my toes. I'd expect nothing less. Say yes."

"Can we maybe get to the appetizers before I commit to such a big decision, Mr. Scott?"

I pick up the white linen napkin on my plate, snap it open, and spread it over my lap. I send her my most winning smile. "Of course. Have some salad. Then say yes."

She laughs loudly, her head thrown back, causing several people at tables nearby to turn their heads and stare.

"I just asked her to move in with me," I explain to the fat guy in a purple velour tracksuit at the next table. He looks like an eggplant wearing a blond wig.

He says, "Well, if she says no, I'm available." He smiles and blows me a kiss.

*God, I love this town.*

"Thanks, man."

I turn my attention back to Grace, who's hiding her face in her hand. Her shoulders are shaking she's laughing so hard, trying to hold it in.

"You see, Grace, I have options. But I choose you."

"So feel special?" she asks between gasps of air.

"Exactly."

"Well, you're not boring, I'll give you that."

She peeks at me from behind her hand, and I grin. Big.

"*The Thomas Crown Affair,*" I say. "One of my all-time, personal favorites. Now you *have* to say yes."

She picks up a dinner roll from the basket in the middle of the table and throws it at me. I catch it before it smacks me in the middle of my chest and take a bite out of it, tearing into it with a wolfish growl.

From the corner of my eye I see the fat guy at the next table make a silent O with his lips.

"Okay, seriously. Let's talk, Brody." Grace sits back in her chair, smooths her hand over her hair, and then folds her hands in her lap.

"Uh-oh. Is this what you look like in session with your patients? Because you're really intimidating right now." I take a sip from my water glass to moisten my dry throat.

Her smile is mysterious. "Tell me about your family."

I cough, almost spitting water all over the table, but catch myself before it can spray out my nose.

Grace looks at me with raised brows. "Touchy subject? As I recall you said you were close with them."

Suddenly I feel like there's a spotlight glaring down into my face and I'm tied to a chair in a bare room, looking at a wall of blacked-out windows that's actually a two-way mirror a row of CIA agents are standing behind. It's a good thing I'm not wearing a tie, because I'd involuntarily loosen it, which I'm sure Grace would take as a sign of something bad.

Which of course it would be.

I set my water glass carefully back on the tabletop and meet her direct gaze. This is a test, one I'm not going to fail. No matter how many hurdles I have to jump over, she *will* be mine.

"I *am* close with them. My mom, Margaux, still lives in the house I grew up in—"

"Wait. Your mother's name is Margaux Scott? Like the children's book author?"

"That's her. Why, do you like me better now?" I tease.

Grace smiles. "Actually, yes. Your mother lends you a distinct touch of respectability."

"Thank you. Now are you moving in with me?"

Her response is a heavy sigh and rolled eyes.

"I'll take that as a maybe. May I proceed?"

Grace waves a hand in the air, a queenly gesture.

"Thank you, your highness. As I was saying. Mother, Margaux. Younger brother, Branson. Older sister, Bronwyn. Branson still lives at home even though he's twenty-five because he is the favorite, is utterly spoiled, and has no reason to move out. Bronwyn lives in Connecticut with her husband and four kids."

When I see the expression on Grace's face, I ask, "What?"

"Your parents named their children Brody, Branson, and Bronwyn?"

"I know. It's awful. We would've been mercilessly bullied when we were young, but we were in prep school and everyone else had equally terrible names. My best friend growing up was named Fenton Farnsworth the third."

Grace laughs. "Was not!"

"Hand to God."

"I can't believe they even have prep schools in Topeka, Kansas! Isn't that farm country?"

"Excuse me, but Topeka is the *capital* of the state, Slick, and very upscale. We even had running water and indoor bathrooms."

Grace smirks. "And here I was picturing you riding bulls and eating deep-fried Twinkies at the county fair."

"Snob."

"Hick."

*"As I was saying,"* I continue, trying not to laugh, "I went to prep school. Then I was accepted to UCLA's music program as a freshman, so I moved to L.A. when I was eighteen."

"With Magda," prompts Grace when I pause to take another swallow of water.

"Yep. My mom was concerned I'd become a male prostitute or a junkie of some sort because she'd seen too many daytime TV movies about runaways in Hollywood, so she sent along a spy."

"What about your dad? What does he do?"

I try, very carefully, to keep my expression neutral. "He was a senator."

Grace watches me, waiting, as it hangs in the air between us.

*Was.*

After a moment, I say quietly, "He died a few years ago from cirrhosis. We weren't . . ." I look down and notice my left hand trembling. I pull it into my lap and make a fist. "We weren't on the best of terms. In fact, we hadn't spoken for years before he passed."

"I'm sorry to hear that," Grace murmurs.

"Don't be. He wasn't a good person."

It's out before I can take it back, an uncensored confession filled with emotion, my voice as harsh as nails scraping down a chalkboard. To stop myself from adding anything else, I clench my jaw.

After a tense moment, Grace says, "Brody."

I inhale a slow breath and look at her. She's staring at me, her expression as calm as a buddha's.

She says, "We'll leave that for another date. Or never, if you prefer. I'm a firm believer that the past is just that: past. And the dead should be left to rest in the ground where we put them. We don't have to share the details of our sad stories. It's enough that we're trying to build better ones."

I don't know why, but that moves me so much my throat closes and my chest goes tight. "Thank you."

The waitress arrives with our appetizers, giving me a much-needed break from having to speak. My vocal cords feel raw, like I've been screaming. We eat for a while in silence, alone with our thoughts, until Grace asks, "What's that tattoo you have, the symbols above the angel's wings on your chest? It looks like some kind of language."

My heart skips a beat. I say quietly, "Kind of . . . part of that past-is-past thing."

I'd have told her if she pushed me for more, but she just moves on to her next question without missing a beat.

"And the necklace you always wear?"

I swallow a bite of my Caesar salad, and absently rub my thumb over the small silver disc resting in the hollow of my throat, suspended from a leather cord. "It's Saint Jude."

If Grace recognizes Saint Jude as the patron saint of lost causes, she doesn't comment. I'm relieved, for a million different reasons, none of them good.

I should've known I wouldn't be let off the hook that easily.

"Where were you right before you came to the hospital the day Abigail was born?"

*Jesus Christ. This woman is as sharp as a samurai sword.*

Panic slams into my gut, making it roll. Sweat breaks out on my forehead. I keep my gaze on my plate, and try to answer with a steady voice.

"Church."

"Oh," she says with a small laugh. "You were surfing! And here I thought it was something sketchy."

The rolling in my stomach worsens. If I ask her why, it could open up a can of worms. But if I don't ask her why, it would be suspicious. So I'm left with no choice.

"Why would you think that?"

With a shrug she says, "Because you acted so weird when Nico asked you what held you up. Like you were embarrassed, or maybe felt . . . guilty."

Her tone and expression are nonchalant, but her gray eyes are soul piercing.

She knows. She set the trap, added the bait, and I took it.

Feeling sick, dreading where this conversation is headed, I set my fork and knife on my plate and sit back in my chair. "I wasn't surfing, Grace," I say, my voice low. "I was at church. Real church."

Mirroring my actions, she puts down her silverware and sits back. To anyone else looking, Grace appears serene, mildly interested, just another woman listening to her dinner companion talk about nothing of particular importance.

But I see how brittle this veneer of tranquility is. That vein in her temple is going gangbusters, and her eyes have turned the color of steel.

She says calmly, "Here's the part where you explain why you, a man who said he and God had their differences and that he hadn't been to church since he was a kid, made a stop at a church between an afternoon barbeque and the birth of your best friend's child. Because, radical honesty time, that strikes me as very strange."

*I was so close. I was so fucking close to having her, and now I'm gonna open my mouth and it's all gonna come out and she'll hate me. It's ruined. It's over. I've lost.*

I can't lie to her. A sin of omission is one thing, but an outright lie, right to her face, is something completely different. I can't do it.

My pulse pounding, I close my eyes and confess.

"Because of the accident."

There's silence on the other side of the table. When I open my eyes, Grace is staring at me in confusion.

"I'm sorry, but I have no idea what that means."

I'm struggling to breathe. The air doesn't want to come into my lungs. The air hates me as much as Grace is going to any second now. "Because after I came back from the bathroom at Nico's, Chloe and Kat told me about your accident, and I . . . I . . ."

Grace's hand flies up to cover her mouth. Her eyes go wide. "You were reminded of *your* accident?"

Time stops. My heart stops. The blood stops flowing through my veins. Wordlessly, dying inside because I know she's going to ask me for details, I nod.

Grace breathes, "Oh, sweetie. I'm so sorry." She stands, crosses the few feet that separate us, and winds her arms around my shoulders.

I'm so stunned I can't speak, or move, or do anything but sit frozen as Grace kisses my cheek. She takes my face in her hands. From my chair I stare up at her, shell-shocked.

In a fierce whisper, she says, "They didn't mean to upset you! They didn't know you'd been in an accident, too!"

Dazed, not understanding what's happening, I manage to rasp, *"What?"*

"I know we haven't talked about what happened to you, and it can be another one of those things on the don't-ask-don't-tell list as far as I'm concerned, okay? I *hate* talking about my accident. I'm sure you feel the same way, right?"

I swallow, and then answer truthfully. "Yes."

"Then we won't talk about it. Not ever, not if you don't want to. I meant what I said earlier, Brody. We don't have to tell each other our sad stories. Fuck the past. Life is in front of us, not behind."

The kiss she presses to my lips is so gentle it brings tears to my eyes. A strange noise leaves my throat. My vision is swimming. And inside my chest, my heart is starting to break.

Because I understand that to Grace, the accident I was in and the thing I told her I did when I was young that I have so much guilt over, that I called myself a coward over, are two different things.

Which, of course, they're not.

# Chapter 32

## Grace

For the next three hours, we talk. About everything and anything, sharing stories, asking questions, getting to know each other better. It's by far the most time I've ever spent talking to one man outside of bed.

We're so engrossed in our conversation we end up closing the restaurant. Still, it's not so much the food or the ambiance that stays with me, but the expression on Brody's face when I told him we didn't have to talk about his accident. He looked so grateful I thought he might cry.

Of course I'm curious about what happened to him. Anyone would be. But I'm in the unique position of understanding exactly why he'd like to avoid discussing it. Talking about your demons can make them very angry.

Better to let them sleep undisturbed than shake them out of their nests.

Before we leave, he asks me one final time over dessert to move in with him, and I tell him I'll think about it. But he's persistent, and promises to ask again in the morning. I try to convince him I'm not going anywhere, so he should relax and enjoy the courting phase of our relationship, a new experience for both of us. His reply gives Kat a run for her Dramarama title.

"If you haven't made up your mind in a week, I'll die of a broken heart."

I tell him it's too bad he's such a terrible actor, because his sense of theatrics is Shakespearean.

When we get back to Malibu and pull into the long driveway that leads to his house, I have to smile.

"This doesn't look like the guest house, Brody."

He turns to me, his eyes shining in the dark interior of the car. "You're so perceptive. Besides your enormous feet that are two different sizes, that's my favorite thing about you."

"My feet aren't enormous!"

His smile widens. "Sweetheart, you make Ronald McDonald's feet look dainty. I think Shaquille O'Neal has smaller hoofs than yours. It's like you're walking around on two life rafts."

I smack him on the arm, and he breaks out into laughter.

Brody laughing is one of my favorite sounds in the world.

I spend the night with him, and the night after, and the night after that. On Monday I go back to work, wearing long sleeves to cover the faint red marks on my wrists where they're chafed from Brody's lovely sand-colored rope.

I can't remember ever feeling so happy.

Or so convinced that things that seem too good to be true inevitably are.

A week goes by, and then another. I work and diligently look for places to live, but still go home to Brody every night. The clothes I keep buying are all in the guest house, but the majority of my time is spent in the main house, with him.

And Magda, my new fairy godmother, who spoils me to within an inch of my life.

"Eat more," she urges in Spanish, hovering over me with a platter of enchiladas *poblanas*. Just looking at the delicious chicken, tortilla, cheese, and green chile dish could add five pounds to each of my thighs. And I've already had two helpings. Another few weeks in this house and I'll be researching liposuction.

"You're killing me, Magda," I groan, rubbing my stomach. "Save it for later, when everyone gets here!"

"I have more food for later." She pokes me in the shoulder with her finger. "You're too skinny. A stiff breeze could blow you over!"

It's little things like this that make me adore her so much. I have no memory of my own mother, but I imagine her like this. Scolding, spoiling, letting me know in a million different ways that I'm her favorite person in the world.

Magda has told me I'm the daughter she never had. I've told her she's my second mother. Brody told both of us he can move to the guest house if she and I would like to continue our love fest undisturbed, to which Magda responded, "I thought you'd never ask."

Which I translated to, "Don't be silly."

Brody only smiled.

The swell is up now, so Brody's out on the waves for the second time today. Truth be told, I'm glad to have the alone time, because it's the dreaded St. Patrick's Day, and I'm in a shit mood.

The enchiladas are helping, but from experience I know that comfort food will only get me so far. As soon as the sun goes down I'm hitting the hard stuff.

Before that even, if the gang ever gets here. Drinking alone always makes me feel like I've failed at life.

I push my chair back and rise from the table. "Thank you, Magda, but I can't eat another bite."

She pouts. On Magda a pout looks exactly like a scowl, which her smiles also look similar to. She has one default expression, and that's general disappointment in the human race.

I kiss her cheek and head toward Brody's bedroom, where I flop on my back on the bed and stare at the ceiling, willing myself not to dwell on the significance of the day. Instead I think about the appointment Brody made with his doctor friend for next week.

I don't want to get my hopes up that he can help me with my memory any more than the other doctors I've seen, but I admit I'm excited. When I read about some of his case studies and his background, I couldn't help but be impressed.

I'm still thinking about the good doctor when Brody walks through the door.

He's dripping wet, still in his wetsuit. His eyes are red. His jaw is set.

Surprised by his expression, I sit up in bed. "What's wrong?"

He swallows and rakes a hand through his wet hair. "Nothing. Why?"

I stare at him, taking in his face and the tension in his body, wondering at the frog in his voice. "Because you look like you've been crying."

"It's just the salt water, Grace," he mutters, stalking across the room. He disappears into the bathroom and closes the door behind him.

I see two of us are in a shit mood today.

I debate following him into the bathroom but decide to give him some space, and his privacy. I hear the shower go on, and wait a tense twenty minutes until it goes off again. After another few minutes Brody emerges, bare chested, a white bath towel wrapped around his waist.

Moving with his breath, the angel's wings across his chest seem to shimmer.

"I'm sorry I was a dick," he says softly, looking at his feet. "It's not you."

His left hand is curled into a fist. The right one is slightly shaking.

"Apology accepted. I got up on the wrong side of the bed this morning, too."

He glances up at me, sitting with my arms around my knees, and offers me a sad smile.

"It's okay if you want to bitch me out, you know. You don't always have to be so understanding."

I shrug. "I'm a relationship counselor, Brody. I've seen the best and worst of human nature. I'm not going to bitch you out because you firmly closed a door and took a shower."

His Adam's apple bobs as he swallows. In a husky voice, he says, "Well, when you put it that way . . ."

This time his smile isn't quite so sad.

I pat the mattress. "C'mere."

Holding the towel closed with one hand, he crosses to the bed, then sits on the edge. I scoot over to him and rest my head on his shoulder.

"Does your mood have anything to do with that nightmare you had last night?" I ask.

His back stiffens just enough to be noticeable.

I press a kiss to his warm skin, inhaling the smell of him, shampoo and soap and clean, masculine man. "Yeah. I thought so."

Brody blows out a hard breath, leans over and props his elbows on his knees, then drops his face into his hands. "Haven't had one that bad in years," he says, his words subdued.

He doesn't have to tell me. He woke up thrashing and screaming "No! No! No!" at the top of his lungs in the dead of night, scaring me half to death. It was nearly an hour before he fell back to sleep, twitching and whining in the back of his throat like a dog.

Oddly, my nightmares have eased over the past few weeks, but Brody's seem to be increasing. It's a surreal experience for me, waking up to someone else's nightmare, comforting someone else's terror, listening to the frantic beating of someone else's heart. I've been alone for so long with my own nocturnal visions it's weirdly comforting to find Brody and I have this awful thing in common. I'm grateful to be able to forget about my own problems for a while and focus on helping him deal with his.

There's a faint voice shouting "Hello, codependency!" from some dark corner of my brain, but for now I'm ignoring it. Once I get past today and all its goblin memories, I'll be able to turn a clearer eye to the big picture.

Rome wasn't built in a day, as they say.

Brody asks, "What time is everyone coming over again?"

"They should be here in an hour. Unless you want to cancel—"

"No." He straightens and looks over his shoulder at me. "God, no. This is your annual thing with the girls, there's no way I'm fucking it up. Besides," he takes my hand and squeezes it. "I can use the distraction."

So can I.

I haven't told him *why* it's my annual thing with the girls, but it didn't require an explanation when I brought it up last week. I said we do this every year, he said great, let's have it at my place. End of discussion.

Had I known a man existed who was exactly as comfortable with ambiguity and equivocation as I was, I'd have started looking for him years ago.

He says, "Speaking of distractions," and pulls me onto his lap.

"Oh, so I'm a distraction now?" I tease, winding my arms around his shoulders.

"Now and forever." His eyes search mine.

I bend my head and softly kiss him. "Sweet talker."

He cups the back of my head and pulls me closer, his mouth eager for mine. Our tongues sweep against each other. His other hand curls around my hip, rocking me against his growing erection.

"I think there's something under your towel that needs some attention, Mr. Scott," I whisper, gazing into his eyes.

But he isn't in a teasing mood. His eyes are intense, drilling into mine. He's not smiling. Instead he says, "When this new album is released, we'll go on tour to support it. The label is booking all the dates now."

"Okay," I answer slowly, unsure where this is going. I wait for him to say more, but for a moment he only stares into my eyes, thoughtfully stroking my cheek with his thumb.

"There'll be US stops, Europe again, too. Most likely we're looking at two months."

I feel a twinge of unhappiness, but smile to cover it. "I guess I'd better update my international calling plan."

With sudden urgency he says, "I need you with me. I can't do it again without you. I won't."

I frown. He's asking me to go on tour with him? Of course that's not happening. "Well, you have to, sweetie. I'm sure your contract stipulates—"

"I love you."

He says it like a confession of a terrible sin, his voice raspy, his face contorted in pain.

A crushing pressure descends on my chest. It's impossible to breathe. I stare at him, shocked past words.

He repeats it again, the words bursting from him like water from a broken dam. "I love you, Grace. I need you with me. Everything makes sense now that I've found you. I've been waiting my entire life for you. I want to take care of you forever. Be my wife. Marry me. Please."

I'm floating outside myself. My body is a tornado of emotions—pounding heart, shaking hands, shallow breathing—but my mind is detached, clinically appraising with narrowed eyes and a raised brow.

Twice before I've had marriage proposals. Both times I laughed. Neither time did I feel as if I were being asked to throw a lifeline to a drowning man.

I cup his face in my hands and softly press a kiss to his lips.

He closes his eyes. His arms around me are crushing. In a ragged whisper, he says, "Please."

With all my heart I want to believe this desperation comes from a place of joy, a natural, healthy impulse to join his life with mine and create a unified future. But there are so many red flags waving in my face I'm blinded.

And *today*, of all days.

Fate has a really vile sense of humor.

"I'm not saying no."

"But you're not saying yes."

We stare at each other, our faces inches apart. His heart is beating so hard I can almost hear it.

"I'm saying—"

The doorbell rings.

When it rings again, Brody drops his head to my chest and groans. "They're fucking *early*!"

Yes, they are, and I'm relieved because this interruption gives me a chance to get my head together before Brody and I continue the conversation.

Something is behind this sudden proposal. Something darker than love. Something connected to . . .

A thought hits me with such force I lose my breath.

*He knows.*

Brody knows the significance of this day to me. One of the girls told him, or one of the guys. Of course. Of *course* he'd know! He must've known all along, since the day of the barbeque at Nico's!

So him declaring his love and proposing to me today is . . . what?

My mind leaps forward at lightning speed. In the space of a few moments I've gone over every significant conversation we've had, every doubt I've felt, every time I've wondered why he was moving the relationship so fast.

Does his whole knight-in-shining-denim thing stem from a hero complex? Am I a project for him, a damsel in distress who needs saving?

*A pity fuck?*

Or, possibly even worse, a Band-Aid for his guilt over whatever made him call himself a coward? Give the poor girl with amnesia a happily-ever-after and get a free pass on your own sins?

My whole body goes cold.

My God, is this entire relationship just Brody's Freudian response to shame?

Magda must have opened the front door, because A.J.'s booming voice echoes through the house.

"Hey, pretty boy! Put your pants on, man, company's here!"

Chloe's softer voice follows, shushing him, and then there's laughter.

Inside my head there's a sound like a thousand wolves howling at the moon.

"I guess this conversation will have to wait." Brody raises his head from my chest and looks at me. His beautiful green eyes are dark, so dark, and full of pain, mirroring the pain inside my chest.

I nod, unwind my arms from around his shoulders, and stiffly stand. My body feels wooden. Numb. Except for the throbbing of my heart, I feel nothing at all.

"I'll let you get dressed."

I walk from his bedroom, close the door behind me, and stand in the hallway for a moment, sucking in deep breaths and trying to get my bearings. Nothing looks familiar. All the beautiful furnishings have taken on a dark, ominous cast, as if they're alive and unfriendly, watching me, smirking at my blank distress.

Magda rounds the corner, wiping her hands on her white apron. She stops dead when she sees me standing still near the door.

*"Cariño?"* she says, peering at me. *"Qué te pasa?"*

"Nothing, Magda," I answer, my voice steady. "Nothing's wrong at all."

I can tell from the look on her face she doesn't believe me, but I force a smile. "Things have never been better."

I walk down the hall, smiling my dead smile, not meeting her eyes, and pass her on my way into the living room. Her gaze is as heavy as sandbags on my back as I walk out to greet my friends, dying a little with every step.

# Chapter 33

Since Chloe gave birth to Abby so recently I knew she wouldn't want to leave the baby at home, and it didn't seem fair not to invite A.J. if Chloe and the baby were coming, and since A.J. was invited it didn't seem fair not to invite the rest of the band, and since they were invited we had to invite Kenji—and of course Barney—so I'm looking at a lot of smiling faces when I walk into the foyer. Even Abby is smiling, nestled happily in A.J.'s arms.

Ethan and Chris couldn't make it because of their annual trip to Vegas for St. Paddy's Day, but I'm sure whatever strip club they're in, they're smiling, too.

Kat takes one look at my face and her smile vanishes.

She keeps her eagle eyes on me as I come in, but doesn't say anything. Yet. As long as I'm surrounded by people I'm safe, but I know she's already plotting how to get me alone so she can grill me.

Kenji imperiously sails past everyone and kisses me on both cheeks. He pulls back to survey me, his hands propped on his hips as he examines my expression. "You're wearing that face again, lovey. I think you need a colonic."

"What I need is a pair of sunglasses, because you're blinding me. I've never seen that color in nature."

"It's *citron*!" Kenji says, offended. He makes spokesmodel hands at his outfit, a costume of top hat and tails in a retina-searing shade of nuclear yellow-green. A clover-pattern vest over a frilly white shirt, tight "citron" leggings, and black patent leather shoes with chunky heels and big gold buckles on the toes complete the look.

Barney says, "What it *is* is offensive to leprechauns."

Kenji mutters, "Ack! Philistines!" Then he waves his hand in the air and stalks off into the kitchen, his shoes clacking loudly against the wood. Emerging from the hallway behind me, Magda follows him, quiet as a ghost.

"You guys are early," I say, my hollow smile firmly in place. "I thought musicians were always late."

Nico, wearing a pair of emerald-green alligator boots with his usual jeans and tight black T-shirt, grins at me. "Musicians who aren't married to drill sergeants who have best friends with punctuality issues are always late. Me, on the other hand—"

Kat smacks him lightly on his shoulder, and he laughs.

Chloe, looking chic in a slim white sheath and a pair of cute kitten heels even though her arms are full of baby paraphernalia and a collapsed stroller, pipes in. "It's actually Barney's fault. He's been barking at us all to get our asses in gear since ten o'clock this morning."

Barney shrugs, his expression impassive. "If I left it up to you people, we'd be getting here sometime next week."

"Exactly." Kat steps forward and gives me a tight hug.

As always, her hourglass figure is stunning, complemented today by a rock-chick ensemble of black leather jacket and designer jeans paired with stilettos and a T-shirt the color of key lime pie, stretched taut over the generous swell of her boobs. Into my ear she whispers, "That's not your usual St. Patrick's Day fake, brave smile, sister."

I whisper back, "It's the best I could do on short notice."

"Oh God. Don't tell me the D is starting to be a disappointment!"

"Hey, no whispering, you two!" booms A.J., looking in our general direction. "And what the hell is 'the D'?"

I'd forgotten Chloe told me A.J. has gained Spidey senses since he lost his sight. Apparently she was spot on.

Chloe scolds A.J. "None of your business, Big Daddy. And stop eavesdropping!"

"I can't help it if I have superhuman hearing now," he replies, sounding unconcerned.

Abby gurgles, kicking her little feet under the pink blanket she's wrapped in. A.J., his long blond hair in a sloppy man bun and a goofy smile on his face, begins to coo down at her, making baby talk and gently bouncing her up and down in his enormous tattooed arms.

"Can I, sweet pea? No, Daddy can't help it if he's got bat hearing now. No, he can't. No, no, no." He makes kissing noises at his daughter. Staring up into his face and flailing her arms, Abby squeals in delight.

I put a steadying hand on Kat's lower back. She's watching A.J. and Abby with a look of intense longing.

She hasn't told me if she's gotten the results back from the fertility clinic yet. As a matter of fact, Chloe hasn't told me if A.J. has had his visit to the doctor yet, either.

Looks like all three of us are up in the air.

I pronounce, "I need a drink. Let's get this party started. Everybody to the kitchen. Follow the echo of Kenji's leprechaun heels."

As Chloe, Kat, Nico, and A.J. move off, Barney stays behind, examining my face a little too closely for comfort.

He's in his regulation black Armani, complete with pristine white dress shirt and black leather shoes polished to a mirror shine. His goatee is shaved with such precision it looks like he uses an X-ACTO blade to trim the edges. I wonder if his entire closet is row after row of the same black and white, and decide it probably is.

He asks, "Where's your boy?"

"Getting dressed. He should be right out."

"Am I allowed to give you a hug before he gets here?"

My laugh is a little too loud. "Why, do I look like I need one?"

Dark eyes burning, he says, "You look like you need something, Angelface, but I'm not sure what it is."

There's a moment of tension between us, a quiet space wherein we simply look at each other. I think about how long Barney has known Brody, how Kat once told me Barney was the keeper of all Bad Habit's skeletons, and wonder with a chill running down my spine if he knows something about Brody that I'd want to know, too.

Holding Barney's intense gaze, I say, "Clarity is what I need. Only as it turns out, I'm finding it really hard to come by."

He glances down the hall toward the bedrooms. His gaze slices back to me. He takes a single step toward me, but stops abruptly, as if he's thought better of it. Keeping his voice low, he asks, "You know you can always talk to me, right?"

My heart thumps hard underneath my breastbone, because my intuition tells me Barney's offering more than just an ear.

"He's your friend."

His answer is instant. "You're my friend, too."

As soon as the words are out of his mouth, he looks away and runs a hand over his short hair, a muscle in his jaw jumping. I get the distinct feeling he'd liked to have said something else.

Something safer, in a tone not quite so gruff.

I ask softly, "Am I?"

His head swivels around. He stares at me, jaw clenched, silent.

If I push it, Barney would tell me anything I wanted to know about Brody, of that I'm sure. But Barney's not the one I should be asking. It's not fair to either of them, so I let it go.

"You know what? Forget it. Let's just go have a drink and relax. Today's my least favorite day of the year, and I just want to get through it."

There's a moment where Barney's eyes register something strange, but his gaze shutters quickly, becoming as expressionless as the rest of his face.

"Sure. Lead the way."

He follows me into the kitchen, where we find Kenji acting as hostess, whistling as he distributes tequila shots. Magda hovers over the food buffet on one counter, filling up plates. A bar forested with bottles of every kind of liquor has been set up on the large island in the center of the kitchen. A galvanized tub of beers on ice sits just inside the patio doors. I wanted to set up everything outside, but it's cold and blustery today, the sky a glowering gunmetal gray as it heads toward nightfall.

Beyond the wall of windows, the ocean is whitecapped and dark, as restless and glum as I feel.

"We need some music in here!" says A.J., settling into one of the chairs around the big kitchen table with the help of Chloe. He grins. "I know this really cool band we should put on."

Chloe quips, "Maroon Five?"

Still grinning, A.J. says, "That's cold, Angel. Ice cold."

She leans over and kisses his forehead. "Hmm. Maybe it'll help cool your raging ego, Big Daddy."

"Omigod, *stop* with the Big Daddy already, girl!" says Kenji. He downs a shot of tequila, and then looks at Chloe in disgust. "Do you know what people think of when you say that?" He makes a lewd gesture at his crotch. "Is *that* what you want people thinking? In front of the baby, no less?"

"Let me guess," says A.J., a smile in his unfocused gaze. "He pointed to his dick?"

"You see!" Kenji shouts, throwing his hands in the air.

Chloe laughs. "Since when did we switch roles and *you* became the prude one?"

Kenji gasps, his long, fake eyelashes fluttering. "Prude? *Prude*! I am *not* prude! I'm . . ." he flails around for a word, until he settles on, "classy!"

"Oh yeah," says Barney drily, dropping into a chair across from A.J. "You've got class coming out of your ass."

Kenji's eyes bulge. He looks as if he just swallowed his tongue. "That's a terrible thing to say to someone, Nasi!"

"Not if you're from Jersey, it isn't."

I say to Barney, "You're from New Jersey? You don't have any accent."

Sitting next to Nico at the other end of the table with an enormous margarita in front of her, Kat asks, "And who's Nasi?"

Barney shoots Kenji a sour look. Kenji sticks his tongue out at Barney, and then flounces back to the bar to pour another shot.

"My real name is Nasir," replies Barney grudgingly. He glances at his Rolex as if counting the minutes until he can leave.

Fascinated, I take the shot of tequila Kenji's holding out to me but don't drink it. "Really? Nasir? That's beautiful. What's the origin?"

"It's Lebanese."

"You're from Lebanon? I thought you just said you were from Jersey?"

"No, I didn't. And I'm not from either one."

Judging by his terse tone, that's as much as I'm getting from him about his origins, so I try another tack. "Does the name Nasir have a meaning?"

Barney's dark eyes flash up to meet mine. His voice thick, he says, "Protector."

From my peripheral vision, I see Kenji looking back and forth between us with raised brows. I quickly look away, mutter, "Interesting," and then shoot my tequila.

"How did I not know this?" asks Kat, peeved. She shoots Nico a pointed look, but he only shrugs.

"This is the first I'm hearin' about it, too, darlin'." He stares at Barney, who sighs.

"I got stuck with the nickname due to an unfortunate choice in costumes one Halloween a *long* time ago." Barney smiles at Kenji, his perfect white teeth gleaming. "And Kenji's the only one who knew. Just like I'm the only one who knows a few things about him."

Kenji blinks, hard. Beneath his layer of perfectly applied foundation, he goes pale. "Don't. You. *Dare.*"

"Then keep your pretty little mouth shut from now on, my friend, or everyone's gonna hear all about that time in Bangkok—"

With a banshee shriek, Kenji flies at Barney, arms waving, top hat sailing off his head.

Barney jumps up from his chair and puts Kenji into a restraining hold. Quick as lightning, he pins Kenji's arms to his sides in a bear hug from behind. As Kenji squirms and curses, Barney chuckles. He says, "Pipe down, princess, you'll hurt yourself," to which Kenji responds with another shriek.

"I see the circus has started without me."

Brody strolls into the kitchen, hands shoved into the front pockets of his jeans. His untucked white dress shirt is rolled up his forearms, showing off his tan. He appears relaxed, he's even smiling, but I sense all the fault lines waiting to crack.

*What a pair we are. Two peas in a fucked-up pod.*

The thought makes my stomach tighten.

Barney releases Kenji, who slaps him on the arm and wags a warning finger in his face. Barney blows him a kiss. Brody greets everyone with a hug or a handshake, depending on the gender of the person, with the exception of Kenji, who gets a pinched cheek. Then he makes a beeline for me.

He pulls me into his chest, kisses me on the temple, and whispers, "Hey."

"Hey, yourself, rock star," I whisper back.

"Tell me you're okay."

"I'm okay."

His lips still hovering near my temple, he whispers, "Uh-huh. Now tell me something honest."

I drop my forehead to his chest and sigh. He winds his arms around me, so I'm enveloped in his strength and warmth, the subtle clean fragrance of his skin. Keeping my voice low so only he can hear, I say, "I'll *be* okay, how's that?"

From behind us, A.J. booms, "What did I tell you about whispering, woman!"

As if in agreement with her father, Abby squeals.

Brody turns my face to his and gives me a gentle kiss on the lips. Looking into my eyes, he murmurs, "Better." Then he heads to the bar and pours himself a big measure of vodka into a highball glass, which he proceeds to chug as if it's water. He immediately pours himself another, and away that one goes, too.

Watching him, I frown. I've never seen him drink like that before. He's always been very controlled with his drinking, with the exception of the night he told me he thought he was a coward.

*Coward.*

It echoes in my head again now, like the tolling of a churchyard bell.

"Pace yourself, brother," says Nico with a shade of tension in his voice.

"Yeah, we don't want a repeat of *last* year," mutters Kenji, sharing a look with Barney. His annoyance with Barney seemingly forgiven as quickly as it came, he flops into the chair next to him and accepts a plate of food from Magda with an excited "Ooo!"

"Or every year before that," Barney says under his breath, glancing at his watch again.

With wide eyes, Kat and Chloe both look at me.

"I'm *fine*," says Brody loudly. He slams his empty glass down on the counter with a bang.

Everyone goes silent. Even the baby, who looks around the room, startled at the noise.

I swallow, my mouth suddenly desert dry. Something scratches on the inside of my skull with tiny, razor-sharp claws, an invisible rodent digging in the dirt for buried bones. On the distant horizon beyond the windows, a jagged flash of white lightning illuminates the dark, choppy sea.

Brody spends every St. Patrick's Day drunk.

*Scratch.*

Brody's going to get drunk again this St. Patrick's Day.

*Scratch.*

Brody had a nightmare last night, the worst one he can remember.

*Scratch.*

Brody asked me to marry him today.

*Scratch! Scratch! Scratch!*

Into the awkward silence Chloe says brightly, "So A.J. and I have good news!"

I can tell from the frozen expression on Kat's face that she thinks Chloe's about to announce her second pregnancy, but I can't give it too much attention because I'm staring hard at Brody, this person I thought I knew, who now seems as substantial as a mirage shimmering off in the distance.

*What's happening? What am I missing? What have I been overlooking all along?*

Ants crawl over my nerve endings. I feel as if I've just bumped into an electrified fence. My mind darts all over the place, hunting for something but not quite deciding what it is.

"What's the news?" asks Nico.

"Well, we finally got into the doctor this week," Chloe says, "and they did a whole bunch of tests, and A.J.'s headaches . . ."

I turn my full attention to her. She's beaming at A.J., who sits smiling by her side.

"What?" Leaning over the table, Kat grabs Chloe's hand.

"They're from dehydration!"

Through a mouthful of food, Kenji asks, "What headaches?"

Magda sets down plates full of food in front of Nico and Kat. She looks at me, and I shake my head. She looks at Brody, glowering at his empty glass on the counter, and shakes her own head.

Nico repeats, "Dehydration? What the fuck?"

Chloe laughs. "I *know*, right? All the tests showed *no* new growth in the tumor, and *no* other abnormalities in his system, and they finally concluded that he was just exhausted and dehydrated because he's been so focused on taking care of me and the baby that he wasn't taking care of himself! All they did was give him a saline IV!"

"Oh thank God! Honey, that's amazing." Kat rises, rounds the table, and engulfs Chloe in a hug from behind. Then she hugs A.J., who scoffs, "I *told* her I was fine!"

I move woodenly from where I'm standing alone by the counter and sink into a chair, not certain my legs can support me much longer. "You guys, I'm so relieved."

Kenji is grousing to himself. "A.J. was having headaches? *I* didn't hear about these headaches. Nobody thought to tell *me* he wasn't feeling well, because obviously I'm as important as chopped liver around here!"

During all of this, Barney looks back and forth between Brody and me with a slight, thoughtful furrow between his brows, as if he's trying as hard as I am to figure something out.

Magda places food in front of Chloe and A.J. Brody pours himself another vodka. A boom of thunder rolls through the clouds outside. A few erratic splatters of rain hiss against the windows.

In an obvious effort to keep the conversation going and gloss over Brody's weird mood and the even weirder vibe between us, Kat says to me, "Hey, sweetie, why don't you show me that photo album Brody started for you? It sounded amazing when you were telling me about it."

When I hesitate, she adds with a laugh, "Unless it's full of nudes!"

"There's one or two," Brody says dully from his spot at the bar. He's holding the glass of vodka in his hand, staring at it, or through it, like he might not even be seeing it at all. He glances up at her and forces a smile. "I don't think I ever properly thanked you for getting me all those pictures of you girls, though."

She smiles back at him. "No thanks necessary. I thought it was a wonderful idea." She looks at me. Her gaze is intense but her voice is casual when she says, "Well, if the photo album isn't fit for public viewing, I'd love to see all the new clothes you've been buying."

Picking up the thread of Kat's train of thought, Chloe says, "Oh, me, too! Why don't the three of us pop over to the guest house real quick before it starts to rain too hard?"

Kenji rolls his eyes. "Chopped liver, what did I tell you."

His attention turned back to his glass of vodka, Brody continues on as if there wasn't a break in their conversation. "The hardest part was finding anything about her before college for the Look Back section. It was kinda like . . . she didn't even exist."

"That's because I didn't."

Everyone looks at me.

It's one of those things I'll wonder about for years afterward, why I choose this particular moment to disclose that particular piece of my past. Maybe it's because everything's already so strange, and adding one more strange thing seems to fit. Maybe it's because of what Barney had revealed about *his* name. Maybe it's because of the gathering storm, or the marriage proposal, or all the unanswered questions I'd lived with for so long.

Or maybe, just maybe, it's because some part of me already knows.

"What do you mean?" asks Chloe, puzzled.

I look at her, and then at each person at the table in turn. Even Kenji has stopped eating to stare at me in silence.

"I mean I go by Grace Stanton, but it's not the name people knew me by when I was growing up."

From the corner of my eye, I see Brody's head lift.

Confused, Kat says, "What? Why?"

For something so long unspoken, it comes out effortlessly.

"The attorneys advised me to change it after the accident, after I received the settlement from my parents' life insurance, to avoid scammers and predators. You know, because I was a teenager, alone. And I was determined to start a new life without that notoriety hanging over my head. I didn't want to be what everyone saw me as, the sad orphan amnesia victim whose parents died in a tragic hit-and-run. I wanted to be anonymous, so a new name made complete sense. And because of the circumstances, a judge granted my name change under sealed order, so if anyone tried to find me from my old name, they couldn't."

A moment of shocked silence follows. Then, in a tight voice, Brody asks, "What name did you go by growing up?"

I turn my head and meet his eyes.

"Diana Van der Pool."

All the blood drains from Brody's face. The glass of vodka slips from his hand and shatters against the floor like a bomb.

## Brody

*The sound of the rain on the roof of the rental car is like a hail of bullets. It's dark, so dark and wet the headlights are nearly useless on the black ribbon of the winding canyon road ahead. We're going too fast, because my father always drives too fast, taking the next curve in the road with a reckless speed that makes the tires spin against the pavement. For one long, terrifying moment we float on the layer of water on the asphalt before the tires find their grip again and the car comes back under my father's control with a hard jolt that slams my teeth together.*

*In the passenger seat, I clutch the armrest and silently start to pray.*

*"Fucking rain!" my father mutters, peering through the windshield as the wipers slide back and forth over the glass. "I thought it never rained in California!"*

*His breath reeks of Scotch.*

*My audition for the UCLA music program went well today. One of the faculty members said he'd never seen an undergraduate perform contrasting Bach suite movements in addition to a Boccherini concerto on the classical guitar, that it wasn't until the master's program that that level of proficiency was usually achieved. I'm almost positive I'll make it in as a freshman like I'm hoping.*

*We flew in last night from Topeka, just my father and me, while Mom stayed home to look after my brother and sister. I watched her face from the taxi window as she stood in the doorway of our house and waved good-bye.*

*I didn't take it personally that she looked relieved we were leaving for a few days.*

*I knew it had nothing to do with me.*

*When my father dropped me off at the audition with the excuse he was going to visit an old friend, I knew the condition he'd be in when he came back to pick me up. This "old friend" he visited in between bouts of sobriety always returned him much worse for wear.*

*And today being St. Patrick's Day, with every bar around campus advertising specials on drinks, I knew the wear would be far worse than usual.*

*When we fly over a rise in the road and I see what's ahead, my heart jumps into my throat.*

*"Dad!" I holler. "There's a car! Slow down! Slow down!"*

*Cursing, my father slams his foot on the brake.*

*Too late.*

*The brakes lock. With the road so wet, the car goes into a long, uncontrolled slide, drifting aimlessly as my father fails to turn the steering wheel because he's frozen stiff in horror by the realization of what's about to happen. His hands are gripped so hard around the steering wheel his knuckles are white.*

*I'll remember that vividly later, his white knuckles.*

*That and all the other body parts.*

*As if the person driving is looking for an address or trying to see the road more clearly, a small white Honda is creeping forward on the road ahead of us. We're headed toward it at top speed, the night flying past in an inky blur.*

*One hundred feet.*

*Sixty feet.*

*Thirty feet.*

*Ten.*

*I scream just before the impact rips the sound from my throat and sends my head smashing into the passenger window.*

*The sounds of shattering glass and metal grating against metal pierce my eardrums with a terrible, inhuman roar. There's a moment of weightlessness, and then my head snaps sideways from the sudden velocity of our car changing direction. The awful grinding noise stops, and then somehow we're going straight on the rocky shoulder of the road, losing speed.*

*Miraculously, my father recovers enough of his senses to guide the car to a coasting stop.*

*Stunned, we sit in silence for seconds that feel like eons, listening to the sound of the rain on the roof. My heart is a jackhammer. I'm shaking violently. I can't catch my breath. A high-pitched buzzing echoes in my ears. Something is dripping into my eyes.*

*When I reach up to touch my face, I realize it's my own blood. My head hit the window so hard it split open.*

*"What . . . what happened?" asks my father, dazed.*

*He looks over at me. His gaze is unfocused and his face is slack, like he's awakening in confusion from a dream.*

*I look over his shoulder to the road behind us. The hot, acid bite of bile rises in my throat.*

*The Honda is upside down, smashed against a telephone pole on the opposite shoulder of the road, the front end crumpled up like an accordion. The wheels are still spinning. One headlight flickers erratically. Smoke rises in billowing gray plumes from the destroyed engine compartment, and, in spite of the rain, small licks of orange flame dance merrily inside.*

*I'm shaking so hard my fingers are almost useless, but I manage after a few fumbling attempts to open my door. I stagger out into the cold March air, my breath frosting in front of my face. I smell gasoline and smoke, sharp and stinging, and cough.*

*Then I see the foot.*

*It's lying alone in the middle of the road, a human foot sheared off just above the ankle, impossibly clad in a red high-heeled shoe.*

*A woman's foot.*

*I lean over and vomit, retching violently until there's nothing left.*

*Crying now, my breath leaving my body in raw, hacking sobs, I wipe my mouth on my sleeve. I stagger into the road, headed toward the Honda, terrified of what else I'm going to find, terrified even more of doing nothing.*

*When I'm a few feet away, the engine erupts into flames with a blood-curdling POP!*

*Shocked badly by the sound, I stumble and fall. I start to crawl to the car on my hands and knees, panic eating my insides. The smell of gasoline is choking me. Smoke billows into my face, burning my eyes.*

*From somewhere far away, I hear the sound of a siren, and then my father urgently calling my name.*

*There's a man inside the car, still buckled into the driver's seat. Even upside down, it's obvious he's dead. No one's head can be at that angle.*

*Beside him, crumpled into a mangled heap, is his wife.*

*I stop and retch, but nothing comes up. When I lift my head again, I see a flash of red in the backseat. My first thought is that it's blood, but as I force myself to crawl closer I realize it's not.*

*It's hair. A long, gleaming sheet of hair, falling from the head of the girl strapped into the backseat.*

*Her eyes are closed. One of her pale arms hangs lifelessly over her head, resting on the inside of the roof, and the other is pinned between her side and the door, folded into a dent. I think she must be dead, too, but then she lets out a soft moan of pain.*

*I almost faint from the relief that floods my body when I hear that sound.*

*Then the fire in the engine exhales a sudden burst of heat.*

*I know what's about to happen. I start to scream frantically at the girl.*

*"You have to get out! I have to get you out! You need to release your belt buckle now!"*

*I'm at the smashed window, reaching through, grabbing her wrist. She moans again, and her eyes flutter. I scream some more.*

*When her eyes open, it takes a lifetime for them to focus on my face.*

*"Your belt buckle!" I pull on her arm, but she doesn't budge. "Release your belt buckle!"*

*There's blood in my eyes, smoke in my nose, vomit in my throat, my hands and knees are cut and bleeding, but all I can think is please, please, please don't die. Please do not die on me, girl, I need you to live I need you to live I NEED YOU TO LIVE!*

*There's another hideously loud pop from the engine compartment. Heat flashes over me, such scalding, ferocious heat I know we're both going to die.*

*With a sudden burst of strength, I force my shoulders through the window, jab at the belt buckle until it gives way, and then give her arm a final, brutal pull.*

*I drag her through the smashed window and clear of the burning car just as the entire thing is swallowed in flames.*

*I run like I've never run in my life, dragging the redheaded girl over the wet pavement by her slim, pale wrist, crying so hard I can't see.*

*Behind me, the car explodes with a noise like a rocket blasting into space.*

*I fall again, this time on top of her, shielding her from the heat and debris raining down. I don't know how we're not both killed, but we survive. Somehow, we survive.*

*And then my father drags me off her with his fists in the back of my sweatshirt and starts to drunkenly scream at me.*

*"We have to leave, get in the car, get back into the car, can't you hear the sirens!"*

*"Are you crazy? We can't leave, she needs help—"*

*He backhands me across the face.*

*My father is a big man, broad shouldered and barrel chested, a man who played rugby in his youth. Even in middle age he's strong as a bull. Even drunk he's still powerful.*

*I'm not strong or powerful. I'm just a skinny kid who doesn't have a lot of friends because he spends all his time playing guitar.*

*His strike puts me on my knees again, stunned and seeing stars. Then he yanks me to my feet and pushes me toward our rental car, still idling on the opposite side of the road.*

*He snarls, "Get in that fucking car and drive, boy, or I'll tell them it was* you *who was driving. You think you'll be going to music school then?"*

No! No! No! *chants my brain,* You can't let this happen!

*But my father, mayor of Topeka, Kansas, embarking next month on his first-ever run for senate, which everyone says he will easily win, is not a man who understands the word "no."*

*He also isn't a man who would hesitate to sacrifice anything, including his oldest son, for his political aspirations.*

*Sobbing, wrecked, in a state of shock I'll never completely recover from, I let my father push me down the road.*

*I don't remember the drive back to our hotel. I don't remember anything about the rest of that night, or the next day, except that when we turned in the rental car my father explained the damage to the front end by saying his son just got his driver's license and didn't have experience on wet roads.*

*Swerved to miss a squirrel and overcorrected, he said. Ran into a retaining wall.*

*Then, smiling, he clapped me on the shoulder and told the young man behind the counter to have his old buddy Jim Rennett, the owner of the company, give him a call. He was going to be a senator soon, and with a growing business, Jim would need a voice in congress.*

*When I checked the papers, sure it was only a matter of time before the police came knocking, I read that there were more than two hundred car crashes in L.A. that night, up significantly from the usual numbers due to the rain.*

*Those sirens probably weren't even for us.*

*How it tortured me to think of that redheaded girl lying alone and helpless on that dark road. How it haunted me to wonder how long she remained there with the bodies of her parents being incinerated in their car, mere yards away. How it killed me to wonder if she'd been badly hurt, or even survived.*

*How I hated my father.*

*How much more I hated myself for being too much of a coward to stand up to him.*

*And how grimly satisfied I was to discover the name of that family in the paper a few days later. Because I not only knew that the girl survived, but I had the means to more properly torture myself. Naming your victims makes them all the more real.*

*Mr. and Mrs. Robert and Elizabeth Van der Pool.*

*And their daughter, Diana.*

# Chapter 35

## Grace

As Magda exclaims at the mess around Brody's feet from the smashed glass of vodka, Brody stares at me, his eyes wild, his face white, his entire body shaking.

He utters a single, choked word.

"*No.*"

Seated across from me, staring at me with the same expression of horror Brody's wearing, Barney breathes, "Mother of God," and makes the sign of the cross over his chest.

I look back and forth between them, all the tiny hairs on my body standing on end.

Brody whispers, "You said you grew up in San Francisco."

Adrenaline screams through my body. That rat inside my skull scratches furiously, clawing into my brain.

Something is wrong.

Something is very, very wrong.

"I did."

"But the . . . the accident was in Brentwood."

Kat, Nico, Kenji, and Chloe are looking at the three of us like they can tell something really weird is up, while A.J. sits silently with his head cocked, as if listening to everyone's thoughts.

"My father had been offered a job at the Rand Institute in Santa Monica. He was a computer analyst. We drove down that weekend to look at neighborhoods . . ."

I trail off into silence because I realize I've never told Brody where the accident occurred.

And that he said "*the* accident," not "*your* accident."

*I once did something when I was very young*, he'd told me. *Something stupid.*

*Oh my God.*

I stand so abruptly I knock my chair over. It hits the floor with a clatter as loud as a gunshot. My vision narrows, the room blackening to a tunnel, until all I can see is Brody's white, wild-eyed face.

I'm punched in the gut by a long-buried memory, a memory that only surfaces in the worst of my nightmares. A memory of a boy, screaming at me through a smashed car window, his face covered in blood.

His terrified eyes exactly like Brody's are now.

Everything comes together with the swiftness of two fingers snapping. Goose bumps erupt all over my body. I feel the single, painful beat of my heat.

I breathe, *"You."*

As if the word is a physical shove, Brody staggers backward. He collides with the kitchen counter and then stands there gripping its edge, his chest heaving, looking as if he's about to pass out.

A bewildered A.J. asks, "What's happening?"

Sitting beside him, Chloe stares at Brody like he's a dangerous stranger. I wonder if she's somehow put it together, too.

Slowly, Barney rises from his chair, his hands held out toward me as if to try to stop me from bolting. "Grace," he says, his voice low and soothing. "Take it easy. Just look at me. Grace. Look at me."

I can't look at him. I can't look away from Brody. Brody, the man I've given my body to. Brody, the man I've given my heart to. Brody, the sweet, thoughtful man who only today proposed.

The man who murdered my parents and stole eighteen years of my life.

His guilt is all right there in his face. It's all over him, like a stain on the inside leaking out through his pores. Blinded by my feelings, I haven't been able to see it until now.

Rage blasts through me, dark and primal.

Hands fisted at my sides, my feet planted on the floor, I open my mouth and scream.

It's a long, raw shriek of anguish, betrayal, and fury that makes everyone at the table jump. Brody's hands fly up to cover his ears. His face crumples. He starts to sob.

"Grace!" Kat leaps to her feet. "What the fuck is going on?"

From my peripheral vision I see Barney moving slowly toward me, but I still can't look away from Brody.

"You . . . you *targeted* me," I accuse in a hoarse, furious whisper, the words as raw in my throat as broken glass. "All this time you *knew* and you *lied* to me—"

"No!" he cries, his body racked with sobs. "Grace, no—"

*"What the fuck is going on!"* shouts Kat.

Now everyone except A.J. is on their feet, standing around the table in confusion, watching Brody and me, witnessing my worst nightmare come to life.

No. Not even in my worst nightmare could I ever imagine that I'd fall in love with my parents' killer.

"Let's just calm down and talk," suggests Barney. He's using the same rational, detached tone I use when I'm dealing with a patient who's emotionally out of control. It snaps the very last thread of my sanity.

I whirl on him. "You knew, too! Didn't you? *DIDN'T YOU!*"

"It's not what you think," he says, still with his hands out. His voice remains calm, but I see all kinds of things in his eyes. Dark, secret things that break my heart.

"You make me *sick*. Both of you make me sick!" Shaking hard, I back up a step, fighting the urge to vomit.

Nico, holding Kat by her arm to keep her from launching herself across the room toward me, growls, "Barney, what the *fuck*?"

My voice shaking as badly as the rest of me, I say, "Tell him, Barney. Tell him how the two of you lied to me. Tell him how you took advantage of me. Tell him how you could have *protected* me from him, but didn't."

The word "protected" makes him wince. His voice rises. "It's not like that! Will you just listen to me—"

"Fuck you." The words are bitten out, as hard as a slap. Barney recoils as if I've struck him across the face. I turn my gaze back to Brody, as pale as stone, still frozen against the counter.

"And fuck *you*, too," I whisper, voice breaking. "You monster. You *murderer*!"

Kat, Chloe, and Kenji gasp.

Nico and A.J. exclaim in unison, *"What?"*

Sobbing, Brody sinks to his knees.

Across the room, Magda stands staring at me. Her gaze doesn't flinch away from mine. *He was a wild thing when he was a boy*, she'd said. *I worried he'd turn out bad.*

She knew, too. Everybody knew but me.

Tears crest my lower lids and slide down my cheeks. I turn around and run.

I'm driving too fast, but I don't care. I have to get away from that house as fast as possible. I can't stand to be anywhere near him. I need to be out of the city, the county, maybe even the state.

"I could move to France," I whisper, ignoring the tears streaming down my cheeks. Along with the rain, they're making it hard to see the road through the windshield, but I don't care about that, either. "I have enough money. I could get on a plane tonight and never come back. I could start over. Again."

I laugh. Even to my own ears it sounds insane.

I'm cracking.

As the car flies around a turn, I pound the steering wheel and shout at myself. "Get your shit together! You're a lion! You're a tiger!"

*You're a fool who fell in love with the man who ruined your life.*

A sob escapes my lips. I shove a fist into my mouth to stifle it.

Headlights appear behind me on the highway. Reflected in the rearview mirror, they momentarily blind me. I squint and hold up a hand to block the light. My car jolts over a rough patch in the road, and I jerk the wheel to correct the sudden, violent swerve.

The headlights of the car behind me flash. The car zooms closer, and they flash again.

It's Brody's Tesla.

Heart pounding, I stomp on the gas. My Lexus leaps forward with a roar. The traffic is light on this stretch of PCH, where the houses are huge and far apart, but once I hit the main part of town it will be gridlock.

I have to lose him before then. I never want to see that bastard's face again.

Then—out of nowhere—a dog is standing in the middle of the road. It's big and white, unmoving, looking in my direction with startled eyes as I barrel straight toward it.

Instinct takes over.

I slam on the brakes. They lock. On the wet asphalt, the tires lose their grip. The car goes sideways. I yank the wheel hard in the opposite direction, desperate to regain control, but the car doesn't respond. I slide down the dark, rainy highway with my hands gripped around the steering wheel, my heart pounding like mad, a scream of terror trapped in my throat.

The dog sprints away and is gone.

The edge of the highway looms through the windshield, flying closer. Beyond is nothing but blackness, the storm-tossed ocean, and the rain.

A cliff.

I sail straight over it and out into the night.

My terrified scream breaks free and echoes all around me, a final requiem as I fall.

*"Higher, Daddy! Higher!"*

*Standing to one side of the metal swing set on our patchy backyard grass, my father laughs. "You'll go too high, Peanut! Pretty soon you'll touch the sun!"*

*But as the swing descends and then arcs up again, he puts both hands on my back and pushes me higher, as he always does when I ask him to. I scream in delight, my bare legs flung out in front of me, my long hair streaming away from my face.*

*The sun shines so brightly. The sky is so blue. There's nothing I love more than the feeling of flying, or the steadying strength of my father's hands on my back.*

*"Dinner's ready!" my mother calls through the open kitchen window. Smiling widely, framed between yellow flowered curtains, she waves at us.*

*Daddy says I get my beautiful smile from her. Same for my red hair.*

*"Be right in, honey!" Daddy calls.*

*As the swing descends again, I beg, "One more, Daddy! One more!"*

*He laughs. "You heard your mother, Peanut."*

*But then his hands are on my back and I get another push that sends me flying high, so high I think I'll touch the sun.*

Cold.

Electronic beeping.

The smell of antiseptic, stinging in my nose.

*God, I hate that smell.*

It's not the cold or the beeping, but the smell that finally forces me to open my eyes, though all I'd like to do is lie here in this blank darkness forever. I have to find out what's causing that acidic stench and make it stop.

A room swims into view. Blank white walls and a white tiled floor, a pale blue curtain hung from the ceiling on a metal rod with rings. A flat-screen TV mounted on the wall opposite me, off kilter a few inches. My lids are heavy, so heavy it's impossible to keep them open more than a second at a time, so I let gravity pull them shut.

After a while, someone speaks.

"Miss Stanton? Miss Stanton, can you hear me?"

With a gargantuan effort of will, I drag my eyelids open again. An older woman leans over me, looking down at me with kind brown eyes. She's heavyset, wearing pink scrubs, her salt-and-pepper hair pulled away from her face in an untidy bun. Glinting in the light, a gold cross hangs from a chain around her neck.

I have the strangest sense of déjà vu, as if I've been here before, right here, lying on my back in an unfamiliar room with this same woman leaning over me, looking at me with those sympathetic eyes.

"Miss Stanton, you're in the hospital. You were in an accident. Can you hear me?"

*An accident. I was in an accident.*

The thought is vaguely alarming, but I don't have the strength to work up a real fear yet. For now it's enough that I'm not in pain. That must be good news, at least. I take comfort in the lack of sensation in my body.

Now that I think of it, the only thing that hurts is my head.

My mouth like cotton, I whisper, "Water."

The nurse nods, disappears from my view for a moment, and then reappears holding a small white cup with a bendy straw. She helps me sip from the straw, her hand cradled under my neck.

"I'll send the doctor in," she says when I'm finished drinking. "He'll be pleased you're finally awake."

*Finally?* I think, drifting back down into my fuzzy awareness.

I don't want to know what she means.

A minute or a week later, a man's voice interrupts my drifting thoughts with a cheerful, "There she is! Welcome back to the land of the living!"

He sounds like a salesman. Whoever this person is, I already know I can't stand him.

I crack one eye open. At the side of my bed is a doctor. Actually he looks like someone playing a doctor, because he's much too good-looking to have wasted his time going to medical school when he could've been making millions selling toothpaste on TV. He's tall and well built, with hair the color of good whiskey and one of those perfect smiles you just *know* cost thousands to create. His smile shines so big and bright I close my eye against its disturbing glare.

"Don't go back to sleep on me now, Grace, we've been waiting for this moment for three long days!"

*Don't call me by my first name, Dr. Chompers,* I think, irritated, but then get distracted by what he's said. "Three days? We?" I repeat groggily, trying hard to correctly form the words.

"You had swelling in your brain so it was necessary to induce a coma to get it under control." He leans over me and switches off some machine that's beeping next to my head. "You might be disoriented or nauseated, both of which are perfectly normal and shouldn't last long—"

"Three days?" I say again, more forcefully this time.

Dr. Chompers gazes down at me, his smile firmly fixed in place. "Yes. Very Jesus-like of you, if I do say so myself."

When I stare at him in silence, he adds brightly, "You know, 'And on the third day He rose again'?" His grin grows wider. "Except in your case, of course, it's 'She.'"

I'm in hell. This is hell. I'm being punished for every bad deed I committed in my life by this fake doctor, who is really the devil posing as a bad television actor and his gaudy, gleaming teeth.

I mumble, "Nice to meet you, Satan. You look exactly like I thought you would."

The toothpaste smile doesn't even waver. "Hallucinations are normal, too."

From his white coat pocket, he removes an instrument the size and shape of a pen, clicks one end, and proceeds to open my eye with his thumb and forefinger, pulling the lids apart without even so much as a warning. He shines a light directly into my eye.

I say thickly, "Why does my head hurt? Am I injured? What happened? Where am I?"

Satisfied by whatever he sees in my right eye, Dr. Chompers moves the light to my left. After a moment, he nods, and then retrieves the uncomfortable-looking plastic chair from next to the small table by the window and sits down next to my bed. He crosses one leg over the other, and looks at me with a serious gaze, his ridiculous smile at odds with the rest of his expression.

"You're in Saint John's Hospital in Santa Monica. You were involved in a car accident on Pacific Coast Highway. You lost control of your car around an unsecured curve and you went over the edge."

Flashes of memory hit me like strobe lights. The rain. A white dog. My Lexus in an uncontrolled slide.

"How am I not dead?"

He chuckles. "You landed on the beach berm. Right on top, like a cherry on an ice cream float. You ask me, that's a miracle right there. Yes, ma'am. A real miracle."

When I frown at him in obvious confusion, he continues.

"You know, the Malibu beach berm, the giant sand dune that runs parallel to that stretch of the highway for about a mile? The state trucked in tons of sand and piled it up to protect the road from erosion during the winter storm months until they can do proper reinforcements this summer."

I have a fuzzy recollection of pictures in the newspaper of tons of sand dumped over the edge of the highway and scooped into huge piles by earthmovers working on the beach.

The doctor continues. "You were saved from more serious injury by the airbags, but that's also what caused the trauma to your head. You have whiplash, a concussion, and had minor bleeding in your brain, along with the swelling—"

I gasp so loudly the doctor stops speaking, surprised.

"My father," I rasp, staring at the blank TV screen, my heart pounding.

The doctor looks at the television, and then back at me. He clears his throat. "As I said, when you're coming out of anesthesia, hallucinations are—"

"No. No, I mean, I *remember* my father." Tears gathering in my eyes, I look at the doctor. "And my mother, too."

And Brody.

I whisper, "Oh fuck," and squeeze my eyes closed in a futile attempt to try to block the memories.

The doctor stands. After a moment he says, "I understand you suffer from retrograde amnesia from an automobile accident you were involved in years ago."

I don't reply. I'm too busy dealing with the onslaught of memories and the overwhelming emotions suddenly raging through me like wildfire. I'm hot, and cold, and sick, and dizzy, and everything else, all at once.

*Brody. God, Brody. No.*

The doctor says, "I'll schedule a memory specialist to see you as soon as possible, but in the meantime, I'd like to run through a few simple tests if you're feeling up to it."

Though I'm feeling anything but "up," I nod silently, putting all my concentration into holding back the tears that threaten to spill from my eyes.

I have a terrible suspicion if I let them loose now, they'll never stop coming and I'll drown.

I'm kept in the ICU for another two days. My plump, caring nurse—her name turns out to be Cuddleby, how perfect—keeps a vigilant eye on me, ruthlessly refusing to let me wallow in what quickly becomes apparent is a devastating depression by bullying me into eating, talking, and interacting with her, when all I want to do is curl up into a ball and die.

"Lunch!" she says to me now, sailing into my room with her motherly smile, carrying a tray that holds various dishes covered in plastic wrap.

"I'm not hungry."

Her smile turns to a frown. "Going on a hunger strike isn't going to help anyone, kiddo, least of all *you*." Blocking my view of the television, she sits on the edge of my bed and uses the fork to stab a blob of unidentifiable meat smothered in an unappealing lumpy gravy from one of the plates. She holds it out to me.

"Eat," she demands.

I stare at the mystery meat on the end of the fork. "If you can tell me with any kind of certainty what animal that is, I'll think about eating it. Until then, no thanks."

She wiggles the fork up and down at me as if I'm an unruly toddler and she's trying to bribe me with candy. "C'mon. If you don't eat, I'll tell Dr. Gold you were seeing Smurfs and Gremlins all over the room."

I glare at her. "That's blackmail."

She smiles sweetly back at me. "Them's the breaks, kiddo. Eat, or I'll report that you're confused and hallucinating, and you'll have to stay here with me and this gourmet food of ours even longer."

I give her some really strong stink eye, but she doesn't wither a bit. So I take the fork, shove the disgusting piece of meat into my mouth, and chew.

"I think it's rat," I say around a mouthful of stringy awfulness.

She watches me for a moment, not satisfied until I swallow, and then asks, "Anything new today?"

With my memory, she means. Since I woke from the anesthesia, memories of my childhood have been coming back in fits and starts, like one of those old crank movie cameras, projecting jittery black-and-white pictures inside my head. According to the memory specialist the hospital assigned me, the new trauma to my brain might have opened old pathways, knocked long-stuck things loose.

He also floated the idea that my amnesia might have been psychogenic—in other words, caused by stress, not tissue damage—but didn't float that hypothesis again after he saw the murderous look I gave him.

"I had a cat named Scooby," I answer. "A raggedy little orange thing with a raspy meow."

I don't add that I loved that cat with the fierce, blind devotion of a child, and cried when I remembered it had been run over by a car in the street in front of my house when I was eleven.

Nurse Cuddleby and I sit quietly until she says, "He's still out there."

My heart jolts into high gear. Trying to control the sudden shaking in my hand, I slowly set the fork down on the tray. "Call the police."

She sighs. "It's a public waiting area. He's not doing anything that would get him in trouble, or disturbing anyone—"

"He's disturbing *me*!"

We stare at each other. Forgoing another mention of Brody, who, according to her, hasn't left the hospital waiting room in five days, she moves on to a safer topic.

"Your other friends are still asking to see you, too. The blonde one with the adorable baby went home for the day, but the other one, the brunette with the gorgeous husband—they're celebrities, right? Security keeps escorting TMZ off the premises, but there's reporters crawling all over the parking lot."

"Kat," I say dully.

"She's back. She went ballistic when she heard you still can't see anyone. The rest of the nurses are afraid of her." She softly laughs. "She's a little spitfire, that one. Small, but feisty. I'm worried she might break down the ICU doors!"

I turn my head away and stare out the window. It's gloomy outside, the sky as flinty as graphite. As cold and lifeless as my soul.

In a way I'm grateful I'm not allowed to have visitors, because I know as soon as I see the girls' faces I'll break down. And I'm not ready to break down just yet. I've got something I have to do first. As soon as they let me out of this hospital, I'm going straight to the police station to file a report.

I happen to know for a fact that in California there isn't a statute of limitations for murder.

I say, "Could you please tell her—"

"Tell her what?" demands a rough voice from the doorway.

Barney stands there, almost unrecognizable in a badly wrinkled white dress shirt, with a week's growth of beard darkening his cheeks and dark circles under his eyes. His shirtsleeves are rolled up, exposing his forearms, which are tattooed with mysterious markings from the inside of both wrists up to his elbows, where the tattoos disappear under his sleeves.

They're exactly like the markings Brody has tattooed across his chest.

Startled, Nurse Cuddleby rises quickly. "You can't be in here! You need to leave!"

Barney says, "I'm not leaving until she hears me out."

My heart beats so fast I'm having trouble breathing.

"Security!" calls the nurse.

I say, "Wait—let him in. It's all right."

She glances at me, examines my face, and then asks, "Is he immediate family?"

Barney and I lock eyes. Finally, my heart still thumping like mad, I nod.

She looks back at Barney and gives him a narrow-eyed once-over, obviously not believing we're related, but unable to throw him out since I've said we are.

"I'll be right outside. You have ten minutes." She moves past him quickly, skirting him as she goes through the doorway, and then waits by the nurse's station in the hallway. She keeps her eye on Barney as he walks slowly into the room.

He stops at the end of my bed and stares at me.

I bite out, "You don't have ten minutes, you have sixty seconds, so make it count."

With a faint smile he says, "Can't tell you how relieved I am to see you, Angelface. You look like shit."

"You look worse. The clock is ticking."

He chuffs out a hard breath, drags a hand over his head, and then begins to talk, his voice rough as if he's swallowed a handful of gravel.

"Brody was twenty-two when he joined the band, right out of college. At first I thought he was just another shallow pretty rich kid, went to school on daddy's dime, had more money and pussy than he knew what to do with."

My face reddens. Barney continues without blinking an eye.

"But he was more serious than that. He worked hard, he was more dedicated to making good music than anybody else, he had his priorities straight." Barney's voice gets lower. "But there was a dark side. One he kept under control most of the time, but that came out without fail every year, on the same day."

I swallow and fold my shaking arms across my chest.

"After three disastrous St. Patrick's Days in a row—we're talking drunken rages, picking fights with guys twice his size and getting his ass beaten bad, waking up in jail kind of disastrous—I forced him to tell me why. The story he told me—"

"Are you asking me to feel *sorry* for him?" I interrupt, sickened. "Did he tell you my father was almost decapitated? That his body and my mother's body were so badly burned the authorities couldn't identify them for days? That I *crawled* for half a mile to find help while my parents' ashes rained down on me?"

Barney inhales a slow breath, and then says quietly, "Brody wasn't driving the car that killed your parents, Grace. His father was driving the car. His father who was shitfaced drunk."

Shock hits me in a cold, hard slap. I stare at Barney, speechless, feeling sick straight down to the marrow of my bones.

His steps heavy, Barney slowly walks around the edge of the bed. He pulls up the ugly plastic chair, lowers himself into it, and sighs.

"He was a local politician in Kansas, a real son of a bitch from what I understand, getting ready to run for senate. He and Brody were in town for Brody's audition at the UCLA music school. His father left him at the audition, got drunk at a local bar, and then got behind the wheel. After . . . he forced Brody to leave the scene. There were no other eyewitnesses."

Barney's dark eyes shine like he has a fever. His gaze drills into mine. "Brody pulled you out of the car before it exploded. He saved your life, Grace. Do you remember that?"

I can't think. I can't speak. I can barely breathe. I make a small sound of horror in the back of my throat.

Barney runs a hand over his hair, sighing again. "After a few days back home, he couldn't stand the guilt that he'd allowed his father to drag him away from the wreck. He went to the Topeka police and told them what had happened. But because his father was who he was, and he and the chief went way back, and his father made a statement that his son had been getting into drugs lately, the police brushed it off as a 'family dispute.' They didn't even investigate Brody's claim."

*Brody wasn't driving. Brody's father was drunk. Brody went to the police, but they didn't believe him.*

*Brody's father killed my parents.*

I can't process it. Any of it. My stomach twists and rolls. I break out in a cold sweat, my palms and underarms clammy. "But . . . their car. There would have been physical evidence—"

"Yeah, there would've been. If they hadn't been driving a rental car from a company owned by a good buddy of Brody's dad. A guy he was in the army with. A guy who, once Mr. Scott was elected into congress, got a very lucrative contract to be the exclusive rental car provider for all the state government's business in Kansas. The rental car they were driving that night got fixed and repainted lickety-split, and Brody got such a severe beating from his father for going to the police that he couldn't get out of bed for days. Those beatings continued until the day Brody fought back and broke his father's jaw. Then he went away to college and they never spoke again."

My head pounds. I close my eyes and squeeze my forehead with both hands, trying desperately to make sense of what Barney is telling me.

But I can't. No one could ever make sense of a thing like this.

"As soon as he moved to L.A., he tried to find you. All he had was a name from the newspaper, an article he cut out and kept in his wallet." Barney pulls his own wallet from his back pocket, opens it, and removes a folded up piece of newsprint. He offers it to me.

I take it, my fingers shaking so badly I almost can't hold it straight.

*Couple Killed in Hit-and-Run Identified*

*Authorities have released the names of the husband and wife who lost their lives in a tragic hit-and-run accident on St. Patrick's Day. Robert and Elizabeth Van der Pool were driving on Beverly Glen Road in Brentwood at approximately six o'clock in the evening when their car was struck by another vehicle from behind. The impact caused the Van der Pool's Honda to veer off the road into a shallow gully, where it overturned and collided with a telephone pole.*

*In a community alert, police say they are still looking for the other car, which most likely has significant damage to its front end. The driver fled the scene and remains at large.*

*The Van der Pools are survived by their daughter, Diana, who is recovering from injuries sustained in the accident.*

My parents' deaths occupy a three-inch-long section of newspaper, unaccompanied by a picture.

A section of newspaper Brody has been carrying in his wallet for thirteen years.

The article grows blurry as tears well in my eyes. "How do I know this is true? How do I know it wasn't him who was driving? That he made his innocence up, pinned this whole thing on his dead father, and sent you in here with more lies?"

Barney shakes his head. "He told me this *four years ago*, Grace, long before your lives intersected again. He asked me back then if I could help him try to find Diana Van der Pool, so he could tell her how sorry he was, how much he hated himself for what he saw as his cowardice, how he would do anything he could to help make her life better. But I didn't have any more luck finding Diana Van der Pool than he did. She was long gone. Vanished from the face of the earth, as if she'd been abducted by aliens."

His voice softens. "And now we know why."

I'm hyperventilating. My mind can't stick to any one thought, and spins wildly from memory to memory as pain crashes over me in waves. I want to scream, and break something, and run somewhere, anywhere, as fast as I can, but all I can do is sit in my hospital bed and stare at Barney as the last pieces of my composure come crumbling down.

I never used to believe in things like Fate or Destiny. I prided myself on my cool, rational mind. But now I think all that rigid control I cultivated so diligently and exercised over my life for so many years was nothing more than castles built in the sand. An illusion, ephemeral as a breath of air.

Fate has had its hands on my steering wheel all along.

My life literally collided with Brody's thirteen years ago, and though I've done everything in my power to forget my past existed, Fate has been determined to bring us back together ever since.

Now the only choice before me is whether to continue the fight, or surrender.

My voice as ragged as the beating of my heart, I say, "Your tattoos—Brody has the same thing across his chest, above the angel's wings."

Barney looks down at his forearms, and then glances back up at me. "He got them the same night he told me that story, after he asked me what mine meant."

"What do they mean?"

His face clouds. He doesn't speak for a long time. Then he murmurs, "It's in Arabic, and not something I'll ever speak aloud again. Brody's tattoo is in Arabic, too, but it says something different."

My heart in my throat, I ask, "What does his say?"

"You should ask him."

"I'm asking *you*, Barney. Tell me what it says."

Slowly, Barney stands. He gazes down at me with an unreadable expression. Finally, just when I think he won't speak again, he does.

"'Unforgiven.'"

That takes my breath away.

*Are you sorry for what you did? Then I forgive you,* I'd told Brody, completely ignorant of what I'd been forgiving.

My face crumples. I start to sob, loud, violent sobs that shudder my body and echo through the room. I lean over, put my face into my hands, and give in to them. Barney rests a comforting hand on my shoulder, and then Nurse Cuddleby barges into the room with a shout.

"What's going on? Get your hands off her!" She turns and hollers out into the hallway. "Security! Security!"

"For the love of God, woman, she's only crying!" Barney shouts at the nurse.

Then like a whirlwind Kat bursts through the door, her eyes wild, her long, dark hair flying around her face. As soon as she spots me she lets out a loud string of curses. She barrels across the room, knocking aside Nurse Cuddleby, who shrieks in panic.

Kat flings herself on me, hugging me so hard it hurts.

"Tell me you're okay," she begs.

I'm crying so hard I can't answer.

Barney says gently, "She's fine, Kat. She's just emotional. Under the circumstances, it's to be expected."

Kat hugs me even harder and starts to cry, too. She wails, "Goddamn it you crazy bitch if you *ever* scare me like that again I'll kick your fucking ass so bad you won't be able to *walk*!"

*"Security!"* hollers Nurse Cuddleby, hurrying from the room.

Through my tears, I have to laugh.

Kat pulls away and cradles my face in her hands. She whispers, "I'm so sorry, honey. I can't even imagine what you're going through."

"So everyone knows everything about . . . ?"

For some reason, it's suddenly impossible to say Brody's name.

Kat nods, swallowing hard. "He and Barney told us everything. And I don't know if this is the wrong thing to say right now, but I think you should know that this situation is killing him. Not knowing if you were going to be okay, not knowing if you would live to hear what really happened, or if you did, if you'd ever forgive him . . . he's a total wreck. He won't eat. He barely speaks. He hasn't changed his clothes or showered in five days."

Her voice drops. "He was the first one on the scene, honey, when you went over that cliff in Malibu. He pulled you out of a wreck *again*. He thought he'd lost you *again*. Can you imagine? I've never seen anyone in so much pain. I'm worried . . ." She bites her lip. "Honestly I'm worried he might do something to hurt himself."

My stomach turns over. I don't know what I expected to hear, but it definitely wasn't that.

Barney says, "He'll be all right. I'll talk to him. Once he knows I've seen you, that you're gonna be okay—"

Kat says, "You can't talk to him. He's gone."

"Gone?" I repeat. "Where?"

She shakes her head. "I don't know. Right after Barney left the waiting room, Brody just got up from the chair he's been in all week and walked out without a word. Even when I called his name he just kept walking like a zombie without looking back."

Barney lets out a long, low sigh. "Fuck."

When Kat and I look at him, he says with quiet resignation, "I think I know where he went."

# Chapter 37

## Brody

I was a fool to believe there could ever be redemption for someone like me. No amount of good deeds can erase the things I'm guilty of. No force in this world can wash away *my* sins.

Not even love.

With a crowd of reporters and cameramen at my back, I slowly walk up the wide stone steps of the Santa Monica police station, pull open the glass door, and go inside.

# Chapter 38

## Grace

Four days after I'm released from the hospital, television news vans are still parked on the street outside Nico and Kat's house, where I've been staying.

"Vultures," mutters Kat as we drive past in Nico's big Escalade, turning our faces away from the blistering eruption of camera flashes our departure provokes.

Sitting in the front passenger seat beside Barney, who's driving, Nico says, "You gotta admit we've given them plenty of interesting stories to report on over the last couple of years."

Next to me, Kat reaches over, grasps my hand, and gives it a reassuring squeeze. "We certainly have," she murmurs, looking at me.

*Yes*, I think sadly. *We certainly have.*

After that, we're all quiet until we're past the news vans and cameramen jostling each other for a closer position and shouting questions at the blacked-out windows as we go by. Once we reach the freeway and are speeding away from the Hollywood Hills toward the lavender dusk of Santa Monica, Kat asks, "You sure about this?"

"I'm sure," I answer firmly.

I've never been as sure of anything in my life. Locked up in the guest bedroom at Kat's, I've spent the last four days pacing, thinking, and agonizing over the unbelievable position I'm in, and I finally came to the conclusion that this is the right thing to do.

As if my heart would give me a choice, anyway.

It takes thirty minutes to arrive in Santa Monica, another ten to get through the heavy rush hour traffic on the streets. Then we're parked in an underground parking garage, and Kat is squeezing my hand once again.

"Okay, sweetie," she says. "We're here."

I meet Barney's gaze in the rearview mirror. He asks, "You want us to come in with you?"

"No." I pull my coat a little tighter around my shoulders. "I need to do this alone. But it shouldn't take long. I'll text you as soon as I'm done, okay?"

Nico murmurs, "Good luck," and Barney echoes it. Kat leans over and kisses me on the cheek.

"Love you, Gracie," she whispers fiercely into my ear.

"I know," I say, my voice cracking. "And you're the best friend anyone could ever have."

Before I ruin my mascara, I open the car door and step out. I take a deep breath, lift my chin, square my shoulders, and smooth a hand over my hair.

Then I take the parking elevator up to the main floor and enter the police station.

The detective who shakes my hand is tall and rangy, with bushy brown eyebrows and a moustache to match. He wears cowboy boots with his conservative dark suit and a bolo tie made from a chunk of real turquoise, and doesn't smile when we're introduced.

I instantly like him.

"Detective MacAllister," he says in a twangy tenor, nodding at me. "But you can call me Mac. Have a seat."

He waves at the pair of battered leather chairs in front of his desk, which is a mess, covered in file folders bursting with papers. A small, bronze longhorn steer acts as a paperweight atop one teetering stack, a black glass armadillo perches on another.

"What part of Texas are you from?" I ask, settling into a chair.

"San Antonio. Best city in the world if you like 'em flat and hot, but the food is for shit."

"That's quite the recommendation. I'll be sure to never go."

Mac sits, fishes a pack of gum that looks like it's been run over from his top drawer, and holds the pack out to me.

"No. Thank you."

"Suit yourself." He unwraps three pieces from their silver wrappers, pops them into his mouth, starts to chew, balls up the wrappers, and, without looking, tosses them over his shoulder into a trash can behind him. Then he leans back in his big captain's chair with his hands folded over his stomach and looks at me.

*Really* looks at me.

"Thanks for comin' in," he says.

"Of course."

Working the gum between his molars, he looks at me some more, his gaze frank and assessing. I can almost see the gears turning behind his eyes. Accustomed to enduring long silences between people, I sit patiently and wait for him to begin.

Abruptly, he asks, "You know how I can tell when a man's tellin' the truth?"

"Because he looks you square in the eye and doesn't fidget, equivocate, or stumble over his words when he answers."

Mac stops chewing momentarily, and then starts up again, nodding. "Yep, he said you were smart."

He's talking about Brody. Heat saturates my cheeks. "That's not exactly rarefied knowledge."

"Rarefied?" Mac chuckles again.

"I'm happy to know I amuse you," I say, my stomach tightening, "but I didn't come here to talk about myself."

The phone on Mac's desk rings. He answers it while looking at me. "Yep." Several moments go by as he listens, and then he says, "Yep," again and hangs up.

"Detective MacAllister—"

"We're not charging him," he interrupts, sounding a little tired. "And I told you to call me Mac."

I feel as if I've been kicked off the edge of a tall building. It's several seconds before I can speak again. "You're . . . not . . ."

"When was the last time you talked to Mr. Scott, Miss Stanton?"

"Call me Grace. And not since the day of the accident. He's been out of contact with everyone," I answer unevenly, reeling from the news.

I've been so certain the police would charge Brody with hit-and-run, or aiding and abetting, or felony something or other, that I can hardly believe my ears.

"Well, Grace, since Mr. Scott came in to see me five days ago and insisted he should be arrested for accessory to murder, I've talked to a lot of folks. Folks who know his family, folks who knew his father, folks on the Topeka police force, folks at Rennett Car Rental who worked there thirteen years ago . . . even Mr. Rennett himself. Who, it bears mentioning, is doing time in a federal pen in Kansas for some unrelated nasty business he was involved in."

My heart is going a million miles an hour, like a crazy hummingbird flying around inside my chest.

Mac continues, his tone friendly. Casual. As if the world itself hasn't stopped spinning on its axis and is standing still in space.

"Under the laws of the State of California, Mr. Scott *might* have been prosecuted for something called accessory after the fact, which basically means there was no criminal intent but the individual somehow assisted a perpetrator in the commission of a felony—which, as you probably know, a hit-and-run resulting in death most definitely is—but because he was a minor, was under duress to leave the scene by physical force from his father, *and* he reported the crime, accessory after the fact doesn't apply in this case."

He leans back in his chair again. "In addition, his total lack of a criminal record and the fact that he's given millions to Mothers Against Drunk Driving in the past decade has led the DA to conclude this is an untriable case. There's not a jury in the world that would put him behind bars."

As I sit stunned and speechless, Mac chews for a few beats, thoughtfully smooths the ends of his moustache with his fingers, and then says, "Quite frankly, it's not only the laws of the State of California that don't apply here. The laws of reason, probability, and sheer dumb luck don't, either. I've been in law enforcement a long, long time, and I've never heard of nothin' like this."

He shakes his head. "You two give 'star-crossed lovers' a whole new meanin'. I gotta say, Romeo and Juliet are lookin' pretty tame in comparison."

Overwhelmed, I close my eyes, pinch the bridge of my nose between my fingers, and concentrate on breathing.

Mac leans over his desk, resting his elbows on the blotter. "For what it's worth, my experience with people bein' what it is, I think he's a good man. I can understand why you'd hate him and want him to pay for what happened, but tryin' to get him prosecuted just isn't gonna—"

"No!" I say, so loudly Mac blinks. "I don't want him *prosecuted.* I just wanted to tell you my side of it, so you *wouldn't* file charges against him. And I don't hate him. I could never hate him. I . . . I . . ."

*Love him*, my heart whispers.

Heat flashes over me in a wave.

I love him.

Even though it's impossible. Even though none of it makes sense and if you tried to tell the tale to a stranger they'd laugh you right out of the room.

I love him, and it's the only really real thing there is.

Tears gathering in my eyes, I stand abruptly. "Thank you, Mac," I say. "I have to go."

He smiles at me. "All right, then. You take care now, Grace. Don't take this the wrong way, but I hope we never meet again."

"You and me both," I say, and bolt from the room.

"Can't you drive any faster, Barney?" I plead.

He glances at me in the rearview mirror. "Not safely, no."

*Fuck safety!* I want to scream, but don't. In the backseat of the Escalade, Kat beside me gripping my hand, I bite my tongue and watch Pacific Coast Highway fly by in smears of color and darkness. Instead of screaming, I start to pray.

*God, if you're listening, I just want to tell you that if Brody isn't okay when we get to his house, I will find a way to make you pay.*

So it's more of a threat than a prayer, but it's the best I can do at the moment.

Nico hangs up his cell phone and from the front passenger seat looks over his shoulder at me. "He's still not answering his cell."

Kat whispers, "Oh no."

"Call the house," I suggest, my panic growing.

"I did. Got the machine. Same as I've been gettin' every time I've tried to call for the last few days."

"Shit." Dread is growing inside my stomach like a nest of tumors. The closer we get to Brody's house, the worse it feels.

I won't allow myself to dwell on all the what-ifs and worst case scenarios my mind keeps thrusting at me in lurid detail, or on the memory of Kat saying she was worried Brody would do something to hurt himself. He's going to be okay when we get to his house. He's just avoiding the paparazzi, that's all. He's lying low. The story that his father, the late senator from Kansas, caused and then covered up the car crash that killed two people thirteen years ago who, in a strange twist of fate, happened to be the parents of his new girlfriend, a fact which neither of us knew, is causing a media sensation.

Add to that my amnesia and identity change and that Brody tried to have himself arrested as an accessory to murder, and you've got the makings of a pulp journalist's wet dream.

Trying to distract me, Kat says, "You're going to sue the hospital for breach of privacy, right? Those fuckers need to pay for leaking information to the press!"

"Coulda been someone at the police station, too," says Barney. "I know TMZ pays a lot of money for a scoop on this kind of story."

It doesn't matter to me who leaked the story. It's out, and it's out of my control. The only thing that matters now is Brody.

Who hasn't been seen or heard from in days.

*Romeo and Juliet are lookin' pretty tame in comparison*, Mac had ominously said.

And we all know what happened to them in the end.

"Barney, please. Go faster," I whisper, but almost as soon as I say it we're pulling up to the large iron gate that leads to Brody's house.

"God, they're everywhere!" groans Kat.

Four white news vans are illegally parked on PCH right outside the gate. When Barney rolls down his window to punch the security code into the black box on a stand on the side of the driveway, half a dozen guys with cameras rush him, shouting questions into his face.

"Eat a bag of dicks!" he growls.

The gate swings open and we pull through.

I'm out of the car before it even comes to a complete stop. I sprint toward the front door, my heart thundering inside my chest. Without ringing the bell or knocking, I throw the door open and run inside. All the lights are on. Wild hope that someone's home surges through me.

"Brody!" I call, running into the kitchen. "Magda! Is anyone home? Hello!"

Magda appears suddenly from the doorway to the garage. I run to her and give her a hug. Breathless, I ask, "Where is he? Is he home? Is he okay?"

She reaches up and sadly pats my cheek. *"Sí. Y no."*

Yes and no. Oh God.

He's not okay.

Panic claws its way up my throat.

"Tell me where he is, Magda, please," I beg, frantic.

She says, "He didn't know. He didn't know it was you, *cariño*."

Exasperated, I shout, "I know! Please, just tell me where he is!"

"In the guest house," she answers, her eyes shining. "With all of your things. He locked himself in there days ago. I tried to bring him food and he told me to go away. He wouldn't even open the door for me."

My stomach drops like a brick. Without another word, I turn away from Magda and bolt.

I pass Barney, Nico, and Kat just coming in the door. I don't answer when they call out to me, I just sprint through the yard toward the guest house as fast as my legs will take me. The trees and garden are crowned by moonlight, the air is thick with the sound of the restless ocean and redolent with the smell of night-blooming jasmine. Ghostly fingers of fog creep low through the grass, clinging to my feet as I run.

When I reach the front door of the guest house, it's locked.

With shaking fingers, terrified of what I'll find when I go inside, I withdraw the key from the pocket of my coat. Fumbling and cursing, I insert it into the lock. The handle turns. I throw the door open and run inside, shouting Brody's name.

Everything is dark. My voice echoes eerily throughout the silent house.

"Brody! Brody, where are you?"

I run through the living room, dining room, and kitchen, but he's not there. When I run toward the master bedroom, I glimpse light spilling out from under the closed door.

My heart stops. Time seems to slip into slow motion. I fly down the hallway as if in a dream, my blood pumping through my veins like wildfire.

I throw open the bedroom door.

There he is, sitting on the edge of the mattress, with his elbows propped on his knees and his head hanging down. He's barefoot and bare chested, wearing only an old, faded pair of blue jeans. The room is dim, lit only by the candles guttering on the dresser. On the bed beside him is my memory book, the album filled with pictures he took of the two of us, open to the first page.

On the nightstand next to the bed is an empty water glass.

In his hand is an empty bottle of pills.

I fly to him, knock the bottle from his hands, and cry out, "What have you done?"

His head lifts. His cheeks are wet. He blinks at me slowly, as if not believing his eyes, and then whispers raggedly, "Grace?"

I throw my arms around him. He's frozen for a moment, but then comes to life with a pained groan and crushes me to his chest. I wrap my legs around his waist and cling to him, so grateful to feel his warmth and strength, so relieved to see him yet terrified he's hurt himself.

"You're here," he whispers, shaking. "You're here."

Then he pulls away and frantically starts to check me for injuries, his gaze darting all over my face and body, his hands roaming me, searching for bruises and breaks.

He chokes out, "Your head—I stayed until the doctor said you were stable and then they said you'd been released and I knew you wouldn't want to talk to me I knew you must hate me so much—"

I kiss him, swallowing his words in my desperation, my palms on his cheeks, the scrape of his unshaven face a rough heaven in my hands. He kisses me back with equal desperation, sobbing when he tries to draw a breath.

"I need to call the paramedics," I moan against his mouth. "You goddamn fool, you idiot, what the hell were you thinking!"

"Paramedics?" he repeats, freezing.

"The pills!" I cry, gesturing wildly to the empty bottle on the floor.

Brody looks at the bottle, and then back at me. His eyes wet and filled with wonder, he shakes his head. "Honey, no—that's just a prescription pain reliever, a little stronger than Tylenol. I only took the last two that were in the bottle, not all of them. I just have a headache. Probably because I haven't eaten in like a week."

My relief is so overwhelming I can't speak. I sag against him, bury my face in his neck, and start to cry like a baby.

"You thought I was going to kill myself?" he asks.

"You wouldn't answer your phone! No one could get a hold of you! You disappeared!"

He whispers, "Oh, witch face, you're way too hideous to provoke something as dramatic as suicide. I was just having a little mental breakdown. Nothing that would've lasted longer than thirty or forty years."

I cry harder.

He flips me over and takes us down to the bed.

Lying on top of me, he kisses me all over my hot, wet cheeks, murmuring reverently over and over, "You're here. You're here."

"Yes," I whisper, my whole body trembling as I stare up into his eyes. "I'm here and I'm never leaving. I love you, Brody. I love you. I'm so sorry I left before hearing you out. I'm so sorry I ran away. I know what happened wasn't your fault, and I'm so sorry about everything—"

He shushes me by pressing a shaking finger on my lips. In a strangled voice, he demands, "Back up. Say that again."

"I'm never leaving?"

His lids flutter. He exhales a shaky breath. "That's a really good part, too. But no. The other part. After the 'never leaving' and before the sorrys. The part you've never said to me before."

I wind my arms around him, this man that I love, this man Fate led me to not once but twice, this man who's saved me in so many ways.

This man who saved my life.

"I love you," I say, gazing deep into his eyes. "I love you, Brody, and though we might have the strangest and most fucked-up love story in the history of love stories, I'm glad I found you. I'm glad we found each other. I don't want to be away from you ever again."

When he squeezes his eyes shut, tears slide down his cheeks. He whispers, "Well, then. Welcome home."

He presses the gentlest kiss to my lips. I arch into him, my body responding as it always does, and the kiss quickly turns passionate. His hands dig into my hair. My fingernails dig into his bare back.

When Kat's worried call echoes down the hallway from the front door, we hardly even hear it.

# Epilogue

## Three months later

"I know. I will. I love you, too, Mom."

Brody hangs up the phone and immediately turns to me and opens his arms. I step into them, rest my head against his broad chest, and give him a hug. He exhales slowly, his heart thudding against mine. A little tremor runs through his body.

I know from experience that he'll be needing a lot more hugs today.

Talking to his mother now makes his demons itchy.

We're in our bedroom in the main house. It's a Sunday in June, one of those crystal clear, blue-sky-for-miles California days they put on postcards. Magda's in the kitchen cooking enough food for an army, and delicious smells saturate the air.

I ask, "You okay?"

"Yeah," he answers quietly, stroking a hand over my hair. "She said to tell you she's really looking forward to meeting you."

We're flying to Kansas next week to visit his family. Even his sister and her husband and kids are coming in from Connecticut. It's the first time Brody will be seeing any of them in person since the news broke, and he's nervous about it, because he knows how hard it's been for them, especially his mom. Interest from the press has died down, there are no more camera crews camped out on his mother's front lawn, but Brody's younger brother, Branson, has told him about graffiti on the driveway, and nasty phone calls, and how a few of his mother's old friends will simply turn away now if they see her on the street.

His guilt over all of that is one of the many things we're working through in our weekly therapy sessions.

Winding my arms around his wide shoulders, I stand up on my toes and kiss him. "I can't wait to meet her, too. She sounds like a very strong lady."

Brody smiles. His skin is tanned and his hair has so many highlights it's not really brown anymore, it's more of a deep golden blond. When he's not with me or working, he spends as much time as possible in the ocean, on his surfboard, finding peace and absolution where he can.

He says, "Speaking of strong ladies, did you hear Kenji's bringing a *date*?"

I shake my head, smiling. "You and your awful segues. So who's the lucky guy? You know anything about him?"

"Not a thing," Brody says. "Kenji's never brought any of his boyfriends around the band so I have no idea what his taste runs to, but we should be prepared for anything."

"Well, your house parties do tend to get pretty dramatic, Kong. I'm sure today will be no exception."

His smile is wry. "Let's hope not as dramatic as the last one."

"I doubt anything could *ever* get as dramatic as that," I say, chuckling.

"Knock on wood," Brody agrees, and raps me lightly on the skull with his knuckles.

I'm grateful we can joke about it. The alternative is too depressing.

"Since you brought it up . . ." Looking at him with a sly smile, I reach between his legs and squeeze.

"Are you referring to my magical love wand as 'wood'?" he asks, brows lifted.

"Anything would be better than 'magical love wand,' my dear."

He grimaces. "And now it's 'my dear.' How old-fashioned. You sound like my grandmother."

I squeeze again, feeling him growing stiff under my hand. "Really? Your granny gives you a boner, huh?"

He laughs. "Number one, that's gross and you're demented, and number two, my granny hasn't given *anyone* a boner in about two hundred years." He stops and blinks. "I hope."

I tease, "You never know, Mr. Scott, there's a kink for everything."

His eyes get hot, his arms tighten around me, and his voice gains that growly, sexy edge I love so much. "We never did explore my teacher-student fantasy, did we?"

Though I pretend nonchalance, my heartbeat picks up its pace, as it always does when he looks at me the way he's looking at me now. "Hmm. I honestly can't recall. We've had so much sex it all just blends together in my memory, one vague, bland—"

"Bland!" he exclaims, eyes widening. Then his expression changes. The wolf peers out from behind his eyes. His voice dropping another octave, he says, "Oh, sweetheart, you're gonna pay for that."

*Exactly as I hoped.*

He grabs my ass, pulls me harder against him, and takes my mouth.

I kiss him back hungrily, desire rising as fast as the bulge beneath my palm. There's always this wonderful craving that simmers between us, a smoldering heat that takes a mere look to erupt into flame. My nipples harden, and I rub my breasts against his chest. He makes a sound low in his throat, threads a hand into my hair and makes a fist, and then pulls my head gently back so he can kiss me even deeper.

Then the doorbell rings, announcing the arrival of the gang.

Brody groans. "They have the *worst* timing!"

"Agreed," I breathe. "Let's tell Magda to turn the sprinklers on them, buy us a few minutes."

He bites my lower lip, and then runs his tongue over it, teasing away the sting. "We're gonna need a lot longer than a few minutes for what I've got planned for you," he says softly, eyes glowing.

Now it's my turn to groan.

Brody gives my ass a light slap and smiles. "C'mon, Slick. Time to play hostess."

"I'd rather be playing Hot for Teacher," I grouse.

I get a soft kiss on my cheek. "Later," he whispers seductively into my ear, giving rise to goose bumps all over my skin.

The doorbell rings again.

When I mutter a curse, Brody laughs. He takes me by the hand and pulls me from the room.

A few moments later we're greeting Kat, Nico, A.J., Chloe, Abby, Barney, and Kenji at the front door.

And a stunning, petite Asian girl who Kenji introduces as his date, London.

"Hello! Welcome!" I say to her, vigorously shaking her hand as I try not to fall over in shock. Judging by the way she's looking at me, she probably thinks I'm a lunatic.

"Thank you so much for having me. Your home is beautiful," she says politely, in a low, melodic voice created to make angels weep.

She's dressed in a body-skimming gold jacquard sheath dress, knee-length and sleeveless, that accents her slender figure to perfection. Her black hair is pulled back in a sleek chignon, which shows off her long, elegant neck, incredible cheekbones, and flawless skin. Her eyes are dark and huge, canted up at the corners like a doe's.

She looks ready for an evening at the opera, not a beach barbeque with a bunch of rowdy musicians and their significant others.

Standing right behind her, Kenji smirks at me. "Oh, close your gaping mouth, lovey, you'll catch flies."

Wearing a long, royal blue caftan with a burgundy chest sash and a lot of chunky gold jewelry, his bald head polished to a mirror sheen, he steps forward and hugs me.

I whisper into his ear, "I have questions."

Giggling, he whispers back, "I'll bet you do."

"The main one being, why are you dressed like Yul Brynner from *The King and I*?"

Pulling away, he throws his arms wide and says, "Aha! That's *exactly* what I was going for! Oh, I'm so good." Then he makes a low, sweeping bow, and comes up grinning.

With a disarming giggle, London says something to him in what sounds like Japanese.

Kenji blushes. He *blushes*, from his neck clear up to the top of his smooth head.

God, I can't wait to get to know this girl better.

"Everybody come in," invites Brody from behind me, resting his hand on my lower back. "Where are Ethan and Chris?"

Nico gives both of us a hug, and then says, "They drove separately. Said they had to stop by some chick's house on the way over to pick something up."

"Probably a few STDs," mutters Kat under her breath, and then throws her arms around me.

I hug her back, laughing. "Those two really do everything together, don't they?"

A.J., holding Abby in his arms, snorts. "You have no idea."

"Nor do I want to. Kat, you look amazing."

When she pulls away, she's got color in her cheeks and a mysterious light in her eyes. "Do I? Must be the new skin cream I'm using."

When Nico laughs, wraps his arms around her shoulders, and kisses her on the neck, I think I must be missing something. I share a look with Chloe, who shrugs.

She comes forward to embrace Brody and me, and then I look at Barney and hold out my arms.

"C'mere, big guy. Bring it in."

With his slight limp and a lopsided smile, he strolls over and hugs me, briefly but hard. "You're looking pretty amazing yourself, Angelface," he murmurs.

"Yeah, happiness'll do that for a girl. You doing good? I haven't talked to you in a while."

When we disentangle, he's nodding. "I was just telling the rest of the crew on the way over my big news."

"News? What news?"

He looks proud but a little sheepish when he says, "That I got a new gig. I won't be with the band after next month."

I'm floored. The thought of Barney not being with the band is like . . . I don't even know what. Peanut butter without jelly? Batman without Robin? Bogie without Bacall?

"Wow, that's . . ." I bite my tongue so I don't say "horrible." "I'm happy for you, Barney. What will you be doing?"

"Working with a high-level security outfit based in Manhattan called Metrix. It's run by this badass ex–Special Ops guy who provides personal security for a lot of heavy hitters. They specialize in extractions."

I repeat cautiously, "Extractions?"

Barney smiles. "You don't wanna know."

Funny enough, though, I do. I'm not sure how I feel about him leaving. Part of me is worried that it has something to do with me.

Barney sees my expression and says softly, "It was just time to make a change, Angelface."

There's more to it, I can tell, but with everyone standing around all I can say is, "I'll miss you."

He looks at Brody, smiles, and then glances back at me. "I'll miss you, too. It's gonna be your job to keep this bozo in line now."

Brody sniffs. "Tch. I'm a fucking delight."

Then suddenly Kat screams.

Everyone jumps and turns to look at her. Her eyes wide, she points at my left hand. "Omigod. Omigod. Is that what I think it is?"

Blinking innocently, I raise my hand and wave it around like a jewelry model. "Oh, this old thing?"

Kenji crows, "Called it! I *knew* there was a reason we were celebrating today!"

Brody laughs, grabs me from behind, and pulls me against his chest. "Okay, so maybe this *wasn't* just a random weekend get-together."

Chloe takes my hand and stares at the diamond ring on my finger. It's exactly what I wanted, understated in size but with a flawless brilliant-cut center stone that catches all the light and scatters it into a million tiny rainbow beams.

"Holy shit sticks, Grace! You guys got engaged? Congratulations!"

She throws her arms around Brody and me. Then Kat does the same, jumping and squealing in glee, and everyone starts laughing and talking at once.

Until Magda rounds the corner from the kitchen and shouts, *"Ai!"*

When we turn to look at her, she gestures into the kitchen with the spatula in her hand. In Spanish, she demands, "Are you monkeys all just going to stand there making noise, or come in and eat?"

She disappears back around the corner.

Still laughing, Kat says, "Magda's a little scary, you guys know that, right?"

"A little?" repeats Kenji, hand at his throat. "The woman makes Godzilla look like a bunny rabbit. What did she shout at us?"

"I think she wants us to go get some food," suggests Brody. When I turn to him with a brow lifted, he shrugs. "I'm getting better at deciphering the insults."

I say, "All right, gang, everybody to the patio before Magda starts throwing things."

We troop through the house and out onto the patio into the sunny afternoon, everyone happily chatting, Kenji and London holding hands. Chloe has dressed Abby in an outfit that matches hers, a yellow sundress covered in tiny daisies, but Abby also has a headband with a big fake sunflower teetering over one ear. A beaming A.J. follows with his hand on Chloe's shoulder as she leads the way.

Under the shade of white umbrellas, Kenji and London settle into a pair of chaise lounges by the pool and instantly fall into a deep conversation. The rest of us gather at the long wood dining table Brody and I eat our meals at when the weather's good. It's shaded by umbrellas, too, set off to one side of the patio where the view of the ocean is unimpeded by palm trees.

"So have you guys made any plans for the wedding yet?" asks Chloe, taking the baby from A.J. so he can relax.

Sitting beside me, Brody wraps an arm around my waist and smiles. "Not really. Grace doesn't want a big to-do, so we were thinking something small. Maybe just have it here, with you guys. I'd fly out my mom and brother and sister, but other than that I think we're going for the intimate vibe."

Nodding, A.J. says, "Yeah, we're thinking the same thing. Keep it small. Just family."

Surprised, we all look at him. Over the past months, neither he nor Chloe have brought up the subject of their wedding. Every time Kat or I have asked her, she's just shrugged and said, "We're not in a rush," or "It'll happen when it happens."

Trying not to make a big deal of it, Kat says jokingly, "You guys should have a double wedding!"

Blushing, Chloe kisses Abby's head. She says softly, "If we could pull it off before I start showing, that would be great."

Wide-eyed, Kat and I look at each other, and then at Chloe. Kat breathes, "Honey . . . you're pregnant?"

As if we couldn't already tell by the smug, chest-thumping look A.J.'s wearing.

Chloe nods. "Seven weeks. A.J.'s convinced it's a boy this time."

A.J. says, "Oh, it's a boy all right. I know this woman's body better than I know my own. She's carrying my son." He throws a huge arm around her waist, drags her against him, and gives her a passionate kiss as the baby squeals happily in her arms.

Everyone congratulates them. Laughing, Barney slaps A.J. on the back.

Then I'm terrified of how Kat's going to react, because the last thing she told us about her infertility treatments was that they were still ongoing, and she wouldn't offer more. She's been frighteningly tight-lipped about the whole thing, to the point where I've been worried there's something terribly wrong.

I think I might have been right, because Kat's eyes are filling with tears.

But why is Nico smiling like that? He's wearing almost the exact smug expression as—

It hits me like a brick dropped on my head.

I shout, "You're pregnant, too?"

Nodding, Kat bursts into tears.

Nico puts his arms around her, laughs, and tucks Kat's head into his neck. "We didn't want to say anything until we were past twelve weeks, but yeah. We're pregnant. Turns out there was nothin' wrong with either of us, I just needed to wear looser briefs."

Clutching his T-shirt in her fists, Kat bawls into his chest.

Brody says, "Wow. I guess me and Grace better get to work."

I start to laugh and can't stop. Then we're all laughing, until Kenji shouts over at us, "What's so funny, psychopaths?"

From inside the house, Magda grumbles an agreement.

"Come over here and we'll tell you!" I call.

Kenji's about to get up, but London leans over, rests her hand on his arm, and whispers something into his ear. Something that makes Kenji's face go flaming red again.

He sends us a huge smile, waves a dismissive hand in our direction, and settles back into his chaise. "In a minute!"

Impressed, Brody says, "That's a first. Kenji takes direction?"

Gazing at London admiringly, Barney says, "I'd love to take some direction from that one."

"She's so pretty, isn't she?" I murmur.

Kat wipes her face, sniffles, and whispers, "Gorgeous. That skin!"

A.J. asks, "Who're we talking about?"

Trying not to be obvious that I'm talking about her in case she looks over, I smile brightly at A.J. and say between stiff lips, "London, Kenji's date. She's this really beautiful Asian girl with perfect—"

A.J. chuckles, and then starts to laugh, his big shoulders shaking.

"Why are you laughing?" I ask, confused.

He leans over the table. His voice low, he says, "I hate to break it to you, but London's not a girl."

Barney, Kat, Chloe, Nico, Brody, and I look at each other silently. No one dares to glance away from our table. I whisper, "A.J., I know you can't see her, but she is *definitely* a girl."

"Oh yeah?" He leans back, slings his arm around Chloe's shoulders again, and says, "Okay. Tell me what size shoe she's wearing."

Everyone stares at me expectantly.

I hiss, "Why is this my job?"

Kat whispers, "Because you're facing in the right direction! If we turn around it'll be too obvious."

But Brody beats me to it. He quietly says, "Holy cow. I had no idea they made heels in that size."

A.J. says, "Told ya."

Chloe leans in and whispers confidentially, "Spidey senses."

A.J. shakes his head. "Nah. While you guys were all yammering in the car on the way over, me, Kenji, and London were in the backseat having a nice conversation about if waxing or shaving is the best way to get the hair off your balls."

I drop my head onto my arms on the table and dissolve into such gales of laughter I can hardly breathe.

When I can catch my breath, I look up into the smiling faces of my best friends in the world, these people who know all the worst and best parts of me, and experience a profound sense of gratitude, so huge I feel moved to say a silent little prayer.

I look up to the sky, close my eyes, and think, *Thank you.*

The best churches don't have stained glass windows or statues of dead saints or even ceilings and walls. You don't need a building to find forgiveness. You don't need communion wafers and holy water to be blessed.

And miracles are everywhere.

All you have to do is look.

# Acknowledgments

First, to my developmental editor, Melody Guy, I owe you a tremendous debt of thanks. You are such a smart, warm, talented, wonderful lady. For all the ways you make my books better, for all the things you catch that I've let fall through the cracks, for all your insight, humor, and tactful suggestions, I thank you from the bottom of my heart.

Anyone reading this who hates a book that ends in a cliff-hanger should also thank Melody. At the end of chapter thirty-five when Grace flew over the cliff off PCH, I wanted to end the book right there and leave you all "hanging" until the next installment. (Get it? Cliff-hanger?) I was clapping my hands and cackling in glee at the thought, until Melody sent me a very lovely email pointing out that not only was that not a nice thing to do to my readers, but a *literal* cliff-hanger was kinda funny.

And not the ha-ha kind of funny.

So thank you, Melody, for letting me know in the nicest possible way when I'm off my rocker, and saving me from a lot of hate mail from angry readers.

To my team at Montlake Romance who has been so amazing since I was first published four years ago, big hugs. I am eternally grateful for the support you've given me. Maria Gomez, my sharp-as-tacks acquiring editor, and Jessica Poore, author support gal supreme, I appreciate you and am so happy to know you personally as well as professionally. You're both stars.

To all the other people at Amazon Publishing who work so hard—the cover designers who are so patient with my endless revisions, the copy editors who have to slog through my ragged prose, and the marketing and advertising teams I never speak to but whose efforts I reap the fruits of, thank you. I'm sure there are more of you I'm forgetting, but please give me a pass and know I truly appreciate you all.

Eleni Caminis, I love you. Full stop.

Dad, though you're gone, thank you for that star in the sky, and that dream, and that phone call. You were always the best at making sure everyone else was okay.

Mom, thank you for teaching me to speak my mind, laugh at haters, give zero fucks, and to not mess with a Jersey girl. Invaluable lessons, all.

Whew! Where are we? Oh yes—JAY.

There is a reason why every. Single. One. of my books is dedicated to you, Mr. Geissinger. That reason might be that I'm building a case for my innocence after I murder you in your sleep, burn down the house, and flee to my new life in Cabo San Lucas, but it might also be that you are the sole reason I am who I am, can do what I do, and am happy. Thank you for your constant support and for making me laugh every day.

To my readers and fans who are part of Geissinger's Gang, thank you for supporting my work, spreading the word about my books, and spending time with me on social media. I write for myself but also for you, too, and your enthusiastic feedback is invaluable. Thanks for making my journey so fun!

# About the Author

J.T. Geissinger is the bestselling and award-winning author of contemporary romance, paranormal romance, and romantic suspense. She has received the Prism Award for Best First Book and the Golden Quill Award for Best Paranormal/ Urban Fantasy, and was a finalist for the prestigious RITA Award from the Romance Writers of America. J.T. has also been a finalist for the Booksellers' Best, National Readers' Choice, and Daphne du Maurier Awards.

As both an admitted bookaholic and lover of wine, J.T.'s idea of heaven is reading undisturbed in the bathtub with a glass of Syrah. Check out her website, www.JTGeissinger.com, or join her Facebook reader's group, Geissinger's Gang, for the chance to take part in live chats, contests, and giveaways, and to get more information about her works in progress and advance reader copies.